A Storm in a Teacup

Rachael Gray

BLOODHOUND BOOKS

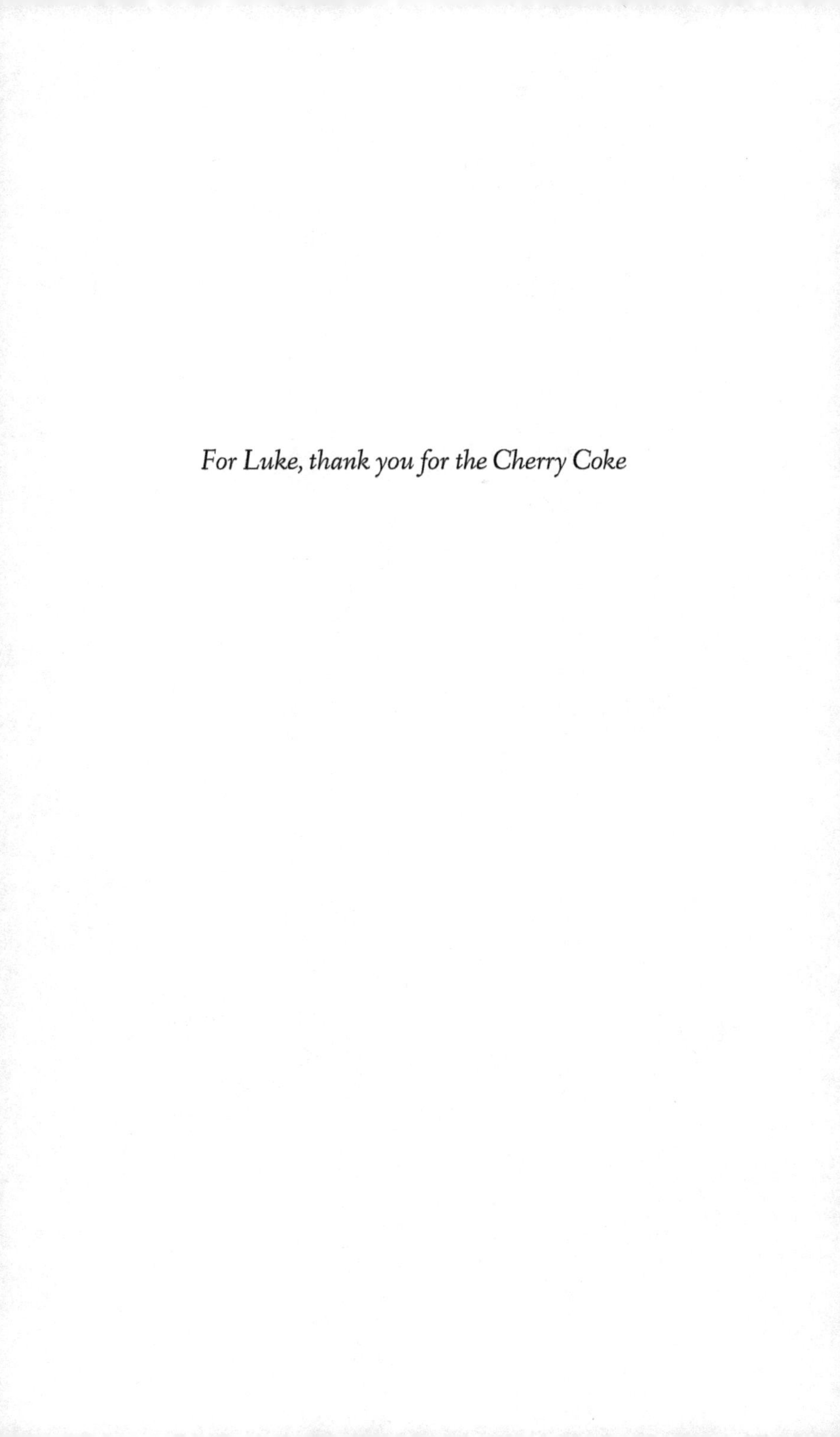
For Luke, thank you for the Cherry Coke

Chapter 1

Laurel

Nestled in the soil was a single yellowed sliver of bone. It wasn't much to look at, but the animated faces around the hole shone with anticipation as everyone strained to see.

No-one was speaking, but Laurel would bet everyone was imagining – hoping – that this find was something special. Maybe even *the* something special all archaeologists, detectorists, and treasure hunters dreamed of.

'Okay, before we get carried away, let's have a proper look,' Dr Delgado said in a soft accent. South American, Laurel thought. A solid man in khaki cargo pants and a faded Elvis Costello T-shirt, he stepped softly into the depression. 'It's an excellent find, Lin.' He patted his team member on the back. 'You've done a lovely job of exposing the bone. It could be from an animal; it's quite near the surface. Certainly not as deep as we'd expect if this were part of a burial.' The sun bounced off his bald head as he bent his face close to the fragment. 'Can I have your brush, please?' He held out his hand. 'And can everyone move back a bit?'

The observers shuffled perhaps an inch or two, then leaned forward all the more, determined not to miss a thing.

Laurel held her breath as he swept the bristles over and around the piece of bone.

Albert whispered to her. 'It's probably from a deer again, like those bones they found up at the Hall the other year.'

Penelope appeared on Albert's other side. 'Dr Delgado will know if they're human or not. He's incredibly experienced and actually an osteoarchaeologist.'

'He knows human bones.' Albert clarified.

'Yup.'

'Did they expect to find human remains here?'

Penelope shrugged. 'I don't think so, but like you never know with these things.'

Only a couple of years back, Penelope had been a black-clad goth teen. Laurel was amazed at the transformation. Tanned, wiry, and attractively confident, her brown hair held up in a messy knot on her head, and streaks of mud on her cheeks where she'd brushed grimy hands over her face.

'There's no barrow here, or any other sign that this is a burial site, but that doesn't mean it's not. There's still so much we don't know about this area, and it wouldn't be the first time something amazing has been found in East Yorkshire. In 2014 in Wold Newton, not that far from here, a metal detectorist found a clay pot with an absolute load of copper coins. I think about two thousand, dating from the fourth century.' Penelope's eyes sparkled. 'Then there was a developer near Pocklington who uncovered an Iron Age cemetery. Not only were there loads of bodies, but all kinds of shields, swords, and jewellery.'

'I remember reading about it,' said Albert.

'I doubt this will be anything like that, but...' she trailed off, her eyes drawn back to the bone.

The lead archaeologist ceased his brushstrokes and backed away. A little more of the yellowish object had been revealed, but its shape remained indistinct, to Laurel at least. 'Lin,' he said to the young woman who'd made the find, 'congratulations, you might just have discovered your first human burial.'

Lin's face was alive with exhilaration and thrilled murmurs rippled through the crowd.

'Now tell me, as we've determined this bone is probably human, and chances are, there's more to uncover, what are our next steps?'

Laurel suspected this was a test. Dr Delgado, the expert, was assessing his team member's knowledge.

Lin, a slight woman in her early twenties with short, choppy hair and ears all out of proportion with her narrow face, bit her lip, her delight replaced with a furrowed brow and scrunched up nose. Then she relaxed. 'The bones are unexpected. This isn't consecrated ground, it's not a known burial ground, and we already have an osteoarchaeologist on site,' she gestured to her boss who bobbed his head. 'But we need to contact the police?' She'd lost her confidence, the uplift in her tone making it a question.

'Excellent,' said Dr Delgado, clapping the dirt from his hands. 'Until we've done that, everyone out, away.' He shooed the onlookers, adding, 'And let's get a cover over this trench.'

In no hurry to leave, Laurel, Albert, and Penelope dawdled to the edge of the meadow where they lingered.

'This is so exciting,' said Penelope as she hopped up to sit on the wall. 'Five days into my first dig and we might have found an actual burial.'

'At least these bones aren't from a murder victim, or if they are, the killer will also have been dead for centuries,' said Laurel with a wry smile.

Albert leaned back against the stones and ran a hand through his unruly white wisp of hair as he muttered, 'Goodness knows there's enough dark secrets buried in this village.'

Trying to copy Penelope and sit on the wall, Laurel made it

to the top, but only after an ungainly struggle. Once she'd wiped the dust from her hands, she asked, 'Is this a summer job then, or something to do with school?'

The young woman beamed. 'I'm a volunteer. I want to get onto the Historical Archaeology degree course at York Uni, so I'm here on a summer placement, which I hope will look good on my UCAS form. I got into it after my class had a field trip to Robin Hood's Bay and Dr Delgado gave a presentation about smugglers to our sixth form class. I got to chat to him afterwards about his work at the university. He was super nice and he and Beth, his wife – that's her, over there – were kind enough to suggest I volunteer on one of their local digs. So far, I'm loving it.'

'They make a handsome couple,' Albert observed.

'Don't they,' agreed Penelope. 'They're amazing. He's from Peru, she's from Alabama in the US, and they've worked all over the world.'

Laurel had follow-up questions about Penelope's goals. 'Forgive me for being uninformed: what's historical archaeology exactly? Isn't all archaeology historical?'

'It's basically archaeology concerning the past two thousand years, the period for which we have like texts and documents and stuff.'

'I see, instead of ancient archaeology, the old, old stuff? I thought there was just archaeology. I didn't realise you could study different types.'

'Yeah. There's also archaeology and heritage, and bioarchaeology courses.'

As Penelope chatted away about the differences, Laurel was distracted. She could feel eyes on her. She shifted her position, but it took her a moment to locate the watcher. When she did, she lowered her gaze and met a baleful stare.

'Hello, Aroon,' she said, a frosty edge to her words as he approached. 'It's been a while.'

He paused, then blinked at her, but remained mute.

'How are you?'

He cocked his head and took a step closer.

Laurel lifted her feet out of reach.

Aroon stopped at the base of the wall, let loose a triumphant crow, then turned and strutted away.

'Rude,' she called to his retreating form.

'You know you mustn't show weakness. Don't let him bully you.' The lines around Albert's mouth and eyes crinkled.

'Your cockerel is a menace,' she pouted making Penelope giggle.

Lapsing into silence, they watched the activity in the field before them. The July sun had baked the earth to a dusty ochre kicked up by booted feet. People's movements were sluggish in the smothering heat. Dr Delgado was instructing his team members to continue in the other trenches and shooing away the stragglers from the village who hadn't left yet.

'I'd better go ask what he wants me to do,' said Penelope. 'I'll see you later.'

'See you.' Laurel raised a lazy hand in farewell.

'I shall be sad to see this meadow go,' said Albert. 'I do enjoy seeing the cat's ear and yellow rattle; such vibrant flowers. Still, a farm shop to benefit a children's charity is as good a cause as any.'

Laurel shaded her eyes and looked around. 'At least it was Dandelions who got Elderwick Hall and not some soulless hotel chain, or worse, that rich bloke who wanted it.'

Albert took a white handkerchief from his pocket and wiped it across his forehead. 'I'm wilting like a snowman in summer. You know, I don't think we'll miss anything if we slip away for a while.' He pushed away from the wall. 'Shall we adjourn to The Pleasant Pheasant for tea and cake?'

Laurel was reluctant to leave in case they missed further developments, but the heat was uncomfortable and nothing much was happening. Slipping down from the wall, she cursed as she snagged her skirt on a jagged edge. She inspected the small tear and hoped no-one would notice until she could go home and mend it.

'I'm glad we were here to witness their first find.' She adjusted her skirt, so the hole wasn't obvious. 'I hope it turns out to be a significant one.'

'This is Elderwick,' replied her friend. 'Be careful what you wish for.'

Chapter 2

Laurel

Reaching the café in the village centre, Laurel and Albert snapped up the last available table outside on the terrace. Under a pink and white striped umbrella, they settled in with sighs of pleasure. There was a light breeze from across the village green, a delicious respite from the oppressive heat. The proprietor, and talented cook, Jo, bustled outside to take their order. Albert opted for a cup of green tea and a fruit scone with jam and cream, Laurel deliberated over a piece of sticky ginger cake or a piece of Aussie crunch.

'I'll go for the Aussie crunch with a glass of raspberry lemonade, please.' Satisfied with her decision, she added, 'And a piece of ginger cake to take home. Thanks, Jo.'

Jo grinned at her, flipped closed her notepad, and headed back indoors to the kitchen.

'Excuse me a second, would you?' asked Albert. 'I meant to tell Jo I've got some extra peas from the garden if she wants them.' He rose and followed her indoors.

Laurel was in no doubt Albert was telling Jo about the bone uncovered in the meadow and not garden peas. He loved to be the first with village gossip.

She let a soft smile play on her lips. In that moment, there was no place she would rather be. The village of Elderwick had been her home for some time now and, barring the odd murder – she winced at the memories – it was a tranquil spot nestled perfectly in the gentle East Yorkshire landscape.

While she waited for her food and Albert's return, she indulged in a spot of people watching. Most of the other customers were people she was used to seeing round and about, except for a man and woman at one of the far tables. She snuck glances at the man's face as he chatted away, but she could only see the back of his companion. Blond hair hung in soft waves down to her summer-bronzed shoulders. She was dressed in a loose but stylish pale blue sundress, and her ears and wrist jangled with bright jewellery. Then she turned and her features sparked a memory.

Her stomach in freefall, Laurel eased up from her chair and switched seats, taking Albert's. Her instinct was to leave the café altogether, but she didn't want to draw attention to herself. Nor could she abandon Albert without an explanation for her departure. She would have to sit tight, keep her back to the other table, and pray she wasn't spotted.

'Come on, Albert. Come on, Albert.' She repeated under her breath whilst wiping her damp palms on her skirt.

'Right, all sorted.' Albert plopped into the empty chair.

She pasted a smile onto her face.

He studied her. 'Are you all right, Laurel?'

No!

He'd said her name loud enough to be heard over the muted chatter. While she wanted to freeze, to become invisible, she was compelled to look. The woman she was sure she'd recognised became very still. Then swivelled in her seat to look across the terrace, past the other patrons, her eyes skimming faces until they met Laurel's. All Laurel could hear was the rushing of blood in her ears.

'I have to go,' Laurel gabbled as she grabbed for her belongings.

'Laurel? Laurel Nightingale?'

Her feet rooted themselves to the ground as though she were a rabbit caught in headlights, and like an oncoming car, there was no stopping the elegant blonde who stood and headed her way.

Reaching Laurel, the woman beamed. 'It *is* you. Oh my goodness. How long has it been? It's me, Jayne, Jayne Clement.' She clasped her hands together.

Offering a weak smile, Laurel pushed out the word, 'Hi.'

Jayne reached for her and pulled her into a hug. There was no point in resisting, but Laurel's skin tingled where she was touched and she had to fight the urge to break away.

'And who is this dapper gentleman?' asked Jayne, addressing Albert once she'd released Laurel.

Dressed in knee-length denim shorts paired with an acid yellow short-sleeved shirt, dapper wasn't the word Laurel would have gone with, but Jayne had made Albert smile. *That's what she does,* Laurel thought. *Everyone likes Jayne.* Her eyes rolled before she could squash the impulse. Thankfully, neither of them was paying her any attention.

'Albert.' He held out his hand and made a small bowing motion. 'It is a pleasure to meet you. And might I say, you look as radiant as the harebells in the meadow at dawn.'

Jayne swatted his arm. 'You are a charmer, aren't you?' Flashing dimples in both cheeks, she helped herself to a spare chair and sat down between them. 'So, tell me everything, Laurel. What are you doing here in East Yorkshire?'

Banking on Albert backing her up, she lied. 'Jayne, I am so sorry. I have a meeting I have to get to. Perhaps we can catch up another time? Are you here for long?' Her fingers were crossed beneath the table. *Please say no.*

With devilish timing, Jo reappeared, bearing a tray loaded with drinks and the sweet treats she and Albert had ordered. 'Here you go, you two. Enjoy.' She laid the plates before them, and asked Jayne, 'How are you getting on, can you I get you anything else?'

'No, thank you,' she replied. 'I'm still enjoying the scrumptious piece of cake over at the table with my friend.'

'Lovely. Give me a shout if you need me.'

As Jo walked off, Jayne pounced. 'It looks like you don't have to rush off quite yet? At least let's have a quick catch-up while you eat your cakes.'

Down but not out, Laurel seized the next excuse she could summon. 'We can't possibly keep you away from your friend. Really, we can do this another time.'

'You're so thoughtful.' Jayne touched her hand. Laurel didn't remember her being so touchy when she'd known her at school. 'As it happens, I'll be in Elderwick a lot over the next few months, so let's definitely put a time in our diaries to sit down properly.'

'Yes, let's.' Relief raised its head. And sank again as Jayne pulled her phone out of a pocket. *A dress with pockets! She still has the best clothes.* 'Oh, you mean now?'

'Yes, we mustn't let this opportunity pass. Of all the places... it's so wonderful to run into you. Why don't you give me your number and as soon as I know my schedule, I'll give you a bell. We can arrange a full afternoon of gossip and laughs.' She was waiting, fingers hovering over the touch screen.

'Sure, that's a great idea.' *When one door closes,* thought Laurel, *the Elderwick mobile-signal-free-zone comes to the rescue. Jayne would never be able to get through.*

After another hug, Jayne waved goodbye and returned to

her companion. Laurel stuffed a chunk of Aussie crunch into her mouth.

'She seems delightful,' said Albert.

He was so predictable and she was annoyed he hadn't seen through the sugar-so-sweet act. 'She's fine. We weren't that close when I knew her before.' Maybe she could divert him. 'What do you think of these bones they've found, then?'

Albert levelled a stare at her.

'What?' She hated the sulky tone in her voice.

He studied her for a few seconds more. 'If you want to talk about it...' He didn't need to finish his sentence; they both knew what he meant. Message delivered, he busied himself with spreading jam onto his warm scone.

Now Laurel felt bad for being annoyed with him. Albert was the kindest, most considerate man she'd ever met, and the best neighbour she could have hoped for. And it made her *want* to tell him, but she bit her tongue. 'Thank you.'

She was hyperaware of Jayne's continued presence a few feet away. She took another bite of her chocolate treat, but her dry mouth meant she struggled to swallow. That had never happened before. The Pleasant Pheasant was popular for a reason. The savoury dishes whipped up by Jo were legendary in the village and surrounding areas, and the cakes and pastries provided by The Plump Tart bakery were sublime. Laurel was convinced she'd gained about a stone since moving to Yorkshire from Somerset, but she was avoiding the scales so didn't know for certain.

'I might be an old worrywart,' Albert began, placing his napkin on his plate when only crumbs remained, 'but I have a bad feeling about these bones. Bodies don't rest easy in Elderwick.'

Laurel frowned over her glass. 'That's a bit out of the blue, isn't it? Are you thinking this might be another of the Hartfields' victims? I suppose it is a grizzly possibility.' She thought of the many dark rumours and suspicions attached to the wealthy dynasty who had owned Elderwick Hall since the 1700s.

'It's a feeling not solely borne of my gut, unfortunately.'

Her mouthful of lemonade turned sour.

Albert pointed over her shoulder. 'I'll wager they're not here for a casual visit.'

Laurel's pulse spiked as she followed his finger to see two police cars turn onto North Street and glide past in an ominous cortège.

Chapter 3

Maggie

Maggie snapped the lid closed on the container of sugar, popped it back onto the shelf and heaved a sigh. Her feet were aching and her eyes were gritty, but it had been another great class.

'You all done?' Constance's head appeared round the door. 'I heard everyone leaving. Sounds like they had a good time?'

'I think so.' Maggie flushed. 'And their strawberry tarts came out amazing.'

Constance wheeled her chair all the way into the room. 'You've cleaned up already. You know you don't have to do that by yourself.'

Maggie flapped a dishcloth at her. 'The class helped, so it didn't take us long.' She put down the cloth and picked up a plate. 'Want a piece?' She proffered the tart. The pastry was golden, crisp, and the strawberries glistened under their glaze of jam. The whole kitchen smelled fruity and Maggie was desperate for a taste of her creation.

'Oh, go on, just a small one.'

'With cream?'

Constance tutted. 'Don't ask silly questions, Maggie.'

As Maggie dished up – two substantial slices each topped with a generous dollop of cream – she listened to Constance, who was gossiping about the people who had been into the bakery that day. Constance and her sister, Hetty, ran The Plump Tart together, and were a wellspring of local information and rumour.

'And a minute ago,' the baker balanced her plate on her lap and pointed, 'two police cars headed up along North Street. I wonder where they're going?'

Maggie bit her lip. Ever since the fire at her old house, The Grange, sirens, police cars, and fire engines set her on edge. She swallowed her mouthful of tart without tasting it.

Constance must have caught her anxiety. 'Don't worry, I'm pretty sure they turned right onto Church Lane. They weren't going towards your place.'

After the fire, she hadn't the heart to rebuild and return. In part because of the damage, but mostly because it had been the house she'd shared with her now ex-husband, Nicholas. The memories of their life there together were not ones she cared to hold on to. Instead, she'd bought herself the charming Thatcher's Cottage at the edge of the village. It was far smaller than she was used to, but it was all hers and she could fill it with colour, and books, and whatever else she damn well pleased. No more Nicholas controlling every detail of her life.

'Hey, maybe they've found something at the dig?'

'Maybe.' Maggie hoped that was it. In her experience, the police turning up in Elderwick usually meant something awful had happened. 'If they have found something, we should know about it soon enough. Albert and Laurel were heading over there to see how the archaeologists are getting on.' She'd lost interest in the sweet treat on her plate. 'Actually, if it's all right with you, I might pop on up myself, see what's happening.'

'Of course. Oh, and before I forget, we're only stopping in

for a quick one, but will we see you at the pub tomorrow? Hetty's bringing Florence.'

'Definitely. Have you got exciting plans for later in the evening?'

Constance nodded. 'I've got my art class. It's the last one now until autumn, and Hetty and Florence are going out to The Bay Horse in Cherry Burton for the pub quiz.'

'The Snooty Fox should do a quiz. We should suggest it to Sam.'

The bell over the bakery door tinkled. 'Duty calls,' said Constance, and she manoeuvred herself back through to the front of house to serve the latest customer.

Maggie untied her apron, lifted it over her head, and hung it on a peg. She picked her bag up off the floor and glanced around the kitchen to make sure there was nothing she'd forgotten. Constance was surely right, the police cars hadn't had their sirens blaring, so it couldn't be anything serious. Still, she'd feel better once she'd seen for herself.

As hot as the day was, there was a welcome breeze outside. It lifted the hair on the back of Maggie's neck, and she paused for a second to luxuriate in the sensation. A late Saturday afternoon drink in the shady beer garden was something pleasant to look forward to on what was forecast to be another sticky day. She could almost taste the apple-scented bubbles of the local cider made at Drumble's Hive busting on her tongue. She swallowed. Her throat was dry. She dug in her bag for the bottle of water she knew was there somewhere. When she sipped, it was tepid, but it soothed the scratch.

Taking the shady back way, Maggie passed the school and pushed on to the fringes of the village where the meadow was a hive of activity. Constance had been correct. The police cars were there.

'Maggie!'

Dorothy was heading towards her. She blanched. On a good day, she could handle the woman, but she was tired and wilting under the fiery summer sun.

'Dorothy, it's lovely to–'

Ignoring Maggie's attempts at the traditional pleasantries, Dorothy interrupted. 'Where's that Laurel girl gone now?'

'Excuse me?' Maggie pronounced the words deliberately and paired them with eyebrows pointedly raised. Laurel had saved the woman's life not so long ago, and yet here Dorothy was talking about Maggie's best friend as though she were an errant child.

If Dorothy noticed her tone, she paid it no heed. 'I saw her hanging around with Albert earlier. The police are here, and they want to speak to her.'

Forgetting her annoyance, Maggie gasped, 'Why? What's happened?'

'Never mind. I bet they went to the café. I'll find them there.' She made to step past Maggie.

Maggie shot out a hand and grasped Dorothy by a bony elbow.

'Ow!' the older woman complained.

Maggie dropped her hand as though scalded. What was she doing? Dorothy was tiresome, but that was no reason to assault her. *What's wrong with me?* she thought. 'Sorry, Dorothy. I... I don't know what came over me.'

Dorothy was rubbing her arm. Her lips pressed together.

'Are you hurt? I'm so sorry.'

'I'm fine,' was the waspish reply.

Relieved she wasn't injured, and driven by concern, Maggie risked pressing her. 'Please, can you tell me what's going on and I'll help you find Laurel?'

With a dramatic sigh, Dorothy acquiesced. 'They found bones in one of those ugly holes they've been digging all over the place and now the police are here bothering innocent folk all over again. Ever since your *friend* moved here, we've been tripping over dead bodies.'

Without waiting for a response, Dorothy strode off up the lane and Maggie followed.

'First, you can hardly blame Laurel for the–' She didn't like to say the word *murders*. '–unfortunate events. Second, I don't understand. Surely, it's not unusual to find bones during an archaeological dig? Why are the police involved?'

'Who knows, but when I told them Laurel had been there when they were found, the officers said they would need to speak to her.'

'And you're being a good citizen by going to find her and deliver her to them?'

Oblivious to the sarcasm, Dorothy marched ahead. Maggie had to hustle to keep up and by the time they reached the edge of the village green, from where they could see Albert and Laurel sitting on the terrace of the café, Maggie's lungs were protesting. Sweat was pooling in her bra and running down her back.

'Dorothy.' Albert sounded pleased, but Maggie saw the twitch at the corner of his mouth. Not that he didn't like her; Albert got on with almost everyone, but even for such a genial man, Dorothy Little was hard work.

'Albert, Laurel.' Dorothy nodded to them, then wasted no time in sharing the bad news. 'I should have known you wouldn't be far from the meadow. I suppose you were hoping they'd come across a corpse or two so you could reprise your little detective act? No wonder the police want to question you.'

'Question me?' Laurel echoed. 'What? Why?'

Maggie frowned at Dorothy and spoke to Laurel. 'I'm sure if you go to see them, this will all get sorted out. They're probably speaking to everyone who was in the meadow.'

Albert rushed back inside to pay, and a clearly frustrated Laurel stood up from the table.

Dorothy tutted. 'You have a hole. It's rather slovenly of you.' She pointed at Laurel's skirt and her mouth puckered.

Easily in her eighties, Dorothy was a constant surprise, usually an unpleasant one. And to Maggie's annoyance, Dorothy stuck with them as they returned to the meadow where the officers of the law were waiting.

'Oh no,' Maggie whispered when she recognised the female officer in plain clothes. 'It's DI Coral, isn't it?'

With two spots of red high on her cheeks, Laurel nodded and sighed. 'As soon as Dorothy told me they were asking for me, I had a bad feeling.'

Maggie took Laurel's hand and gave it a squeeze.

'*Doctor* Laurel Nightingale, so glad you could join us,' called Coral. Her partner, DS Hill, stood slightly behind and to the side of her. He was looking at the ground and shifting from foot to foot.

Laurel moved to the front of the group. 'What's this about? Dorothy said you want to speak to me.'

'Yes, we have some questions about the remains uncovered, and how it just so happens that you were present when they were found. Just as you were there on three other occasions when a body has turned up in this village. It's beyond a coincidence. Don't you agree, Hill?' DI Coral smirked at her partner.

Hill shrugged, non-committal, but made some sound which could have been taken as agreement.

'You need to return to your home and wait there until we come round to take an initial statement,' the DI said to Laurel before issuing orders to Hill. 'Call scene of crimes and ask them what's taking so long. We need them to secure the scene so we can get on.'

Hill moved away, muttering into his radio.

'This is ridiculous,' Maggie began.

Laurel clenched her fists, and Albert reached out to steady her with a touch on the shoulder.

Coral didn't back away. She leaned in and hissed, 'You need to return to your home and wait there until we can come and take a statement. You're not going to get to run around playing Jessica Fletcher this time.'

'What are you talking about?' spluttered Laurel. 'Over some ancient burial? Why would I?'

Sensing triumph in the grin breaking across Coral's face Maggie braced herself.

'Ah, but here's the thing, the bones aren't ancient. Far from it. They're much more recent.' Coral paused before her final pronouncement. 'Which means this is now a murder investigation.'

Chapter 4

Albert

After Maggie had ushered Laurel away, Albert did what he did best in such situations; he played the harmless little old man, blending into the background, meandering his way closer to the action.

He remembered DI Coral and DS Hill from the last time there had been a murder in Elderwick. Hill seemed like a decent chap, but Coral, he felt, was too single-minded. He watched the two of them now as they coordinated their colleagues in setting up a cordon around the meadow and got them started with taking details from the members of the archaeology team.

'Excuse me, sir, I'm afraid I have to ask you to leave the area.' A baby-faced PC approached Albert, a hand held out, directing him towards the gate.

'Don't you need to take my details, young man?' Albert leaned into his act, laying it on thick. He was enjoying himself.

'No, you're okay, but thank you. You should be getting along, though.'

Typical, he'd been there when the bone was uncovered, but this whipster evidently didn't believe an older gentleman could have anything important to impart. Resisting the urge to tut, Albert spotted Aroon, who by then was at the far side of the grassland and making a beeline for one of the trenches. Thankfully, not the one with the bone. 'Aye, I will, lad. Just need to fetch me friend, first.' He waved a hand in the general direction of the bird.

'Your friend? Do you mean your dog?' The PC had dropped into the sing-song tone Albert so often heard used when youngsters spoke to those over fifty.

Bored with his game, and insulted, he favoured the plod with the lecturer's voice he'd perfected in his years teaching at University College London and fixed him with a steely stare. 'I mean my bird. That cockerel over there who'll be off with your evidence if you're not careful.'

The lad spun round, searching until he spotted Aroon. His eyebrows lifted. 'Oh, right, of course.' He looked to Albert, then back to the bird. 'Um, you wait here. I'll fetch him for you.'

Before he could run after Aroon, Albert cautioned, 'I wouldn't. He doesn't know you, and he has a bad habit of attacking below the belt, if you catch my meaning?' That stopped the PC.

'Ah.' He all but put a hand over his crotch. 'In that case, perhaps it's best you fetch him yourself, but then you have to leave.'

'Sure, sure.' Albert wandered off, humming the theme from the American TV show, *COPS*.

He let Aroon carry on with whatever he was doing, and moved closer to the two Delgados, their heads bent in urgent conversation. He was still a few metres away when Beth spotted him. The couple fell silent. 'Edrik, Beth,' he nodded.

'Albert.' Edrik waved. 'And please, like I said before, you can call me Rik.' He chuckled. 'Are you enjoying the excitement?'

'Indeed, though a touch macabre for a Friday afternoon.

What's the latest, if you don't mind indulging a curious senior citizen such as myself?'

'You're such a ham.' Beth smiled at him. 'You're fishing, aren't you? I saw how– what's-her-name, the woman officer? I saw how she treated your friend.'

'Yes, she does rather have a bee in her bonnet about Laurel. And yes,' he did his best to twinkle at them, 'I am *floundering* about the *plaice*, hoping to catch a *dab* or two from someone who is prepared to *carp* on.'

They stared at him.

'Not familiar with fish, then?'

'No,' Rik drew out the word. 'Oh, *fishing*, I get it, very funny.' He grinned. 'Bad news though, the police have warned us not to share any details.'

Albert pursed his lips and thought about what he knew. 'The bone was found near to the surface. I suppose it being a shallow grave supports this murder theory?' Albert didn't know Rik all that well, having only met him a few weeks back when the archaeologist had first visited the site to plan the excavation, but he'd clocked Rik's talkative nature. All he needed was a willing audience and a bit of a nudge.

'It does. Especially with the grave – if that's what it is – being so close to the village. It's not as though someone could have died of exposure and their body lay undetected for long enough to decay into the soil. Due to the positioning of these bones, I think we can say with some confidence, they were buried deliberately.'

'It is a body, then, not just a single bone?'

'We don't know for certain yet, but it's definitely more than just a finger.'

'And how, pray tell, do the police already know it's a modern burial?'

Rik's face lit up, 'You'll like this: we found a ring which we know for certain isn't more than around fifty years old, and–'

'Rik.' Beth hip-checked him.

He shot a look over to the growing number of police. 'On second thoughts, maybe I'd better not say any more.'

Chapter 5

Laurel

Laurel was cheered by knowing how much it would annoy Coral that she hadn't gone home as instructed.

They were quiet on their walk to Maggie's place, and it wasn't until they were cocooned in the cheery pale-yellow kitchen that Laurel unclenched her fists. 'First Dorothy, now the bloody police.' She perched on one of the stools at the breakfast bar and put her head in her hands. 'Today started out so well.'

Why did people insist on warning her against being an amateur sleuth and telling her not to play detective? First, she never intended to get involved with crimes – somehow she got pulled in despite her best efforts to avoid them – and second, she got everything wrong more often than she got it right.

'I'm sure it will all work out. Everyone can see what nonsense it is to think you had anything to do with the... you know, the bones.' Maggie plopped down beside her with two glasses of lemonade. 'It's too hot for tea.'

'Thank you for the drink. I'm not sure I share your optimism about the police, though. But, let's talk about something else for a while, can we? How did your class go today?'

Maggie brightened. 'You know, I never thought I would have the chance to cook or bake professionally. I feel like I'm finally living *my* life, not the one Nicholas had mapped out for me. The kids are coming to visit in a couple of weeks too, and they have both remarked how I seem much happier than I was before.'

'Do you hear from Nicholas anymore?'

'No. The kids still see him, though they're angry with him for what he did.'

'Which bit?'

'All of it, but mostly, what he did to me. I don't know how I didn't see it. You'd only known me for a couple of weeks and you could tell what he was doing. Why couldn't I?'

'Hey, come on.' Faced with her friend's distress, Laurel's self-pity dissolved. 'He worked on you for a long time. It wasn't your fault. You know that, right?'

'Oh, I know, it's just every now and again I feel... happy...' There was surprise on her face as she said it. 'And then I question why I didn't do anything sooner. Sometimes I hate myself for not seizing opportunities earlier in life. For wasting all that time.'

'But you're doing it now.' Laurel clasped Maggie's hands.

'I am, aren't I.' A tentative smile started at the corner of her lips.

A soft tap at the back door made them look up.

Laurel's first thought was that Coral had tracked her down. 'How...'

'I don't think it's the police,' said Maggie, getting up. She opened the door to two young faces peering in.

'Penelope, hi again.' Laurel greeted the young wannabe archaeologist.

'Hi. Sorry, we've been looking for you. Albert said you'd left, but we...' She looked to her companion who nodded in encouragement. 'We know you've like solved mysteries before.'

The other visitor spoke up. 'And we thought you'd want to know the latest about the bone?'

'This is Lin,' said Penelope. 'Lin, this is Laurel and Maggie.'

Lin sketched a wave and said, 'Hi.'

'Hi,' Laurel and Maggie chorused.

Penelope and Lin made no move to go inside; there wasn't really any room.

Maggie solved the predicament. 'It's cramped in here. Let's sit in the garden.' She ushered them all outside. The small grassy area at the back of the house only had space for a square wooden table with four spindly chairs and a couple of flower beds, but the low fence marking the rear border gave out onto the rolling fields that stretched between Elderwick and Dalton, making the garden glorious.

'Congratulations on finding the bone,' said Laurel to Lin. She noticed how Lin's exuberance had faded since making the find.

'Thanks. It's a bit of a downer though. They've got to shut the dig down while the police have the remains excavated and removed. Dr Delgado is sending the rest of the team back to York, but he said I can stay on with him and Beth.'

'And I live here, so obviously, I get to stay too,' Penelope grinned.

Laurel was burning to know what information it was they wanted to share. 'What's the latest, then?'

'Go on, Lin, you tell them,' Penelope prompted.

'You saw me find the bone?'

Laurel nodded.

'Well, Dr Delgado went back in and exposed more of it after sending everyone away. I think he was too excited to wait like he said we should. So, he carried on with the brush and there it was, this glint of metal, of gold. It's a finger bone, one of the proximal phalanges, and there's a gold ring on it. Obviously, all the skin from the finger has decomposed.'

Maggie put a hand to her mouth.

'But you could tell the ring belonged to this finger because the bone really was right through the middle.'

The young women looked at each other.

'There's more?' asked Laurel.

'You won't tell the police we told you? I don't think we were meant to overhear them,' said Penelope.

'Not a chance.' Laurel didn't even have to think about it. 'Maggie?'

'I won't say a word.' She mimed zipping her lips.

Lin leaned forward and spoke quietly. 'When the police went to look, the older officer was saying how the ring proves the burial can't be that old.'

'How did he know?' Maggie quizzed, matching Lin's posture.

'I'm not sure. We just heard him telling Beth and Dr Delgado that it's a signet ring engraved with the words Accrington Standley.'

'Accrington *Stanley*?' Laurel corrected.

'Exactly,' said Penelope.

Laurel sniggered.

Lin frowned. 'What's Accrington Stanley?'

Stifling her giggles, Laurel explained that they were a football club. 'Some clubs have been around for a long time though, so I don't know what date we're talking about.'

Maggie went inside to fetch her phone and looked them up. 'They were only founded in 1968, so the remains can't be more than... what, around fifty-five years old.'

Laurel tensed. Now it made sense. No wonder Coral had

been so quick to declare this a police matter. Although, fifty-five years sounded like a pretty cold case.

Maggie gave a delicate cough. 'Do we know, is there a whole body down there?'

'Dr Delgado thinks so, and I guess the police do too,' Penelope answered.

'If true, it can't have been buried recently, since there's no... the body is... that is, the remains are clean.' Maggie was squirming in her chair, her hands clasped in her lap and her mouth downturned.

Laurel was filing the information away. She would find a notebook when she got home and collate all the data they had so far. *Stop,* she commanded herself, *you're not getting involved.* The mystery of the bones was nothing to do with her. She spun one of her own silver rings round on her finger, wondering what else would be discovered as the rest of the remains were revealed. 'Is there anything else you can tell us?' she asked. 'Does Dr Delgado think the body is male or female? Was there any sign of clothing or hair? Is–'

'Woah, hold on,' Penelope interrupted. 'That's like literally all we know.'

'It must be kind of creepy,' said Lin, 'finding out there's been a dead body buried in the village all this time and no-one knew.'

Laurel shuddered. 'Someone knew.'

Chapter 6

Albert

As luck would have it, Albert had extracted as much information as he believed he was going to get from Rik and Beth before the officer caught up with him. The same whippersnapper who'd tried to send him packing earlier gave him short shrift. 'No respect for their elders these days,' Albert grumbled.

Seeing no way of giving the fuzz the run-around for a second time, he retrieved Aroon, his delinquent cockerel, and set a course for Saint Stephen's in search of the Reverend Christopher Ibori. He was in need of soothing company to aid decompression and was looking forward to a good chinwag with Christopher. Between the vicar's busy schedule and Albert's own packed calendar, it was only once every couple of weeks they winkled out a time to sit down together.

Albert bypassed the grand entrance on the north side of the building, an anomaly in a church, the north traditionally being considered the devil's side. Instead, he used the worn wooden doorway on the far side. He pushed through into a damp, chilly corridor. Like most churches, this one was in need of repairs and upgrades, but the collection plate was barely full enough to stretch to a new can of furniture polish once a month.

'Is that you, Albert? Come on through,' called a voice.

Albert went into the vestry and lowered himself onto the vacant chair with a sigh. 'Have you heard, then?'

Christopher removed his glasses and marked his place in the book on his lap. 'What calamity has befallen the village today? Is Dorothy incensed once more by untidy parking or is there an unauthorised poster on a lamppost?' He chuckled.

Albert allowed himself a wan smile. 'Unfortunately, no, not this time.' He described the uncovering of the bone and the implication of the ring. 'The police are there already, which in itself is not an issue, but the one in charge has a devilish grudge against Laurel.'

'I think this calls for a cup of sweet tea,' said Christopher. 'The kettle's just boiled, unless you want something cold?'

'No, tea is grand, thank you.'

Mugs in hand, they settled into their chairs, ready to put the world to rights.

'You weren't living here in the late sixties?'

Albert shook his head.

'Do you know who was?'

'I've been mulling it over, and there are a few people who come to mind.' He reeled off a list of names. 'Dorothy; Sam Porritt from The Snooty Fox; then there were the Hartfields, of course. You arrived after Marcus and his wife, Petra, left. They were the last of the family to live up at Elderwick Hall. However, in the sixties, Marcus was but a baby, and his father, alive then, has long since passed. Derek Fisher, Marcus' contemporary, is gone too. He lived here his whole life.' Albert's stomach gurgled sourly at the memory of Derek, the cantankerous old grouch.

'And there'll be others who lived here but have since moved on.'

'Undoubtedly.'

Christopher picked up a pencil and twiddled it in his fingers. 'The police are going to have quite a job ahead of them unless they can identify the remains. The ring is the only evidence?'

'They may find more as they continue with the exhumation.'

'Not much for Laurel to go on if she intends to reprise her number one ladies' detective agency.' Christopher scribbled a note in a pad on his desk. 'Will she, do you think? She did a better job than the police with the whole Hugh Quintrell affair. I have to admire her, even if she suspected me for a while.' He smirked.

'Mayhap she'll want to steer clear this time, what with that policewoman, DI Coral, being involved. Laurel does not care for her.'

'Which is probably why Laurel will end up getting herself involved, even as she protests her reluctance.'

Albert chuckled. Christopher had her pegged.

'More tea?' the vicar offered.

Cup refilled, Albert broached a question he wasn't sure he should ask a man of the cloth. 'As a vicar, being involved in burials and whatnot, do you have any idea how long it takes for a body to decompose?'

'I see, it's not Laurel we need to worry about, it's...' He broke off and studied Albert, 'Poirot? No wait, more like an elderly Hardy boy.' He creased up, his shoulders shaking. 'And don't think I don't see you rolling your eyes at me.'

'I was thinking more along the lines of Morse or Jonathan Creek, at the very least,' was Albert's rejoinder.

Wiping his eyes, Christopher said, 'Well, you're neither a detective nor a designer of stage illusions for a magician, so...'

This was just what the doctor had ordered; a good laugh in good company. He was unsettled by the discovery in the field, and worried about his friend.

'Perhaps I should pop up there,' said the reverend, his tone serious again. 'I mean, there's not a lot I can do, but these are someone's mortal remains after all.'

Albert was amused to see the vicar reach for another ginger nut instead of making a move.

'Before I go though,' he said once he'd finished crunching, 'you promised you'd tell me how you've been getting on with your – what are we calling it – your project? You claimed you were making great strides the last time we spoke.'

Albert took his time taking another sip of his drink. 'Let's just say it may be prudent to pause for a while.'

Christopher dunked another ginger biscuit in his tea. 'You know I'm here if there's anything I can do.'

'I know. Thank you.' Albert drained his cup and settled it back on the saucer. 'Now, I think your idea of heading over to the meadow is an excellent one. I find myself at a loose end, therefore, I shall accompany you.'

'They asked you to leave, didn't they? You want to use me as your way back in.'

'My dear man,' Albert clasped a hand over his heart, 'never would I stoop so low!'

Chapter 7

Laurel

Laurel rubbed her hands over her face. The news from Penelope and Lin had been interesting. The ring put the bones at around fifty-five years old at most, and the body was thoroughly decomposed. So, unless the police had other information marking the actual death of the ring's owner as *much more recent*, as Coral had claimed, it was absurd for the DI to suggest Laurel could be involved. But Laurel didn't think Coral really believed it anyway. It was just another excuse for the woman to harass her.

'Much as I'd like to stick two fingers up at the police after how I was treated earlier, I think I'm going to go home and wait for them to come round and take my statement,' she said to Maggie. She'd been backwards and forwards over the best course of action and had decided it probably wasn't smart to antagonise the people in charge of a murder investigation.

'Are you sure?'

'I'm only going to sit and stew over it if I stay here. Besides, if it's someone other than Coral who comes round, maybe I can tease some more details out of them.' She had a funny feeling, though, that Coral would enjoy being the one to take her statement and wouldn't miss out on the experience by delegating.

'Shall I come with you?'

Laurel picked at a nail as she considered the offer. It would be sensible to have a witness, but was Maggie the right person? Laurel was anxious enough as it was. She didn't want Maggie worrying for her too, or worse, getting pulled into whatever ridiculous vendetta Coral was pursuing.

'Thank you, but I'll be fine.'

'If you're sure?'

It was galling to have Coral implying she was an interfering busybody and warning her off from something with which she had no intention of becoming involved. It wasn't as though she had an empty life and needed distraction.

Since her move to Elderwick, Laurel's priorities were friendships and living a rewarding life. She had a busy clinical psychology practice but organised her diary to leave plenty of time away from the office. For those clients she took on, she charged a low, or even sliding scale, fee. As long as she had sufficient to cover her bills, a little for a shopping trip now and again, and a bit left over for all the wonderful edible treats she indulged in, then she had all she needed.

Maggie was observing her the way one might watch an accident waiting to happen.

'I'll be fine, I promise. I'm pretty beat today, but how about you and Albert come to mine for dinner tomorrow night, and we can compare notes? I bet Albert will have something to tell us by then.'

'Dinner?' said Maggie with a grin.

'Tea, I mean.' She still lapsed into *Southern Speak,* as Maggie called it when she teased her over a slip. 'I'll make tarragon chicken with new potatoes.'

Maggie licked her lips. 'That sounds yum. And I should have time to whip up a lemon meringue pie for dessert.'

'You mean pudding, not dessert, surely? Afters, even.'

Maggie swatted at her.

'I said I'd meet Constance and Hetty at The Fox for a drink tomorrow. Do you want to join us before we eat?'

Tempting as the offer was, Laurel opted out; she didn't want to chance running into Jayne again. 'Thanks, but I might give it a miss this time. Give them my love and tell Hetty I'll be in for a couple of pains au chocolat on Monday.' As she said it, she caught sight of her reflection in the window. *On the other hand, I'd better stick to porridge,* she thought, sucking in her stomach.

'I will. I'm meeting them around six, so I can come to yours around seven-thirty?'

'Perfect. That's settled then. I'll stop by Albert's and let him know the plan. If he's not home yet, I'll leave him a note.' Standing to leave, she dabbed a couple of crumbs off her skirt, then bent to hug Maggie. 'Wish me luck.'

'Luck.'

Despite the lingering heat of late afternoon, Laurel hurried up the lane. It would only make matters worse if Coral had already been to Myrtle Cottage and found it deserted. Her earlier glee at disregarding the instruction now felt hollow.

Speed walking along South Street, she nipped down the tree-lined path that skirted the church and continued round the back of the primary school. It was shady and out of sight of anyone on the road. As she exited onto West Lane, she passed the gates to Elderwick Hall and approached the bottom of Birch Lane. She let out a relieved breath. There was no sign of a police car in front of her cottage. She might have got away with it.

As she closed the garden gate at the bottom of the short flagstone path, Coral came striding round the corner from the back of the cottage. Had she been trying the rear doors, or was she peering through windows? Laurel tamped down the flare of indignation, fearing she would say something she would regret.

'I told you to come straight back here. We're in the middle of a murder investigation. We do not have time to be chasing round after you.'

To say they were in the middle of an investigation seemed rich. It was barely two hours since the bone had been uncovered. Nevertheless, Laurel overlooked the rebuke, and acting the good hostess, invited the detective inspector inside.

'Can I get you a cold drink? You must be hot?' Laurel could see beads of sweat on the other woman's forehead, and she would bet she was sweltering under her unflattering suit jacket.

Laurel stood in the kitchen, poised to open the fridge, but before Coral answered, Hill let himself in behind her.

'Sorry,' he said. Then, with a hopeful ring to his voice, 'Did I hear there was a drink on offer?'

Coral's mouth became a single sharp line and her cheeks hollowed.

Hill accepted a glass of lemonade, and Laurel poured one for herself, then led the two through to the living room. She unlocked and pushed open the French windows as her visitors took up positions in the two armchairs. Left with only the sofa, Laurel sat, perching on the edge so as not to sink back into the yielding cushions.

Laurel waited. She'd played this game before. She wasn't going to be the one to break the loaded silence that had descended over the trio. She and Hill sipped their drinks. He appeared to be as comfortable with the quiet as she was. She imagined Coral's muscles quivering as the tension built. She lingered over another mouthful of cooling lemonade and allowed a deliberate sigh to escape softly into the chasm between them.

Coral broke first. 'Explain how you came to be present this morning at the archaeological dig.'

Hill put his glass down – on a coaster, Laurel was pleased to observe – and reached into a pocket for his notebook and pen.

She was tempted to be belligerent, but if she was cooperative now, perhaps Coral would get this nonsense over with quickly. 'I went to see what was happening. To see if anything interesting had been dug up.'

'Did you know there were human remains buried in the meadow?'

'No, of course not.'

'But you *happened* to be there at the exact moment they were uncovered?' The emphasis made her scepticism obvious.

'Yes, I *happened* to be there. A few people were around. Are you interrogating all of them, too? I didn't hear you tell Albert he had to go home and wait for you? I didn't know there was a body there; but even if I had, how could I have known when it would be uncovered? This is ridiculous.'

Coral ignored her questions. 'So, how do you explain knowing it's a body? No-one said anything about a body. As far as I am aware, a single bone from a human hand was the only item discovered this morning.'

The woman's being ludicrous. 'Everyone's talking about *the body*. Whether it's a whole body, who knows. It's a figure of speech.' She hit on something that she knew would rile the DI further. 'Besides, a second ago, you said "remains", plural, had been uncovered, and back at the meadow, you asked how come I'm always around when a "body" is found.' *Parry and thrust.*

Hill's pen hovered over the page.

Coral rallied. 'And I ask again, how is it you have been present, not only present, but the first person to discover three dead bodies in the last few years?'

This was old territory; they'd been over this before when

Laurel had been interviewed at the police station in connection with previous murders.

'I wasn't alone when any of the people who'd been killed were found, you know that. And in each case, the murderer was identified and they're all in prison.' She was struggling to keep her voice from rising. She wanted to shout but wouldn't give Coral the satisfaction of knowing she was rattled. 'How do you know this is a murder?' She threw back, hoping the DI would give up the information about the ring.

'I can't discuss the details of the case.' Coral smirked and Laurel desperately wanted to wipe it off her face. 'That will be all for now, but we'll be watching you. Stay away from the meadow, stay away from my investigation. If you don't, I'll haul you into the station quicker than you can say Miss Marple. This is real life, not a game. I will not tolerate you running round playing amateur sleuth again.'

Words burned in Laurel's throat. She was itching to remind Coral that she had been the one to identify the killers in the past, when the police had failed to do so, but she squeezed her lips together and said nothing.

Chapter 8

Maggie

'Is everyone all right for drinks?' Maggie asked early Saturday evening as she sat herself down next to Constance at the wooden picnic table in the beer garden of The Snooty Fox. The surrounding tables were all occupied, and there was a cheerful hum of conversation in the air.

'We are, thank you,' said Hetty, raising her glass. 'I'm glad you could make it. We heard about the police showing up yesterday. I hope you've come prepared to share the latest?' Florence poked her and she giggled. 'Florence thinks we gossip too much in this village.'

'Too much!' exclaimed Florence. 'It's practically a full-time occupation for most of the locals. You three especially. If someone buys a croissant in the morning, by lunchtime the entire village knows how many crumbs were left after they ate it.' She threw her head back and laughed.

Maggie didn't think she'd ever known anyone who actually did that, really threw their head back so much you could see their fillings. She liked Florence, and it was obvious how happy she made Hetty.

'What is that you're drinking?' She nodded at Hetty's glass.

'This,' she held it up, 'is another of Sam's experiments. It's a rhubarb mojito. I thought you only got them in mint, but apparently not. He's got a whole range: rhubarb; raspberry; coconut; ginger; mango; and even lavender. I'm not sold on the idea of a lavender one, but maybe I'll work up to it.'

Maggie licked her lips. 'I was going to have a cider, but a coconut mojito sounds worth a try. I'll be right back.'

At the bar, Sam chatted away with her as he made her drink. 'You'll have heard about the body they found then? Complete skeleton, old Jacob said.'

'That's not what I was told,' said a gentleman seated on a bar stool to her left. 'It was most of the bones, but no head.'

His companion next to him leaned forward. 'No, it's the other way round. It was just a skull, and there was hair still on it.'

An argument began over the precise contents of the trench in the meadow. Unfortunately, none of the dig team were around to shed factual light onto the rumours.

'Thanks, Sam,' she paid the bar manager and made her escape back to her friends and the relative peace of the garden.

'Come on then,' demanded Constance. 'What were the police here for? What did they find up at the archaeology site?'

Maggie was about to tell them what she knew when she spotted Lin coming into the garden accompanied by a stranger. They were casting around for some spare seats.

'That's one of the people from the dig,' she whispered, motioning to Lin. 'Shall we invite them to join us?' When there were no objections, Maggie called out, 'Lin, do you and your friend want to sit with us?'

'Hi,' said Lin as they reached the table. 'Are you sure you don't mind? We don't want to intrude.'

'Nonsense.' Hetty waved them into the spaces on the bench.

'Ah, but be warned,' chuckled Florence. 'This lot,' she

pointed to the two bakers and Maggie, 'will want chapter and verse about the drama in the meadow and what the police were doing back there today.'

Maggie gave her an exaggerated eye roll before introducing Lin. 'Everyone, this is Lin.'

Hetty, Constance, and Florence gave their names and waved hello.

Beckoning her companion closer, Lin said, 'This is Jessica Marumo. She got here this afternoon.'

Jessica greeted them, 'Nice to meet you all.'

'Are you an archaeologist, too?' Hetty asked.

'No, I'm a student at York Uni, like Lin, but I'm studying anthropology, post-grad. I'm doing my masters.'

Lin expanded on Jessica's statement. 'Jess is not just doing her masters, she's up for the super prestigious Lawton Grant this year to do her PhD.'

'It's not a big deal, and there are thousands of other applicants.'

'She's being modest,' said Lin. 'Also, I should say, I'm not a proper archaeologist yet: I'm only an undergrad.'

'You're as good as,' Jessica shot back. 'Always top in her class and already has a full-time job lined up for after graduation.'

Lin blushed.

Maggie liked Jessica's compliment. Lin reminded her a bit of herself when she was younger, afraid to push herself forward and take credit for her achievements. It was good she had someone like Jessica to champion her.

'Jessica, how is an anthropologist involved with the dig?' Florence sounded eager to know more.

'Actually, Lin called and asked if I was interested in coming up. I've been working on a study of how communities and individuals react when people go missing. You know, the impact, the suspicion, the way some people are shunned if there are suspicious circumstances, what happens if the person returns, or is found, versus if they never come back. We've covered some of the high-profile disappearances, such as Suzy Lamplugh, and now we're looking at local cases. As you can imagine, it's delicate stuff, so we're working with old cases where there are contemporaneous records and accounts.'

'Gosh, that sounds like valuable work,' Maggie commented.

'I like to think our work will be of benefit,' said Jessica. 'And when Lin told me about the remains discovered here I knew I had to take it to my supervisor. She agreed that this could be an amazing opportunity to observe how a close-knit, rural community behaves when a missing person is found deceased.'

'We don't know that they're from Elderwick.' Constance pointed out.

Jessica was shaking her head. 'Doesn't matter. This is about the unanswered questions until the person is identified. Obviously, if it turns out they're connected to someone here, we'll reassess how we continue.'

'I don't mean to be rude,' said Hetty, 'but it seems a bit insensitive. There are a lot of people who've lived in the village for decades. This could be someone they know.'

'No, I totally get that, and I'll be getting consent every step of the way. The other thing is, though, we've got a whole database of people who've gone missing in the area over the last like, fifty years. We think we might be able to help.'

Disliking confrontation, Maggie appealed to Hetty. 'That could be very useful, don't you think?'

'True,' Hetty granted her. 'You'll be careful how you go about it, though?'

'Absolutely. I'll need to speak to Dr Delgado first and get his permission; and the police. We'll be liaising with them. So, actually, could you keep this quiet until I've had chance to do that?' Jessica scanned the faces around the table.

Florence raised her eyebrows. 'They'll try.'

'We will,' Maggie reassured.

Florence winked at Jessica and stood. 'Let me get you two a drink.'

Once they were all furnished with refreshments, Lin recapped what had turned up in the dusty earth the day before. She only mentioned the finger bone, not the ring, and Maggie wasn't about to betray her confidence, despite the twinge of guilt over keeping the information back from her friends.

'We, the team, haven't been allowed back yet. I think the police have been there all day today, probably with the forensic anthropologist.'

All eyes turned to Jessica. 'Different type of anthropologist,' she clarified.

'So, another murder investigation is underway in Elderwick. At least the body isn't fresh this time.'

'Hetty! You can't say that.' Constance set down her drink with a thud, spilling a little on the table. 'A person is dead and has been buried in our meadow. It might have been some time ago, but I think we should show a little respect.'

Hetty lowered her eyes, but there was a quirk to her mouth. 'Yes, dear,' she sing-songed. To Lin and Jessica, she explained, 'Constance likes to pretend she's more sensitive than I am. But she's right.' The sardonic smile slid from her lips. 'I deal with discomfort by being flippant, and it is upsetting to think someone was buried there for so long and no one knew.'

There was a lull in the conversation until Maggie couldn't hold back and voiced what she suspected the others were already thinking. 'There is somebody who knew about the body, because they put it there.'

'Thanks, Maggie,' said Constance. 'That's going to give me nightmares.'

'Wait.' Jessica was frowning. 'What did you mean when you

said *another murder investigation?* Has there been a murder here before?' She'd been peeling the label off her bottle of cider, but her fingers stilled as she gawped at the locals.

There was a pregnant pause as the three Elderwickians round the table looked at each other.

'How long have you got?' asked Hetty.

Later, and another drink into their evening, Lin and Jessica had been fully briefed on the events of the last few years.

'Wow, that's pretty dark,' said Jessica. 'Laurel sounds amazing. She should go into business as a private investigator or something.'

Maggie swelled with pride for her friend. 'Being a psychologist, she's brilliant at picking up on clues, for instance, when people don't get along, or a person has a secret. That's how she solved the other murders.' She paused as an idea popped into her head. If Laurel were with them, she would undoubtedly have more questions for Lin. As that wasn't the case, she would ask in Laurel's stead. 'I know it's unlikely that anyone involved in the dig could have a link to these remains, but are you aware of anything or anyone suspicious connected with the project?'

Lin frowned but shook her head. 'Not that I can think of.'

Mulling over other possible queries, Maggie heard the church bells chime. 'Oh heck, how is it seven fifteen already? I'd better be making a move. I've got to nip home and collect a pie, then I'm having tea with Laurel and Albert.'

Hetty, Florence, and Constance also made noises about having to head off.

Standing, Maggie dithered over whether to invite Jessica and Lin to accompany her. It wouldn't be fair to spring two extra guests on Laurel, but it would give them more time to probe into Jessica's project. Besides, the two students could probably do with a good home-cooked meal.

'Would you two like to join me at Laurel's this evening?'

'That's so kind,' began Lin, 'but we're staying at Drumble's Hive and they've promised us a veggie barbecue tonight.'

Maggie thought of the rough but sturdy huts virtually hidden amongst the trees up on Elder Hill. It was hardly a luxury hotel, but the women were young, and the members of the commune were generous and welcoming to like-minded visitors. 'I've never had a vegetarian barbecue before. You'll have to let me know what they cook. I'd like to make more veggie dishes myself.'

'Absolutely,' Lin replied. 'I'm excited to see what they'll serve up.'

As they gathered their things, Constance asked, 'Maggie, have you got a second?'

Thinking it was going to be about the classes she led at the bakery, Maggie plonked herself back down. 'Sure, if it's quick.'

Constance waited until everyone else had said their goodbyes and were on their way out of the garden, then produced her phone. 'Promise you won't laugh at me?'

'Of course I won't.' Maggie was wounded that she'd even asked. 'What is it?' She edged closer so she could see the screen.

Constance signed into the pub wifi and brought up a website. 'I could download the app, but I don't want Hetty to catch sight of it on my phone. I'd never hear the end of it.' She navigated through a couple of menus to bring up a photo. 'What do you think?'

'Wow, he's hot,' said a voice from behind, causing them to jump.

Constance tried to hide the phone but fumbled and dropped it on the grass.

'Crap, sorry,' said Jessica. 'I guess I wasn't meant to see that? I just came back for these.' She picked up her sunglasses, then retrieved Constance's mobile for her. 'Is it a dating site?'

Constance grimaced.

'Oh, that's what it is,' Maggie grinned at her. 'You're right, Jessica, he is hot. Let's have another look.'

After a moment of hesitation, Constance allowed them another look at the picture. 'His name's Carter Braidwood. He's a chef.'

Maggie admired the handsome, dark-haired, blue-eyed man on the screen. 'Carter Braidwood,' she repeated. 'That's a lovely name.'

'Jessica, come on,' Lin shouted from the gate.

Constance shoved the phone back into her bag.

Maggie stood again and said out-loud, 'Yes, we'd all better get going.' And quietly to Constance she added, 'We'll talk more about this later, you dark horse.'

Chapter 9

Laurel

With Maggie and Albert comfortably ensconced at the table, Laurel added a final sprinkling of tarragon and a swirl of cream to the pot, and she was ready to serve. If it were winter, they would have been balancing the plates on their knees in the living room, her cottage not being big enough for a dining table, but since it was summer, they were out on the terrace in her back garden.

'Here we go.' She set a plate in front of each of them and nipped back inside to grab the chilled bottle of rosé she knew was a favourite of Maggie's. Pouring generous glasses, she realised the tightness in her shoulders had finally released and the pounding in her head had abated.

'Cheers.' Laurel raised her glass and toasted the others.

They clinked.

'Wait, I forgot the bread rolls.' She hurried back inside to take them out of the oven where she'd put them to warm. 'Here we go, fresh from The Plump Tart.' She set the basket down in the middle of the table. 'Oh, speaking of the bakery... I meant to ask, Albert, are the new photos on the wall you're doing? The ones of the bakery before it was the bakery?'

'They are. I came across them a while back and felt they should be in their proper home.'

'Hetty and Constance love them,' said Maggie. 'And it's fun seeing what the building was like before they took it over.' She reached for a roll, tore it in two and dipped it in the sauce on her plate. 'Heaven,' she sighed.

'Not that I want to detract from your delectable cooking, but shall we finish eating before updates or...?' Maggie deferred to Laurel.

'We can eat and talk. My head has been spinning, so it would be good to get your thoughts. I'm so glad Penelope and Lin came over to visit us yesterday. If I didn't know about the ring, I'd think Coral had completely lost the plot. Strike that. I still think she *has* lost her marbles.'

'I believe they're a little in awe of you and your detective abilities,' said Albert.

Maggie put down her fork. 'Did you find out anything else when you were still up at the meadow?' Maggie asked him.

Laurel had a mouthful of tender chicken, but she was barely tasting it.

'Nothing worth reporting, I'm afraid. Rik – Dr Delgado – let slip about the ring, but I couldn't get a word out of the police officers who were there taking peoples' details.'

'This delay won't be doing the archaeology team any favours. How is Dr Delgado taking it?' Laurel asked.

'In his stride. I shouldn't imagine they usually dig up bones this recent, but he appears well versed with the protocol. It's only a couple of times that I've met the chap, but he seems a sensible sort.'

'How did Dandelions find him? I don't know how it works with these archaeologists and new developments. I certainly don't remember Marcus having anyone checking the Elderwick

Hall grounds when he wanted to build his hotel and golf course.'

Albert wiped his lips with a napkin and had a mouthful of wine. 'That's because Marcus didn't bother with official channels. I suspect your ex-husband *eased the way* for him,' he said to Maggie.

Maggie shuffled in her chair and Laurel almost said something. Maggie wasn't responsible for her ex-husband's unethical business dealings, even though she continued to act as though she were equally guilty. If Nicholas ever turned up in the village again, Laurel had a few choice words she'd like to share with him.

'From what I've heard, Dandelions didn't find him. Rik came to them,' he finished.

Laurel paused in her chewing. 'How did Delgado know they needed an archaeologist?'

Albert shrugged. 'I'm in the dark on that one. But I could ask. I'm due to meet with the Dandelions managers on Monday. Do you think it's important?'

'Maybe. It seems odd that Dr Delgado volunteered his team, and they just happen to come across a murder victim?' Laurel pushed back in her chair. 'Hold on, I've got a notebook inside. I want to write this down.'

She went in through the French windows and returned moments later with two notebooks, one pink, one turquoise. She held them out to Maggie. 'I am not saying we should investigate this latest murder – if that's what it is – and Coral specifically warned me off, but I bought these a while back, so we may as well use them. Would you like one?'

Between them, they already had four notebooks crammed with clues, theories, and questions from the previous occasions when they had played amateur detectives. Emphasis on the *amateur*. Laurel cringed at the memories. She'd been so wrong about so many things, and had even put herself in danger twice. No, she was quite happy to leave the police to do their jobs this time.

Maggie's eyes travelled backwards and forwards between the two books. 'I love the turquoise, but you choose, Laurel.'

Laurel grinned. 'And I love the pink, so that works out well.' She handed the turquoise one to Maggie and sat back down at the table. Her guests' plates were clean; her own was only half empty, but she wasn't hungry. The leftovers would freeze well and do for another day.

Stroking the soft leather cover of her notebook, Maggie queried, 'So, tell us, did the police show up to take your statement yesterday?'

Laurel pulled a face and relayed her account of the visit she'd received from Coral and Hill. 'I didn't learn anything new from them and Coral was deliberately woolly on the details. The whole thing was an excuse for her to warn me off again. Goodness knows what she thinks I'm going to do. Like I would even want to get involved!' As she spoke, she opened her notebook and wrote: *To follow up* at the top of the first page, and underneath added: *Dandelions re: approach from Dr Delgado.*

Maggie watched, then rooted round in her bag for a pen and scribed the same into her book. 'Oh, I didn't say, I ran into Lin in the pub before I came here and she had a lovely friend with her, Jessica Marumo.'

'And she is...?' Laurel prompted.

'An anthropology student at York University. A very bright young woman, she's in the running for what must be a prestigious award, the Lawton Grant, to do her doctorate. Lin called her after the bones were found because Jessica's involved in a project concerning missing people. I forget the exact details, but she thinks she might be able to help put a name to the remains.'

'Interesting,' said Albert.

'Oh, but I don't think I'm supposed to mention it until she's spoken to Dr Delgado and the police.'

Albert chuckled.

Laurel scribbled down Jessica's name. She was getting an itchy sensation on the back of her neck, and her thoughts were fizzing. These were bad signs. Dangerous signs. Best change the subject before she suggested something that would get her into hot water. 'Can we talk about something else?' she asked, when she eventually put down her pencil and closed the book. 'That's enough bodies and murder for one evening.'

Maggie jotted a couple more notes, then copied Laurel in closing her book. 'I agree. Let's have a piece of lemon meringue pie and think about nice things. Laurel, shall I do the honours?' With Laurel's enthusiastic assent, Maggie cleared the table and bustled off to the kitchen to get the pie and clean plates.

'Laurel,' whispered Albert, checking behind him for signs of Maggie returning. 'I assume you don't want to talk about Jayne from the café?'

'Not really. Thank you for not mentioning her within earshot of Maggie.'

'Not a problem, my dear.' He patted her on the hand.

'There are some people from the past who should stay in the past, and Jayne is one of them.'

'Jayne who?'

Ears like a bat, that woman.

'Sorry,' mouthed Albert.

'Nobody. Nothing, we were just...' Her words dried up. She couldn't think of an effective diversion. 'Just someone I bumped into. Someone I used to know.'

Maggie handed round plates of pie, which consisted of a golden pastry base heaped with intense yellow curd and topped with clouds of meringue. Laurel's teeth ached just from looking at it. However, appetite magically restored, she was going to enjoy every bite. Nothing would put her off one of Maggie's desserts, not even Jayne.

'Come on, you should know by now, you're not going to get away with that. Who's Jayne and, more importantly, why don't you want to talk about her? No wait, more important even than that, how does Albert know about her, and I don't?' Maggie's naturally sunny face was sending mixed messages, caught between a scowl and a smile.

It was a losing battle. Laurel resigned herself to divulging some details to get them off her back. Albert, she could tell, was as curious as Maggie. Why else had he mentioned Jayne in such proximity to Mrs Bat-Ears? She shot him a look. He beamed back at her, the picture of innocence.

'Fine.' She ran a hand through her hair and deliberated over how to begin. 'But it's nothing exciting; she's just a person I knew at school. We didn't get on very well. I saw her at the Pleasant Pheasant and unfortunately, she saw me too. That's it.'

'Why didn't you get on at school?'

'There was a clash of personalities.' The least she could do was to make them work for every morsel of information.

'She seemed perfectly nice to me.'

Laurel sighed; she wasn't surprised by Albert's opinion. 'Well, you only met her for a few seconds.' She could sense her ears getting hot and hoped they weren't visibly red. This topic of conversation was churning her stomach. 'Sorry, I didn't mean to snap. Jayne's fine. We didn't get on at school, and I'm not interested in getting to know her now.'

Maggie seized on her words. 'Is she going to be around for a while, then?'

'She mentioned something about being in Elderwick for a few days, I think.' Laurel would bet Maggie was already planning to 'accidentally on purpose' run into Jayne if she possibly could. 'I promise you, there's no juicy story here. If you want to meet her, be my guest, but please don't engineer any meetings.'

Maggie squirmed.

Busted.

Later, after her friends had finished all the food and wine, and they'd exhausted safer conversational grounds, they said goodnight and left Laurel alone with her memories. The lack of a mobile signal would take care of any attempts by Jayne to contact her by phone, but she knew she would be looking over her shoulder for the next week or so. There were things about her relationship with Jayne that belonged in the past. The last thing she wanted was to face them again, here in the midst of her new, happy life.

Chapter 10

Maggie

Maggie tapped on the door. It was Sunday and the bakery was closed, but Constance had called and asked if she could go round. She'd sounded upset and so Maggie had pulled on her lightweight linen trousers and a pretty cotton top in pale green and hurried through the early morning hush of the slumbering village.

Constance opened the kitchen door and ushered Maggie inside. 'You must hate me for calling so early, and on a Sunday.'

Maggie noted Constance's red nose and trembling chin. 'Don't even mention it. I'm always awake early. Now what's wrong? Are you okay? Is it Hetty?'

'Hetty's fine. It's just... look, come on through.' Constance wheeled back behind the counter and into the kitchen. Through another door on the far side was a hallway complete with a compact elevator. 'Hetty stayed over with Florence. We can talk in the sitting room where it's more comfortable.'

Maggie climbed the stairs and waited whilst Constance rolled her chair into the lift, and backed out again when it reached the first floor of the flat above the bakery where she and Hetty lived.

'Cup of tea? Coffee?'

'No, I'm fine. Please, just tell me what's the matter. You've got me worried to bits.' Maggie sat down on the sofa, her hands clasped in her lap, knuckles white.

'You're going to think I'm such a fool.' Constance picked up a laptop and handed it to her.

She received it with a puzzled frown. Her heart rate slowed. No-one was hurt, ill, or injured, and if Constance had time to worry about being daft, then this wasn't a life-or-death situation. Curiosity replaced her fear.

Constance reached over and tapped a key to bring the screen to life.

Maggie recognised the website. 'Oh, this is the dating site. Is this about your paramour, Carter Braidwood?'

Constance didn't answer her question immediately. 'This is *Salt 'n' Pepper*. It's specifically for people in the culinary sector. Bakers, chefs, cooks, people who love food and don't necessarily live the nine-to-five life.'

'Okay.'

Constance kept her head low, eyes down. 'I feel like such a fool. I know it's ridiculous, a thirty-seven-year-old woman, a woman like me thinking she could meet someone online. But a friend tried it, and she said it wasn't that bad.'

'Hmm.' Always good with computers, Maggie was navigating the site like a pro. Internet dating wasn't a thing she'd ever contemplated for herself. Since divorcing Nicholas, she'd needed time to learn who she was now he was gone. Who she was other than a wife and mother. It had been a while, though, since they'd separated. Was it time for her to get back out there?

She spied a tab called *Complimentary Flavours* – the company was heavily leaning into the whole food schtick. 'Are these your matches?' Three thumbnail photos popped up and Maggie clicked on Carter.

Constance relieved her of the laptop and put it on the coffee table, but didn't close it.

Maggie refocused. 'Why is it ridiculous? You're a very attractive, intelligent woman. You run your own successful business. You're a catch. This is how loads of people meet their partners these days – so Albert tells me – and even I've heard of Tumble.'

Constance snorted. 'I think you're confusing Tinder and Bumble, but yes, I know this is the norm these days. But only stupid middle-aged women get scammed.'

'What do you mean scammed?' Maggie's heart sank. There were many injustices and hardships faced by women at the hands of men – she should know – and it made her furious to think her friend had been targeted in the very moment she'd made herself vulnerable in the search for love and companionship. She waited until Constance was ready to talk.

'I've been chatting with Carter,' she inclined her head to the laptop, 'since Tuesday. He came across as funny and sweet, and every day I've looked forward to hearing from him. He said he worked the breakfast and lunch shift in a boutique hotel in York, so he was always free in an evening. And you know Hetty and I are up at the absolute crack of dawn then finished by five. So, even in a short time, it felt like we clicked, practically and emotionally.'

Maggie was braced for the *but*.

'But last night he messaged me and said he was at the vets with his seriously ill dog, and he'd forgotten his wallet in his panic to get her there. He was desperate, but said the vet was prepared to call me and take payment details so I could pay the bill for him until he got home when he would pay me back.' Constance rubbed her eyes and exhaled loudly. 'He said he totally understood if I didn't want to because he needed nearly four hundred pounds. He knew that was a lot, and he even said he'd think it was sketchy if it was the other way round.' She lapsed into silence.

'And the "vet", Maggie made air quotes with her fingers, 'called and you gave them your details?'

Constance nodded. 'How could I have been so incredibly stupid? I mean, what kind of moron falls for that? I've never met this guy. I've not even been messaging him for a whole week yet. Why on earth did I give him my card information? But I liked him, and we'd talked so much. I thought he was a genuine guy, you know? God, I'm so embarrassed.' She put her head in her hands.

'How much?'

'Three hundred and seventy-five pounds.'

Expensive dog. Maggie thought about how to ask her next question. 'How did you find out that it was a scam?'

'I haven't heard from him since. I tried messaging him this morning, but I don't think he's even been back on the site. If it wasn't some kind of scam, why hasn't he been in touch?'

Maggie chewed over the possibilities. It sounded like a con, but... 'Well, maybe he's been busy with his poorly dog. It's only,' she squinted at her watch, '8am. If he hasn't been on the site, it's possible he hasn't read your messages yet. I mean, it would have been polite to be showering you with thanks and paying you back right now, but...'

Constance's face fell. 'I really liked him. Since Hetty and Florence got together, I've been feeling more and more like a spare part. It's difficult meeting people, you know, with the chair, but he didn't seem phased in the slightest.'

'Why would he be?'

'Come on, you know how people are.'

'What do you mean?'

Constance rolled her eyes. 'People see me in my chair, this

visual sign of a disability, and they're unable or unwilling to see beyond it. They don't even try to get to know *me*.'

'Well then, they're not the kind of people you need to waste any time on.' Maggie declared.

Constance clucked her tongue. 'Exactly, but that's why I was hopeful this time. Carter was still keen even after seeing pictures of me with Bert and Ernie–'

'Who?'

She gave her arm rest an affectionate pat. 'This is Bert, my big chair, and Ernie's my little one.' She sighed. 'I should have known it was too good to be true.'

Momentarily thrown, and tempted to ask why Constance had chosen the *Sesame Street* names, Maggie shook her head and returned to the problem at hand. 'Let's not write him off just yet. It sounds dodgy, and I know I don't have to tell you to never give money to strangers you meet online...'

Constance stuck out her tongue.

'But maybe he's one of the good guys? How about you send one more message? If he replies, you make sure you get your money back and you take it steady if you keep communicating with him. But maybe cancel your bank card anyway, just in case.'

'I've already done that,' she said. 'And if I send another message and he doesn't reply?'

'You should report him.'

Constance gave a wan smile. 'For all the good it will do.'

Maggie's heart broke at the defeated look in Constance's eyes. She was waffling on about details when what her friend needed was a hug. She scooted over, closer to the wheelchair, Bert, and though she banged her shins, she gripped Constance and held her tight.

When Constance wrestled free, Maggie said, 'Send another email, or whatever it is, and keep me informed. If he is a scammer, we can get him blocked on *Salt 'n' Pepper* and at least stop him from preying on other women on there.'

'Or...' Constance smirked.

'Or?'

'Or I could try to get my own back.'

Maggie plastered on a grin; she didn't like the sound of that. 'Let's not go full vigilante just yet.'

Chapter 11

Laurel

While the dew still clung to the grass, Laurel had gone out for a walk, hoping to enjoy some exercise before the heat returned and it became too uncomfortable to do anything more strenuous than lounge in a deckchair. Unfortunately, she wasn't the only person to be out in the cooler air.

'Laurel?'

What was it with people she didn't want to see or speak to? How did they keep finding her?

'Ben, hi.'

He wasn't in uniform, but his navy short-sleeved shirt and smart jeans were hardly casual.

'How are you?' he asked, moving closer.

His hair shone silver in the sun and his chin was grazed with the perfect amount of stubble. She'd forgotten his eyes, his gold-flecked hazel eyes. He had a few more laughter lines, but they only added to his appeal. She gave her head an imperceptible shake. It hadn't been a good idea then, and it wasn't a good idea now.

'I'm...' She'd been about to say she was fine, but she wasn't. The night had dragged, hour after interminable hour as images of bones rising from the earth had plagued her thoughts. 'I'm fine.' What good would it be to say otherwise?

The last time she'd spoken to him properly was when she'd found out who had been sending her a series of threatening letters. Letters which had arrived at her door during the same period as two murders had occurred in the village. It had got so bad she'd contemplated leaving Elderwick because of what she'd been accused of in the poisonous notes.

'You're back then?' She couldn't help stating the obvious.

'Yes, I decided it was time to come home. I've missed Elderwick.'

Laurel knew he'd rented out his cottage and had taken a secondment with the much larger police force in Leeds. Whether he'd been running away from her or memories of his ex, she wasn't sure.

'That's good. And how are you?' She stuck her hands in her pockets to hide the shake.

'I'm fine,' he echoed her response.

She'd run out of banalities and if she didn't go soon, she was afraid she'd blurt out what she was really thinking.

'Anyway,' he said.

'Yeah.'

'Nice to see you.'

'You too.'

'Okay.'

'Right, I'd better...'

'See you around.'

'Sure.'

She had to walk past him. It would be weird if she turned round and went back the way she'd come. She started forward, her gait felt unnatural, as though she'd forgotten how to walk. She was convinced her discomfort was obvious. She went as fast as she could without breaking into a jog, her breath caught in her chest. Only when she turned the corner and was out of his sight did she pause to take a gulp of air and wait for the stars dancing in her vision to fade.

When she could see straight again, she carried on up Manor Road. She would keep away from the meadow and the dig. Instead, she'd go left and head up to Elder Hill, past Drumble's Hive. It was one of her favourite walks, the road becoming a single-track lane, and eventually a rough trail bordered by cow parsley and foxgloves amidst the desiccated fronds of wild grasses. There was a bench part way. It would be an agreeable place to rest and soak up the peace, away from any chance of being seen by Coral or Hill.

Knocked by her unexpected encounter with Ben, Laurel tried to analyse her response to him. Being a psychologist could be a tedious merry-go-round of analysis and self-reflection, when sometimes, all she wanted was to feel without having to damn well think about it. She slowed her pace and focused on her body. Her fingernails were digging into her palms, her shoulders were up by her ears, and her stomach was in knots.

She liked Ben. No, that wasn't right. She was attracted to him. However, she had no desperate desire for a man in her life.

Besides, who was to say he was even attracted to her?

The warming sun helped as she consciously eased the tension from her body. She swung her arms and with each out breath, flexed her fingers and imagined her troubling thoughts drifting away. By the time she reached the bench, she was at least moderately relaxed and at ease.

She sat and closed her eyes, tilting her head, letting the sun warm her. The wings of birds burred as they flitted in and out of the hedgerow, chattering amongst themselves. Somewhere in the distance, was the drone of farm machinery, and above that was another sound. The crunch of footsteps. With reluctance, she opened her eyes and squinted at the approaching figure.

A tall, solidly built young woman in shorts, cotton blouse, and heavy-duty leather hiking boots marched along the trail. She didn't look familiar. Laurel wondered if she was from the dig.

'Hey,' the stranger called as she drew closer, coming to a halt a few feet away. 'Isn't it a gorgeous day?'

'It really is,' Laurel agreed, hoping she didn't have to share the bench and her moment of peace. 'Are you just starting your walk, or on your way back?' she enquired. It was only polite to make brief small talk.

'I'm on my way up to the village, up to the meadow. I'm working with the archaeology team. I'm Jessica,' she said, moving closer and offering her hand.

'Laurel,' said Laurel as she shook. So, this was Lin's friend, Jessica, who Maggie had mentioned.

'Mind if I sit for a second?'

Maybe it wouldn't be so bad to share for a little while. 'Sure, help yourself.' She shifted along the seat to make more room. 'I think you met my friend Maggie in the pub yesterday evening?'

'I did. She seems like a lot of fun. They all do.' Jessica smiled.

In her head, Laurel was already trying out options for steering the conversation towards the body with no name. 'How are you enjoying Elderwick?'

'It's so beautiful around here, and now they've found those bones...' Jessica stopped and her expression turned pained. 'I'm not sure I'm meant to talk about it. You probably know already, though?'

'In this village?' Laurel laughed. 'Nothing is a secret here for long.'

Jessica leaned back and grinned. 'I've been warned about the gossips.'

'Speaking of gossip...' *Here goes nothing!* 'Maggie said you might be able to help identify the remains?'

Instead of answering, Jessica asked a question of her own. 'Is it true, what Maggie, Hetty, and the others told me about you? That you've solved a ton of murders here in the village?'

'Not a ton, and I'm not sure I'd say I solved them exactly.'

'And you're a psychologist?'

'I am.' She wondered where this was going.

'I was thinking, maybe we could team up on this? Your local knowledge and detective skills would be such a help. Providing I get the go-ahead from the police and Dr Delgado, that is.'

'I really don't...'

Jessica ploughed on, leaving little room for objection. 'And if we find out who it is, buried here, and if there are living relatives, I would feel a lot happier if I had a professional guiding me. My supervisor has confirmed there's a small discretionary fund we can use to pay you. It won't be much, but I promise I won't take a lot of your time.'

Laurel plucked a blade of long grass that was tickling her leg. Why was the world so desperate for her to get involved in another murder?

'It sounds fascinating–'

'Don't say *but*,' Jessica pleaded.

'But DI Coral, the woman in charge, hates me. If you tell her I'm involved, she will do everything she can to derail you.'

Jessica fiddled with a button on her blouse. 'Unless,' she faced Laurel, her eyes bright, 'we don't tell her. There's no reason we can't keep your participation under wraps.'

It sounded like an exciting challenge. 'Can I think about it?'

'I'll take that as a yes.' She bounced to her feet and announced she had to run. 'Let's meet up soon. I'll call by your office tomorrow. What time is best?'

'Midday. But, no, wait... it's not a yes.' But Jessica was away, off up the lane, waving goodbye.

Chapter 12

Albert

Albert was tempted to laugh at the expression on Christopher's face. If asked he'd describe it as horrified.

'She's invited me to lunch. You have to come with me,' the vicar pleaded.

'Who, Dorothy?'

'Yes. Look, you know I care for every member of my congregation, but I don't know if I can eat another meal with Dorothy. Not alone in her home, while she informs me of the sins of the rest of my flock. She cares not a jot for John eight, verse seven.'

'She's a character, that's for certain, a character out of a Dickens novel, perhaps.'

'Madame Defarge.' Christopher put a hand to his mouth. 'Sorry, I shouldn't have said that.'

Albert chuckled. 'I don't think she's knitting a hit list of villagers' names yet.'

'You never know,' Christopher replied. 'Here she comes.'

Over his shoulder, Albert saw Dorothy approaching.

'Please.' The vicar mouthed.

'Dorothy, how lovely to bump into you again, and what a delightful hat. Is that an antique pin I spy?'

Dorothy blushed. 'Thank you, Albert. Yes, it is.' She touched her hat. 'It belonged to my mother. It's an opal. I do like to make an effort for church, unlike the rest of the lazy know-nothings who show up in jeans and tracksuits.'

'Well, you're an example to us all.' He knew he was laying it on thick.

'It's such a shame we don't see you in church on a Sunday, Albert, isn't it, vicar?'

'Not my thing,' said Albert, not leaving Christopher to answer her censorious question. 'However, a lovely luncheon after the fire and brimstone *is* my cup of tea. I was planning on asking the reverend to join me, but he informs me he's already spoken for.'

Dorothy lifted her chin. 'Indeed, Reverend Christopher will be lunching with me today.'

'Ah, I understand.' Albert did his best to look downcast.

When Dorothy didn't reply, Christopher stepped into the conversational lull. 'Perhaps Albert could join us? I know he would be most interested to hear your opinion on the sermon this morning.'

Albert grasped the baton. 'It would be very gracious of you.' Christopher was going to owe him big after this. If that was, Dorothy could be cajoled into extending the invitation.

Dorothy narrowed her eyes. 'I suppose that would be acceptable, but it's a cold lunch. Don't be going expecting a roast chicken and the full works.'

The deal was done.

Notwithstanding the delicious spinach and feta quiche served with a green salad and crusty homemade bread, Albert quickly came to appreciate why his friend had been desperate for a buffer; an additional person to dilute the bile.

'Dorothy, Dorothy,' he interrupted her mid-flow. She was decrying the young single mother who had recently moved into one of the new flats on the edge of the village, and he couldn't sit quietly any longer. 'Can we leave Annie alone, please? She's a lovely mum and her daughter is a delight. Let's talk about you.' Was he inviting trouble? 'Let's focus on you today. How are you?'

Albert had known Dorothy since growing up in the village as a child. After spending his working life in London, he'd retired and returned, and she was still there, albeit in a different house.

Her tone was sharp. 'What do you want to be knowing about me for?'

Christopher jumped in. 'Albert's right, and it would be lovely to hear about your week. You are a stalwart volunteer at the church, but you don't speak often about what else you enjoy.'

Albert observed the colour return to her cheeks and she smiled at him. A smile not accompanied by a cutting remark was a rarity with Dorothy.

'That's very kind of you, vicar. I do like to do my bit for my community, especially the Christian community.' She paused and frowned. 'I'm not sure what you would want to know?'

A twinge bloomed in Albert's chest. Could it be that no-one ever made time to speak to Dorothy? Truly, they all heard her complaining – there was always something she was cross about – and he knew many of the locals would avoid the woman when they could. But did any of them ever enquire after her health and wellbeing? She could easily be stereotyped as a bitter old woman. She had a sharp tongue and a habit of being unkind, but did anyone ever show her kindness anymore?

Beyond Dorothy, out of the dining-room window, was her garden. It was large and wooded with mature plants in the sweeping borders. A lot of work went into maintaining the order and beauty of a plot like that. 'Your garden is looking lovelier than ever. How do you keep it so well-ordered?'

Albert sat back and let Dorothy chatter about her garden. Her hands flew through the air, gesturing as she spoke of sunflowers and love-in-a-mist, mulch and woodchip. Christopher, he noted, appeared more relaxed now, too. Everything was going so well until she got onto the subject of weeding.

'Speaking of digging out weeds,' she said, 'what exactly do that lot in the meadow think they're doing?'

'What do you mean?' Christopher voiced the question before Albert had chance to get a word in; he would have tried to nudge her back to gardening. Now, all bets were off.

'Well, what's this with digging up old bones? As if Elderwick doesn't have enough skeletons in the closet. We certainly don't need any more. Why can't folk who've departed be left in peace? That's what I want to know.'

Albert raised his hands in defeat. Christopher was on his own.

'You know the police have declared it a possible murder?'

'Well, bodies don't bury themselves, do they, vicar?'

The reverend drew back as Dorothy unleashed her acid tongue. 'No,' he fumbled, 'but what should they have done, then? I'm not sure I understand.'

Dorothy gave him a pitying stare. 'Leave well enough alone is what. Nobody wants strangers coming round uncovering things best left forgotten.'

'You almost sound as though you know something about the remains, Dorothy?' challenged Christopher.

She snorted. 'Don't be obtuse. I know no more than you do. But I know digging around in the past never brought anyone any peace or happiness around here. The sordid affairs of the Hartfields of Elderwick Hall have left a dark enough stain as it is on this place and the people. The murders, the disappearances, it's enough to make your blood curdle. And Albert, you're one of them that keeps the stories alive. You keep on telling all and sundry – like that Laurel woman – when what the village needs is to let the past lie.'

Albert didn't have the energy to argue, and maybe, he was loath to admit, maybe she had a point. The village had certainly played host to more than its fair share of dastardly deeds. Was there anything to be learned or gained from repeating the older tales? The last of the Hartfields had left. Elderwick Hall was to be taken over by a children's charity, and there were no lessons to be gleaned from the unpleasant history of the family or their ancestral home.

'I understand how change can be challenging, frightening even,' said Christopher. 'And you were outspoken in your opposition to the charity, Dandelions, moving into the village. Are your objections to the archaeology team coming from the same place? Are you afraid there will be an impact on your life if the farm shop is given the go-ahead?'

Albert wouldn't have dared say it himself, but Christopher was right. Dorothy had not been alone in her criticisms, but she had been the most strident amongst the resistance.

'Afraid? An elderly woman, living alone, who has already been brutally attacked in her own home once. Now what would I possibly have to fear from gangs of delinquent children marauding the streets, drinking their cheap cider, mugging pensioners for their giro?'

'Now hold on.' Christopher pushed his chair back from the table and threw down his napkin. 'These *children* are among the most deprived in our inner cities. That does not make them thieves or hooligans. It's attitudes like yours that...' He stopped, inhaled a long slow breath, then exhaled even slower. 'Dorothy, thank you for lunch, but I think I should go.'

Albert's friend stalked through the kitchen and out of the back door. How he resisted slamming it, Albert didn't know.

'That's the thanks I get for inviting the man for a home cooked meal. I never. I suppose you're leaving too?' She glared at him.

Albert chewed his lip until he came to a decision. 'No, I'm not leaving just yet, unless you want me to?'

'Suit yourself,' she huffed.

'Dorothy, I've got to ask, what do you think should happen with Elderwick Hall? You were against Marcus Hartfield's plans for a hotel, golf course and whatnot, and now you're against the Dandelions charity.'

'It doesn't matter what I think, does it. The decisions have been made. The renovation is underway.' She was twisting her napkin in her fingers. 'And I don't take kindly to being called a bigot.'

'He didn't call you a bigot.'

'He didn't have to use the word; I know what he was getting at. I suppose you agree with him. I know you're a bleeding-heart liberal.'

He thought for a moment. 'I'm not calling you anything, but I am disappointed in your prejudices against these children, whom you've never met, I might add. I appreciate you had a terrible experience the other year, but it wasn't children from the inner city, or anywhere else, who attacked you. Dandelions is not only a worthy organisation who do a great deal for their community, they will also bring new jobs to the village.

Something we're badly in need of for our own youth. I can't expect everyone to feel the way I do, but I ask you to withhold judgement, and to not make assumptions based on zero evidence.' He wasn't sure if he was getting through to her.

'I have an idea,' he said. 'Why don't you come with me to meet some of the team? I'm having coffee with them tomorrow. I'm sure they wouldn't mind you tagging along.' *What are you doing, Albert?* He would call them and forewarn them. Better to have Dorothy onside, if at all possible, than have her continue stirring up the Victor Meldrews of the locale. Dandelions didn't need that.

Dorothy looked like she was chewing on a lemon, but she agreed.

'Excellent.' He rose from his seat. 'Now, thank you for lunch, but I must be getting on. I'll see you tomorrow.'

Chapter 13

Laurel

Laurel tried to picture how Coral would react if she knew about her conversation with Jessica. How she'd hit the roof if she thought Laurel was getting involved. Her amusement faded. The sensible thing to do would be to persuade Jessica the answer was no.

She sat a while longer on the bench until the sun grew too strong. Wishing she'd thought to bring a hat, she decided to cut short her planned walk and instead retraced her steps towards Elderwick, sticking to the shady side of the lane. Back home, in a cool corner of her garden, away from prying eyes, she took out her notebook, powered up her laptop, looked up what it was anthropologists did, and wrote herself a summary. Next, she added a list of questions she had for Jessica before she could make a final decision. Though the answer would definitely be no.

After a light lunch, Laurel grabbed the novel she was reading and had just finished battling with her new sun lounger when a voice called her name.

'Laurel? Hello, are you in the garden?'

She grinned. 'Hey, Maggie. Yes, I'm back here.'

Her friend rounded the corner, hefting a bakery box in one hand and a large tote bag in the other. 'I come bearing gifts.' She dropped the tote on the ground, placed the box onto the bistro table with great care, and lifted the lid. 'Two chocolate éclairs and two jam doughnuts.'

Laurel's mouth watered. She debated whether she should have one of each. 'The bakery's closed on a Sunday, isn't it?' The familiar lettering on the side read *The Plump Tart,* so unless Maggie was reusing one of their boxes, she knew something Laurel didn't. It was bad enough having the temptation of Hetty and Constance's creations call to her six days a week, add in a Sunday, and she would be shopping for a new wardrobe in no time.

'Don't worry, it's still closed on a Sunday, but I was over visiting Constance this morning and she insisted I take these away with me.'

'She insisted, did she?'

'Practically threw them at me.'

'In that case, shall I get plates?'

'Oh, no need to be fancy. It's just us and the crumbs are only going to fall on the ground. Aroon might even wander over to clean them up for you.'

'Bloody bird,' Laurel muttered. 'Four o'clock this morning he was crowing in my garden. Not in his own garden, oh no, in mine! I swear he does it on purpose.'

'He'll be showing off to your chickens.'

'Ha,' Laurel cackled. 'My girls know better than to consort with a rogue like Aroon.'

'Speaking of rogues...' Maggie's eyes glittered, 'a little bird tells me you were chatting up our local policeman this morning. I'd heard he was back. He didn't waste any time.'

'Honestly, MI6 want to send their agents here to train in

intelligence gathering. Or maybe *intelligence* isn't the right word.' She could have sworn no-one had been around when she'd bumped into Ben. If she lived in the village long enough, perhaps one day she'd be inducted into this secret art of knowing everything the moment it happened. 'I ran into him as I was out for a walk, that's all. I wasn't chatting him up. After what he did, I'm not interested. Not that he's interested in me. You can forget that.'

'Hmmm.'

Laurel reached into the bakery box and selected the larger of the two éclairs. They were Maggie's current favourite pastry; that would teach her.

Maggie opened her mouth, but apparently thought better of continuing that particular conversation.

'How is Constance?'

'She's okay. I wanted to talk to you about her actually.'

Laurel had her mouth full of cream, but she waved her hand, encouraging Maggie to go on.

'You mustn't tell anyone I told you, but she's been trying some online dating on a site called Salt 'n' Pepper, of all things, and she thinks she got scammed. She was so upset and embarrassed, but I told her there was no need for her to be. Besides, it might not have been a scam.'

Knowing it made her sound cynical, Laurel couldn't help saying, 'It probably was.'

Maggie batted away her words. 'Even if it was – and we don't know yet – then it's the... nasty person who scammed her who should be embarrassed.'

It was sweet how Maggie avoided swearing in all but the most dire of circumstances. Between her gentle euphemisms and Albert's love of older English words and literary quotes, Laurel sometimes felt she needed a translation app to understand them both.

'How much money?' She'd polished off the éclair and was eyeing the doughnuts.

Maggie told her the whole story and finished by touching on Constance's urge to turn vigilante if Carter didn't finally reply to her messages.

'Has she reported him?'

'No, and I don't think she wants to. She doesn't want people knowing how silly she was. Even though she wasn't silly; she was taken advantage of.'

'Which is what these people count on. That and the fact that most people want to believe the world is fair and everyone is truthful.'

'And what is so wrong about wanting to believe the best of people?'

'It's naïve.' Laurel reached for the doughnut. She was earning her sweet treats today. Between bites, she said, 'Would she speak to Ben, off the record?'

Maggie finished licking the chocolate off her choux. 'I think she would be okay with Ben. What a good idea. I knew you'd be able to help. When I see her again, I'll ask.'

Laurel saw what was about to happen next but couldn't move quick enough to avert disaster. Maggie had spotted her notebook and was reaching for it.

'Hey, have you been making more notes? What have you got?' Before Laurel could react, she'd opened it and was flicking through the pages. 'What's this about Jessica?' she asked, alighting on the list of questions Laurel had made.

'Nothing, just things to follow up on, you know, about her anthropology project.' She held her hand out for the book, but Maggie wasn't finished.

'No, it's not. What's this about you joining up with her? To do what? Laurel, what is this?'

'It's nothing...' She hesitated. Maggie wasn't stupid. 'Okay, you have to swear you won't mention this to anyone else?'

'My lips are sealed.'

'I'm serious. You can't tell anybody.'

'I'm capable of keeping a secret.' She sounded piqued.

Laurel wasn't convinced. 'I don't even know if I'll say yes yet.' She told Maggie about Jessica's appeal for a collaboration. 'She knows I'm a psychologist and I'm local, so she figured I could be useful. I told her about Coral, but she proposed we keep my involvement quiet. *If* I get involved. And it's a big if. Which is why you mustn't breathe a word of this to anyone.' She should have been more careful with her notebook. She had to hope she'd got through to Maggie the importance of keeping schtum.

'You know who we should ask?'

'No, we can't ask anyone.' She pinched the bridge of her nose.

'Hear me out. We should ask Albert. He knows more about the history of this village than anyone.'

'Maybe, but please don't say anything to anyone, not until I've seen Jessica again.'

Maggie sulked. 'Fine, but I thought at least you and I would be working together on this.'

'There is no *this* that we're working on.'

Maggie's face fell. Laurel relented.

'But maybe there is something we could do together.'

Maggie brightened.

'We could have a look ourselves, online, and see if there are any reports of people going missing from this area during the relevant time frame. I'm not sure how much is online from the late sixties and into the seventies and eighties, but I imagine some old papers have been uploaded? Or we could go to the library. The last time I needed to do some research, the librarian was incredibly helpful.'

'The library doesn't open again until Wednesday afternoon.'

'Really?'

'Yes, cutbacks. It's only open Wednesday, Thursday, Friday afternoons, and all day Saturday.'

With a pang, Laurel recalled the many hours she'd spent in libraries over the years. Youngsters these days would probably never know the pleasure of walking into the hush of a library, of the faint vanilla smell of old books. Sure, it was convenient to order her next read on her Kindle whilst lying in bed, but it wasn't the same. Bookshops were vanishing too.

'We could start now.'

'Could we?' Maggie's enthusiasm was returning.

Settled back at the table, Laurel with her tablet, and Maggie using Laurel's laptop, it wasn't long before Laurel realised it would be no simple search. 'I don't even know where to start. I've found a Wikipedia page with mysterious disappearances from 1910 to 1990, and lots of stuff about high-profile missing persons. None of it's helpful.'

'What if we look up the local paper and the term *missing persons*?'

Maggie's idea was a good one, but the results were disheartening. 'It says here that in 2018/19 alone over five thousand people went missing, and that's just in our area. I don't think this is going to work.' Laurel swiped through the rest of the article. 'And there are reports of how even when remains are found, identities aren't always established. God, it's depressing. Their poor families.' She scrubbed her hands over her face. Maggie was being very quiet. She had a look of intense concentration on her face. 'Maggie?'

'How long ago do you think the body had to have been buried to have decomposed as much as it has?' she asked.

A quick internet search provided the answer. 'Ten to fifteen years, depending on a million and one factors,' Laurel read from the screen. 'Which means we're looking at a significant time period, from 1968, the earliest it could have happened, up to say 2008, the latest the body could have been buried. That's forty years!'

'I've lived here for nearly twenty-five years, and I am confident no bodies have been buried whilst I've been here. I'm sure I would have noticed.'

Laurel didn't point out that, whenever the body was buried, apparently no-one had noticed. Still, a smaller range would be more manageable as a starting point. 'In that case, let's say from 1968 to 1998. And I say we focus on men. Women can wear football club signet rings, but on balance, I'm guessing our skeleton is a man. Also, let's rule out children for the same reason. Besides, someone would have mentioned it already if the bones appeared to be those of a child. I'm sure the archaeologists would have known from the size of the finger.' She wasn't confident about her assertion, but she couldn't face the notion that the body might be that of a child.

They turned back to their search, Maggie typing and Laurel swiping page after page.

Fifteen minutes of intense Googling later, Maggie spoke. 'It could be nothing, but here's an old piece from *The Yorkshire Post*. There are three men mentioned who disappeared in the right time frame and have never been found. The results only go back as far as 1970 though, so there could have been others before that.'

'Who are they?'

'Anthony Scrivener, last seen in 1991, aged twenty-five. Tariq Loftus, last seen 1974, aged eighty-three. Harold Emmerson, last seen in 1983, aged thirty-six.' Maggie gasped and pulled her hands away from the keyboard. 'They've included the original piece in the local paper from when Harold first went missing. Listen: *Harold Emmerson, well-known resident of the village of Elderwick near Beverley, missed by his wife, Dorothy, a nurse at Beverley Westwood Hospital.*'

'Dorothy?' Laurel's mouth had gone dry. 'As in Dorothy Little, our Dorothy? She was a nurse, wasn't she?'

'Yes, she was.'

Chapter 14

Albert

Albert had his key in the lock when he heard Laurel's door opening. He glanced over the garden wall and saw Maggie stepping outside. A quick chat with a friendly face, he thought, would do him good after lunch with Dorothy. 'Maggie, how radiant you are today,' he called.

Maggie looked over but said nothing until she'd left Laurel's pint-sized front garden and joined him in his own. 'Can I tell you something in confidence?' she asked.

It wouldn't matter if he said no, she would tell him anyway. He knew her well enough to recognise the signs: her eyes darted between his face and Laurel's front door, and her knuckles were white as she gripped the handles of her large bag.

'Do you want to come inside?'

'That would probably be for the best.' She crowded into the entrance hall and chased his heels as he led the way through to the back of the house.

Ushering her into his compact but perfectly appointed kitchen, he caught sight of the cat flap swinging closed. He wasn't sure if it had been Aroon or his rabbit, Lago, prowling around, but his money was on the bird.

'Have yourself a sit down.' He pulled out a chair for Maggie and then took his own seat. 'What is it you need to tell me?'

She placed her bag on the floor and folded her hands. 'You understand, I'm not a gossip?' With wide eyes, she proclaimed her innocence, 'But I have news. The young anthropologist, Jessica, evidently has a database of people from Yorkshire who have gone missing. What's more, she's asked Laurel to assist her in narrowing down and maybe even confirming the identity of the deceased in the meadow. You can't tell anyone, though.'

As she paused for breath, Albert was able to get a word in. 'Has Laurel agreed?'

Maggie ignored his question. 'Second, even without Jessica's database, we – Laurel and I – already have a possible identity for the bones.' She leaned forward and whispered. 'Harold Emmerson.'

'Harold Emmerson?'

'Yes, a man called Harold Emmerson went missing from Elderwick in 1983, and get this, he was married to a nurse called *Dorothy*.'

'Dorothy?'

'As in Dorothy Little. It has to be.'

He swallowed. 'You think Harold was our Dorothy's husband?'

Maggie looked fit to burst. 'We might have solved the mystery already.'

'You'll forgive an old man from worrying, but might I caution you to keep this information under your hat?'

'Naturally. Did I not just say the same to you?'

'Only, you could be mistaken, and Dorothy would not take kindly to such a rumour being spread around.'

Maggie pouted. 'We will be circumspect. I am only speaking to you now because you know the history of our little village backwards. In fact, I hear you're collecting old mementoes, photos, and suchlike from the older residents for a local history project?'

He shouldn't be surprised she knew. Having been born and brought up in the village, even with some years away in London as a lecturer in linguistics, he was acutely aware that no-one minded their own business in Elderwick. It was both a blessing and a curse.

Maggie hung on, no doubt waiting for him to tell her more about his new pastime, but he would disappoint her. He didn't want to be dragged into raking over the past now these bones had surfaced.

'Besides,' she gave up waiting for him, 'I... we wanted to ask, you must remember Dorothy being married to a Harold Emmerson? It would have been around the late seventies, early eighties?'

He pretended to think. 'No. No, I can't say as I do.'

Chapter 15

Albert

A heavy but brief shower overnight had kept Albert awake later than usual, but he rarely slept late thanks to Aroon's morning chorus. Over a healthy breakfast of fresh fruit and some toast drizzled with honey from local bees, he contemplated his day. He had invited Dorothy to join him on his visit to Dandelions in the hope he could sway her opinion. The charity coming to the village was a boon, and he wanted to bring Dorothy on side. Alas, he didn't anticipate smooth sailing.

Adding further storm clouds to his usually sunny outlook was Maggie's revelation that she and Laurel had been digging into information about missing persons and Dorothy's ex, Harold, had popped up. However, he wasn't going to mention anything to Dorothy. Not yet.

When the doorbell rang, he steeled himself.

'Dorothy.' He greeted her. 'You're spot on time.'

'Of course I'm on time,' she retorted.

He could tell the visit to Dandelions was going to take Anthony Eden levels of diplomacy. 'Shall we go?'

'No point standing around here all day, is there.'

Even Eden had failed on occasion.

Albert escorted Dorothy to the gates of Elderwick Hall. 'We're meeting the senior management team, a Mrs Pinker, and a Mr Galanis,' he said as they began the long walk up the lengthy approach. From either side of the driveway, the old oaks offered welcome shade. It was another scorcher.

'Galanis... What's that, Greek?'

Albert picked up the pace. If she was out of breath perchance she wouldn't talk so much. But Dorothy easily kept stride and kept talking.

'I hope you're not expecting me to sit there nice as pie and pretend I'm in favour of this nonsense? I will not fawn all over these London types who come up here with their elite educations and ideas they impose on us. We know what's best for our village.'

He couldn't let it pass without rebuttal. 'Firstly, they're both from the North; Mrs Pinker is from Northumberland, and Mr Galanis is from Leeds. Born and raised,' he added. 'Secondly, and possibly you forget, I whiled away many of my years at an *elite* institution in London.'

'And it shows.'

Would it hurt, he wondered, if he banged his head on the nearest tree trunk?

They made it the rest of the way without any injuries – self-inflicted or otherwise – and crossed the cobbled courtyard to the grand front steps of the Georgian house. Built of grey brick, cold compared to the warm red-orange of those in the village, the building loured over them with menace. With a shiver running across the back of his neck, Albert was relieved when the heavy oak door swung open to reveal the smiling face of a short, stout man with a shock of black hair and a monocle clamped firmly over his left eye.

He clapped his hands and came down to meet them. 'You must be Albert,' he said, seizing Albert's hand and pumping it up and down with vigour. 'And this must be Dorothy.' She had her hands behind her back and declined to shake. After an uncomfortable moment, their host withdrew but appeared unperturbed.

'I'm Alexis Galanis. Please, call me Alex. Come in, come in. Have a look at what we've done with the old place. What do you think?'

He paused as he gestured to the stately entrance hall. Gone were the clean lines, polished furniture and extravagant vases of flowers of Marcus and Petra Hartfield's residency. In their place were gigantic murals painted directly onto the walls. Bucolic scenes of nature at its most green and docile. There were chairs in bright plastic rainbow colours, and low tables strewn with books. The stately central staircase was bare where the carpet had been removed to leave the varnished wood exposed, and at the top of the first flight, commanding the attention of everyone who entered the building was a larger-than-life cow painted in yellow and white with a green hat on her head.

'That's Dandelion, our mascot,' said Alex, following their astonished gazes. 'At first, we were going to go with a lion, you know, because Dande*lion*, but we thought it might be too scary for the younger kids. Instead, we have a cow eating a dandelion. I know it's a little odd to have her eating a dandelion, but no-one has complained yet.' He laughed loudly and it echoed around them.

'It's amazing, quite a transformation.' Albert observed, knowing Alex was waiting for a reaction. 'Very child friendly. Who did the paintings? They're...' he reached for the right word. He wanted to say twee, but settled on, 'charming.'

'We were lucky enough to find an incredible local artist. Aren't they something?'

'They're definitely something,' groused Dorothy.

Alex's grin dimmed a fraction. 'Well, let's head up and I'll introduce you to Jayne Clement.'

Albert was startled by the name. It was the woman from the tearoom, Laurel's old school chum. He allowed himself a secret smile; the cat would be amongst the pigeons when Laurel found out.

'Jayne?' He queried. 'I thought Mrs Pinker was your co-manager?'

'Ah, yes, she was. Change of personnel. Jayne's new to us but has been in the charity sector for donkey's. We're very fortunate to have her join our team. You're going to love her.'

As Alex led the way up the stairs, Albert gave Dorothy a hard stare, but he didn't think it registered.

Turning left, it was the library to which Alex led them. Inside, Albert was relieved to note the books had remained. They had not been victims of the revamp. The oversized modernist desk of Marcus Hartfield, the previous owner and last in a long line of Hartfields, was gone, though, and in its place was a battered pedestal desk with a green leather top. Behind it sat Jayne, who rose to welcome them.

'Oh, my goodness, it's Albert, isn't it? We met the other day, at the café.' She came round to their side and went straight in for a hug.

Happy to meet another who wasn't afraid of affection and of showing it, Albert hugged back. Jayne, he thought, was the ideal person to work for a children's charity; she was warm and friendly and had a mouth made for smiling, which she was doing now.

'It's lovely to see you again. And this must be Ms Little?'

And she was an excellent judge of character. Dorothy had retreated a few steps, but Jayne's pivot to being more formal had worked.

Dorothy shook Jayne's hand.

'I'm so glad you're both here. We're thrilled to introduce local people to our new centre and the work we're going to be doing here. I appreciate it's a big development for Elderwick, but we know our centres, and others like us, can make a world of difference to children living in hardship and challenging circumstances. For them to visit somewhere like this, in the countryside, a place just for them, where they can run, and play, and try new things, and be safe and warm and fed, it's more than a holiday, it's a necessity. We are only too aware we can't always improve their home situations, but if we can give them a week, even a few days, of a secure, fun place, well, I think that's worth it, don't you?'

Albert recognised a pitch when he heard one. He suspected Jayne used this one often, and she was right to do so, and right in what she said. He watched for Dorothy's reaction. He believed Jayne's words were directed at his prickly companion.

Dorothy gave a slight tilt of the head. 'When you put it like that, I suppose so.'

Score one for Jayne.

'Come on, let's give you the full tour.'

For the next half hour, Jayne and Alex led them around the house and grounds. Albert was impressed at how much they'd done and how much fun it all looked. If he was only thirty years younger, twenty even, he'd have been up in the treehouse, clambering across the rope bridges and singing through the canopy.

'And this,' said Alex with a flourish, 'is our kitchen garden.'

Albert hesitated at the gate. They couldn't have known, could they?

'When we arrived, we found this place half demolished. But the stones were all still here and although it's a little way from the house, it really is the perfect place to grow all of our fruit and vegetables. Albert, you'll know, was it originally an orchard?

We found the stumps of old apple trees. We've planted some new ones, and a pear, cherry, and a plum.'

It was a moment before he could answer. 'Yes, it was an orchard.' He said no more. He didn't want to taint Alex and Jayne's work or enthusiasm with old ghost stories.

The orchard was the site of the darkest chapter of Elderwick's history, the mysterious death of a child in 1725. Her body was found by her father, Archibald Hartfield, at the foot of the Apple Tree Man, the oldest apple tree in the orchard. In his rage and grief, Archibald destroyed all of the fruit trees, sealed the orchard, and in the decades that followed, only weeds had grown there.

The two Dandelions managers stepped into the garden and set off along the pathway between raised beds.

'Are you going to tell them? Or shall I?' hissed Dorothy.

'Neither of us is going to say anything,' Albert whispered back. 'I thought you were the one saying we should let the dead stay buried?'

Dorothy cackled. 'Touché, old man. But someone will tell them sooner or later.'

He grunted. She was probably right.

'Come on,' shouted Jayne, 'I want you to see our greenhouse. We've got tomatoes already fruiting in there.'

Surrounded by the earthy, red-green smell of tomato vines, Dorothy's face lit up. Albert left her quizzing Jayne about the varieties, feed, and watering of the plants while he drew Alex further into the glass house and brought up the archaeology dig.

'It's come as quite a surprise, what they've found in the meadow.'

'I know, it's awful. To think, that poor person, buried there for who knows how long,' said Alex, clasping a hand to his chest.

'Will it cause you much of a delay, do you think?'

'Who knows, but that's really not a worry or priority.

Besides, it'll be a while until we're producing enough to sell in the farm shop. What's important is the police investigation. I hope they can find out who it is. Their poor family, I can't imagine...'

'I'm sure they've got the best people on it.' Albert crossed his fingers behind his back. 'And I understand Rik, Dr Delgado, is an experienced osteoarchaeologist, so right from the start, they've had an expert involved.'

'Oh, I didn't know that. Yes, that is good.'

'How did you find him, if you don't mind my asking?' He had targeted Alex for his questioning, reasoning Jayne was a much newer addition to the charity and might not know.

'Serendipity,' said Alex. 'We knew we would need to commission a desktop archaeological survey and possibly more depending on the results, but we hadn't reached out to any teams when out of the blue Rik got in touch. Said he'd heard we'd purchased Elderwick Hall and were we open to having him bring a team down for a full excavation? Said he's always on the lookout for suitable sites to bring his students. I think he thought this would be a good practice dig for them, not too far from the university and all that. We're all for providing opportunities where we can, so we were happy to accept his offer.'

'His offer? You're paying though?'

'We are, but not the full going rate. That was the deal. He said he couldn't charge us the full rate since we're a charity.'

'That's splendid.'

'I'll say. Between you, me, and the gatepost, this is our largest project by far and I think our finance guy is feeling the heat. But he is a worrywart.'

'You're not in any financial difficulty, though?'

'Not at all. It's more a case of it being like the advert says, *every little helps.*'

Albert filed his denial away for further scrutiny at a later time.

'It certainly was a stroke of luck, given what a small dot we are on the map. Did Rik mention how he heard about Elderwick Hall?'

Alex bent over a bed of fragrant herbs and plucked a few leaves of mint, releasing the cool perfume into the air. 'You know, he did. He said it was one of his students had told him. Seems we have her to thank for our good fortune.'

'Did he mention a name?'

Alex stood up, his dark brows knitted together. 'Is there anything I should know? You seem very interested.'

'No, no. Don't mind me, I'm a bit of an amateur historian and I like to know the ins and outs of village life. Many of us here knew the latest Hartfields well, before they moved to France. I suppose I'm just being a bit nosy. Too much time on my hands.' When telling a lie, he knew it was best to keep it simple and short. He worried he'd oversold it.

Luckily, Alex's clouded expression cleared. 'I hear you. My granddad's the same.' He handed a sprig of mint to Albert. 'Smell that, isn't it fantastic?'

Albert relaxed. Alex had dropped his guard.

'Lin, that was the student's name. Lin Cheng.'

Chapter 16

Laurel

Relishing the luxury of waking before she needed to get up, Laurel grabbed her phone from her bedside table and checked her diary for the day. She scanned through the names booked into the one-hour time slots and reminded herself of the presenting problem for each.

9.30-10.30am – Mary Streeter. Needle phobia

11am-12pm – Nick Jameson. Chronic pain

1-2pm – Sanjay Gunawardena. Weight management

2:30-3:30pm – Gertrude Bell. New assessment – relationship difficulties

Not bad for a Monday. She was well into her work with Mary, Nick, and Sanjay, and all of them were progressing brilliantly.

After eight sessions, Mary could hold a syringe with a needle attached without panicking. Nick and his wife were about to embark on a holiday to Spain and he had a plan for managing his pain whilst away. And Sanjay, lovely, shy Sanjay, had identified the root of his difficulty with food. Laurel was working with him on his self-esteem and, though weight loss wasn't their immediate goal, Sanjay had already lost fifteen pounds.

Gertrude was an unknown, but Laurel enjoyed new assessments and it would be a gentle way to end her working day.

The sun was already pouring through the gap in her bedroom curtains and in the slice of sky visible there wasn't a single cloud to tarnish the blue. She should get up and go for a walk. She didn't know if Coral and co. would be at the dig again, but she thought avoiding the meadow entirely would be the better course of action. If she went up North Street to Elder Lane, it would be shady and cool at this time, and rather than continue on towards the commune, she could take the path between Elderwick and Cherry Burton which would bring her to her second favourite bench where she could stop for a short spell before heading to the office.

She had yet to pass a single other person when she reached the stile into the field where a trod – a fairy path, more gold than light green owing to the weather – led to the mature woodland that would take her almost all the way to the neighbouring village.

Humming Sting's 'Fields of Gold', Laurel was fifty feet into the field when she became aware that she wasn't alone. She froze. Twenty or so cows were watching her. Big, innocent-looking cows. But she knew better. Only a few weeks ago, she'd read in the paper of an elderly man in Hampshire who had been trampled to death by apparently docile cows. She didn't trust cows.

She gauged the distance back to the stile, then checked

ahead to see how far she was from the gate and the safety of the beech trees. She mustn't run, she remembered that.

If she went forward, she would have to take a lengthy detour to get back to Elderwick on her return, so backwards made more sense. Keeping as many of the creatures within sight as possible on her right – and praying there were no calves that they were protecting – she turned round and edged back towards the stile. One step at a time, slowly, no sudden movements. Was she meant to make noise? Would it scare them away or agitate them? She couldn't remember.

Almost there. Her heart was racing, and her palms were slick with sweat. A few of the herd moved. She arced away from the path, putting more space between her and the outliers. They weren't blocking her escape, but until she was over the wall, she wouldn't relax.

She stumbled, her foot slipping into a large divot caused by hooves, giving her ankle a nasty wrench. Righting herself, she tried to slow her breathing and ignore the pain. Plenty of people passed through the field unmolested every day, but she couldn't shake her alarm at being so close to these hefty beasts.

Nearly there. Nearly there. Nearly there.

Only twenty steps from the stile, she froze for a second time, and all thought of cows evaporated in the face of what was lying in the shallow ditch alongside the wall on her left. If she'd kept to the path, it would have remained hidden from her, but she couldn't miss it now.

'No, no, no,' she whimpered. Having been a palliative care psychologist, she was no stranger to death, but not like this. This fragile body, limbs outstretched, lifeless and still.

It was too late. There was no need to get closer.

'Oh, Jessica.'

She was equally relieved and horrified that it was Ben who arrived first on the scene.

She hadn't wanted to leave Jessica alone, and of course her phone had no signal – she wasn't even sure why she carried it with her anymore – so she'd had to wait in the field, one eye on the cows, until a passer-by strayed near enough to hear her shouts. As they ran to call for help, Laurel bowed under the weight of what had happened.

Jessica could only have been in her mid-twenties; her whole life, and a promising career in anthropology, ahead of her, all taken away in a moment. Laurel wondered if Jessica had family, and who would visit them to break the harrowing news.

'Ben.'

'Laurel, are you okay? Sorry, stupid question.' He rubbed a hand over his eyes. 'I'm going to get you away from here as soon as possible, but right now I need you to stay exactly where you are whilst I check for signs of life.'

'It's a bit late for that.' God, she sounded disrespectful. 'Crap, ignore me. I'm not thinking right. Sorry.'

'Hey, you've had a nasty shock. Don't worry about it.'

He picked his way closer to Jessica.

'Careful, it's muddy over there.'

He leaned down and, with fingers encased in blue nitrile gloves he'd conjured from his pocket, he pressed against Jessica's neck, searching for a pulse. He wouldn't find one.

'Right.' He stood up and backed away, slipping slightly in the patch of claggy mud around the body. 'I need to ask you some questions, then I'm going to get you to go back over the stile.'

She nodded, not trusting her voice.

'Where you are now, is that as close as you got to the deceased?'

She was grateful for his use of the word deceased, instead of reducing Jessica to a body, to meat. 'Yes. I was keeping out of the way of the cows, and I saw her, and just stopped. I should have checked; she might have still been alive. I didn't think...'

'It's part of my protocol that I have to check, but we both know she's been gone for some time. Don't beat yourself up about any of this.'

Tears pricked her eyes. She blinked rapidly.

'You didn't touch her skin or any part of her clothing?'

'No.'

'Okay. Now, moving real slow, head to the stile and go on over. If you can do it without touching anything with your hands, that would be great.'

She did as directed, leaving him in the field, the only object between Jessica and the curious cows who were moving steadily closer.

'What about the cows?' she asked.

'Farmer's on his way to shift them. Hopefully, he'll be here before the DI.'

'The DI? Who is it?'

Ben's mouth twisted. 'Coral.'

'Great.'

'Yeah.'

The unspoken hung in the air between them.

'But it was an accident... the cows, right?'

'I'd say so, but it'll be up to the coroner to confirm cause of death.'

'And why is Coral coming over?'

'We have protocols to follow.' He sounded as glum as she felt. Perhaps Coral was no more popular amongst her colleagues than she was with Laurel.

Laurel forced herself to look again at Jessica's lifeless form. She felt selfish for being grateful she wasn't the one lying there, body trampled and beaten by the animals who even now were edging ever closer. She shivered, glad to be back on the other side of the wall.

She wasn't superstitious, but that was two deaths associated with the archaeology team. She hoped to goodness there wouldn't be a third.

Chapter 17

Maggie

Maggie had arranged to meet Constance a little later than the previous morning. Her hope being she would not be as tempted by the sweets and pastries of the bakery if she'd already eaten breakfast. Unfortunately, before she'd even made it inside The Plump Tart, she knew she had made a serious error. No fullness of stomach would dissuade her from desiring these delicious baked goods.

Cardamom and caramel scented air wrapped her in its irresistible embrace and wafted her to the counter.

'Hi Hetty,' she breathed, unable to tear her eyes from the display case.

'Hey, Maggie. Constance is upstairs. You can go straight on up. She won't tell me what you're up to, but if you spill the beans on your way back down, I'll put a couple of these cardamom and caramel spice cookies aside for you.'

Maggie licked her lips. 'I could take some up with me, save you the trouble.' She could practically taste the cookies on her tongue.

'No trouble. They're only just out of the oven anyway, far too hot to hand over yet. And remember, you need to pay the price. If I give them to you now, I'll never know what you pair are up to.' She snapped her tongs at Maggie and chased her away through the kitchen.

Damn Hetty.

'Maggie, is that you?' Constance called from the top of the stairs. 'Come on up.'

They got themselves settled at the dining table in front of the laptop.

'I heard back from him,' she blurted before Maggie could say a word.

Maggie smiled, but then noticed Constance's expression wasn't a happy one. 'Isn't that good?'

Constance showed her the various tabs she had open on her laptop. 'You'd think so. However, I've also found him on three other dating sites so far. Same photos, saying he lives in the same general area, but a different name each time.'

'Oh no, that's rotten. I'm sorry, Constance.'

Constance's lip wobbled, but she clenched her fists. 'Whoever he is, I think he's local, which gives me a fighting chance of finding him.'

'You're actually planning to track him down?'

'*Hunt* him down,' Constance corrected.

Maggie was unnerved by her friend's choice of words, but she could understand her anger. 'In reality, he could be from anywhere, couldn't he? What makes you believe he's local?'

'When we were chatting, he talked about places around here. Not *here* here, like Elderwick, but Beverley and Hull. He obviously knows the area. Clearly, he doesn't really work at the hotel in York, but I'd bet anything he lives somewhere between here and there.'

'It's a pretty big area.' Maggie pictured a map in her mind, labelling all the towns and villages she knew between their corner of Yorkshire and the cathedral city.

'Not in the world of online dating, it's not.'

'If he's local, doesn't he risk someone identifying him?'

'The photos aren't actually of him.'

'I see.' Maggie was glad she'd never dipped a toe into online dating. It sounded like a shark tank. 'Go on then, when he messaged back, what did he say?'

'I'd made out that I had no idea he'd conned me out of money. I just asked about his dog and said I hoped to hear from him soon and he swallowed it. I'm not the only gullible sap. He said he was sorry he hadn't been in touch again straight away and that his dog is doing better but might not be out of the woods. I'm pretty sure he thinks I am a soft touch and that he might be able to take me for more. Little does he know, I'm on to him now.'

'And what do you intend to do?'

'Like I said, I'm going after him,' Constance snarled. 'He picked the wrong person to screw with this time.'

Chapter 18

Laurel

'You're kidding me, right? This is some kind of sick joke?' DI Coral's face turned puce the moment she set eyes on Laurel. 'Are you telling me she was the one who found the body?' she spat at Ben.

'Yes, guv.'

'And why the hell aren't you in uniform?'

His silver hair was neat, recently cut, and he wore his jeans and grey shirt with casual elegance. The DI was rumpled, her hair stringy and tangled, her face free of make-up except for heavily mascaraed lashes.

'I'd just come off duty when the call came in. I live nearby, so they asked me to attend until you got here.' He was about a foot taller than Coral, who had got up close, pushing into his personal space. Even though this had him looming over her, it was clear who was in charge.

Laurel wished she could disappear. She held her breath as though being quiet and small would make Coral forget her presence.

'Hill,' Coral barked at her partner, 'get an initial statement and arrange for her to come down to the station as soon as.' She jabbed her thumb in Laurel's direction. 'You,' she pointed at Ben, 'wait for the team and keep the looky-loos away until we've got a cordon in place.'

Ben shot a glance at Laurel as he went off to do as instructed.

Laurel talked DS Hill through her movements and how she'd found Jessica's body. 'No, I didn't see anyone else at all. The meadow was deserted, and there were no other walkers. Too hot, I guess, even this early.'

'Would you usually walk this way at this time of day?'

She explained that it wasn't her habit, that it was a spur-of-the-moment idea. 'I wouldn't even have seen her if I hadn't come off the path. I've never trusted cows.'

'Got to be careful around farm animals,' he agreed. 'We see it once in a while. A walker spooks them, or more likely, their dog agitates the cows and people get hurt. Dog always gets away, mind.'

She gave him a wan smile.

'Did you touch the body or anything around the body?'

'No, like I told Ben, I kind of froze when I saw her. The closest I got was about six feet.'

Hill made a note in the pad he'd pulled out of his pocket. 'Okay, that's really all I need for now. Can you come down to the station later?'

'Crap.' Laurel looked at her watch. 'I have clients due at the clinic all day. Would half four be all right?'

'It's not my place, but you might want to think about taking the day off. You've had a nasty shock. Why don't you let Ben walk you back home, have a cup of tea, then come through to Beverley? We can get your statement and you'll be back home in time for lunch.'

'Or locked in the cells, if Coral has her way.'

Hill checked over his shoulder and guided Laurel a little

further away from where his boss was ordering around the farmer who had arrived to round up his herd. 'I know she's been tough on you.'

'That's an understatement.'

'Don't let it get to you. She doesn't really think you're responsible for these murders.'

'So why does she keep reacting the way she does? I know it's weird how I keep finding dead people, but it's not like I go out looking for them. If I were a serial killer, I'd have to be pretty stupid to be the one who reports the death every time. Anyway, Jessica wasn't murdered, and since I did not magically arrange for a bunch of cows to crush her, why is Coral being an arse again?'

Hill blew out a long breath. 'Between us, she was involved in the team investigating that murder of Lily Armitage, and she was one of the people arguing it was an accident. What with you kicking up a fuss and then it turning out to be murder after all...' he trailed off, shrugging.

'She's upset because I was right and she was wrong?' *Unbelievable.*

'I know, I know. I don't understand her reasoning. I'm only telling you what I know.'

Relieved by a team of uniformed officers who turned up and set about securing the site, Ben wandered back over. 'Why don't you let me walk you home?'

'Exactly what I suggested,' agreed the DS. 'Good man.'

They both looked at her expectantly.

The adrenaline had worn off and Laurel's hands were shaking. She stuffed them in her pockets. 'I need to go to the office. You can walk me there.' She didn't want to be in Ben's company any more than necessary, but, in that moment, neither did she want to be alone.

'If you're sure. Come on, let's get away from here.'

'If you insist on working, make it four at the station?' Hill called a reminder.

'I'll be there,' she said without looking back.

They walked in silence. At first, Ben had tried a couple of gentle openers, but her monosyllabic responses didn't invite further attempts at conversation. She stared at her feet, barely glancing up, trusting Ben to lead the way.

'Do you want me to come in and wait with you or is there anyone I can call?' he asked when they reached the door to her office building.

She regarded his mud caked shoes. 'I'm fine, thank you and the cleaner would kill me if I let you walk muck all over the carpets.' She couldn't meet his searching stare. The shakes were worse. She badly wanted someone to put their arms around her and tell her it would all be okay. Not him, though.

'Okay, but call me if you need anything.'

'Sure.' She put the key in the lock, let herself in and closed the door on him. Heaving a deep sigh, she leaned against the wall and let the tears fall. She let two minutes pass, then wiped her cheeks, grasped the banister, and hauled her aching body up the stairs. There were three offices on the first floor, each opening off a shared waiting area, but on a Monday, she was the only person working, so there was no one to disturb her or see her puffy eyes and red nose.

She should cancel her appointments. She was in no state to conduct psychological therapy, but she hated to let people down, especially a potential new client. She checked the clock on the wall. Mary, her first client, would arrive in twenty minutes. No, it was too short notice. She would see her, explain there had been an unexpected event and that they would need to cut the session a little shorter than usual. As compensation, she wouldn't charge her. After that she'd see how she felt, but she would probably keep going and keep busy.

Decision made, she had a drink of water, splashed some on her face, and regained a modicum of equilibrium. As soon as she was finished with Gertrude at three-thirty, she would head to the police station. Get it over with.

Her first three sessions went smoothly, and she even managed to force down a bit of lunch. Thankfully, she'd had a packet of crisps and a snack bar in her desk drawer. She didn't fancy emerging from the safety of her office and facing any kind of bombardment over Jessica's death. However, two-thirty came and went with no sign of Gertrude. She rose and went to the window overlooking the village green. There were parking spaces outside, but the only vehicle there belonged to Sam, the manager of The Snooty Fox. There were no strangers loitering around, only a couple of chattering mums with buggies on the terrace outside the tearoom.

At two-fifty, she gave up. Ms Bell had changed her mind or been unable to attend for whatever reason. She would follow-up with a phone call tomorrow. For now, she was relieved.

Chapter 19

Laurel

It was quiet inside the pub. Most of the customers were out in the garden enjoying the evening sun. Laurel picked a table in a corner furthest from the bar and waited for Maggie and Albert to arrive.

Her interview at the police station had been brief. There wasn't much she could tell them, and try as she might, she couldn't get Coral or Hill to give anything away. As soon as Coral had said she could leave, Laurel had called Maggie and asked if they could meet. Maggie in turn had called Albert, who had suggested they rendezvous in The Snooty Fox. She hadn't mentioned Jessica; it wasn't the kind of news one broke over the phone.

Lost in thought, she didn't notice Maggie had arrived until her friend plopped down beside her. She had a drink in a fancy glass with an umbrella which she handed to Laurel.

'It's one of Sam's lavender mojitos. I'm not brave enough to try it.'

Laurel sniffed the liquid. It smelled wonderful, but she wasn't convinced it was a scent she wanted to ingest. She had a sip. 'Mmm, thanks for this.' Her mouth puckered. It tasted like soap. She put it down and pushed it away. 'Not one of his best.'

Maggie didn't reply. She was busy knocking back a large glass of wine.

'There you are, dear ladies,' said Albert, wandering over to their table. 'I see you're both furnished with beverages. I'll be back in a tick with one of my own.'

'Get me a glass of chardonnay, would you?' Laurel called to his retreating back and he lifted a hand in acknowledgement.

Laurel sat on her news until he returned, but when he did, she knew she couldn't put it off any longer.

'Sorry to be the bearer of bad news.'

Maggie's eyes swam with instant tears. 'We already know. That poor, poor girl. I can't believe it.'

Albert patted her hand. 'It is tragic. And Laurel,' he turned, 'I'm most dreadfully sorry you were the unfortunate soul to discover her. Were they terribly trying at the police station?'

'I survived. They asked a lot about what Jessica was doing in Elderwick. I told them to speak to the university, and Dr Delgado and Beth.' The knot in her stomach was already easing now she was back in the company of her friends. 'They have to ask their questions. I understand. I only wish Coral wasn't such a cow about... oh, no, I didn't mean that. Bloody cows.'

'I've cautioned people about the cows before,' said Albert. 'However, I've walked through that particular field umpteen times with no bother. There are no calves in there and I don't believe Jessica had a dog with her, so I'm at a loss as to what could have spooked them so badly? That said, animals are unpredictable. I should know, my cockerel is a law unto himself.'

It earned him weak smiles from his audience.

Laurel bit her lip, then blurted out the question that had been plaguing her since finding the body. 'Is it me?'

Maggie studied her. 'What do you mean?'

'Since I moved here, people keep dying, and I don't mean older people dying of natural causes. I mean healthy people who wind up,' she lowered her voice, 'murdered.'

'Oh no, don't say that. Jessica dying was an accident, and the bones they dug up, well, they're from long before your time.'

'I know, it's just, my dad died when I was little, then my mum got sick and died. I ended up working in palliative care...' She swallowed hard. 'Next, I move here and,' she counted on her fingers, 'Four people have been killed, and at least three were nearly killed, plus the bones. I honestly think that I... I don't know... that I attract death.' Her rational brain understood a correlation didn't equal causation, but the bodies were stacking up. 'During the whole Hugh Quintrell saga, when everything was getting a bit scary, I was ready to leave Elderwick to protect you guys. Maybe it's not such a crazy idea.'

Albert smacked the table and made them jump. 'Don't you entertain such an idea for a moment. You are not responsible for any of this. True, we've had more than our fair share of bereavements, as have you in your personal life, Laurel. However, the only people who hold any responsibility for the murders are those irredeemable creatures who took lives, and they are locked away. If anything, your presence here is serendipitous.'

'How do you work that one out?' She wasn't convinced.

'Without you, would we ever have identified the killers in our midst? The police were flailing in all the cases, and it's only thanks to you the guilty parties were apprehended. If you choose to believe in fate, perhaps your fate is to be the unmasker of villains?'

She wasn't entirely persuaded. 'I appreciate your counterpoint. Logically, I know it's nonsense, except it's hard to hang on to logic when I'm the one who keeps finding the bodies.'

'I concede to you there. In light of which, and far be it from me to tell you your job, however, I am wondering if you would benefit from some professional support yourself?'

'Albert's right,' Maggie said. 'It must have been ghastly to find Jessica. We are always here for you, but...'

Laurel reached over and clasped their hands. 'Thank you. If I need help, I have a network of people I can go to, but for now, I have everything I need right here.'

Maggie reclaimed her hand and smothered Laurel with a hug. 'Do you want to talk about it? Because it's okay if you do...' she offered, her voice partially muffled.

Releasing herself from Maggie's clutch, Laurel contemplated the overture as she absently sipped the lavender mojito. The drink hadn't improved with age. 'It might be helpful to tell you guys about it. If not for me, then at least you can correct people when they start embellishing the story.'

'Was it awful?'

'Maggie,' Albert warned. 'Let Laurel tell it.'

She considered her words. 'It was a surprise. I was too focused on the cows to notice her before I was... before she was... right there.' The image of Jessica's unstirring body surrounded by hoof prints clawed back to the front of her mind and settled there. 'You know how they say people appear peaceful in death? Well, she didn't.' She broke off. 'You know, you don't need to hear this, and I don't think I do want to go over it again. The only thing it's worth knowing is she was gone by the time I found her. I wish I'd been there sooner so I might have been able to do something, or so that at least she wouldn't have been alone.'

Silence fell between them, and into that silence crept a

niggle. Something about the picture in her head was wrong. A detail wasn't where it should be, or what it should be. She tried to identify it, but the incongruity kept slipping away.

'What are you thinking?' asked Albert softly.

She sniffed and didn't answer immediately. She almost had it. 'Nothing.' It wouldn't come. 'For a second, I thought I'd missed something important about what I saw. I'm tired though, I'm sure it's nothing. In fact, let's change the subject. You two tell me about your days. What have you been up to?'

Albert deferred to Maggie, who said she'd been to visit Constance. Evidently realising Albert didn't know the latest, Maggie filled him in on the online dating saga.

Laurel smiled to herself. Poor Constance, Maggie could not keep a secret.

When it was Albert's turn, he told them about his meeting with the Dandelion managers and dropped a bombshell. 'Laurel, you won't want to hear this, but that old friend of yours, Jayne Clement, is one of them.'

'One of what?' She was drained by the events of the day and a glass of wine and half a mojito down and couldn't process why Albert had brought up the topic of Jayne.

'She is one of the managers with Dandelions. A recent change in personnel, I understand.'

Oh crap.

'I must say, she is a charismatic and convincing woman. I swear, she almost won Dorothy over when we were there.'

'Why was Dorothy with you?' asked Maggie.

'I thought if she saw the work they've done to the Hall, and if she could speak with the people from the charity, she might stop being such a gnashgab about it.'

Maggie snorted.

'How come Dorothy was so taken with her?' *Typical,* Laurel thought, *another person charmed by Jayne.*

'Like I said, Jayne is very convincing. She obviously takes pride in the charity and her faith in the good it can do shines through. Not to mention, they have an impressive set-up. There's been a substantial amount of money poured into this project. Though I was discomforted to learn where they've built their kitchen garden.'

'It's not?' Laurel put it together.

'Where? Where is it?' Maggie's head swung back and forth between Laurel and Albert.

'In the old orchard. They rebuilt the section of wall taken down when Marcus was developing the place, and they've even planted some new apple trees. It gave me quite a turn to be back in there. That said, it could be good to bring new life to such a blighted place. We'll know if it's worked with the first crop of apples. If they're sweet, all is well. If they're deformed and worm-eaten, mayhap the rot is resistant to being ousted.'

Laurel wasn't one to believe in ghost stories, but her own encounter in that ill-fated space was enough to make her ponder the idea that a place could absorb bitterness and misery. It had been shortly after she'd arrived in Elderwick that she'd taken an ill-judged jaunt to the orchard. In the darkness of the night, she was sure no-one else was there, but somehow, she hadn't been alone in that desolate and damaged place. An icy finger slid down her spine.

'You know, maybe it's not me that attracts death after all; maybe it's Elderwick Hall.'

'We're certainly well versed with the Hartfield ancestors and the dreadful acts they've perpetrated over the decades,' sniffed Albert.

'I don't mean the owners. What if it's the actual building and the grounds?'

'Like in Stephen King books, where people are always going

and building on top of old Native American burial grounds?' said Maggie.

'Maybe. Think about it: every time that old orchard is disturbed, bad things happen.'

Chapter 20

Albert

Once he'd escorted Maggie and Laurel safely home, Albert pottered around his garden, putting his menagerie to bed: his rabbit, his chickens, and a new addition, a juvenile crow who'd been injured by a marauding cat. He was hoping the bird – Crowanna Lumley – would be ready to fend for herself soon, but for now, she still needed a bit of TLC.

Aroon, never one to be corralled, set his own timetable, doing as he pleased. That particular evening, what he pleased was to perch on the fence between Albert's garden and Laurel's, strutting back and forth in full view of her chickens.

'You'll push your luck too far one day, my lad,' Albert warned.

As he went about his comforting evening ritual, his mind was busy puzzling over the pickle in which he found himself.

Once all was secure outside, he went indoors and upstairs to the small room at the front of his cottage that served as his study. He sank into his worn desk chair and brought his PC to life.

So far, he'd managed to scan around a third of the photos he'd amassed for his project, including the one that was causing him a problem. He had the original safely filed away, but with his eyes not being what they used to be, it was easier for him to zoom in to the picture on the screen and increase the brightness to illuminate the dark corners.

On its own, the photograph was innocuous enough, but to the right – or should that be wrong? – person, it showed how and when a crime had been committed. It was dangerous. Not quite evidence, but enough to lead an informed individual to a conclusion he hoped they'd never reach. He was minded to destroy both the physical and the digital versions, but it wasn't his decision to make.

Ten minutes later, he retraced his steps towards the centre of the village, but rather than turn right and return to The Snooty Fox, he continued straight ahead onto East Street. Halfway down a quiet side lane, he ducked under an arch cut in a hedge, crossed the neat garden, and went round the side of the house to the back door.

'I know it's late,' he said when his knock was answered, 'but we need to talk.'

Chapter 21

Maggie

Maggie spotted her quarry a couple of hundred feet away. She hitched up the hem of her summer dress and set off in pursuit.

The conversation the previous evening had left an ache in her heart. She knew how dismayed Laurel was after finding Jessica, but that night, back home, she'd had an idea. What Laurel needed was a win, and what better than for Laurel to be the one to deduce the identity of the skeleton in the meadow? She would help her friend to accept that Albert was right; she was the investigator the village needed, and she'd be completing the work Jessica had planned before her untimely end.

Her target was getting away.

'Ben,' she shouted, not caring who turned to stare. 'Can you spare me a minute?'

He stopped and waited for her by the pond. Puffing, she reached him and collapsed onto the bench to catch her breath and cool off. It was going to be another hot one.

He eased down beside her. 'You okay?'

She fanned her face with a hand. 'Fine, just give me a moment.' It was only now she was realising she hadn't thought about what to say. Ben wasn't even in charge of the investigation, but he would do for starters.

'It's about this business with the bones.'

Ben grimaced. 'I can't talk to you about an ongoing investigation. You know that, Maggie.'

She grinned in triumph. 'You've not solved it yet? That's interesting.'

'Solved it?' he laughed. 'No, not yet.' His eyes narrowed, but he was smiling as he asked, 'Why? You're not on some Miss Marple kick again, are you?'

'I beg your pardon.'

His smile faltered.

'I'm hardly old enough to be compared with Miss Marple. I believe she was seventy-five years old in the earliest novels!'

Ben's mouth fell open.

She punched him on the arm. 'I'm teasing you. I know you would never dare suggest I was a day over... let's say forty.' She was amused to see him look relieved. He was lucky he hadn't said something similar to Dorothy. She was in her eighties, but woe betide anyone who mentioned it in her presence.

'On a serious note, though... In light of these bones, and as a concerned citizen, I would like to know if I should be worried about a possible murderer in our midst?' Despite her lightness of tone, Maggie quivered at the thought the bones were there as the result of a murder.

Ben's eyes were searching. She kept her mouth shut and waited.

'It happened a long time ago.'

'There are people who've lived here for decades,' she countered.

'All the more reason not to sensationalise, Maggie. You'll get people scared when we don't even know for certain what caused the person's death.'

Maggie squirmed; this wasn't going the way she'd imagined. 'We didn't mean any harm. We've just been talking and–'

'Who's *we*?'

'Me, Laurel, and Albert,' she supplied the names in a quiet voice.

'Huddled round a cauldron, were you?'

She made a face.

'The police have to investigate, emphasis on *police*. His family, if we can find them, deserve answers.'

Maggie pressed her lips together. Ben had unwittingly confirmed the skeleton was a *he*.

'And you're right, there might still be people in Elderwick connected to the deceased. Think how they would feel if, out of nowhere, people start running around making wild speculations or even accusations. You know how that happens in a place like this. Which is why I would appreciate you not talking about it anymore. Do you understand?'

'I understand.'

<hr>

'Albert?' Maggie hammered on his door.

'Easy does it. You'll have the paint off with all that knocking,' he said as he answered. 'Are you quite all right?'

'I've tried Laurel, she's not in, but I need you both to know what I've just heard from Ben.' She lowered her voice and checked around her, making sure there was no-one nearby to overhear. 'He didn't mean to, but he referred to the body in the meadow as being that of a man.'

'In you come.'

As he held the door for her and she passed him, she thought she heard a muttered *again*, but she didn't have time to remonstrate. As her foot crossed the threshold of the living room, he flung out his arm and blocked her passage.

'It's a terrible mess in there. Let's go into the kitchen.'

'Okay.' Albert's cottage was perpetually cluttered, but in a homely way. It was like a voyage of discovery exploring the objects and books he had scattered around his living space like leaves on an autumn lawn. She'd never known him to be worried about a bit of untidiness.

He led her through to the kitchen and filled the kettle. 'Let's have a cup of tea, shall we?'

'Albert, is everything all right?' He was taking cups and saucers from the cupboard and retrieving the milk from the fridge, his face hidden.

'I'm tickety-boo. A bit of a restless night is all and whilst I couldn't sleep, I took it upon myself to reorganise some old bits and pieces. Now there's not a surface in there free of flotsam.'

'But you're okay?' she asked again.

'Like your good self, I am heartsick about the death of that young woman which has produced a certain melancholia, you could say.'

'Melancholia... that's the word. I'm feeling it too, especially since speaking to Ben. He warned us not to speculate about the bones. Do you know, I felt quite told off?'

Albert blinked. 'I wonder if Ben isn't correct, that we should leave this to the professionals?'

Maggie blanched at his tone. 'But I thought you and Laurel should know what he said.'

Albert put his hand to his chest. 'I apologise. I didn't mean to be brusque. Perhaps the lack of sleep has taken a greater toll than I realised. Let me get you your tea and when we've drunk up, what say we pop over to Laurel's office? I saw her heading out to work this morning. We might be able to catch her between patients to relay the latest intel and Ben's instructions.'

'We could do that.' Mollified, Maggie accepted her Earl Grey with a squeeze of lemon and inhaled the floral vapour drifting from the china cup. 'Lovely, thank you.' It was impossible to be annoyed with Albert. 'Oh, and biscuits too. You are spoiling me.'

'I am. They're the chocolate ones. None of your rich tea in this house.' Albert leaned against the worktop and turned his face to the window overlooking his back garden. 'It's a crying shame for Laurel to even entertain the idea that she is some kind of malign influence in Elderwick. It won't be long before she thinks twice about so much as venturing from Myrtle Cottage, lest she should stumble upon another corpse.' He came to the table and sat. 'Do you know the religious significance of myrtle?'

'No.'

'It represents fertility and life.'

'That's rather ironic. I mean the life bit, not the fertility. I mean, I know Laurel doesn't want children – and there's nothing wrong with that – but the life bit...' She lost her thread and her sentence petered out.

'I didn't know she didn't want children, but then, it's not the sort of thing a young woman discusses with her aged neighbour. And speak of the devil, here comes one of mine.'

'One of your what?'

'One of my children.' Aroon popped through the cat flap and strutted over to Albert, twisting about his legs and butting him with his sleek head, his red comb wobbling.

'I don't know about him being a child, but devil is right,' muttered Maggie, keeping one eye on the cockerel and a protective hand over her biscuits.

Albert stroked Aroon's head and the bird purred.

Maggie could feel his golden eyes watching her as she ate her last two biscuits. 'Shall we go?'

Albert finished his tea, gathered up the cups, and placed them in the sink. 'Ready when you are.'

It was a short stroll to the village green, opposite The Pleasant Pheasant, where Laurel had her office. They rang the bell by the discreet entrance and were buzzed inside. Laurel was waiting for them at the top of the stairs as they ascended.

'Have you two finally accepted that you need professional help?' she laughed. 'You're in luck. I have a free slot so I can see you now. I warn you, though, it won't be a quick fix.'

'You're bright-eyed and bushy tailed this morning,' Albert remarked.

'You might think so. Frankly, I'm running on fumes. I was awake most of the night thinking about Jessica.' Laurel flopped down onto a chair as they followed her into her consulting room. 'I was thinking, there's still the mystery surrounding this body in the meadow. Jessica wanted me to help her identify the deceased and maybe even support any living relative, so although she's gone, I think I should try to do just that. In her memory.'

Maggie looked at Albert.

'What is it?' asked Laurel.

'Maggie ran into our local bobby this morning.' Albert offered the second chair to Maggie.

Maggie sat and waited for Albert to wheel over the desk chair for himself before she said, 'From what Ben told me, the remains are those of a man.' She heard Albert cough, but she wanted to share the important details before she had to tell Laurel they'd been instructed to leave well enough alone. 'I don't think he realised he'd slipped up and told me so.'

'And he told Maggie she shouldn't be talking about it.'

'Albert thinks we should leave it to the police this time.' Despite having been warned off once already by DI Coral, Maggie didn't think Laurel would be able to let it lie, especially not now. None of them *wanted* to get involved in another murder investigation, but... 'But, you said it yourself in the pub, Albert, Laurel is the unmasker of villains and I don't think it's too much of a stretch to say we – you and I – are her trusty sidekicks: Charles and Oliver to Laurel's Mabel.'

'Oh, I love *Only Murders in the Building*.' Laurel perked up. 'But Charles and Oliver aren't sidekicks, neither are you guys. It's always been the three of us together.'

'Are we doing this?' Maggie crossed her fingers.

'Much as I hate to admit it, we make a good team, and I have to be honest, the police haven't covered themselves in glory in previous cases.' Laurel addressed herself to Albert. 'What do you say, Albert?'

He steepled his fingers. 'I will do what I can in the interests of humanity.'

Maggie wasn't sure if that was a yes. 'Is that a yes?'

'It's Poirot.' Albert replied with a glint in his eye. 'And yes, I'm in.'

Chapter 22

Laurel

After Maggie and Albert's visit, Laurel found it difficult to concentrate. Luckily, she had only two clients booked, and both sessions went smoothly. She toyed with the idea of contacting Gertrude Bell, her no-show from the day before, but decided not to. She would leave it up to Gertrude to call and reschedule if she wished. She wasn't hard up for business. There was no need to be chasing clients.

Decision made, she straightened her office and locked up. She and Albert had been invited to Maggie's for tea, so she crossed the green to make a stop at The Pleasant Pheasant. She wanted to pick up a bottle of the cloudy cider made at Drumble's Hive that Jo sold in the tearoom.

Bottle obtained, she scanned the faces at the café tables whilst waiting for her change. She had been hoping to run in to Dr Delgado, Beth, or Lin to pass on her condolences and to offer her support if anyone in the team wanted to talk. None of them was present, and thankfully, neither was Jayne Clement. It had been bad enough seeing her once, but now Albert was saying Jayne was part of the Dandelions team, it meant she could be around the village for who knew how long. It was a headache she could do without.

Cider safely stowed in a carrier bag, Laurel said goodbye to Jo and had got as far as the corner of Manor Road when she heard the rapid footsteps of someone running and Lin came barrelling out of Dorothy's driveway.

'Lin,' she cried as the young woman nearly collided with her.

Lin lifted her head. Her cheeks were streaked with tears. 'Shit, sorry,' she said.

'Is there anything...' Laurel began, but Lin was already past her.

Laurel walked to Dorothy's gate and peered down towards the house that could just be seen beyond the ugly leylandii bracketing the driveway. The owner was nowhere in sight. What had happened to make Lin race from the house the way she had? It wasn't any of Laurel's business, but knowing Dorothy, she was worried the older woman had said something offensive or hurtful to cause Lin's rapid escape. She would try to catch up with Lin sometime soon and extend her offer of support.

Back home inside her cosy cottage, Laurel had a quick shower and changed into a cute pair of pedal-pushers and a cream cotton smocked top. Entering the living room, her attention alighted on her new pink notebook. She felt a twinge of guilt over Ben's admonition that they should stay away from the case – Coral's identical warning didn't trouble her in the slightest – but they weren't going to interfere. They were only talking, and only amongst themselves. What harm could it do?

Laurel lifted her nose and inhaled. 'It smells heavenly in here. What are we having tonight?'

'Molasses-coated chicken thighs with a Moroccan inspired couscous,' said Maggie, handing her a glass of cider. 'Albert's out in the garden if you want to join him. The food will be ready in ten minutes.'

'Can I help with anything?' Laurel hoped the answer would be no.

'No, it's all under control. Go and relax, but don't talk about the case without me.'

Somehow, they refrained from discussing the case throughout the meal. It hadn't felt right to talk about death over such wonderful food.

Collecting up the plates, Maggie said, 'Let me get my notebook, and then let's see where we're starting from with all of this. The washing up can wait until tomorrow.'

She returned to the table within seconds, her turquoise book in hand, pen at the ready. 'Who wants to start?'

'Do we know anything more about the bones?' asked Albert. 'The ring, and the time frame it gives us, is compelling, but does it move us in any particular direction? We should be cautious not to jump to conclusions as they may lead us a merry dance down the wrong track.'

Maggie rubbed her forehead. 'Can we give the bones a temporary name, to make it easier?'

'What, you want to call him Fred or something?' Laurel teased.

'Napoleon Bone-apart,' suggested Albert.

Maggie snickered.

To prevent further wandering off track, Laurel pressed on. 'We have two angles of approach: we consider who went missing from around here at the right time, or we see if we can arrange access to this database of missing people Jessica has compiled at the university.'

Albert cleared his throat. 'Did Jessica not share any names from her list?'

Laurel shook her head. 'We hadn't really got that far in our conversation. She might have said something to Lin, though. We should ask her.'

'Laurel and I already found reports for three missing people from this area in the right time period,' said Maggie. 'I think we should consider each of them, with particular attention paid to Harold Emmerson, if he was Dorothy's husband as we suspect. I don't suppose you had the opportunity to sound Dorothy out when she accompanied you to Dandelions the other day?'

'Afraid my mind was elsewhere,' Albert answered.

'How would Albert have known to ask Dorothy about Harold Emmerson?' Laurel pinned Maggie with a stare. She didn't know whether to laugh or sigh in exasperation. 'I take it you told him already?'

Maggie flushed, and Albert chuckled.

'Never mind,' Laurel absolved her friend. It was just Maggie's way. Besides, they were a team. Albert was safe to bring into their confidence.

Quickly recovered, Maggie pressed on. 'Albert, you must know if she was married to a Harold, though? You've known her for years.'

'Dorothy is a very private woman, and as I said before, I don't recall her being married, but then, I was away from the village for quite some years, throughout the seventies and eighties.'

Maggie looked surprised. 'You didn't come back to visit at all during that time period?'

'I was teaching in London. I had no particular reason to be back here. I don't recall that I made any visits.'

Laurel frowned. Albert knew *everything* about Elderwick and the people who lived there, even the things that had happened whilst he'd been away. She was aware of Albert watching her and heat flared in her cheeks.

'I think the cider's gone to your head,' Maggie giggled, pointing at Laurel. 'You've gone all red.'

'It's strong stuff.' Her voice sounded strained to her own ears. 'It should be easy enough to check public records to find out if Dorothy was married and we could always ask her directly. Maggie, let's put it on our to do list.'

'I can speak to her, if one of us must,' said Albert. 'Not to stir the pot, but Laurel, I think we both know she wouldn't tell you, and Maggie, I simply couldn't send you into the dragon's den. I shall arm myself with every charm I can muster and see what I can learn.'

'Brilliant.' Maggie looked relieved.

Laurel put Albert's name next to the task. He'd been quick to offer when she'd suggested they ask Dorothy outright. Was there a reason for that? She pushed the thought away. 'Maggie, could you arrange to bump into Ben again? See if there are any new developments?'

'Will do. But wouldn't you like to be the one-'

'Great.' Laurel wasn't about to let her finish that sentence. 'And I'm going to approach the archaeology team to offer support over the loss of Jessica. Whilst I'm there, and of course only if it's appropriate, I can ask around and see if Jessica had chance to confide in anyone in particular.'

'I've thought of one more thing,' said Maggie. 'We should make a list of everyone who was opposed to the farm shop being built in the meadow. If anyone in the village knew the bones were buried there, they wouldn't have wanted the project to go ahead.'

'Excellent point. Albert, you know the council guys. Could

you quiz them over any objections they received, or perhaps ask the Dandelions people in case anyone went direct?'

Albert signalled his assent.

'Maggie, at your next WI meeting, will you ask your ladies if they have anything to contribute?'

'Of course. We're meeting this Thursday as usual. We have a busy agenda, but I know the members will all be twittering about the bones and Jessica, so it'll be no bother to ask a few questions.'

Albert clapped his hands. 'We have an action plan,' he beamed. 'You know, I do believe we will have this solved in record time.'

Chapter 23

***

Laurel

Laurel had no regular clients booked in for Wednesday morning, so she was heading out to find the archaeology team. She'd make the meadow her first port of call, and if no-one was there, she'd double back and go up to Drumble's Hive, where some of the archaeologists, and Jessica, had been staying.

For a change, the weather was cooler with a few feathery clouds in the sky. Summer was not Laurel's season of choice; she didn't like the heat, the bugs, or the sticky nights. She longed for autumn when the breezes turned fresh, and the shadows lengthened towards winter.

She pulled in irritation at the linen dress she was wearing which kept shifting about so the neckline was no-longer straight. It wasn't a garment designed for a woman with boobs.

Even from the bottom of Church Lane, she could tell there was activity at the dig site. Going by the glimpses of fluorescent yellow, it was probably the police. She wavered. DI Coral had told her to stay away, and while she wasn't worried about disobeying – it was a public lane she was on – she didn't want to be summoned to another interview at the station for no good reason. She backtracked, cut through the church graveyard, and nipped through the gap in the low wall to join the dirt path that led along the back of the cottages that faced the lane. From the hidden pathway she would be able to observe much of the meadow whilst remaining inconspicuous behind the trees. Hopefully, unnoticed by anyone official.

Once in what she judged to be the best position for reconnaissance, Laurel crouched down to settle on a handy log from where she could peer through the foliage. She scanned the people milling about. There were only two members of the police team. Neither of them was Ben, nor were they Coral or Hill. They seemed to be overseeing activity in the trench with the bones. She shifted to get a better view and caught sight of Dr Delgado and his wife, Beth, coming out of the white tent that sheltered the grave. Once out, two other people manoeuvring large plastic trays went in, emerging again moments later.

Busy watching the tray carriers, she lost sight of the two archaeologists.

'You get a superb view from the church tower,' said a voice behind her.

'Bloody hell!' She lurched forward and fell off her perch. Brushing her hair out of her eyes, she swivelled round and blurted an apology, 'Sorry for swearing, but you gave me a proper fright. Why are you creeping around?'

Christopher laughed and invited her to join him back on the handy stump-cum-seat. 'I could ask you the same thing. Not spying on our local constabulary, I'm sure?'

She blushed.

'Is anything happening?'

'I think they're removing the bones. She pointed to where the trays were being loaded into an unmarked van.'

The vicar bowed his head. Laurel thought he was praying.

'I do hope they uncover the identity,' he said when he was

finished. 'I imagine there is a family somewhere who have been waiting many years for answers.'

'Do you think it's better to know, even if you learn your loved one was murdered?'

'Is that what they're saying? I suppose it must be suspicious,' he answered himself. 'Bodies don't bury themselves, and it evidently isn't an old burial, by which I mean Saxon or Roman.'

'You know about the ring?' She wasn't surprised.

'Come now, you've lived in Elderwick a little longer than I. We both know news spreads more easily than soft butter in this village. No doubt, this very moment, over pieces of cake in the teashop, people are speculating about the vicar and the psychologist huddled together in the undergrowth.' He shook with silent amusement and his face creased with well-worn laughter lines. 'Forgive me, I shouldn't make light.' His expression clouded. 'Especially after the death of that young woman. You found her, I believe?'

She didn't want to talk about it. 'I did, but, if it's okay, I'd rather not—'

Christopher held up a hand. 'Say no more. My door is always open should you be in need of a listening ear.'

'Thank you.' She liked the Reverend Christopher Ibori. True, he'd been on her suspect list the last time there was a murder in the village, but he was a good friend of Albert's and that was as good a recommendation as it was possible to have.

'Did you see it's in the papers today, about the remains? I'm surprised it took the press this long to get wind of it.'

She hadn't even thought to look. 'No, what do they say?'

'Not much, only that the complete skeleton of an adult male has been found in Elderwick. They didn't include any mention of the ring, but they said the police enquiries are underway.'

'No new information then?'

'Not in the papers, no.'

'Not in the papers, but...?'

'Strictly entre nous,' he whispered, 'I bumped into Rik – Dr Delgado – yesterday who told me they found a coin under the remains which he and the police believe may have been in the pocket of the deceased.'

'A coin?' This was new. How had she not heard about this already? 'With a date?' It could be crucial information.

'1981. Does that narrow down your timeline a smidge?'

'It certainly does. We...' She stopped. 'I don't have a timeline. Why would I?'

'Why indeed,' he twinkled.

Laurel knew she wasn't fooling him.

'Vicar.'

'Please, you know you can call me Christopher.'

'Christopher, can I ask you something in confidence?'

'Of course.'

'It's about Albert.'

'I see.' He spent a moment knocking a spot of dirt off his trousers. 'Why don't we head back to the vestry and have a chat? The chairs are far more comfortable than this lump of wood, and afterwards, if you're still interested, I'll show you that view.'

'You weren't joking? I didn't think people were allowed up the tower.'

'In general, they're not, but I can make an exception.'

Back at the church, she hesitated for a fraction of a second before crossing the threshold, chilled by memories of a near-death experience she'd had at the hands of a determined killer in that very building not so long ago. She ignored the quake in her legs and hurried after the vicar, only relaxing when they reached the vestry.

Christopher handed her a freshly brewed cup of tea and proffered the biscuit tin. 'You're lucky, I think there are some chocolate Hobnobs left.' He helped himself to a Jammy Dodger and dunked it in his mug. 'What is it you want to ask me about Albert?'

Laurel knew Albert and the vicar had become close since Christopher's arrival in the village. She was desperately hoping he would calm her fears and confirm she was being nuts for suspecting Albert of deception. 'It's about all the weird stuff that's been going on here. And, you know I love Albert, and I know he is the most honourable man for miles around – present company excepted – but last night Maggie, Albert and I were discussing the case... I mean the bones and who they might be. But I could swear Albert was lying about something.' She winced. 'Lying is a bit strong, but I'm certain he knows more than he was telling us.'

'When you say *case*, do I take it to mean you're... How shall I put it? ...conducting your own enquiry?'

Laurel fidgeted. 'We were just talking about what's happened. We're not interfering.'

'Far be it from me to suggest that you are.' A ghost of a smile played on his lips. 'Let me ask a question.' He placed his mug on the table and leaned back, getting comfortable in his chair. 'Do you trust Albert?'

She mirrored his posture as she thought. The answer was obvious. 'Yes, absolutely.'

'Then you can cease fretting. *If* Albert is concealing information, we can assume he has good reason and will tell you once – if – he is able. Does that help?'

For a long time in her life, Laurel had struggled to let people get close for fear of leaving herself vulnerable. It wasn't until she'd moved to Yorkshire that she came to understand how much she was shutting herself off and what she was missing out on by keeping people at arm's length. Maggie and Albert were the closest friends she'd had since primary school. And Christopher was right, whilst Albert was undoubtedly holding something back, he would have good reason.

'It helps.'

All the same, she remained intrigued. What was he concealing?

'Good. Now how about we go look at what's happening in the meadow? How are you with heights?'

The stone steps were steep and in the absence of a handrail, Laurel pressed as close to the outer wall as she could. She didn't like to think how it would be when they came back down. They reached the belfry, and she thanked her lucky stars the three sizeable bells weren't due to ring again for another ten minutes.

'We can't see much from here,' she observed.

'We have a little further to go yet,' replied Christopher as he placed a battered wooden ladder beneath a trapdoor in the ceiling. 'Are you game?' He was grinning.

'I've come this far,' she said, tamping down her nerves.

'Great.' And he was away up the ladder, through the hatch, his feet disappearing. A second later, his head reappeared above her. 'When you're ready. Don't worry, the ladder's safe.'

She was sceptical. Nonetheless, up she went.

'Oh! My goodness.' She spun round, drinking in the view. It was the village she knew so well, but the new perspective was entrancing. She could see all the way past the school to her cottage. She could make out the roof of Elderwick Hall above the trees, and they had a perfect view of the meadow.

'Watch your step. It's a bit uneven up here and the parapet is low.'

Placing her feet with utmost care, she shuffled along to where she had the best view of the figures amongst the trenches. One of them – Laurel thought it was Beth – glanced up towards the tower and after a beat, waved. She and Christopher waved back.

Her enjoyment of the lofty view paled when the flapping tape of the police cordon caught her eyes in the distant field where Jessica's body had lain. The cows were gone.

'They had dogs in the meadow on Sunday.'

'Dogs?' she echoed.

'Cadaver dogs, I believe.'

Of course, she thought. Where there's one unexpected set of skeletal remains, they would need to check for others. 'Did they find anything?'

'I don't think so. Not whilst I was watching at any rate.' He hemmed. 'Please don't think I'm a ghoul. I come up here to...'

'Hide?'

He chuckled. 'You could put it that way. I find it very peaceful. I can marvel at God's creation and know I won't be interrupted for just a little while.'

They lapsed into silence as another vehicle pulled into the dusty layby alongside the meadow. A bulky man emerged and stood arms folded, observing the activity in front of him. From their perch, his face was hidden, but something about him was familiar. He sported a full head of grey hair and was dressed smartly in beige chinos and a pale blue shirt.

'Who's that?' asked Christopher.

She shrugged. 'Not sure. I don't think I've seen him around here before. He could be another police officer?'

As she spoke, one of the constables on site noticed the arrival and walked over to the wall where he engaged him in conversation. The older man began gesturing, and his voice was raised, but she couldn't make out what he was saying. The uniformed officer retreated a couple of paces, his body language suggesting he was uneasy. He lifted what Laurel assumed was his radio to his mouth and spoke, turning a few degrees away from the visitor, who took up pacing alongside the wall. Laurel dug in her pocket for her phone and opened the camera.

'I'm just curious,' she whispered to the vicar. She zoomed in as far as she could, and at the precise moment the grey-haired man turned and revealed his face, she snapped a photo. Lowering the phone, she looked at the screen and gasped.

Vincent Tillow. The ex-chief superintendent of the local police force, one time council colleague of Maggie's former husband, and father of someone she would rather forget. What was he doing at the crime scene? Had he been involved in the local missing persons cases during his time on the force? Was that what had brought him to the meadow?

The hand holding her phone shook and she was seized by an urgent need to get her feet back on solid ground. 'I need to get down. Now, please.'

'Ah,' said Christopher, blocking her way to the ladder. 'You might want to...'

His words were lost as the clock struck the hour and the bells rang out over the rooftops.

Chapter 24

Maggie

Maggie slipped on her oven gloves and pulled out a tray of macarons. 'Voila, perfectly baked, and see how the colours stay so bright?'

Around her, seven heads bobbed up and down.

'Once they're cooled, you're all going to fill your own macarons with the lemon and white chocolate ganache you made. However, we then have to leave them for about twenty-four hours until they're ready to eat.' She grinned at the groans this disclosure elicited from her bakery group. 'But they'll be worth it.'

It didn't take long for her students to finish up. Once they'd wiped down the surfaces and put the bowls on the side to be washed, they filed out of the door, each bearing home a tin of their own jewel-like meringue-based sweets with which to impress their family and friends.

'Hiring you to run these courses was an inspired idea,' said Hetty, coming into the kitchen. 'Whose idea was it again? Oh, that's right, mine. Well done me.'

'I love them, and I love you for letting me do this.' Maggie gave Hetty a peck on the cheek. 'And since you're so happy with me, can I ask a teeny-tiny favour?'

'I knew it was too good to last. What do you want?' She mock-scolded as she ran the hot water to wash up.

Maggie found a clean tea-towel and stood by, ready to dry. 'I was hoping you could spare Constance for about an hour? The early morning rush is over, and I'll have her back before you get busy for lunch.'

'Constance didn't mention anything. Are you doing something fun? It'll do her good to get out. She's been moping around like a deflated balloon recently. Do you know what's wrong with her? Because she still won't tell me.'

Standing side by side, Maggie was able to avoid looking Hetty in the eye. 'No. I saw she was a bit down, though, so I thought I'd take her out. Try and cheer her up.'

'You're not roping her into any amateur sleuthing with Laurel, are you? I know what you two are like when you get your heads together.' Her tone was jokey, but Maggie knew Hetty worried about her younger sister.

'Nothing like that, I promise.' It wasn't a complete lie. She wanted to talk to Constance about the internet scam artist, Carter.

Hetty pursed her lips. 'Okay, but you crazy kids be back in time for the lunch rush. Oh, and we're eating at the pub at seven if you want to join us? Lin and Penelope from the archaeology team were in this morning and I've invited them too. I think they could do with a pick-me-up after everything that's been happening.'

'I'd love to.' Maggie experienced a flicker of shame that she was agreeing in some measure for the opportunity to question Lin and Penelope again.

Before she had time to dwell further on her ulterior motives,

Constance appeared. 'We all set, or did my jailor refuse me time off for good behaviour?'

'You're reprieved. As you well know, because you've already got your bag ready to go,' remarked Hetty with a flap of the dishcloth. 'Go, I'll get back out front, but you're helping me with the rest of this washing-up when you're back.'

Maggie convinced Constance to go with her to Ben's cottage first. Though curious, Constance wasn't keen, but agreed on the condition they wouldn't talk about the online dating with him. Which was fine, since Maggie had her own agenda. In the event, there was no answer when they knocked at his door, and he wasn't in the back garden when Maggie peeked through a gap in the fence.

Meandering back to the village centre, Constance suggested getting ice lollies from the tearoom and eating them on the green. While Maggie ran in to get them, Constance said she would stake out a pleasant spot by one of the benches in the shade.

'What's the latest with Carter?' Maggie asked on her return, handing over a Funny Feet and unwrapping her Fab.

'I've found him on two more dating websites. It was stupidly easy. He really has used the same photos and exactly the same blurb. No creativity at all.'

'And you've reported him to the admin of the services?'

'Not exactly.'

'What do you mean, *not exactly*?' The churning had started up again in her stomach. She had convinced herself Constance was speaking in anger when she'd talked about going after this Carter person, that she hadn't meant it.

'Calm down, let me explain my plan before you get your knickers in a twist.'

Oh dear. 'This Carter could be anyone. He could be one of those crazy swindlers they make those documentaries about or a ruthless drug dealer. Not someone to mess with,' Maggie implored.

'This is East Yorkshire, not Baltimore.'

'Baltimore?'

'Isn't that where that series is set, The Wire?'

Maggie didn't think Constance was taking it seriously. 'Are you drunk?' The conversation was getting away from her.

'Drunk like McNulty.'

Maggie put her head in her hands, narrowly avoiding getting her hair sticky with melting strawberry ice. She'd never watched the programme but knew McNulty was the alcoholic, obsessive detective and main character. Not someone to aspire to emulate. 'Start again,' she implored. 'Tell me what you've done.'

'I thought, since Carter has multiple profiles, I would do the same. I mean the nerve of him. His search area is still set to within ten miles of Beverley. I'm guessing he's tech savvy, so I didn't want to use photos I just found online, so... and I know I should have asked first...'

Maggie reeled back, her spine connecting painfully with the wooden slats of the bench. 'You better not be about to say what I think you're about to say?'

'It'll be fine, and it was the only thing I could think of.'

'I can't believe you put photos of me on a dating website. No, worse than that, I can't believe you sent them to some... some weirdo who will probably stalk and kill me now.'

'Woah, hang on, I didn't use your photos. I'd never do that.'

That brought Maggie up sharply. 'If you didn't use mine, whose did you use?'

'Hetty's.'

'Very clever,' Maggie deadpanned.

Constance looked smug. 'I know. Two can play at this game.

I've called her Sylvia in the new profile. She is stunning in this picture. No way will Carter ignore her DM.'

Maggie's head was spinning. 'Eww, a DM, isn't that when a man sends a photograph of his you-know?'

Constance gaped at her, then howled with laughter. 'Direct message,' she wheezed. 'It means direct message. Oh Maggie, you crack me up sometimes, you really do.'

Chapter 25

Laurel

As she emerged from under the lychgate, Laurel's attention was still on the meadow and Vincent Tillow, and she almost ran into Jayne Clement.

'Laurel! Am I glad to see you,' declared Jayne. 'Isn't it simply dreadful?'

There was no escape. 'Hey, Jayne. It could be better.'

'And this is such a quiet little village.'

Laurel was surprised to hear Jayne was unaware of the recent history – come to think of it, the recent *and* the older history – of Elderwick. Then she remembered Albert saying Jayne was a newcomer to the Dandelions charity. Presumably, no-one had fully briefed her on the murky underbelly of the location of their newest centre.

'Most of the time it is.' Despite everything, she didn't want to talk down her home, even if it hadn't been all things nice since she'd moved there. 'The people here are the loveliest you could ever meet, and as for the food, there must be something in the water to produce so many talented cooks and bakers.' If she could, she'd keep the topic of conversation firmly away from murder, and history. The history between her and Jayne in particular, was not a place she wanted to visit. 'Albert tells me you're one of the new managers for the Dandelions Centre. Will you be based here permanently?' *Please say no.*

'I'm not sure yet. The initial plan was for my colleague, Alex, and me to coordinate the opening, then he would run the show, and I would be back at HQ in Leeds.'

Jayne's non-answer failed to soothe her nerves. 'And the plan has changed?' Not wanting to linger on Church Lane when Vincent Tillow might drive past at any moment, Laurel set out at a gentle pace back up the lane, away from the police activity behind them.

'Maybe. But enough about me. I can't believe it. Of all the places and all the people, I stumble across you here. You're looking well and it's truly marvellous to see you again.'

The worst thing, Laurel thought, was that Jayne sounded as though she meant it. 'You too. It's good to see you,' she lied. 'And Dandelions is amazing. It must be incredibly rewarding to do such valuable work?'

'I could say the same about you. I hear you're a doctor of psychology, and you run your own practice here. Impressive.'

Laurel flinched. She was flattered by Jayne's praise, but she had never been comfortable accepting compliments. 'Were you going somewhere? I don't want to hold you up.'

'I was out for a stroll, that's all. No particular destination in mind. I admit, I was drawn towards the meadow, but in all honestly, it was out of morbid curiosity. On reflection, I don't think I want to see it as it is now. I don't even know how I feel about having the farm shop there after all that's happened.'

Laurel could sympathise. Would anyone want to stand checking the ripeness of tomatoes on the spot where a skeleton had risen from the ground? 'Will this affect Dandelions?' No matter her personal history with Jayne, Laurel didn't want the charity's plans derailed.

Jayne walked on a few steps before replying. 'I shouldn't think so. Whatever happened to that poor person they dug up, it happened a long time ago.'

'Have the police been in touch with you?'

'Alex and I had a visit from them yesterday. They wanted information about the archaeology dig, how far ahead it was planned and so on. They even wanted to know if we're aware of any objections or obstructions to our project.'

'Were there? Are there?'

'Objections? We've had the usual suspects with their baseless fears about,' she made air quotes, 'inner city hooligans running riot in the countryside.' Her face spoke volumes. 'NIMBYs, you know the sort.'

'I do. I think I even know one of them. You met her the other day.'

'Ms Little? Ha, she needed a bit of sweet talking, that's all. I don't think she'll be causing us any problems.'

Laurel wouldn't bet on it, but she held her tongue.

'Look, we're almost at The Pleasant Pheasant,' Jayne pointed out. 'Why don't we drop in for a bite to eat? It's almost lunch and I'm craving another of Jo's delicious cakes. You were spot on regarding the food in this place.'

Laurel considered saying no, but she was hungry. This way, she could get it over with, her catch-up with Jayne, and be done with it. On cue, her stomach rumbled. 'Sure, why not?'

'Perfect. I spy a table with our name on it. You know, if I do put down roots in the village, I could easily see myself having lunch here every day.'

'That is the downside of Elderwick. If you're anything like me, you'll gain weight and spend half your waking hours either here, at the bakery, or the pub.'

'I think that's a price I would be willing to pay,' Jayne grinned.

Jo had made a chilled minted pea soup served with freshly baked crusty rolls. 'It's going fast,' the server said when he arrived to take their order.

Soup and drinks on their way, Laurel dropped her guard a centimetre and smiled. Good food had that effect. If only they could make it through the entire meal without talking about–

'It's been a long time since Shawcroft.'

Damn it. Their old secondary comprehensive school, Shawcroft. For Laurel, her years there had been a mess of crippling insecurity and maladaptive coping strategies. Feeling forever alone, yet surrounded by prettier, smarter, more popular people. It had not been a great period in her life, but it had got her to university and from there, on to her doctorate. So, it hadn't been a total waste of time.

'Do you keep in touch with anyone from back then?' Jayne searched her face.

She felt as though she were stepping out onto a barely frozen pond. 'I hear from a few people now and again.' It wasn't true. The people she had spent most of her time with in school had been more acquaintances than friends, and she was guilty of not doing a lot to stay in contact with them over the years.

'Me either.'

'Really?' She hadn't meant to sound so disbelieving.

'Really.'

Their lunch arrived and the conversation paused.

Laurel's mind was turning over Jayne's pronouncement. Great though her shock was, her first taste of the heavenly combination of thickly buttered bread with the intensely green soup broke through. 'Oh my god, this is even better than the last time I had it.'

Jayne's eyes were shining. 'That's it, I'm moving to Elderwick. I mean, it's just cold soup, but it's... it's... better than sex.'

Laurel swallowed and nearly choked from laughing.

'Seriously, it is.'

When she wrestled back control of her breathing, Laurel declared, 'Wait until you try the pepper and parmesan one Jo does in autumn.'

'I might be tempted to give up men altogether if I could cook like Jo.'

In spite of herself, Laurel was enjoying their chat, but couldn't help interrogating what Jayne had said before the soup. 'Not that I want to move away from discussing your sex life, but I'm surprised you haven't kept in touch with anyone from the old days. You were super popular.' She hoped the bitterness under her words wasn't noticeable.

Jayne stirred her soup and Laurel braced. But when Jayne spoke, it wasn't what Laurel had expected to hear.

'I know I was part of the popular group in school, but I never quite felt I fitted in. Those girls I spent time with, they were nice enough, but I...' She paused her stirring and let the spoon clink against the side of the bowl. 'I didn't like them all that much.'

Laurel had a million questions. Jayne, from the moment she'd arrived at Shawcroft aged thirteen, had been one of the popular, successful pupils. Never without friends buzzing round, picked first in netball *and* hockey, lead in the school play, and ultimately, head girl.

'Don't get me wrong, we had fun together, and they were loyal friends,' continued Jayne. 'But it was like they all believed they were better than everyone else because they were popular.'

'It does kind of follow, though, doesn't it? If you're intelligent, and nice, and fun, and pretty,' she shouldn't have added *pretty*, she sounded pathetic, 'you have lots of friends and you win at life, or life at school, anyway,' she finished, cringing inside.

A smile played at the corners of Jayne's mouth. 'You thought I was intelligent and pretty?'

'Of course you were.' No sense denying it.

'Which bothered you more, that I was smart or that I was pretty?'

The thin ice cracked. 'What do you mean?' Laurel focused on the piece of bread she was dunking, but she'd held it in the soup too long and it disintegrated. She didn't dare to look up.

Jayne sighed. 'Perhaps now isn't the time.' She retrieved her spoon and resumed eating.

Laurel did the same, but there was a stone in her stomach, and she'd lost all sense of pleasure in the meal.

'What were we talking about before?' Jayne's brow furrowed. 'Ah yes, our visit from the police.'

Laurel blinked hard, trying to keep up with the change in direction.

'And speaking of crime, what I hear on the grapevine, is you're something of a whizz at solving them?'

Mute, she nodded, forgetting to parrot her usual caveats and denials.

'Which is why I'm going to share this with you.'

That caught her attention. 'What's that?' she croaked, her voice thick with anxiety.

'Please know, I am not trying to sow suspicion. I know the people of Elderwick are your friends and neighbours, but if this business can be put to rest, as it were, I believe it would be better for all concerned. Don't you agree?'

Again, all Laurel could do was nod.

Jayne leaned in. 'The police didn't only ask about objectors. They also asked Alex and me if anyone from the village has shown a particular interest in the development, especially the archaeological dig. Beyond the usual curiosity and people stopping by to watch the action, that is.'

Laurel cleared her throat and, with a dry mouth, asked, 'And is there anyone?'

'Yes, two people, in fact.'

'Who?' It came out as a whisper.

'Albert, and your favourite person, Dorothy.'

Chapter 26

Albert

It was Wednesday evening before Albert judged it safe to make the house call he couldn't avoid.

Dorothy let him into the kitchen with a sour look. 'What do you want? I'm in the middle of something.'

For once in his life, Albert wasn't sure how to begin. He hovered by the kitchen table, unsure if he should sit or stand.

'Would you sit down? You're making the place look untidy.' Dorothy folded her arms and stood over him. There was no offer of a drink.

'I'm sorry to have to do this,' he stammered, 'but I need to ask you about your ex-husband.'

The colour drained from Dorothy's face, and she dropped onto one of the wood-backed dining chairs. She raised a hand to her throat and stared at him, open-mouthed. 'Is it... is he...'

'No, it's not that. This is about what happened... before.'

'Before...' she repeated. Her hands were worrying at the buttons on her blouse. 'Do we have to?' The words fell from her lips like stones into a still pond.

'I'm sorry.' And he was.

She got to her feet and walked over to open one of the

cabinets above her kitchen worktop. From inside, she retrieved a bottle of vodka. Not bothering with glasses, she grabbed two mugs and poured them each a generous measure of the spirit. 'This is what he used to drink. I don't even know why I keep it in the house.' She sloshed the clear liquid around. 'It's all going to come out now, isn't it? After everything... after everything, he's going to destroy me for good this time.'

'Not if I can help it,' stated Albert. He sipped at his drink, and the fiery liquid burned down his throat. They were going to need all the fortification they could get in the next few days and weeks.

'And what can you do? What can either of us do?'

He didn't know, but he was determined to come up with a plan if he could.

'Is it little Miss Amateur Sleuth? Is that who I have to thank for this? I should have known. The minute those bones showed up, I knew this was going to happen. You can't keep an old bastard down, right Albert?'

Perhaps what was required in that moment, more than a stiff drink, was a clear head. He put down his mug and pushed it to the side. 'Sit back down, Dorothy. We can figure this out together.'

She sat and knocked back the remaining contents of her own mug, then poured some more.

'And no, Laurel doesn't know for certain, but she's come across his name.'

'And the police?'

'You know how news spreads around here? I imagine they'll be knocking on your door soon enough if we don't head this off. I didn't want to do anything without speaking to you first, though. I don't know how you want to handle this?'

Dorothy's knuckles were white. 'What do they know?'

Albert sighed and laid it all out for her. 'Laurel and Maggie were researching cases of missing people from the area, and they came across Harold. The date he went missing is within the range suggested by the ring. Leading them to believe he could be... that the bones could be Harold's remains. I don't know if they've heard yet about the 1981 ten-pence piece that was also found with the skeleton, but when they do, it will only reinforce their conclusion. And if they've made the connection, I can only assume the police have, too. Or will do soon.' He tugged on his left earlobe. 'However, none of that is our biggest problem.'

'Well, obviously,' Dorothy bit back. 'I'm not an idiot.'

'Precisely. And we need to be prepared for their questions.'

'There's no *we*, though, is there. This is me, my life.'

He could hear panic now in her voice.

'Dorothy.' He reached for her hands and held them in his. 'We may not always see eye to eye, but I am right by your side on this. You don't have to do this alone.'

'But what if...'

'Let's deal with the *what ifs* if it comes to that. Meantime, let's do everything we can to ensure it doesn't. Okay?'

'No, but what choice do I have?'

'We're going to get through this.'

Chapter 27

Maggie

Maggie was the first to arrive at the pub that evening. Sam, the manager, showed her to the table he'd reserved for Hetty, Constance and company.

'I've put you inside since there's a fair chill in the air this evening. Is that okay with you?'

'Yes, thanks, Sam.' It was her favourite table, nestled in the far corner with a huge bench seat on two sides. Plenty of room for everyone.

'Can I get you a drink while you're waiting for the others?'

'Go on then, I'll have a raspberry mojito.'

'I'll bring it right over.' He winked and wandered off.

Only a few of the tables were occupied. As she glanced round the room, she couldn't help but wonder with a shudder if the person responsible for burying the bones was amongst them. A few years back she wouldn't have believed that a quiet little village like Elderwick could harbour a killer, but that misapprehension had been well and truly turned on its head. She gave herself a mental shake. It didn't do to be entertaining those kinds of thoughts. What she wanted was a fun night with friends, and no talk – or thoughts – of villainy.

Sam was back with her drink and a copy of the specials menu, giving her the perfect distraction. As she studied it, she caught a movement in the corner of her vision. Thinking it was one of her dinner companions, she lifted her head with a smile.

'It's Maggie, isn't it? Sorry for intruding, but I saw you here on your own and wanted to say hello.'

The brawny man towering over the table was immediately recognisable, though he was dressed quite differently than when she'd last seen him, knee deep in dust with a trowel in his hand. 'Yes, and you're Dr Delgado. It's a pleasure to meet you properly.' Then she remembered. 'And I want to say how dreadfully sorry I am about Jessica.'

His face fell. 'I appreciate it. She wasn't a member of our team, but I knew her from around the university campus. She'll be missed. In fact... do you mind?' He indicated the space beside her.

'Be my guest.' Maggie moved her bag so he could sit.

'I still can't believe it. One minute we find those remains and everyone is excited. The next I know, they could be the body of someone murdered around fifty years ago, and then Jessica. I feel like I have whiplash. You must think I'm horrible for being in the local pub drinking at a time like this?'

'Not at all. Company can be beneficial at difficult times. Are you here alone?'

He brushed his hair off his face with the back of his hand and Maggie noticed how callused his palms were. They spoke of long days – years – of hard, physical work.

'I am. Beth, my wife, is at our hotel in Beverley. She couldn't face coming back, but I had to meet DI Coral and DS Hill at the meadow. After half an hour with them, I am sorely in need of this.' He held up his glass of Guinness.

'I'm meeting some friends for tea–'

'Ah, sorry. I'll get out of–'

'No, no,' she cut him off. 'I was going to say you're welcome to join us. If you want company, that is?' She could listen to him all evening, speaking in his gentle accent. He sounded Spanish to her untrained ear, though she knew he was Peruvian.

'You know what, Maggie? I really would. Thank you.'

Before they could engage in any further conversation, Hetty, Constance, Lin, and Penelope arrived and instituted a flurry of activity as they got settled around the table. Dr Delgado announced he was going to the bar to get everyone drinks, leaving Maggie to explain he'd be an extra guest for tea.

'I appreciate he's your boss,' she said to Lin and Penelope, 'so I hope it's okay with you?'

'Totally,' said Lin.

'I think it'll do him good,' added Penelope. She lowered her voice. 'Jessica's death has really hit him hard, and to be honest, I don't think Beth is dealing with it very well either.'

'What do you mean?' Maggie's gaze bounced back and forwards between them.

Penelope answered first. 'It's none of my business, but Dr Delgado has been like super supportive of everyone, whereas we've hardly seen Beth.'

'And when we did see her, she didn't speak to us. She just had a row with him and stormed off,' finished Lin in close to a whisper.

Maggie's radar was pinging. 'Do you know what they were arguing about?'

They both shook their heads.

Frustrated to see Dr Delgado returning, meaning she had to cut short her quizzing of them, Maggie reapplied her smile. While he set down the drinks, she introduced him properly to Hetty and Constance, who also gave their sympathies.

'Will the dig continue now?' Hetty asked.

The team leader plucked a napkin from the table and wiped

the Guinness foam from his top lip. 'I think so. Naturally, our work was put on hold whilst the remains were removed, and to give the police time to check the rest of the meadow, but I think we'll get the go-ahead to restart within the next couple of days.' To Lin and Penelope, he said, 'But no-one has to return if they don't feel comfortable. Bones are one thing, but for a fellow student to... pass away... I... we would understand if you would rather leave?'

The two younger women caught each other's eyes and as one affirmed they were staying.

'It's horrible, what happened to Jessica, but it was just an accident,' Penelope explained. 'And, to be fair, I didn't know her. Not that it makes it any better, but you know...'

Lin shrugged. 'It's my first dig. I don't want to leave. I'm broken up about Jess, though.'

'Does she have family?' Dr Delgado asked. 'I spoke to her advisor in the anthropology department and understand she was working alone on her missing persons project, but I am sure there will be colleagues who must be devastated.'

Lin sniffed. 'She doesn't... didn't have any close family. Her dad left years ago to go back to Botswana. She hasn't... hadn't seen him since she was seven, and her mum died two years ago. God, it's all so sad.'

Dr Delgado shared a sympathetic smile with her. 'No brothers or sisters?'

'No.'

'That's such a shame,' he continued. 'I was hoping to send flowers on behalf of the team. I imagine she would have been a real boon, to us and the police, in tracing the identity of the um... of the dead... body.'

'Had the police given her the go-ahead?' Penelope asked. 'I saw her talking to one of them on Sunday afternoon.'

'Did you happen to hear the conversation?' Dr Delgado studied her.

'I was too far away. You spoke to her right after, though, I thought?' said Penelope.

Dr Delgado clasped his hands. 'Did I? I know I spoke with her that morning and gave my blessing for her to be on site, providing the police gave her the all-clear. But I'm afraid I don't remember speaking to her later on. I would like to follow up with the officer, though. Do you know who it was?'

'It was an older man,' supplied Penelope.

Maggie was pleased to be able to assist. 'That would be DS Hill. He attended when the bones were first found.'

Dr Delgado gave her a warm smile. 'Thank you.'

'Speaking of the bones, Dr Delgado,' Constance chimed in, 'did they find anything else in the field?'

'Not a thing. We were able to borrow a GPR, sorry, a ground penetrating radar, from the university, since the local force couldn't locate one they could use. Nothing came up. Certainly no more bodies. Thank goodness.'

Hetty was frowning. 'If there's nothing else there, is there any reason for you to keep digging?'

Lin made a sound of dismay.

'Don't worry,' he said to her. 'So, we know we're not going to find a Roman hoard or a Saxon burial, but there may still be artifacts for us to uncover. Maybe signs of human activity, or soil changes that suggest features no-longer present. It's all good practice and Dandelions are happy for us to continue as contracted.'

Dr Delgado didn't sound disappointed, but from the expressions on Lin and Penelope's faces, Maggie could tell they were disheartened.

'We heard there was a ring with the bones. Did you find anything else? Any other evidence which could point towards an identification?' Constance had shifted her chair so she was almost knee to knee with the archaeologist.

He stroked his chin. 'I didn't realise the ring was common knowledge.'

Maggie bit her lip, and Lin and Penelope flinched.

'Sorry, I didn't know it was a secret.' Constance didn't sound the least bit sorry. 'It dates the remains to no earlier than 1968, is that right?'

Dr Delgado's face softened. 'Since you already know all there is to know, I suppose it'll do no harm to confirm that yes, we found a gold signet ring that dates from 1968 at the earliest. Although we believe it originates a little later than that, perhaps the 1980s. However, I honestly can't say more whist there's an investigation going on. The police gave us strict instructions.'

'Were they a murder victim?' Constance pressed her luck.

A flicker of distaste crossed Dr Delgado's face and Maggie was compelled to intercede. 'I think we should order some food and focus on less upsetting topics.' She said it loud enough to attract a server hovering nearby. His arrival at the table provided the desired deflection.

There were murmurs of agreement and the menus were passed round. They all ordered, then Dr Delgado excused himself to use the facilities. In his absence, Hetty and Constance chatted away to Lin.

Penelope shuffled closer to Maggie. 'You know I said I saw Jessica speaking to that police officer on Sunday afternoon?'

Maggie bent her head to hear what she was saying. 'A minute ago, yes.'

'Well, I don't see how Dr Delgado could have forgotten he saw her because five minutes after I saw Jess with the policeman, I saw Jess and Dr Delgado having a very...' she wrinkled her nose, 'shifty... no, not shifty exactly... you know... um...'

'Agitated?' suggested Maggie.

'Yes, an agitated conversation until Beth showed up, and when she did, you should have seen Dr Delgado's face. He looked super sus. But I don't think I should tell anyone, should I?'

Maggie chewed it over. 'Did you hear what they were saying?'

'No.'

She noted the archaeologist was already heading back. 'I imagine they were talking about Jessica's project. It would have been a delicate arrangement with lots to discuss.'

'I'm famished,' Rik announced, retaking his chair and nodding to the approaching member of staff bearing loaded plates.

Penelope shuffled away again, the food was distributed, and the condiments were passed round. Delicious as her steak and ale pie was, Maggie was distracted. Deep in thought, she only realised she'd lost track of the conversation when a voice broke into her reverie.

'Maggie? Are you still with us?'

She blinked. Five faces around the table were peering at her. 'Sorry, I was miles away. What were you saying?'

Penelope giggled. 'Dr Delgado was asking, not very subtly, if you're married?'

Maggie blushed. 'Um, yes. That is, no. I used to be, but no, I'm not now. Why?' She didn't understand. Dr Delgado was married to Beth. Why did her marital status concern him?

'Thank you, Penelope,' he waggled his eyebrows at her, 'but I wouldn't put it that way exactly. I think you've got Maggie worried.'

'No, it's fine.'

'I have a friend, that's all. I was planning to invite him down for the weekend, and I don't know, something makes me think you two would hit it off.'

Maggie's cheeks burned hotter. 'I'm... no, I'm not... it's not for me right now. Thank you. It's Constance who's looking for love,' she blurted.

'Maggie!' Constance exclaimed.

'Is that so?' asked Delgado, turning a wolf-like smile on Constance.

Discomfort twisted Constance's expression. 'I'm so sorry,' Maggie mouthed, earning a scowl.

'I didn't know you were in the market,' teased Hetty.

'I'm not. Can we just leave it?' Hands on the wheels of her chair, she was inching back from the table.

'Just be careful of using any of those online dating sites,' Lin advised. 'Jess was telling me about a lecturer at uni who got scammed recently.'

'Me too,' Penelope chimed in. 'One of our teachers got taken in not long back. It was such a shame because she's super nice.'

Constance shot Maggie a despairing glance, and Maggie reached for the only topic she could think to avert the disaster she'd set in motion. 'I wasn't going to say anything, but Laurel and I think we might have uncovered the identity of the remains.'

Chapter 28

Laurel

It had been four days since the bones had been uncovered, and only two since Laurel had stumbled upon Jessica's body, but time, she felt, was racing by. Yet she had no sense that the official police investigation was progressing at speed, and she didn't know how much priority would even be given to a cold case such as this. She certainly wasn't about to hold her breath with DI Coral in charge.

In her office, Laurel swivelled back and forth on her chair and half-heartedly considered reading some of the latest research in the *British Journal of Psychology* but couldn't quite muster the enthusiasm. On her fifth swing, her eye fell on the whiteboard on the wall. She used it a lot during sessions, drawing out diagrammatic representations of vicious cycles or formulations of her client's difficulties. She had a couple of hours before her afternoon clients, perhaps the time could be put to good use.

With a black pen she wrote the 'name' of the victim, though of course he was still in want of official identification. As a placeholder, she used Albert's joke suggestion of Napoleon Bone-apart. Under this, she drew a timeline and marked when the body was unearthed and what information she'd gleaned since. She stretched the line back to 1981 to reflect the date on the coin found with the remains, and marked 2008 as the likely latest point at which the body could have been buried. All they had were skeletal remains, so it... he, she corrected... couldn't have been put in the ground much after that, probably.

At the bottom of the board, in brackets and blue ink, she added the names of the missing people she and Maggie had discovered in old news reports. Then she drew a line through Tariq Loftus' name. Already eighty-three when he went missing in 1974, his whereabouts were unknown long before the 1981 coin had been minted. She underlined Harold Emmerson and drew a dashed line linking him to where, in red, she wrote the name Dorothy Little. Presumably Dorothy had reverted to her maiden name if they were right and she had been married to the missing man. Harold's disappearance in 1983 was comfortably within her date range. But she had to be cautious not to disregard other possibilities.

She stepped back. She had a mess of lines and writing adding up to a whole lot of nothing.

Appending a box to the right of the main diagram, she labelled it *Clues*. So far, she had only two: the gold signet ring and the 1981 coin. The final heading she included was *People of interest*. Her pen hovered as she contemplated the names given by Jayne. After a moment of hesitation, she scribbled Dorothy's name for a second time, and Albert.

This kind of exercise always worked best with Maggie contributing. Laurel had her hand on the phone and was about to try calling her when it rang. She jumped as though bitten. As was her habit in the office, she let it go to voicemail, but she turned up the volume so if it was urgent, she could pick up.

'Hi, this is Michael Wishart. Um, I um, don't know what to

say. I'm Jessica's colleague from York Uni, and I think that you... knew her?'

She snatched the receiver from the cradle. 'Hello, Mr Wishart, it's Doctor Nightingale here.'

'Oh, hi. Look, I know it's no notice at all, but I'm in the area. Is there any chance I could come over to your office? I'm in the car about ten minutes away. I could really do with someone to talk to.'

She checked the clock. There was ample time. 'Of course. Do you know where to find me?'

'Yes, I think so. Right, see you soon.'

He hung up before she could say anything further. She had to prepare. He was probably grieving for his fellow student, but he was also a man who might provide some answers regarding the missing persons project. She surveyed the room: the tissues were stocked; the bin empty; no client files open on her desk or computer. She nearly missed the whiteboard.

'Damn,' she hissed. With her mobile, she took a photo of the notes she'd made so she could recreate it if necessary, then with a couple of tissues, she wiped it clean.

Five minutes later, the bell rang at the bottom of the stairs. She buzzed to admit Michael and waited by her office door to greet him. He was a shortish man with sandy-brown hair and a distinct birthmark visible by his left ear. He held out his hand and they shook. He fit her image of a student with his messenger bag over his shoulder, faded jeans, and a T-shirt for a band she'd never heard of.

'Thanks for seeing me. I shouldn't have called, but I don't know anyone round here and I...' He blew out his cheeks.

'Sit down.' She guided him into one of the comfortable chairs by the window and nudged the box of tissues closer. 'Can I get you a glass of water?'

He nodded. She busied herself getting a glass and filling it from the tap over the basin in the corner of the room, giving him a moment to gather himself.

'Here you go.'

He accepted it and drank half in a single gulp. 'I don't even know what I'm doing here. I'd been trying to reach Jess since Monday, but...' he tailed off. 'I can't process it. Even the way she died. Some stupid accident.'

Since there were no words to salve his pain, Laurel remained silent, allowing him space.

'I went into uni yesterday, we share an office in the department, and the whole day I kept turning round to tell her stuff. I kept forgetting.' He finished his glass of water and exhaled a long, shuddering breath. 'I should probably explain why I'm here.'

Laurel was curious to know how he'd come to arrive at her door. Jessica hadn't mentioned a colleague.

'Jess called when she got here on Saturday. She knew I'd be in the office. I live in a student house and it's a circus at weekends; I can never get any work done. Anyway, sorry. She called and told me what had been found here and, to save her from having to come back to do it herself, she asked if I could pull her missing person's database and email it to her. Which I did.'

He played with his empty glass. 'She told me about the body and mentioned the name of the village. It rang a bell with me. I'd seen her working on the database before, and I thought I remembered the name Elderwick. It's pretty unusual. I went back to look, and I found two people reported as having gone missing from here in the early eighties.'

Two people missing from Elderwick. That was interesting.

'And two others, Anthony Scrivener and Tariq Loftus, from pretty close by. It should be easy to rule out Scrivener, though, because he had a prosthetic leg.'

Laurel recognised the names from the online search she and Maggie had undertaken. If the skeleton had been missing a leg, she was sure she would have heard about it by now, through one channel or another. Which meant Anthony probably wasn't their man and the list was getting shorter. 'And we can rule out Tariq,' she said. 'A coin dated 1981 was found with the remains, but Tariq went missing in 1974.'

'Okay, cool,' he said, sounding downbeat. 'Anyway, that's why I was calling her, to give her those names and maybe save her some time.'

'And you called me because she'd mentioned me to you?'

'She sent a message on Sunday to say she'd met you and asked if you would be involved.'

'I see.' Laurel didn't, not yet.

'She was so excited that her project might have a real-life impact, you know. And actually, she would have been brilliant. Her research is ridiculously comprehensive.' He reached down to pat his bag and Laurel dared to hope he might have brought the research with him.

'That's why I'm here. I think she would want someone to see it through, and I was hoping... I... it would be... do you think...' He gave up, his cheeks scarlet. 'You probably think it's weird, right?'

'I don't think it's weird. I think it's very thoughtful.' She was dying to ask the names of the two people missing from Elderwick, the ones not yet ruled out, but was worried it would be insensitive.

'You'll help, then?'

It was her turn to need a glass of water. 'Excuse me a second.' As she sipped, she reviewed her options. She could accept his request for help, knowing it would get her into trouble with Coral if the DI found out, or she could do the sensible thing, and send him away with her condolences.

She made her decision. 'Michael,' she sat back down across from him, 'I will do what I can, but you should know, the police won't be thrilled about my involvement. I can explain it to you sometime, but for now, suffice to say, you'll need to take the lead.'

'That's fine with me.' His eyes were red, and he kept swiping at his nose, but for the first time since he'd walked into her office, there was a spark in his eyes. 'Jess would love it if we were the ones to figure out who the remains belong to.'

Second thoughts were already clamouring for attention. Before she could back-track, she located a business card in the drawer of the coffee table. 'Here,' she scribbled on the back and handed it to him. 'This is my office number and my home number. There's no mobile signal in the village, but you'll be able to reach me on one of those.'

As though the air had gone from his body, he sagged. 'Thank you.'

She sat with him until he was ready. There was so much more she wanted to know, but for now, it was enough to share in the sadness of this young man who had lost someone for whom he obviously cared.

With a last blow of his nose, he picked up his bag, pulled out a blue folder, and held it out to her. 'It's not a lot to go on, but I printed off the info on the other two missing people I identified. If you want to have a read through it, maybe we could arrange another time to meet after... *if* I get the go-ahead from the police?'

She reached for the folder, noting how light it was. 'Absolutely. Will you be heading straight back to York in the meantime?'

'Yeah. Well, via the police station in Beverley, then I need to get back, but I can come over again at the weekend?'

Plans made, Laurel's curiosity and eagerness got the better

of her. 'Do you remember the names of the men missing from Elderwick?' She held her breath as she waited for the answer.

'Sure, Harold Emmerson and Jurgen Sturm.'

'Jurgen Sturm? That's quite a name, though my money remains on the bones belonging to Harold Emmerson,' Maggie declared down the phone when Laurel finally reached her once the afternoon clinic was over.

Laurel had struggled to concentrate after Michael's visit but had done her best to set aside her eagerness to dive into the file of information he'd left with her. It had to wait. She owed her other clients every ounce of her attention.

'We should keep an open mind. We don't know anything about this Jurgen Sturm, and the bones might be Harold's, but they could be someone else entirely. Look, are you free tonight to get together again with our notebooks?'

'Fiddlesticks. It's the WI meeting this evening.'

Of course, she'd forgotten.

'I wish I could cancel.'

She could hear Maggie drumming her fingers.

'But I simply can't, they rely on me, and I want to ask around about opposition to the development or the archaeologists, like we discussed. Should I ask about Jurgen now, too?'

Maggie was right. The WI meeting was a good chance to tap into the village grapevine – what the women of the WI didn't know wasn't worth knowing – but Laurel didn't want Jurgen's name out there yet.

'Hang off on the name for now, and for goodness' sakes, especially don't mention Harold. I have to admit, Albert's right, we shouldn't throw names around until we know more.' She pulled the phone away from her ear as Maggie made a strangled sound.

'Don't be mad,' she said when she'd stopped making noises.

Laurel massaged her temple with her free hand.

'I was at the pub last night and Dr Delgado was there, and he was asking about dating and Constance was getting cross, and I had to change the subject.' Maggie's speech sped up as she neared the confession Laurel knew was coming.

Count to ten.

'And I told them we thought we knew the identity of the buried man.'

'And his name?'

In a small voice, Maggie admitted that yes, she had shared the name. Before Laurel could respond, she rushed on. 'And also, I think they found something else in the trench with the bones, but Dr Delgado avoided the question when Constance asked him.'

'They did. Christopher told me they found a coin dated 1981.'

'I knew it! And that narrows our timeframe.'

'Wait a sec. We can discuss that later.' The names Maggie had mentioned filtered through. 'Dr Delgado and Constance were there?'

Maggie's voice was small. 'And Hetty, Lin, and Penelope. Sorry.'

Laurel was quiet as she tried to foresee the implications of so many people knowing. 'Look, it's been a long and draining day. Let's have brunch tomorrow and talk it through. Just you and me, like old times,' she suggested.

'No Albert?' She heard surprise in Maggie's voice.

More than anything, she wanted to be wrong about Albert, but no matter what the vicar said, she could not shake the feeling her neighbour knew more than he was letting on and that it had something to do with the bones. 'I'll catch him up later, but I think it would be nice if it was just us girls.'

After a beat, Maggie said, 'Yes, why not? I'll bring the croissants.'

'And I'll make a lovely pot of tea.'

They said their goodbyes and Laurel put the phone down. Had she been religious, she would have said a prayer asking God to protect Maggie when Dorothy found out that Maggie had leaked the name Harold Emmerson.

Chapter 29

Laurel

Laurel resisted opening the file Michael had given her until she was back home at Myrtle Cottage, sitting in the garden away from prying eyes – all that is except for those of the cockerel on the fence once again.

She'd brought a tall cool glass of elderflower cordial out with her, which she sipped as she laid out the papers.

She flicked through the information on Harold first. The document to jump out at her immediately was his marriage certificate. It was confirmation he had been married to Dorothy, their Dorothy Little of Elderwick. A sense of triumph sparked but quickly faded. How could Albert not have known? She rubbed at a sharp pain in her breastbone.

Also included were a copy of *The Yorkshire Post* article she and Maggie had seen online, and a copy of the original missing persons report which had been filed by a Mrs Maud Emmerson. Harold's mother or sister perhaps, and not by Dorothy, his wife, which was noteworthy. The last item concerning Harold was a handwritten note – written by Jessica, she assumed – with a list of facts to be tracked down or checked.

> *Contact details for Mrs M Emmerson – if still alive?*
>
> *Contact details for Mrs D Emmerson née Little – if still alive?*
>
> *ID of any local police officers who worked on / were aware of the case – need to know of any updates since first reported missing.*

The newspaper article had been published in 2000 after he'd been missing for seventeen years, but it appeared Jessica didn't have any information dated later than that.

The remainder of the papers in the folder concerned Jurgen Sturm. There was a photo of a severe man, blond-haired, slim but strong looking. She guessed he would have been about thirty when the photo was taken. Then there were more hand-written notes and a short timeline neatly drawn in blue ink on graph paper of the type that used to be used in schools. On the first page, Jessica had written:

> *Interview with Brendt Sturm (62), Jurgen's younger brother.*
>
> *EOD @ St Helen's. good days and bad*
>
> *SW, Samina Khan, agreed to me taking copies of attached documents.*
>
> *NB. SW contacted dept. in resp. to ad. re: project. Brendt EOL (<2 years) and desperate to trace brother. Acc. to Brendt, Jurgen v wealthy. SW stated, if deceased, any remaining money could be used to fund Brendt's care.*
>
> *No MPR*

Laurel translated the abbreviations as she went. EOD, was early onset dementia. SW must be Social Worker, and EOL was end of life. Brendt had not been well when Jessica had spoken to him. It wasn't that long ago, but he might even have died since then. She was interested in the mention of Jurgen's wealth and wondered if Jessica had meant bank manager wealthy, or Rishi Sunak stinking rich.

Unlike Harold, there was no MPR for Jurgen, no missing persons report.

Laurel moved onto the timeline:

> *? January 1981 – Jurgen begins working in Beverley*
>
> *? June 1982 Brendt visited Jurgen in Hull for two days.*
>
> *Christmas Day 1982 – Phone call from Jurgen, said he's met someone, going to be staying in Humberside, as was – now E. Riding of Yorks.*
>
> ** 22nd Sept 1983 – letter from Jurgen (included in file)*

Laurel rifled through the documents until she found the letter. The letter itself was not illuminating, detailing as it did the mundanity of his day-to-day life and a brief section in which he asked after his brother's wellbeing. However, attached to the letter was a flyer, and it was a flyer for the Elderwick Autumn Fair. That must have been the mention of the village name that had stuck with Michael. Someone – Jurgen maybe – had scrawled across it. She squinted and thought she could make out the words:

This is the most exciting thing that happens here!!!

Not a fan of village life then.

Returning to the timeline, she read the last entries.

? December 1983 – Brendt gets photo in post from Jurgen of him with a woman. Possibly a wedding pic (not found).

It was frustrating that the photo wasn't available. She might have recognised his bride.

She scribbled more notes, her hand cramping there was so much to get down. In particular, if Jurgen had been married, why hadn't his wife reported him missing?

**May 1985? (postmark smudged) Postcard to Brendt from Jurgen – sent from Germany.* (included in file)*

She studied the postcard against the letter from September two years earlier. The letter was neatly written, whereas the postcard had the feel of a missive dashed off in a hurry. She put the two pieces of correspondence aside.

The timeline ended there, but paper-clipped to it was a list, like the one for Harold, outlining the other steps taken by Jessica. She hadn't been able to obtain a copy of Jurgen's birth certificate, but had scribbled the question: *In Germany? Will they send a copy?* She hadn't been able to find a marriage certificate or a death certificate either. She had tracked down some old phone books but hadn't found a listing for any Sturms, or indeed Emmersons, in the area.

Laurel sat back in her chair glad it was late enough in the day that her garden was in dappled shade and the fierce burn of the afternoon sun had passed.

'I guess we need to look for Jurgen's wife, if she's still here,' she said aloud to Aroon, who hadn't moved from his perch and who was being uncharacteristically quiet.

He blinked at her.

'And why would Albert lie to me about Dorothy's husband?' she asked him.

Aroon cooed.

'I know. I don't want to believe it either.'

Chapter 30

Maggie

Maggie waved Albert off from the steps of the village hall. He'd stopped by to help her set up for the WI meeting and had promised to return again at the end to clear up. As he left, she noticed Dr Delgado's wife, Beth, lingering by the bus stop. 'Beth?' she shouted. 'How are you?'

'Um, as good as can be expected, I guess,' Beth called back as she approached and looked Maggie up and down. 'I was just wondering what was happening? It sounds like a lot of fun in there.'

She was right. Raucous laughter spilled out through the doorway into the still evening air.

'It's our WI meeting. You're welcome to join us as a guest if you'd like. It must have been a difficult few days for you? Maybe good company, tea, and cake will help?'

Beth chewed her lip. She was an attractive woman with large features that suited her height. Maggie was five foot nine, making Beth about six foot.

'Is that allowed?'

'Of course.' Maggie ushered her inside. 'It's my meeting and the more the merrier, as they say. Here, this is Babs. Babs, this is Beth. Babs, would you be a star and make Beth a cup of tea and introduce her around?' Leaving them to get acquainted, Maggie went to check her materials were set up for the meeting. She loved running the local WI, but it was a lot of work.

'Maggie, wait up.'

Constance was waving to her from beside the stage, she must have come in the back way. 'You look flushed,' Maggie commented, reaching her side. It was more than that, Constance was red and sweaty, but she didn't want to be unkind.

'I'm knackered. I wanted to catch you before you start, so I got over here in record time. I wanted to tell you as soon as possible. I've been talking to Carter.'

'I'm really sorry about the other night at the pub,' blurted Maggie.

Constance waved away her apology 'It's fine. Listen, Carter, Harrison, Louis, take your pick of the fake names he's using, but yes, our internet dating scam artist. He's taken the bait and he's flirting with *Sylvia*.'

'Your fake profile using Hetty's photo?'

'Yes. I sent him a couple of pokes and reeled him right in.'

Maggie grimaced.

'I can't understand what I ever saw in him though, he's so cheesy. He's even using the same lines on *Sylvia* as he did on me. Can you believe it?'

Maggie could believe it. She blanched. What Constance was doing was a bad idea. There was no way to know what kind of person this Carter was, but given that he'd already scammed Constance out of money, he was hardly going to be in the running for the good Samaritan of the year. 'I think you should leave it. I know I've said it before, but you don't know what he might do if he finds out you're trying to set him up. I'm worried about you.'

Constance's mouth set in a firm line. 'Why? Because you don't think I can take care of myself? I'm a grown woman.'

'Of course you are, I know that. What I mean is, this man conned you, and that must feel lousy, but what you're doing now... I mean, what's your goal? Do you want to meet him in real life?'

After blowing out a breath, Constance apologised. 'I'm sorry, and honestly, I don't know. I just feel like I've got to do something. And I know you're right, and this could be dangerous, but I've been such a moron. I need... I need to feel powerful again and in control. I'm still bloody angry and I want him to pay. Besides, he's never going to meet anyone in real life, is he? That's not what this is all about. Sooner or later, he'll try to get more money out of me, well *Sylvia*, but this time, maybe I can get him to do it in a way that he can be tracked or something.' She pouted. 'So, I haven't thought it all the way through, but it's something that I'm getting him to waste his time on me instead of going after some other innocent woman.'

'If it's an organised thing, he's probably talking to lots of women, and men too.'

'Oh god, you're so sensible.'

Maggie smiled. 'Be careful, that's all.'

'Yes, mum.'

'Are you staying for the meeting?'

Constance twisted her lips. 'I wasn't planning on it...'

'Go on, stay. You might even enjoy yourself. Beth's here for the first time. You should go sit with her.'

With a smirk, Constance asked, 'Are you wanting me to do some digging in case she lets slip anything new about the bones?'

Maggie blushed. The thought had crossed her mind. 'No, but if she does say something, let me know?'

Laughing, Constance rolled away.

Maggie called after her, 'Get yourself a drink and we'll catch up again at the end.'

Despite Constance's reassurances, Maggie was worried for her. She knew first-hand what it was to be taken in by a man, a man who professed to love and care for you. When the scales had finally fallen from her own eyes over her ex-husband, Nicholas, her overriding emotion had been shame. Shame she hadn't seen him for who he truly was, and shame that she was the only one to have been blinded for so long. Everyone else, even Laurel, who'd only met him a handful of times, had known what a monster he was.

It had taken her a long time to realise the shame wasn't hers. He was the one who should be ashamed. Though she doubted he was.

She shook her head free of the past and turned her attention to her group. It took a while to call the meeting to order. Gossip and theories were careening round the room. Everyone was sad about Jessica's accident, and they all had an opinion and an idea about the identity of the body found in the meadow. And as soon as the main agenda for the evening was complete – a talk on the many uses for old pairs of tights; a vote on the correct amount of sherry in a trifle; a raffle draw for a bottle of old Jacob's infamous rhubarb wine, only no-one owned up to having the winning ticket – the speculation whipped up again.

'If everyone could be quiet for a while longer, we can have some questions. I know you're all curious about what's been happening on the Dandelions farm shop site.' She'd been careful not to draw attention to Beth, and hoped the newcomer wasn't distressed by the gleeful interest people were taking in the recent events.

As a semi-hush finally descended, a woman raised her hand. 'Melanie,' Maggie acknowledged her. 'What do you want to say?'

'First, it's dreadful what happened to that young girl. I think Mr Pickersgil should be made to keep his cows elsewhere, not in a field with a public footpath right through the middle. I've been harassed by those buggers myself, more than once.'

Murmurs of agreement bubbled amongst the group.

'Second,' Melanie continued, 'I want to know what the police are doing? It might have been years since that body was put in the meadow, but there are lots of people who have been in Elderwick for a long time. How do we know there's not a killer living right amongst us? No-one in here, naturally,' she was quick to add. 'How are we meant to sleep safe in our beds with another murderer on the loose? That's what I want to know.'

Maggie's mood plummeted. Tension was building. She didn't want the meeting to end with everyone leaving to accuse their neighbours or feeling compelled to sleep with a carving knife under their pillow. 'Hold on, let's not get carried away. If the police believed there was a threat, they would have told us.'

'Would they, though?' someone shouted.

Dorothy cleared her throat loudly.

Maggie had known her luck couldn't last. She could only hope the woman wasn't aware of the speculation over a certain Harold Emmerson. She crossed her fingers.

'It seems to me,' Dorothy said, 'this village has become a dangerous place to live over recent years. And I think we have to ask ourselves why?'

Maggie didn't like where this was going, but she wasn't sure what to do. Then, like a guardian angel, she caught sight of Albert slipping back into the hall, right on time for clearing up and possibly bouncer duties if Dorothy got out of hand. Distracted, she didn't immediately notice that Beth had stood up and was waiting to be acknowledged.

'Beth?' Maggie interrupted Dorothy, who had moved onto failures in local policing, and invited the newcomer to speak.

All eyes turned to the statuesque woman. She had a rich speaking voice still laced with a lilting Alabama accent, easily heard throughout the hall. The twittering masses subsided.

'I'm not a member of this WI, nor a resident of Elderwick, but Maggie kindly invited me to join you this evening. My name is Beth Delgado. Some of you may know me. My husband, Rik, and I are the lead archaeologists on the Dandelions dig.' She waved a hand in the vague direction of the meadow.

Dorothy opened her mouth again but Maggie motioned her to be quiet. She wanted to hear what the archaeologist had to say.

Despite her searing glare, Dorothy relented, acknowledging Maggie's authority as chairperson.

Beth had paused, waiting for the go-ahead to continue.

'Please, carry on. We'd like to hear your perspective. It's been a difficult time for you and your team,' said Maggie.

Beth closed her eyes for a moment as a grimace contorted her features. 'It has been dreadful, more so because of the loss of Jessica. We had only just met, but she seemed a delightful woman determined to help. I can't imagine the devastation her death has brought to her family and colleagues.'

The members around the hall declared their sympathies likewise.

'What I would like to say, though, speaks to your concerns about the remains we uncovered and the investigation the police have begun. I appreciate it must be unsettling for you all to know a body, possibly the victim of a murder, has been buried in your village.'

There were nods of agreement.

'But I'm glad this person has been found. Somewhere, there must be people who are missing, have been missing, a friend or a relative, and now there is the chance for them to learn the truth. Sad though the truth may be. There's also a chance the police will apprehend a killer, a person who has been able to live undetected all these years. A person who has escaped justice. Until now.'

'Hear, hear,' shouted Babs from her place by the tea urn.

'So, yes, it might feel as though my team have brought nothing but trouble, but what we do, what we're doing here, is bringing into the light events from years past. Whether that be one thousand years, or forty, we are here to tell the stories of those who have gone before us. I would hate to think there is a murderer hiding here in plain sight, but if there is, knowledge is power, and the police are investigating. We've been able to provide them with a number of pieces of evidence, including the recently recovered key, and I'm confident they'll keep you informed.'

'What key?' one of the younger members, Daniella, asked.

Maggie couldn't tell for certain, under the fluorescent lights, but she thought Dorothy had paled.

'Oh dear,' Beth stammered. 'I assumed you'd already know. Perhaps I shouldn't have mentioned it.'

Chapter 31

Laurel

Her heart hammered in her chest as the phone rang on the other end.

'Hello?'

Sweaty palms meant she nearly dropped the handset. 'Ben, hi, it's Laurel.'

'Hi.'

There was an awkward pause as she marshalled her thoughts.

'Hi.' *Spit it out!* 'Sorry to call you about work when you're at home, but is there any chance I could pop round? There's something I need to show you.' She winced. She hadn't meant to sound so suggestive.

'Um, sure. There's, er... someone here at the moment, but I should be free in about half an hour. You can come round then.'

She pressed her fingers to the bridge of her nose; she'd interrupted a date. Could this get any worse? 'You know what, it's not urgent. You've got company and I don't want to intrude.'

'Honestly, it's fine. Half an hour. See you soon.'

'Brill.' *Brill?* She hung up and went straight to the bathroom to splash cold water on her burning face. What was it with Ben? Why was she constantly making a fool of herself around him? It wasn't as though she was attracted to him. Okay, she was attracted to him, but not like that. He was just a good-looking guy. Nothing more.

She caught sight of her reflection. A touch of make-up and a nicer dress wouldn't hurt. It was good manners. It wasn't as though she was making an effort for him.

By the time she'd changed, smoothed her hair, added some lipstick and blusher, and brushed her teeth, she was late heading out. Which was good because the last thing she wanted was to run into his guest as they were leaving.

Ben answered the door wearing jeans and a black T-shirt which showed off his toned upper arms. 'Hey, come on in.'

He had on a subtle woody aftershave and Laurel had to concentrate on not reacting and wished she'd had a glass of wine before setting off. Then she remembered he wasn't dressed that way or smelling so delicious for her benefit. A jolt of envy shot through her.

'How can I help?' he asked as he led her into the dining kitchen at the back of the house. 'Wine?' He held up a half-empty bottle of red.

'Please.' She sat at the table and put her hands in her lap so he couldn't see them tremble. There was no reason for her nerves, or the ridiculous envy. She wasn't interested in him... anymore. Sure, she had been in the past, but he'd had a girlfriend then, not to mention the whole issue with his lying. He was a complication she did not need in her life.

He poured two large glasses and placed one in front of her. She spied a third glass on the draining board by the sink but couldn't tell if the smudges on its surface were lipstick or fingerprints.

'It's about these bones.' She had the folder that Jessica's

university colleague, Michael, had left with her in her bag but she didn't bring it out yet.

'I can't talk to you about the case. I'm not even working on it.' Ben's tone was amused. 'But...' he crossed his legs and leaned back in his chair, 'if you have information to share, I can pass it on?'

She drank from her glass and swore when a dribble ran down her chin. *Smooth.* 'I didn't go looking for this. He came to me.' It was important to get that straight before Coral started breathing down her neck again.

'Who did?' Ben was less relaxed now, a tension in his face.

'Michael Wishart, he works at the university. He knew Jessica.'

'Okay.'

He wasn't giving anything away, but this had to be a two-way street. Despite his declaration, Laurel wanted some information from him if she was going to hand him the file.

'He said he was going to speak to the officer in charge.' She repeated the assurance Michael had given her.

Ben paused. 'If you say so. Like I said, not my case. Can you tell me what this is all about?'

She placed the folder on the table and talked Ben through the contents. 'He told me he'd emailed the missing persons database to Jessica, but he'd also recognised the name Elderwick and pulled up these two specific cases: Harold Emmerson and Jurgen Sturm.'

Ben finished his drink and poured another. He lifted the bottle to her glass, but she put her hand over the top.

'Not for me.' She wanted to keep a clear head.

'Let me make a call.' He left the room, pulling the door closed behind him.

While he was making his phone call, she surveyed his kitchen. She'd been in his house before, but only in the living room. The kitchen was neat and clean. There was a bowl of fruit on the table, a smoothie maker on the counter, and a rack of herbs and spices by the hob. She was contemplating sneaking a quick peek into his fridge when he came back.

'I spoke to DS Hill. He said this Michael hasn't been in.'

'Oh. Maybe he spoke to Coral?'

Ben sat down again, facing her, arms resting on his thighs so he was leaning towards her. 'Not according to Hill.'

She shivered.

'You said you're going to see him again? Is he your patient?'

'Client? No, not a therapy client. He wants me to help him finish Jessica's work and identify the person who, you know, the bones.'

'And you said yes.' It wasn't a question.

Her mouth was dry. Maybe a few more sips of wine wouldn't hurt.

'When are you meeting him next?'

'At the weekend, after I've gone through Jessica's research.'

Ben opened his mouth, then closed it. He opened his mouth again. 'If I tell you this, you have to keep it in confidence. Seriously, you can't even tell Albert, and definitely not Maggie.'

She didn't like the sound of that, but she'd promise what she had to, to hear what he was about to say. 'I promise.'

'According to Perry–'

'Perry?'

'DS Hill. It's short for Peregrine, but don't ever let him know I told you that.'

She enjoyed the wicked glint in his eye.

'According to Perry, the pathologist is uncertain about the cause of Jessica's death. There are signs of a blunt force trauma to the back of her head.'

Laurel lowered her head and concentrated on her breathing. She didn't want to throw up in Ben's kitchen.

'Are you okay?' His voice was close to her ear.

She pressed her lips together and gathered herself. 'I'm okay.'

'Did you really believe it was the cows?' he asked, touching her on the shoulder.

She met his eyes and admitted, 'No. I wanted it to have been an accident, but let's be honest, accidents in Elderwick are rarely what they seem.'

His closeness to her in that moment, the intimacy was overwhelming, and she slid back in her chair putting a little distance between them. 'When will they know for certain?'

'The lab needs longer to check it out, but unfortunately, Coral had already made up her mind. Even with these results, she's digging her heels in. Her take is that the cows knocked Jessica over and she hit her head on the wall, which killed her.'

Questions crowded her mind. 'And DS Hill?'

'Perry isn't convinced by the accident explanation. He said he has a feeling something is off, and...'

'And?'

Ben gave a half-hearted laugh. 'He said I should ask you your opinion, since you were the one who found her and, in his words, *you're bound to have some theory.*'

With the almost confirmation that the death wasn't due to misfortune, Laurel's original misgivings reasserted themselves. 'I knew it. The day I found her, that evening, I was talking to Albert and Maggie about it, and there was something I couldn't put my finger on. It's just like Hill said, something was off. You saw her, too. Do you have any ideas?'

He slumped. 'No.'

'What shall we do?'

'Have another drink first,' he said, emptying the last drips from the first bottle and pulling a second from a wine rack. 'And there is no *we*, okay? You're not here and we are not discussing this.'

'Got it.' She swirled the liquid around in her refilled glass and the words spilled from her mouth. 'This could mean she was murdered, then?'

Ben rubbed the back of his neck. 'We don't know anything for certain. The post-mortem isn't complete, and we'll need to revisit the scene to see if we can identify a spot on the wall where she might have hit her head. Unlikely as that is. I know they didn't find anything the first time round, but that could be because it was missed, or it's not there.'

'What else did the pathologist say?'

He pulled the wine bottle towards him and picked at the label.

Laurel waited him out. There must be more.

He finally spoke. 'He said there were no defensive wounds on Jessica's hands, which there should have been. A herd of cows doesn't sneak up on you. She wasn't wearing earbuds, so there's no chance she was unaware of them. Even if they knocked into her quickly, she would have...' He lifted his hands as though warding off a cow to demonstrate what Jessica would have done. 'There would have been some marks.'

'That's it. That's what was bugging me. I can't believe I didn't realise. Of course. No marks on her hands, and she didn't look like she'd been... trampled. You know?'

Ben lifted a shoulder, conceding the point.

Another thought struck her. 'Oh, but there was only one set of shoeprints by the body, and they were presumably Jessica's? I don't understand how someone could have got close enough to hit her and not have left prints? Do you remember, there was rain the night before leaving the ditch wet, and how muddy your shoes were when you had to get near enough to check for a pulse? You left prints. And that is what we're saying, isn't it? If it wasn't the cows knocking her into a wall, it was someone with a lump of stone.' She stopped as the image resolved in her mind. *Who would do that?*

She finished her drink and held out her glass for a top-up. 'I can't believe there might have been another murder in Elderwick.' The hand holding the glass shook and she had to put it down before it spilled. 'If Jessica was murdered,' she said, sifting through the facts and conjecture, 'could her death be related to the discovery of the bones?'

'I don't follow?'

'I suppose I'm making another assumption, but let's take it as read that the bones are also from a murder victim. Now that he's been dug up, whoever killed him absolutely won't want him identified if there's anything that could link the two of them. But along comes Jessica, who says she might be able to help with that identification, and five minutes later, she turns up dead.'

Looking rattled, Ben grasped her hands. 'This is exactly why I shouldn't have told you. Laurel, look at me. You can't go round saying Jessica was murdered. Do you understand?'

She pulled away from him, stung by his rebuke but galvanised by a possible link between the deaths. 'Are you going to tell Coral about Emmerson and Sturm?'

'Of course. But it worries me that this Michael Wishart didn't.' He pursed his lips. 'Until we know more about him, I'm not sure you should meet with him again.'

Chapter 32

Laurel

The moment she opened the door to her friend, Laurel knew Maggie was bursting with news. Her cheeks were flushed as she rushed through the usual pleasantries: *good morning; how are you; I'm fine.* With her signature flair, Maggie was dressed in cream linen trousers and a butter-yellow tunic which skimmed her slim hips, her hair pinned up in an elegant chignon. Laurel brushed a self-conscious hand over her grubby jeans and wished she'd not pulled on the T-shirt with the hole in the hem. In her defence, she'd been out in the garden early, checking the chicken coop for eggs, and she knew better than to wear nice clothes for the dusty job.

'Croissants.' Maggie all but dumped them into her hands. 'I have so much to tell you! You will not believe what else they found with the skeleton.'

She flashed a grin Laurel couldn't help but return. She loved Maggie's enthusiasm, but her churning gut wasn't soothed. Should she tell Maggie that Jessica's death might not have been the accident they thought it was? She'd promised Ben not to reveal any sensitive information – like the blow to the back of Jessica's head – but she hated to keep anything from her best friend. And they needed to talk about suspects. Laurel felt the ticking clock more keenly than ever; the man to whom the bones belonged might have been killed decades ago, but now she feared his killer was back in business.

Undecided, Laurel focused on Maggie's revelation. What else had they found in the shallow grave? 'I've set things out on the terrace, but let's exchange news first, then I'll put the kettle on,' Laurel suggested as she led the way to the bistro table still shaded from the morning sun.

The moment she sat, Maggie whipped out her notebook and launched into her account of the WI meeting.

Laurel's mouth dropped open as she learned of the key. 'That could be a pretty solid clue. Imagine if it still fits a lock somewhere in the village.'

Maggie was nodding with vigour. 'Absolutely, the key could be the key, if you'll forgive the pun. I asked Beth after the meeting, and she said it was found underneath the bones.'

'Same as the coin,' added Laurel.

'I don't think she meant to tell us. Apparently, the police were trying to keep those details quiet. Do you think they'll be trying the key out in doors around the village? It's a bit like a morbid Cinderella, *whose lock the key fits...*'

'With so many years having passed, there's a fair chance the door to which the key belongs is long gone, or the lock has been changed, but it's something else to go on.' Her face clouded. 'I just hope no one we know is implicated.' She doodled with her pencil. 'I'm still concerned it might turn out to be Dorothy's missing husband, but now I suppose we should also consider this Jurgen Sturm, don't you think?' Maggie asked.

'Speaking of Jurgen Sturm, I had a chat with Ben last night.'

Maggie's eyes twinkled. 'Did you indeed?'

'Not like that.' Laurel blushed and inwardly cursed. 'I had questions, and it's a good job I saw him because it turns out

Jessica's colleague, Michael, wasn't entirely truthful when I met him.'

'Why? What did he lie about?'

'Well, he told me about Harold Emmerson and Jurgen Sturm. He gave me a file containing the information Jessica had put together on them. He said he was going to meet with the police to ask their permission for him to proceed with Jessica's plan.'

'And?'

'Ben checked with DS Hill, who said neither he nor DI Coral have heard from anyone called Michael. Which doesn't make sense.'

'What did Ben say about that?' Maggie had put down her pencil, no longer taking notes, but listening, brow furrowed.

'I think he found it suspicious. But then we got distracted.'

Maggie's lips broke into a delighted grin. She nudged Laurel. 'Did he get saucy?'

Laurel flushed. 'Not that sort of distraction. I meant distracted by...' She hesitated. If she crossed this line and told Maggie about the pathologist's suspicions, the whole village would know about the question mark over Jessica's death.

'Distracted by...?' Maggie prompted her again.

'A bottle of wine,' was her lame reply.

Maggie stuck out her tongue. 'I honestly thought for a moment there you might have softened and given in to a dash of romance in your life.'

'No, thank you.' The conversation needed redirecting before Maggie quizzed her further. 'Anyway, while Ben briefs Coral and Hill, I suggest we put all our efforts into looking at Harold and Jurgen and see if we can rule out one or both of them.'

'We need to speak to Albert again,' Maggie declared. 'In

fact, I wanted to ask why you were reticent about inviting him along this morning?'

Laurel didn't know what to say.

'You think he knows something he's not telling us, don't you?' Maggie was on form, and her sharpness in catching onto Laurel's anxiety only increased the sour guilt in Laurel's stomach.

'It crossed my mind.' She tensed, waiting for her friend's reaction.

'You could be correct.'

'Oh.' It wasn't what she'd expected.

'But *if* he does, he must have a good reason for not telling us.'

Maggie sounded like Christopher. Why couldn't she trust Albert unquestioningly, too?

'I think we need to have it out and ask him. We shouldn't be suspecting him of things behind his back.'

Laurel recoiled.

'Let's go now.'

'No, I don't think... what if...' She had no good excuses, but she was horribly afraid of what they might learn.

***

Albert answered the door. His hair was askew – more so than usual – and he had a dusting of flour on his chin. 'To what do I owe this unexpected pleasure?' he beamed.

Laurel cowered behind Maggie. She didn't want to have this conversation.

'Mind if we come in for a quick chat?' asked Maggie.

'Of course.' He led them into the kitchen, where whisks, butter, flour, and a huge bowl of strawberries decorated the table. 'I've got more Royal Sovereigns than Wimbledon, so I'm making pies and jams and shortcake.'

For once, Laurel's stomach didn't rumble at the talk of food. Her appetite had entirely deserted her.

'Sit, sit,' said Albert, rearranging his baking accoutrements making no discernible difference.

'Ouch, these blasted shoes.' Unable to look Albert in the eye, Laurel bent down to fiddle with her left sandal, going so far as to slip it off. She willed Maggie to grasp the nettle and get it over with, to ask him what she wanted to ask. When nothing happened, she lifted her head to see Maggie was glaring at her while Albert had busied himself making a pot of tea. Maggie inclined her head in Albert's direction, but Laurel pressed her lips together and mimed that they should wait.

As Albert turned back to the table with the teapot, Laurel squealed. Something soft had brushed against her foot.

'You'll need to watch him. He'll be away with...'

He didn't finish. It was already too late. Aroon streaked out from under the table, Laurel's sandal clamped in his beak.

'Come back here you little... terror,' she yelped, setting off in pursuit of the feathery menace who legged it down the hallway and through a gap in the door into the living room. 'Got you now,' she gloated. The bird wasn't getting back past her.

From behind, Albert shouted, 'Don't go in there.'

Laurel squinted in the gloom. The curtains were drawn, leaving only a sliver of sunlight trickling through a narrow gap. 'Where are you?' She guarded the doorway whilst scanning the dark corners until she caught sight of items laid out on the coffee table. Taking a step closer, she forgot all about the sandal thief.

The photographs, some in colour, many in black and white, almost covered the surface, but there was one singled out in a space of its own, and it was impossible to miss.

Albert, followed by Maggie, crowded into the room behind her.

Laurel picked it up by the edges, careful not to cause smudges.

Albert, his voice uncharacteristically flat, said, 'You may as well have a good look.' He strode to the window and pulled back the curtains.

Maggie nestled in beside Laurel, and they studied the photo. Laurel's heart constricted as the implications sank in. Had Albert not reacted as he had, if she hadn't already been suspicious, she might have missed the significance, but it wasn't to be. She was positive she knew why he hadn't wanted her to see this image from the past.

'A couple of months ago, I started a project,' Albert informed them. 'People are always saying I should write a history of the village, so I thought I'd give it a go. I've been asking some of the long-term residents for memories, photographs, mementos from their lives in Elderwick. That,' he indicated the photo, 'came from Derek Fisher's collection. All the notes and documents relating to Elderwick's history we found in his bungalow after he died.' He sighed and sank into his armchair. 'When the bones were discovered, I was worried. I came back to look through everything I had amassed, and I found that.'

'It's Elderwick,' said Maggie. 'What's that say?' She jabbed at a banner captured by the photographer. Leaning closer, she read, '*Autumn Festival 1984.*'

'Yes.' He gave a tired laugh. 'It's all there, isn't it. It may as well be a smoking gun.'

Maggie sat on the sofa and pulled Laurel down beside her. 'What do you mean?'

'Do you want to explain?' he asked Laurel.

Pointing at the features in the photo, Laurel decoded the

scene. 'You're right, Maggie, it's obviously Elderwick. That's the meadow, though it's got a fence here, so the wall must have been built later. There, you can see a pit has been dug in the ground, I'm guessing the spit over the top means it was the fire pit for a hog roast or something like that.' Focusing on the irrelevant details was futile, but she was compelled to delay the inevitable because she didn't want to examine what it meant.

Albert nodded.

'And the people?' Maggie asked. 'Is that Dorothy? And next to her, I think it's Jo?'

'I wasn't sure who the women were, but I'd say you're right,' said Laurel.

'You have a good eye,' said Albert.

'Who's the man, though? I don't recognise him.'

'There are two men,' Laurel corrected her. The muscular blond was older, but recognisable. 'Based on the photo Michael gave to me, I'd say that's Jurgen Sturm standing next to Dorothy. And that,' she pointed to a figure in profile almost out of shot, but not quite, 'is you, Albert. You did come back to the village in the eighties.'

'How can you tell it's Albert? It could be anyone.'

Her heart breaking, Laurel asked, 'Who else would have a crow on his shoulder?'

'Crowco Chanel, a predecessor of Crowanna Lumley. I'd rescued her a few years before that photo was taken, and she recognised me every time I returned to the village.' Aroon had come out of hiding and hopped up onto Albert's knee, his beady eyes fixed on Laurel as Albert smoothed his feathers. 'If it's any consolation, I'm sorry I lied, but I had no choice.' His hands were shaking. 'I can't compel you, but I ask you, as my friends, can you keep this to yourselves?'

'Why wouldn't we?' Maggie looked from Albert to Laurel

and back again. 'It's not a crime to forget you were back here in the eighties.'

'Albert didn't forget.' Laurel put the picture down. She wished she'd convinced Maggie to stay back in the garden of Myrtle Cottage, enjoying their brunch so they would never have found themselves in the situation now facing them. 'I think it's Jurgen he didn't want us to see.'

'But why?' she persisted. 'I admit, Albert, I thought you were protecting Dorothy over this Harold Emmerson, but why don't you want us to see a picture of you with Mr Sturm?'

'Maggie,' Laurel wanted to put it gently, 'I believe Jurgen might be the body in the meadow, and I believe Albert thinks so, too.'

Chapter 33

Albert

Albert sat immobile in the chair long after Laurel and Maggie had left. For the first time in a long time, he was struck with indecision. It wasn't his place to go to the police – though he knew he would be criticised if not condemned for not doing so – but he wasn't sure he could risk contacting her again to ask what she wanted him to do. The last thing he wanted was to leave a trail of breadcrumbs straight to her door.

He joked about it often, but the speed with which gossip spread in his home village was formidable. He wanted to believe the promises made by Laurel and Maggie that they wouldn't tell another soul about Jurgen or act without returning to speak with him first, but once brought to light, secrets in Elderwick spread faster than the bindweed in his garden.

'What do you think, Aroon?' he asked the bird still perched purring on his knee. He wished he could talk with Christopher, but he baulked at putting his friend in a compromising position. Since Albert wasn't a practising Christian, he didn't think he could claim the confidentiality afforded to a penitent making a confession. 'Whatever shall I do?'

He reached for the incriminating photograph and held it in

his unsteady hand. The idea of destroying it, forefront in his mind, was nonetheless a step too far and wouldn't do anyone any favours. Not now it had been seen by others.

He'd told her about the picture, when it had turned up amongst the late Derek Fisher's belongings. He hadn't known then the implications of holding on to it. But then the body was found, rising to the surface like the proverbial bad penny. He should have destroyed it when he had the chance.

Aroon, tired of the inactivity, hopped down and strutted from the room, no doubt seeking mischief elsewhere. An hour must have passed whilst Albert deliberated, turning over every possible course of action. However, the decision was made for him when he heard a car draw up outside.

He'd been fortunate to never have had heart troubles during his seventy-odd years, but now, the beating in his chest was painful and the blood rushing in his ears close to deafening.

What had they done?

Chapter 34

Maggie

From the bench on the village green, Maggie watched in horror as someone she'd known for years was taken away by the police.

She wrung her hands. Had she and Laurel made a mistake in promising Albert their silence over the photo? Had Laurel changed her mind? Was that why the police had arrived? Had Laurel betrayed Albert and the confidence he'd guarded all these years?

'Maggie, what's happening?' Constance called as she buzzed past The Pleasant Pheasant and over to the bench. 'Hetty thought she saw Dorothy being driven away in a jam sandwich?'

'It's been at least ten years since the colour scheme on police cars changed, you know.' Usually, Maggie would enjoy joking around.

Constance ignored the correction. 'Why? Is this something to do with the bones?' she pressed. 'Is this about her husband, Harold?'

Whatever Laurel had done, and however much of a friend Constance was, Maggie didn't want to break her oath to Albert.

'I expect the police want her help. She's lived here for years. I bet she's helping narrow down the possibilities on the identity of the remains. It doesn't mean it's Harold.' It sounded like a reasonable explanation, and was maybe even true, but her distress wasn't eased.

Constance scowled. 'That would be just like the fuzz, to haul her away. She's a pensioner, for heaven's sake.'

'Hey,' came a deep voice from behind. 'Mind if I join you?' Dr Delgado plopped down next to Maggie.

Constance shifted to say hello and as she did, Maggie saw a piece of paper drop from her chair to the ground and flutter along in the breeze. The archaeologist scooped it up.

'Sorry, did I drop that?' Constance said, holding out her hand.

Dr Delgado leaned over to hand it to her.

Constance smoothed it out on her lap and wrinkled her nose. 'I'd forgotten I had this. It's Jessica's. I saw her drop it outside the bakery on Sunday. She'd gone by the time I got outside. I was going to get it back to her, but...' Her face fell. 'Guess I won't be able to now.'

'Is it something important?' asked Dr Delgado.

Constance lifted a shoulder. 'Probably not.'

Maggie caught a glimpse of a list of initials and a gobbledygook word at the bottom before Constance shoved it back down the side of her seat cushion. 'Poor Jessica,' she sighed. 'And poor you, Dr Delgado. I bet this isn't what you and your team expected when you came to Elderwick?'

'Hardly,' he replied. 'And there have been more developments this morning. Do you know what's happening?'

'We were just talking about it,' said Constance. 'The police have taken Dorothy away. Maggie thinks she's helping with enquiries over the remains you dug up.'

'Helping with enquiries? Really? What's the saying?

There's no smoke without a fire?' Disbelief dripped from his words.

Maggie shifted so she was face on to the tall archaeologist, her upset curdling into anger. 'Why didn't you tell us about the key you found with the skeleton?' she demanded. She was pleased to witness his smile dissolve.

'She – the officer in charge – asked us to keep quiet about it. Beth shouldn't have mentioned it to your group, but it's probably a moot issue now.'

'Why?' Maggie cringed a little at how combative she sounded, but Dr Delgado was an outsider and, photo and a missing husband notwithstanding, she didn't believe Dorothy had anything to do with the dead body. Probably not. Either way, he had no right to make assumptions about someone he didn't know.

'It's obvious they suspect her. We all know that helping with enquires is code for *we think you're guilty.*' He chuckled and leaned back, stretching an arm along the backrest.

Maggie stiffened, disliking the proximity. 'You don't know what you're talking about,' she snapped.

'Is that Lin?' Constance interrupted the building hostility, pointing to a figure on the far side of the road by the pond. 'Lin,' she shouted.

With a dazed expression, the young woman crossed the road without checking for traffic and it was only thanks to the empty road she wasn't hit by anything.

'Have you heard?' she asked as she reached them. She was pallid and wide-eyed.

'Come, sit down before you fall down.' Maggie stared at Dr Delgado until he rose and surrendered his place. 'We know the police have taken Dorothy away with them.'

'I was at Dorothy's when they arrived,' Lin sniffed. 'They were awful to her.'

Maggie wanted to ask what Lin had been doing at Dorothy's, but she held back the question. Now wasn't the time.

'They were saying she had to go with them to the station to answer questions about her missing husband. Then they were messing around with her front and back door. I don't know what they were doing. Who's going to look after her cat?' She lifted her face to Maggie, worry writ large.

Maggie patted her hand. 'Don't you worry, she'll be back home in no time, and until then, we'll make sure her cat is okay.' She debated the wisdom of asking with others present, but she needed to know. 'The thing they were doing with the doors, did they look pleased, like they'd got what they wanted? We think they might have been trying a key in the locks.' She knew she wasn't the only one holding their breath as they waited for an answer.

'Um, no, I don't think so. I heard one of them say they'd have to try at the other house.'

Maggie gasped.

'And I think I heard them mention Albert.'

Maggie fumbled for more information while she processed the latest revelation. 'You said the police were awful to Dorothy. What did they do?' She disliked pushing the young woman, who was clearly upset, but the more knowledge she had, the better.

Lin shuddered. 'There was that older guy there, the one I saw Jess speaking to before she died. He was the worst. He was shouting at Dorothy, telling her he'd always known she had something to do with her husband's disappearance and now he was finally going to make her face justice. He sounded like a bad TV cop. Dorothy was winding him up, you could tell. She was going on about how he wouldn't know a criminal if one lived under his own roof. He went ballistic. I really thought he was going to hit her, but she stood there and didn't even flinch. She was incredible.'

It was the nicest thing Maggie had ever heard anyone say about Dorothy.

'Is this about the bones?' Lin addressed Dr Delgado. 'Are they Dorothy's missing husband? I can't believe she would have anything to do with a murder.'

Dr Delgado folded his arms. 'I think we'd best leave that up to the police. They wouldn't arrest a person if they didn't have good cause.'

'Hold on, no-one mentioned arrests.' Constance said before asking Lin, 'Did they say they were arresting Dorothy?'

'No, definitely not.'

'So, please don't add fuel to the fire, doctor,' Maggie scolded.

He held up his hands. 'Either way, she must know something. Once the police find the door the key unlocks, they'll have their man, or woman.'

Maggie dearly hoped the key didn't fit the lock of anyone she knew. 'Was there anything else said that we should know?'

Lin thought before confirming that no, there was nothing else to share. 'But do you know anything about her husband who went missing?'

Maggie averted her eyes. 'No, not a thing.' In her peripheral vision, she caught Dr Delgado's eyes narrowing.

'Albert would know,' said Constance. 'He's lived here forever. In fact, so has Dorothy. Oh...'

'Yes, well, we can hardly ask them now, can we, not if the police are already at Albert's?' Maggie saw Constance flinch at her sharp tone. 'Sorry, I'm worried about them. You know how DI Coral can get.'

'I wonder who put the police on to them, and why?' Delgado wondered aloud.

Maggie thought of Laurel and felt wretched.

Chapter 35

Laurel

Laurel stood back from her bedroom window and peered out at the car. It was a police car, and it had come to a halt in front of Albert's cottage. DS Hill exited the vehicle and walked through the small front garden to Albert's door. Albert had it open before Hill had lifted his hand to knock.

'Maggie, what have you done?' Laurel groaned. 'Why did you go to the police?'

Her window was closed so she couldn't hear everything being said, but she didn't hear any raised voices. A uniformed officer followed Hill inside the house. She hovered and was rewarded when the officer emerged and fiddled with the door. Her view wasn't good enough to see exactly what he was doing, but she could guess.

She held her breath.

He stepped back and from the slump in his shoulders, she assumed he'd been unsuccessful. Thank goodness.

He disappeared along the path around to the back of the cottage. She wished him a similar disappointment. The suspicion she and Ben had cooked up, that the bones in the meadow and Jessica's death could be linked, had seemed reasonable at the time. But that was before she'd seen the photograph in Albert's living room.

Albert was no killer. The idea was absurd. She knew that. She hoped Ben knew that. But would DI Coral view the situation in the same way?

Laurel opened the window, then sat down on the edge of her bed, waiting for whatever happened next.

She was afraid cars were arriving outside Jo and Dorothy's houses, too. Had the key already been tried in their locks? As soon as the police left, she would check on Albert, then call round to Dorothy's, then Jo's. Or maybe she could dispatch Albert to make sure Jo was okay.

The sooner this issue of the identity of the remains was resolved, the better.

Fresh sounds from down below alerted her to the fact that her plan to check on Albert would have to be deferred.

Breaking into a cold sweat, she moved back to the window and saw Albert being folded into the back of the car.

Hill climbed into the driver's seat then powered down the window and spoke to the uniformed officer who had returned from the rear of the property.

Laurel held her breath and pressed as close to the window as she dared.

'Get that key over to the place on East Street, and then Tulip Cottage, because I don't think they thought to check it. Afterwards, get a lift back to the station.'

She recognised the name Tulip Cottage. It was Dorothy's holiday cottage.

She chewed on her lip. She was considering calling Ben. It was a bad idea, and he would be unlikely to tell her anything, if he even knew what was happening, but she had to act, to do something.

The car pulled away from the curb, did a three-point turn,

and headed back towards the centre of the village. She could just make out Albert's hunched form. In spite of his earlier subterfuge, she was still struggling to believe Albert could be involved with the bones, let alone Jessica's death.

Then again, she'd been dangerously wrong about a killer before.

Demand for clinic appointments was typically low during the summer months, and Laurel was pathetically relieved to have another free afternoon. It meant she could spend the rest of her day at home, inside or in the garden, always with an ear out for Albert's return.

She tried calling Ben, Maggie, and even the number for The Pleasant Pheasant, but no-one was answering on any line. She could have a go at tracking them down in person, but she didn't want to leave the cottage in case Albert was brought back and she missed him.

When he hadn't returned by seven that evening, she went next door and into his back garden, where she fed Lago the rabbit and Crowanna Lumley. She spied Aroon lurking in the undergrowth at the bottom of Albert's vegetable patch, but he wouldn't come near her. She put out some of the dry food Albert kept for him in the shed — she smiled at the name above the door, Tumbledown Cabin — and called goodnight. As annoying as she found the bird, she felt sorry for him. He was never far from Albert's side and wouldn't understand what was happening. She hoped his owner would be home soon.

At eleven she gave up and went to bed and it wasn't until 1.57 in the morning that she was awakened by a car and voices. Without turning on a light, she tiptoed to the window and saw Albert disappearing inside his cottage and the car driving away.

She thought about going round to check if he was all right, but while she was deliberating, his lights went off and stillness returned to the lane. He would need sleep. She'd go round first thing.

Sleep eluded her as the hours dragged by. She thought about the photograph and what it meant. It proved Albert had been in Elderwick in the autumn of 1984, even though he'd claimed he hadn't visited in the eighties. Jurgen Sturm was in the picture, proof Albert, Jo, and Dorothy, all knew him. How close their relationships were with him was impossible to tell from a snapshot of a single moment in time, but the way they were arranged, they didn't look like strangers. Albert hadn't wanted her and Maggie to see the image, and when they had, he had implored them not to tell anyone.

Logically, it wasn't much. It was a far cry from evidence of Albert's involvement in any crime, and the same could be said for Dorothy and Jo. Why then had Albert withheld the information and the photograph? Was it because he was afraid people – the police – would jump to conclusions?

Nothing was making any sense.

She tried again.

The remains in the meadow had to have been placed there deliberately, but surely, someone would have noticed a grave being dug or a mound of disturbed earth afterwards? The question caused the details in the photo she'd originally dismissed as immaterial to resurface, and a grim explanation took shape.

The fire pit dug for the 1984 Autumn Festival would have been perfect cover for someone to bury a body. As far as she could recall, the pit was in the right place. The same place as the trench. She put a hand over her mouth. It was a grisly idea.

Her phone was on the bedside table. She'd saved the newspaper article about Harold Emmerson's disappearance. She consulted it again. He'd been reported missing in 1983. If the fire pit in 1984 was the grave – and unless his body had been hidden elsewhere for a year – this was confirmation that the bones from the meadow didn't belong to Harold.

Chapter 36

Albert

Tired as he was from the unpleasantness at the police station the day before, Albert rose with the lark and spent some time soothing the fur and feathers of his animal companions. He could tell someone had fed them the previous evening – Laurel, he presumed – but Aroon was giving him the cold shoulder.

When he'd done all he could, and with a promise to be home soon, he stepped lightly through his front garden and out of the gate, anxious to avoid being waylaid by his neighbour. He wanted to get over to Dorothy's for a debrief. Naturally, the officers he'd spoken to at wearisome length had warned him not to discuss the case with anyone. However, he wasn't under arrest and so they couldn't stop him.

He snuck a peek at Laurel's as he beetled past. Her curtains were closed downstairs, but open upstairs, as was the window. He wasn't sure if that meant she was up and about. He increased his speed and was out of sight within moments.

For years, he had feared this day would come. Then as the years became decades, first two, then three, he'd dared to believe they'd got away with it. He'd felt no triumph, only a tempered relief. Of course, all that was shattered now.

Mayhap, in his heart of hearts, he had known the truth would be revealed one day. Even the darkest secrets didn't stay buried forever in Elderwick. Was that why he'd come back after winding down his university career? So he'd be here to take the brunt and shelter his friend? *Friends,* he amended.

Not a soul was in sight as he slipped through the gates and up the drive to Dorothy's house. He hoped Jo was already there. They had a lot to consider.

Two tear-stained faces greeted him as he let himself into the house and tiptoed through to the drawing room.

'Oh Albert, I'm so sorry,' wept Jo. 'This is all my fault.'

Chapter 37

Maggie

If anything, Maggie was feeling even more off-colour than she had the day before. She was sick to think of Albert and Dorothy being in trouble with the authorities. It was obviously a ghastly mix-up, and everything would be put right in short-order, but what if... No, she didn't want to go there. There was nothing to be gained by predicting the worst.

Admittedly, she and Laurel had enjoyed spinning theories and suppositions about murder and murderers in the past, but this time it was their friends and neighbours who were being drawn in. Which was simply too much.

Had Laurel gone to the police about the photograph? As far as Maggie knew, she and Laurel were the only people – barring those captured in the image – who were aware of its existence. However, there was no reason for Albert to have told anyone about it, and she certainly hadn't spilled the beans herself.

She pushed aside the toast she'd been trying to eat and resolved to take action. What action she hadn't yet determined, but she couldn't sit around the house all day twiddling her thumbs.

The Pleasant Pheasant occurred to her as the obvious place

to start. It was the hub of the village, and where, no doubt, she would find Jo. It was early yet, but the breakfast crowd would be in, and chances were, one or more of them would have a piece of the puzzle they'd be eager to share with her over a pot of tea.

The anticipation of one of Jo's bacon sandwiches made her mouth water, stomach upset already forgotten. Everything would work itself out. It always had in the past.

Passing the village hall, where South Street became North Street, Maggie's pace slowed. She could see the café terrace and a few people milling about looking lost. She squinted, the door to the tearoom, always left open at this time of year, was closed and the blind drawn over the window. Where was Jo?

Her heart rate kicked up a notch. She put on a burst of speed, eager to catch the loitering few and ask if they'd seen the proprietor.

Maggie called out before she'd barely reached them, but they each shook their heads. No-one knew why the tearoom was closed and no-one had seen Jo. They had all heard about people being escorted away by the police the day before, though, and gossip bubbled from their lips. Had Jo been taken too?

'I heard they arrested Dorothy Little over those bones and Jo is a witness against her,' confided Babs from the WI.

'No, you have it back to front,' corrected her husband. 'Jo was arrested. The remains are Dorothy's husband and Jo killed him in a jealous rage.'

His wife smacked him on the arm with her handbag. 'Don't talk nonsense, Oscar. You're making things up. Jo would never do such a thing.'

'But Dorothy's husband did disappear all those years ago, don't you remember? You both lived here then.' This came from a short, dapper gentleman, Rupert. He and Maggie would often run into each other in The Plump Tart. They shared a devotion to chocolate éclairs.

Babs gasped. 'So he did. It was in all the papers. Ooh, I bet that's what it's all about. The remains *are* Dorothy's husband. She must have killed him and buried him there and not said a word about it all these years.'

Her husband and Rupert were nodding along. Oscar added, 'She used to be a nurse, you know. If anyone would be able to bump someone off, it would be a nurse.'

Maggie thought she ought to halt the speculation, but perhaps these older residents would know something about Jurgen. He was just as likely a candidate as the body in the trench. 'Do any of you remember a gentleman called Jurgen Sturm living in Elderwick? It would have been in the eighties.'

Her query silenced the group. Babs, Oscar, Rupert, and Pratiksha, who had wandered over to join them, all put on a show of thinking. Oscar mouthed the name a couple of times.

'Sounds German,' said Rupert. The collective nodded. 'You're thinking this Herr Sturm could be the body in question? Why's that then?'

She didn't want to give too much away. In fact, she worried she already had by mentioning the name when Laurel had implored her to refrain from doing so. Then again, if the police were going round strong-arming people off to be questioned, people she'd known for years, her friends and neighbours, perhaps the time for softly-softly was over.

'He's someone I saw in a photograph. It was taken in Elderwick in 1984 and...' she trailed off, trusting the gossips to steam ahead.

But then, they didn't.

'I don't recall anyone by that name. No, no, I'm certain this Sturm fellow never lived in the village. We'd know.' Rupert spoke for them all.

'Quite so,' agreed Babs. 'Now come away Oscar, if there's no food on offer here, I'll do you a nice bowl of porridge at home.'

Oscar's face dropped, but before he could be led away, Dorothy and Albert appeared at the top of West Street.

'Now we'll get the full story,' said Rupert, his interest clearly piqued once more.

As one, they turned to watch Dorothy and Albert approach. Maggie thought Dorothy faltered, but Albert's shoulders were squared, and his head held high.

'Good morning, all,' he said. 'I've no doubt you're waiting on tenterhooks for the juicy details?'

Babs laughed, a high, brittle sound, broadcasting a discomfort Maggie shared.

'Is Jo all right?' Maggie asked first. She didn't want Albert to view her as just another of the chattering masses with nothing better to do, and she was genuinely concerned.

'I don't know. Is the tearoom closed?' he asked, bending to look at the door beyond her. 'Perhaps she's taken a day off. Best thing is you all pop off home and fend for yourselves.'

Oscar disengaged his arm from his wife's and stepped forward, but before he could speak, Dorothy swore. Maggie's mouth dropped open, Dorothy never used bad language. She must be truly rattled. Gathering herself, she turned to track the direction of Dorothy's gaze. Laurel was jogging up to the growing crowd.

'Dorothy, Albert, I'm so glad you're okay. Are you okay?' She was breathless and flushed.

If Laurel was the one who had spilled the beans about the photograph to the police, Maggie thought she was showing poor judgement to be asking now if people were okay.

'This is all your fault.' Dorothy rounded on Laurel, poking her with a bony finger. 'Don't think we don't know it was you. You can't keep your nose out of other people's business, can you? Never could. Not since you first arrived here. I know you think you're some sort of amateur sleuth, but let me tell you–'

'Dorothy, please. I didn't mean... I didn't...'

'You didn't think, is what you didn't do. Telling the police about that photograph meant Albert and I spent all day yesterday being accused of being liars and worse. And I'll tell you this for nothing. Everything that happens next will be your fault.'

Maggie caught Albert's eye, asking him a silent question. What was going to happen next?

Albert, usually quick to defuse tense situations, was making no move to do so.

Maggie knew she too should be jumping to her friend's defence, but Dorothy also had a point. Wrestling with indecision, she was spared having to choose sides by one more addition to the gathering: an attractive woman with shoulder-length blond hair and an eye for stylish summer wear. Maggie didn't recognise her, but Laurel, Dorothy, and Albert evidently did.

'Jayne,' Albert bobbed his head in acknowledgement.

'Hello, Albert, Dorothy.' Her greeting was warm.

Now she'd heard the name, Maggie could place her. This was Laurel's old school friend and manager of Dandelions, Jayne Clement. By way of filling the space so Dorothy couldn't relaunch her attack, Maggie introduced herself and received an effusive smile in return.

'And Laurel,' Jayne directed her attention to the focus of Dorothy's ire, 'are you well? I feel like I'm interrupting something?'

Jayne must have heard Dorothy's tirade. On whose side would she fall? Laurel had refused to share any details, but there was history between her and Jayne, Maggie knew.

'This doesn't concern you,' growled Dorothy.

'If this is anything to do with the items found by the archaeologists, and the events of yesterday, then I believe it is my business, and your accusations are unfounded,' she told Dorothy. 'What's more, Laurel is my friend.'

'Is she?' Maggie froze. She hadn't meant to say that. It had slipped out. She snuck a peek at Laurel who wore a mortified expression.

Jayne, however, chuckled. 'It's been a long time since we were at school together, but yes, I'd like to count Laurel as a friend. Particularly as I've decided to base myself here permanently.'

Laurel's mouth dropped open.

Whatever this was that was happening, even Dorothy was distracted.

'What do you say?' Jayne asked Laurel.

Laurel shifted from foot to foot. 'Why are you defending me?'

'Why wouldn't I?'

Laurel let out a long breath. 'Because I wasn't very nice to you at school.'

Now Maggie's mouth hung slack. She'd assumed Laurel had been bullied by Jayne based on Laurel's determination not to speak about the woman. She certainly hadn't pegged Laurel as the bully.

Jayne laughed and pulled Laurel to the side. 'I know you didn't like how I showed up midway through the year and suddenly I was top in English lit., maths, and chemistry. I remember the time you pretended you'd thrown away my favourite pencil case, but I also know you didn't throw it away and that it was you who snuck it back into my bag outside the assembly hall. Besides, you were the first person to speak to me when I came back to school after my dad's heart attack. Everyone else, even the teachers, behaved weird, but not you. I don't know what else you did, or think you did, but you weren't that bad. I always hoped we'd be friends, and maybe now we can be.'

Laurel's eyes welled with tears. 'I was such a stupid jealous cow, and here you are even now, being the bigger person.'

'Yes, yes, and you hate me for it,' Jayne laughed.

'How very heartwarming,' sneered Dorothy.

'Now, about the police and yesterday.' Jayne got back on track and Maggie felt she was sizing them up one by one.

'I don't know anything about a photograph, but that's not the reason the police asked you in for questioning yesterday.'

'And what, Jayne, would you know of it?' demanded Dorothy.

Dorothy was still on the warpath, but Albert had inched his way round, so he was standing next to Laurel. Maggie saw him reach out and touch the back of her hand and when Laurel looked at him, he smiled.

'As the managers of Dandelions, Alex and I had a meeting with DI Coral and DS Hill yesterday morning. There was another man present, an ex-police officer, name of Tillow, which was odd. Proper pompous ass he was too. Still, there we go. He wanted to know who amongst the locals had been the most interested in our plans here in the village. I'm afraid we had to tell the truth, that it was you, Dorothy, and you, Albert.'

'Tell the truth and shame the devil,' Albert muttered.

Maggie shook her head and told Jayne, 'He does that, famous quotes left and right.'

Jayne smiled, then continued. 'Unfortunately, this set him off. Tillow that is. Judging by his reaction, he was positively delighted to hear your names. The last I heard as they were leaving was him insisting you both be brought in for questioning. He said, and apologies if I'm not remembering it exact, but he said he knew you, Ms Little,' she pointed to

Dorothy, 'had killed your husband and this time he was going to nail you to the wall. Sorry.'

Chapter 38

Laurel

Emotionally wrung out, Laurel surveyed the loose gaggle of people outside The Pleasant Pheasant. What she wanted, in that moment, was to speak to Jayne in private. To apologise properly for not having been nicer to her when they were at school. It had weighed on her over the years, to the extent that she'd been mortified to learn Jayne was in Elderwick. What would her friends think when they found out how horrible she'd been as a young teen?

There were two other people to whom she also wanted to apologise, Maggie and Albert. She had believed the worst of Maggie, thinking she had blabbed about the photo. However, after watching Maggie's behaviour during Dorothy's rant and Jayne's defence, she had the inkling that Maggie had suspected the same of her.

Certainly, Dorothy had.

'We should probably go,' she said. She could practically see ears flapping in the crowd.

'You can come back to mine. It's closest,' Dorothy said with bad grace, but Laurel was thankful for the offer.

As they walked, Maggie gave her a rundown of what the

villagers had been saying. 'They're adamant that Jurgen Sturm never lived in the village,' she whispered. 'But they know all about Dorothy's husband going missing. They're of the opinion she could have bumped him off.'

Laurel glanced at Dorothy, but the woman gave no indication she'd heard what Maggie had said.

Once they reached Dorothy's and were sitting round the kitchen table, well away from curious bystanders, Laurel asked, 'Did the police take Jo in too?'

Albert was shaking his head. 'No, just the two of us.'

'Ah, I assumed...' Laurel began, but didn't know how to finish without giving anything more away about the photo to Jayne.

Albert shared a look with Dorothy. 'Dorothy,' he said, turning to her with a sigh, 'I think it's time to tell the whole story. It's going to come out now anyway, and better they hear it from you.'

Dorothy's already thin lips compressed further. 'I shouldn't have to talk about this at all. It's no-one's business but my own. However, Albert is right, it will be all over the village by sunset, so you may as well hear it from me.'

Laurel held her breath, afraid to move in case Dorothy took offence and changed her mind. She need not have worried.

Dorothy smoothed her skirt and clasped her hands on the table. 'I didn't marry young,' she began. 'Why would I? Who needs a man? I had a career as a nurse, friends, family. I was satisfied.'

It was interesting Dorothy hadn't said *happy,* but Laurel kept that observation to herself.

'Then, at thirty-eight, I met Harold Emmerson.' She stared off out of the window. 'He was five years younger than me and the foreman at the cattle market in Beverley. It's not there anymore, of course. It was where the big supermarket is now, off

Morton Lane. Harold was strong from his days as a livestock handler, and very handsome. Not that it matters.

'I was a stupid woman who should have known better than to let him sweep me off my feet. We were married within a year. That's when things changed.'

Albert reached out to her, but she batted him away. 'I'll keep it short. It was what you'd call domestic abuse now. Physical and psychological. Beatings, talking me down, isolating me from my family and friends. He wanted me to give up my job and start spitting out babies and when I told him no, he broke two ribs.' She touched her side. 'Like a fool, I let it go on for nearly two years and if it hadn't been for my brothers, I think, eventually, he would have killed me.'

'Dorothy, I'm so–'

'Save your sympathy. It was what it was. I was one of the fortunate few who got away.'

'Because of your brothers?' asked Laurel.

'Yes, they saved my life. They got rid of Harold.'

Maggie gasped.

Dorothy shot her a glare. 'They didn't kill him,' she snapped before lapsing into silence.

Albert stepped in. 'Dorothy's brothers, Dale and Donald, were older and hadn't seen their sister since the wedding. When they made an unannounced visit to check in on her and saw what Harold had been doing, they took it upon themselves to warn him off. And warn him off they did, with menaces, which was no more than he deserved.'

Stunned, Laurel found her voice. 'And he left?'

'He did,' confirmed Albert. 'This was in 1983.'

'I didn't know until afterwards,' said Dorothy. 'I'd been taken out of the way to a friend's house, a friend who still welcomed me even though we'd been distant for months by then. And the only reason you're hearing this now is that Dale and Donald are dead, so they can't be accused of any wrongdoing. Because we all know how it goes with domestic abuse cases.'

Albert grunted. 'Which brings us to Vincent Tillow.'

'Which brings us to Vincent,' Dorothy spat his name. 'In the first few months of Harold's abuse, my matron at Beverley Westwood Hospital saw the bruises and convinced me to go to the police, which is how I met Vincent.' Her lips curled into a snarl. 'He told me...' Her voice cracked. '...he told me it was a husband's right to discipline his wife and that if I wasted police time again, he'd lock me up instead.'

'That bastard,' exclaimed Maggie in the strongest language Laurel had heard her use in a long time. 'So, you didn't report Harold ever again?'

'Not until he broke my ribs. I was so badly injured, I had to have a doctor come out to me. This doctor – I knew him from work – insisted I be admitted as an inpatient. During my stay, the same matron saw me and called the police herself. Again, it was Vincent. He made all the right noises with the staff around as witnesses, but I knew he'd do nothing about Harold.'

'But, then when Harold went missing, suddenly it was all hands-on deck. Because of course, when a *man* is missing, it's a *serious* issue.'

Laurel's hands curled into fists.

Dorothy was shaking.

Once more, Albert picked up the thread. 'Tillow hounded Dorothy, and when he found out about her brothers, he hounded them, too. He was convinced they'd killed Harold at Dorothy's request and disposed of the body. This went on for nearly a year. You went to live with Dale in Lancaster for a while after you were home from hospital, if I remember rightly?'

Dorothy nodded. 'I didn't live in this house then, but a small cottage down School Lane. I loved that place. It was my home, but I had to get away.'

'You came back, though,' said Maggie.

'Oh yes.' Fire returned to her eyes. 'I wasn't about to let Harold or Vincent chase me out of Elderwick.'

'And that's why Tillow brought you in yesterday. He thinks the body in the meadow is Harold.' So many things about Dorothy made sense now. Laurel wished she'd been kinder to her.

'And Albert, because he was... is my friend. Why harass one person when you can harass two?'

Jayne cleared her throat and Laurel jumped; she'd forgotten she was there.

'The others are too polite to ask, but are you saying that the body in the meadow isn't your ex-husband? That's it not Harold?'

'I wish it was, but no, it's not him.'

'Can you prove it?' continued Jayne. In her gentle but firm voice, it didn't sound like a challenge or an accusation, but a hopeful enquiry.

'I don't know,' said Dorothy.

Chapter 39

Albert

It was easy to forget all that Dorothy had been through; she didn't wear her heart on her sleeve and had a hard shell protecting her against the world, but Albert was beset by guilt. He shouldn't have consigned the knowledge to the past. He was ashamed to recall how many times he'd been less than charitable to her. He understood she didn't want sympathy, but he should have been more considerate over the years. At least now, he could be her support, though she was doing an outstandingly good job unassisted. Furthermore, he was hoping her disclosure had thrown Laurel, Maggie, and Jayne now too, off the scent of the bigger truth.

If they could somehow prove that Harold was still alive, or that he had been when he'd left the village in 1983, it would take the wind out of Tillow's sails.

'What can we do to help?' he asked Dorothy.

When she didn't answer, Jayne made a suggestion. 'I've worked in children's services for years, in a variety of roles, and for a while I was involved in a scheme run in conjunction with the UK Missing Children Unit. I'm not blowing my own trumpet, but I know a thing or two about tracing missing people.

Of course, we don't have access to any official resources, but I reckon we could make a good go of tracking old Harold down.

'Given what we now know of Mr Tillow, I don't think we can rely on the police to dedicate sufficient effort to what could be a needle in a haystack task. Dorothy, you said your ex was five years younger than you? Making him about...'

'Seventy-six,' Dorothy confirmed.

'Seventy-six,' Jayne repeated. 'Whilst some older people are very computer literate, many are not. If he isn't, it will make our job harder as he won't have an online presence, but we'll give it a go. Right?' She looked at Laurel, Maggie, and Albert.

Albert was au fait with email, news websites, and on-line crossword puzzling, but he'd left the university before the internet took a stranglehold, and he'd never been one for social media. He'd do what he could, but his skills lay in old school methods. 'I can go to the local library and see what I can dig up. I recall there were various articles in the papers at the time, when his mother reported him missing. And I'll speak to Christopher about checking for a death certificate in case Harold's done us all a favour and died since then. He'll be glad to help.'

Jayne beamed at him. 'Wonderful.'

Maggie and Laurel were enthusiastic about getting started and offered to begin with a trawl of social media

'Did he have family?' Laurel asked Dorothy.

'Only his wicked mother – the apple didn't fall far from that tree – but she'll be long gone. I was always sure she knew how he treated me, but she never offered so much as a word of kindness. She was the one egging Vincent on when her precious son disappeared.'

'Sorry if this is a silly question,' said Maggie. 'But if the police were after you for potential murder, why didn't you tell them at the time how your brothers had run him off?'

'That *is* a stupid question,' Dorothy retorted.

Maggie blinked. 'I didn't say stupid.'

Albert stepped in before things deteriorated further. 'Tillow was out for blood. If Dale and Donald admitted what they'd done, they and Dorothy would have been locked up anyway for assault or some such. He wouldn't have accepted any kind of self-defence explanation.'

'Thank you, Albert,' Maggie said pointedly.

'What about Ben?' suggested Laurel.

Albert and Jayne shook their heads in synchrony as Albert explained, 'Best leave Ben out of it. He won't be able to use police databases unofficially, and we don't know if he can be trusted not to tell Coral what we're up to.'

The disappointment he fancied he saw crossing Laurel's face was unexpected. He made a mental note to ask her about it later. When this was all over, and frivolous pursuits were once again the order of the day.

'Let's get to it.' Jayne smacked her hands on her knees and stood.

'And am I supposed to sit and twiddle my thumbs?'

Even when people were extending assistance, Dorothy couldn't help herself. Albert hid a tired grin.

Jayne responded. 'Yes, that is precisely what you should do. Do not give the police a single shred of a reason to come back on you. Leave this to us. Okay?'

Jayne was steering this ship then. He knew he'd warmed to her for a reason.

Maggie left the group at the end of Dorothy's drive, and Jayne peeled off at the gates of Elderwick Hall.

Alone with Laurel, Albert slowed his pace. 'I need to make amends,' he said. 'I was jargogled, jumbled, and of the mistaken belief that you had told the police about the photograph. I am shamefaced.'

Laurel stared at him for a beat before her features relaxed. 'Don't worry about it, I thought Maggie had.'

He felt lighter than he had been for some time. Truly, they were not out of the woods yet, but his faith in his friends was secure. 'Mistakes are always forgivable, if one has the courage to admit them.'

'Oscar Wilde?'

'Bruce Lee.'

'Speaking of mistakes...'

The knots snarled up once more in his muscles, locking tight with anticipatory anxiety.

'I'm afraid Dorothy might have made one, a mistake that is, by mentioning the photograph in front of Babs and company.'

He slapped his hand against his forehead. That damn photo! Of course, how had he not realised? He knew why not, because he'd been too caught up in the very thing for which he'd just apologised, the mistaken belief that Laurel had disclosed the existence of the picture already. He could kick himself.

He felt Laurel's concerned gaze.

'You've gone very pale,' she said.

He swore he could feel the blood draining from his face.

He pictured the scene the day before: the police car drawing up outside; his error in thinking; his doubt over Laurel's word. It meant he hadn't bothered to hide the photo. He'd left it lying on the coffee table in full view of anyone who should enter the room.

He came to a stop by the gate to Laurel's garden and closed his eyes, walking back through his memory. He'd opened the door to Hill, who had followed him into the kitchen. The other officer hadn't come in but had fiddled about with the lock at the front and then with the one on the back door. Had either of them crossed the threshold of the living room?

'That photo, it is important, isn't it?' Laurel interrupted his panic. 'There's been something you've not been telling me from the start, something you're keeping back even now. Albert, you can trust me, and I think you need to because this all feels like it's about to spiral out of control. Tillow has it in for Dorothy, we need to do whatever we can to help her. Who are you protecting? Is it Dorothy, or...'

He heard the disappointment in her voice.

'...is it yourself?'

There it was. There was nowhere left to hide. He'd done what he could, but the cork was out of the bottle, the cat out of the bag.

'You'd better come in,' he said.

Chapter 40

Laurel

The first thing Albert did was to check the pile of photos on the coffee table.

'Well, it's still here at any rate,' he muttered, his fingers not quite touching the picture as though he were afraid to make contact.

Laurel was catching on. 'You thought that DS Hill or his colleague might have caught sight of it yesterday?'

'I was afraid of that, but maybe we got lucky?' He didn't sound as though he believed his own words. He collapsed into his chair and Laurel offered to make him a cup of tea.

'A jot of brandy might go down better right about now,' he said. 'There's some in the sideboard there, and you'll find glasses, too. Help yourself if you'd like to join me.'

Sneaking a glance at her watch, Laurel judged eleven in the morning too early for hard liquor, but she poured Albert a generous measure and handed it over. As the quiet stretched between them, connections were falling into place: the remains dug up by the archaeology team; Albert's dissembling; the photograph taken at Elderwick Autumn Festival in 1984. She didn't have all the pieces yet, but the puzzle was finally making some sense.

Albert knocked back his brandy but refused a refill. 'I'll need a mostly clear head for this.' His laugh was hollow.

Laurel hated him being brought low, but she was angry with him for lying.

The tension was uncomfortable. She should jump in and tell him what she already knew, and what she suspected. Get it over with. She wouldn't mention Jessica's death, though until the cause was confirmed. She'd circle back if necessary. No need to muddy the waters more by conflating the two cases.

'Shall I tell you what I've worked out?' She wished she had her notebook to consult.

'Please. It might not be so hard if you've deduced the truth without my aid.'

Must he be so cryptic?

'I am counting on you to fill in the gaps, you know.'

'Naturally.'

She braced herself. 'Okay, we've got a body in the ground, buried sometime after 1981, probably in the early eighties, going by the coin found with the remains. We now know a key was also found with him, but I don't know if that's helpful yet?' Albert didn't reply, so she pushed on. 'Dorothy's husband, Harold, was hounded out of the village in 1983 and hasn't resurfaced. However, if what Dorothy told us this morning is true – and you say it is – then he is, or was, alive when he left Elderwick. Meaning we can safely say the remains in the meadow are not Harold.'

'So it follows.'

'Unfortunately, Tillow believed then, and continues to believe that Dorothy and her brothers, possibly with your knowledge and help, killed Harold and disposed of his body.'

'Unfortunately,' he echoed.

She took a second to gather her thoughts for what she was about to say next, which was still mostly speculation. 'Which leaves Jurgen Sturm as the most obvious candidate for the deceased. Thanks to Jessica's notes, we know he's a missing person, missing from this area, and I know what he looked like because of the picture of him in her file. Then, I recognised him in your photo. This photo.' She pointed at the table. 'Which confirms not only was he here for the festival in 1984, but that you, Dorothy, and Jo all knew him. How close you were, I'm not sure. But your...' She didn't want to call him a liar to his face. '... not complete honesty tells me you know something about his disappearance, and that what you know is significant, so I think the four of you were close.'

Albert gave a dry chuckle. 'I appreciate your delicate turn of phrase, but you can speak plain and call me a hugger-mugger; I did practise to deceive.'

Laurel's lips quirked.

'It's a leap, given the lack of evidence, but I'm going to lay out my hypothesis. The skeleton is Jurgen. From Jessica's file, I know he was probably married and I'm going to say he was married to Jo. We know it wasn't Dorothy, and marriage between two men wasn't legal in the eighties, so it wasn't you.'

Albert neither confirmed nor denied.

'I think that sometime shortly after the festival, Jurgen died. Either he was killed, or there was an accident?' She studied him, but his expression was unreadable. She took a deep breath. 'You and Dorothy both know what happened, and you've been protecting Jo by remaining silent ever since?'

Chapter 41

Maggie

Maggie brushed her hair and topped up her barely-there lipstick in the hallway mirror, then ambled to the bakery.

The bell above the door jingled as she went in. Behind the counter, Constance looked up and smiled.

Tearing her attention away from the fresh cakes and pastries, Maggie asked, 'Do you fancy a nice cold drink in the pub and a bit of internet sleuthing?'

'About Carter?' Constance asked after she'd ensured Hetty wasn't within earshot.

'No, about the bones.' It still made her shiver to say it.

'Sure, why not. Give me ten minutes?'

While Constance was in the kitchen, gathering her things and persuading Hetty to take over front of house again, Maggie's gaze was drawn inexorably back to the contents of the display cabinet. Needing to resist, she lifted her head to study instead the photos of old Elderwick on the wall. Did these photos, too, hide secrets?

'All set,' said Constance, reappearing.

Maggie pointed to a gap between frames three and five. 'What happened to the fourth picture?'

Constance rolled her eyes. 'Fumble fingers Rupert wanted to look at it this morning. Then he only went and dropped it. Still, he offered to take it away to replace the frame and the glass, so that's something. Are you ready? There's a mango mojito waiting with my name on it.'

Ten minutes later, in The Snooty Fox, they scoped out the best place to sit. Maggie waved to Dr Delgado and Beth, who were chatting with Lin and Penelope, but declined their mimed invitation for her and Constance to join them. 'Got a bit of work to do,' she called. 'But thank you. Another time, maybe.' The only other patrons were a young man she didn't recognise nursing a pint at the bar and an older couple from Little Wick sharing a sandwich at a table on the far side of the room.

Soon, she and Constance were huddled in a spot by the window, Sam had already provided refreshments, and they were logging onto free wifi.

'How's Hetty?' Maggie asked while they waited to connect.

'She's fine. She's excited about tomorrow night. Florence is taking her to dinner at *Table 12* in Beverley.'

'Fancy.'

'And expensive. Hetty is convinced Florence has something planned. She thinks she might be about to ask her to move in.'

Maggie squealed. 'How romantic. They're such a good couple. But how would you feel about Hetty moving out?'

'Let's see if it happens first, then we'll cross that bridge.' Constance busied herself adjusting the brightness of the screen.

Hetty and Constance had lived together over the bakery for as long as Maggie had known them. It would be a big change. Maggie had been terrified to find herself living alone after years of being married to Nicholas, but once she relaxed and realised she could do what she wanted, when she wanted, and add as much colour to the house as she wanted, she quickly grew to love it. She hoped Constance would, too. If it came to it.

Taking over from Constance, Maggie navigated to the newspaper website where she'd first seen the missing persons report for Harold Emmerson and brought the baker up to date with the events of the last day or so. Since half the village, if not all, had been outside The Pleasant Pheasant that morning, she reasoned that most of the details were no-longer confidential, and she trusted Constance to keep the sensitive aspects under wraps: Harold's identity; his relationship to Dorothy; how he was run out of town.

'We're looking for proof he's still alive, or that he was for some time after 1983,' said Maggie as she opened Facebook and Twitter. 'I won't bother with TikTok or even Instagram because it's mostly just younger people on there.'

'Do you think you'll find him after all this time?' asked Constance. She ripped open a bag of crisps and pushed them into the middle of the table, where they could both help themselves.

Maggie eyed the packet and turned up her nose. She hated prawn cocktail.

'I don't know, but we've got to try, for Dorothy's sake. Laurel, Jayne from Dandelions, and Albert are all looking too, in different places. Between us, I'm sure we'll find something. Or the vicar will find a death certificate, hopefully one dated a long time after the eighties.'

They set about their work, taking it in turns to try out variations on Harold's name. Constance even had the idea to contact the newspaper and ask to speak to the original reporter. She sweet-talked Sam into letting her use the phone. Unfortunately, but unsurprisingly, the paper said the reporter hadn't worked there for years, and no-one could give her any new information.

Drawing blank after blank, they ordered more drinks and a plate of chips. Those Maggie had no trouble wolfing down. She hadn't had any lunch yet – very unlike her – and she was ravenous.

'I think we've exhausted all avenues,' Maggie sighed.

'What about Myancestors.com?' Constance nudged Maggie out of the way, brought up the page and logged in. 'I've got an account already set up, not that I've ever used it for much. Our family is not very exciting. No kings or queens in our family tree.'

A couple of clicks of the mouse and it was obvious they hadn't solved the case. Emmerson was a popular name, and there were so many H. Emmersons it would take forever to sift through the records. They knew his age, but Maggie couldn't remember his exact date of birth. They narrowed the search, reducing the number of hits, but not enough.

'I can get his date of birth from Dorothy or Laurel, and with enough time we can work through them all.' Maggie yawned. She'd been full of hope they would stumble across him within half an hour or so, but she hadn't appreciated how many rabbit holes there were in which to get lost. Maybe Jayne was having better luck.

She let Constance continue tapping away while she surveyed the room. The archaeology group hadn't moved but Christopher had arrived and was in an animated conversation with the elderly couple.

On the verge of suggesting to her companion that they take a break, Maggie's gaze was drawn to the young man at the bar. The pint he'd been working on when they had arrived had been replaced with a new one, but what snagged her attention was his obvious, and growing, frustration with the mobile phone in his hand. He kept pressing at the screen, then holding it to his ear before sighing loudly, lowering it and repeating the process. She was about to go to his aid when Sam beat her to it, telling him there was a complete lack of signal in Elderwick.

'For a quid, you can use the phone at the end of the bar there,' Sam offered.

Maggie checked the laptop screen to see if Constance had made any progress, but she couldn't help but hear the stranger's side of the conversation.

'Doctor Nightingale?'

Oh, he was calling Laurel. This could be interesting.

'It's Michael Wishart, Jessica's colleague. ... Yes... Thank you, yes. Look, sorry to bother you, and I know it's earlier than planned, but is there any chance we could meet now? ... No, I'm at the pub in the village, the erm, The Fox something. ... No, don't worry if you've not had chance to do much yet. The reason I'm calling is... it's about Jessica.' He lowered his voice. 'No, not that.'

Maggie tried not to breathe so she wouldn't miss a word.

'Thing is, I got a call from the police this morning. They wanted me to go to the station. ... Yes, in Beverley. They said– they said that they're treating Jessica's death as suspicious. Something about a lack of footprints and– ... Yes, of course. Thank you.'

Maggie clapped a hand over her mouth to stifle a gasp. She bet the others in the bar were equally shocked as they listened in on the call. Not much more was said, but from what she could gather, Laurel had agreed to meet Michael. Disappointingly, not in the pub.

After he'd hung up and paid for the use of the phone, he lifted a bag from the floor by his bar stool and hurried out of the door. The second the door was closed, the chatter started.

'Did you hear that?' asked Sam to no-one in particular. 'That's the young woman we thought was killed by the cows.'

Beth's chair scraped across the flagstones with a ghastly noise as she stood, her face white.

Dr Delgado reached for her, but she moved, and his hand missed. 'It's okay, it's okay,' he repeated.

'It's not okay, Rik,' she said. 'She was our responsibility and... oh, her poor friend. We should have spoken to him. We shouldn't have let him just leave. How could this happen? How could someone have harmed Jessica deliberately?'

When she paused for breath, her husband stood and took her in his arms. 'It will all be okay,' he murmured, rubbing her back as she buried her head in his neck. 'It's been a tough week for us all. I think we should cancel the rest of the dig and let another team take over. Come on, let's get you back to the hotel.'

Beth sniffed and let him lead her away from the table.

'Lin, Pen, you too. Come on,' he said calling back to them. 'You shouldn't have had to find out like this. Pen, let me run you home, and Lin, I can take you back to Drumble's Hive. You can wait outside in the shade while I get the car. I'm parked just up the road.'

Christopher met the group as they reached the door with an offer of any help and support they might need. Dr Delgado clapped him on the back and Beth thanked him.

'I'll say goodbye,' she added. 'We'll leave what's in the meadow for the next team, but none of us will set foot there again. Take care, Reverend.'

He clasped her hand in both of his. 'God be with you.'

Maggie and Constance watched the archaeologists leave, then gawked at each other.

'Murder,' Constance breathed.

'*Another* murder,' Maggie corrected. 'I feel sick.' She pushed away the bowl, still with a few chips left in the bottom.

Before she could find the words to carry on, the laptop binged. 'What was that?'

Constance blushed. 'I wasn't getting anywhere with the ancestry site, so I logged into Sylvia's dating profile. That was a message coming in. Sorry.' She read from the screen. 'Oh crap,' Constance muttered. 'Carter wants to meet. In real life.'

Chapter 42

Laurel

Laurel rarely panicked, but she was rattled by her conversation with Albert. Fury born of fear quickened her pulse. Although Albert had promised to fill in the gaps in her hypothesis, he'd done no such thing. He'd even refused to confirm whether Jurgen's death was an accident. All he'd said was that it wasn't his place to tell the story and that he was sorry. He wouldn't be drawn further, and she'd stormed out, slamming the door. If he was innocent, or if everything he'd done was to protect a friend, why couldn't he admit it?

Barely back inside Myrtle Cottage, she heard her phone ringing and snatched up the receiver. Michael's voice on the other end caught her off-guard. She'd forgotten they were due to meet. She strove to keep her tone steady as she responded to his news. Jessica's death had been confirmed as suspicious. She swallowed her frustration at Ben for not having updated her himself. Eager to know what Michael had to say about the development and to observe his reaction in person, she readily agreed to keep to their arrangement, despite Ben's caution, and headed out to her office.

Michael had been calling her from the pub. She had to get a

move on. It wasn't far from her home to the office, but it was another humid day, and she didn't want to be a sweaty mess by the time she got there.

He was outside the door when she arrived. His eyes bloodshot and his hair mussed up. Once she'd got him settled upstairs, tissues and a glass of water on the table, she urged him to tell her what the police were saying about Jessica's death.

He gripped his knees, leaning forwards and avoiding eye contact. His voice was rough when he spoke. 'They told me about the post-mortem, and that they found some stuff in the wound.' His hand strayed to the back of his own head. He seemed to realise what he was doing and returned it to his lap. 'They said she was hit, that it wasn't an accident, that it wasn't from a fall or anything. Someone hurt her.' He met her gaze and repeated, 'Someone hurt her, someone ended her life deliberately. Why? She never did anything to anyone.'

'I am so sorry, Michael.' She wanted to ask questions about the investigation, but she restrained the urge. 'Is there anything I can do?'

'No. I don't know. I just needed someone to talk to. I thought they wanted me back at the station to talk more about Jess's missing persons work, but then they dropped this on me. Actually, I was scared they were going to arrest me. I don't think it was a completely informal chat. Jesus.'

'Do you know who it was Jessica spoke to about the project in the first place?'

'She didn't say. The last time I was here, after we met, I went to the station. I was told it was DI Coral in charge of the bones case, so I asked to see her. I was going to talk her through the whole folder, you know, about Emmerson and Sturm, but she wasn't there, so I ended up speaking to her colleague.'

Now she knew he was lying. DS Hill had told Ben no-one

had been into the station to talk about Jessica's missing persons database.

She studied the man opposite. He dressed like a student, he had Jessica's research, but the truth was, he was a complete stranger. She had no proof he was who he claimed to be. Was he even enrolled at the university? It should be easy enough to check, but she couldn't do it with him sitting in front of her. Come to think of it, she was unlikely to reach anyone in admissions in York on the weekend. It would have to wait until Monday.

Could he have harmed Jessica? He was one of the few people who'd known she was in Elderwick, but what motive could he have?

'I only met Jessica the once, but your department must miss her.' She had an idea and wanted to check it out, but she'd have to tread carefully.

'We all do, very much. She was a brilliant member of our team, and her research was amazing.'

'I'm sure yours must be, too? I haven't had chance to ask, what project are you working on?'

His eyes darted to her face, then away. 'I'm looking at people who use dating apps. It's more complicated than it sounds, but I don't want to bore you.'

'I bet it's fascinating. There's a lot of overlap with anthropology and psychology, by the sounds of it.'

'There actually is, so much overlap. Maybe I could tell you more about it some time after all this is... settled. I've got one year left, but I'm hoping to get funding for a PhD next.'

'I'd love to know more. And a PhD too. Is funding hard to obtain these days?'

'Ha, you could say that. Bloody impossible is more like it. There's a lot of competition.'

She had her opening. 'Did I hear Jessica was up for a grant for her PhD?'

Michael's lips twitched. 'She was.' He snatched a tissue from the box and blew his nose. 'Sorry, I'm just messed up after today at the station.'

She would make a call to the university as soon as possible. She was convinced there was something he wasn't telling her. Laurel shifted forward on her chair. 'I can hear how much of a shock this has all been for you.'

He dumped the used tissue into the bin under the table and scowled. 'You know, they really scared me. They actually think I might have hurt Jess.' His hands balled into fists, and he thumped one on the arm of his chair. 'They kept asking where was I the night she was attacked? Had we argued? All that shit.'

'The *night*?' She shouldn't have interrupted, but she was thrown off when he'd said *the night* she was killed. 'Sorry, only I thought she'd died the morning she was... I found her?'

He was shaking his head. 'They said time of death was around midnight. She was seen leaving Drumble's Hive at eleven thirty. They said something about her... dying before it rained.' He screwed his eyes shut for a second. 'Wanted to know if I'd noticed the rain that night. I wasn't even here. I was in York.'

Before it rained? She was trying to remember what time the shower had been that night. She remembered waking up to hear the water rushing through the gutters. But she was sure it had been around eleven.

'Did you talk to them about Emmerson and Sturm today?' she asked. Again, she only had his word he'd spoken to the police.

'Yes, they took another copy of the file, same as I gave you. They flicked through it and asked if I knew anything about a ring or a key with initials scratched onto it. Items found with the bones.'

This was the first she'd heard about any markings on the key. 'Initials?'

'Yes, T C. I told them I've...'

T C... T C... T C. Laurel had stopped listening.

As quickly as she could, Laurel sent Michael on his way, having arranged to see him again on Monday. He'd been insistent. Next time, she'd make sure she wasn't alone in the building with him.

She watched from the window until he got into his car and drove away. After locking up, she dashed up the lane towards Saint Stephen's.

The church interior was gloomy after the dazzling sunshine, but the cool air was a welcome respite from the heat and humidity. As her vision adjusted, Laurel edged inside and closed the door. Although raised Church of England, with all its carol services and harvest festivals, she was unfamiliar with the customs and expectations of being in a church. She had no clue if churches were usually empty on a Saturday afternoon nor if Christopher was likely to be there. If not, she would visit the vicarage next.

'Vicar?' she called in a voice too soft to penetrate more than five yards. She cleared her throat and tried again. 'Christopher?'

'Down here.' The disembodied words floated out of the shadows from somewhere ahead of her.

Emboldened, Laurel walked down the aisle searching for the owner of the voice. 'Ah, there you are,' she said as Christopher materialised beside the church organ brandishing a feather duster.

'Laurel, two visits in one week. Careful, you'll be coming to Sunday services before you know it.' He grinned at her.

Was it impolite to laugh or worse, not to laugh at his joke? What came out of her mouth was between a gurgle and a choking sound.

He set down the duster and brushed the remnant of a cobweb from the sleeve of his blue shirt. 'I told Dorothy she should take the day off, what with everything that's happened, so I'm on cleaning duties,' he explained. 'You're a good excuse for a break. How can I help today?'

On her way over, she'd thought about what she wanted to say, but now, in front of Albert's friend and the village vicar no less, she hesitated. Christopher pointed to a pew, and they sat as he waited for her to summon her courage.

'Do you remember what time it rained last Sunday evening?'

The vicar frowned. 'That's what's so urgent?'

'No, but I would like to know.'

He stared ahead at the stained-glass window behind the altar. 'It was about eleven. I was heading for bed after listening to the *Westminster Hour* on Radio Four and it was just starting to rain. I shouldn't listen to that programme. It gets my blood up and isn't conducive to a restful night, but I feel I have a duty to remain informed and it often provides fodder for a sermon, as you can imagine.'

Eleven, that's what she'd thought.

'But what is it you really came here to say?' he prodded.

Once she started, it all came out in a rush. She told him about Albert, and the photo and her hypothesis, which Albert had refused to confirm or deny. 'I know you said I should trust him, and he'd tell me what he knew if and when he could. Well, he told me some of it, but he's still holding back.'

'I see,' was all Christopher said, before lapsing once again into silence, giving her chance to continue.

'And a few minutes ago, I found out there were initials on a key found with the remains. At first, I thought they must be a person's name, but... if they're not, then I think I might know where the lock is that the key fits.'

'And this lock, it's at Albert's house?'

Her mouth turned down and bile rose in her throat. 'The initials are T C and Albert's shed is called Tumbledown Cabin. T C.'

She wanted Christopher to tell her she was wrong and jumping to conclusions. To her surprise, he reacted with another grin. 'I admit, it looks bad for our hero,' he joked, 'but T C could stand for so many things. And if I'm not wrong, Albert's shed can't be forty-odd years old. I can see you're concerned for your friend–'

'And so she should be,' crowed a familiar voice from the doorway to the vestry.

Laurel jolted in her seat and yelped.

Christopher jumped to his feet. 'Who's there?' he demanded.

DI Coral walked into view.

Laurel's stomach lurched. How much had she heard?

'There was me thinking I was so clever to guess T C might stand for The Church, but I think Albert's shed is a much better prospect. I knew he was in this up to his eyeballs.' She lodged her hands on her hips and sneered at them.

Laurel thought she was going to be sick. Had Coral heard what they'd been saying? Even if she hadn't heard it all, had she just handed this loathsome woman enough to go after Albert?

The DI swaggered forwards, holding up the key itself in her gloved hands. 'I was about to try it out on your locks, vicar, but I think I might just head on over to Birch Lane right now. Get all this cleared up before tea.' She came to a stop by the eagle lectern and tutted, glaring at the key and rubbing her gloved fingers together. 'How is it still covered in bloody ashes?'

Laurel blinked at the mention of ashes. Her theory about the fire pit being co-opted as a grave could be correct.

'Nothing to say?' Coral mocked them.

Refusing to give the woman the satisfaction, Laurel kept her mouth shut and took the opportunity to squint at the key. It was a fight to keep her expression neutral; it was the wrong type of key! When she'd been round to feed Albert's menagerie, whilst he was at the police station, the shed hadn't been locked. However, she'd noticed the lock, and it was the type opened by a cylinder key, not an old brass mortise key like the one Coral was holding.

Coral scowled at her and stowed the key in an evidence bag, which she placed into a pocket. Tugging off her gloves, she located her mobile phone and jabbed at the screen. 'Bloody thing,' she muttered upon discovering the lack of signal. 'Vicar, I need to use your phone. Tell you what, why don't you make me a nice cup of tea while I make some calls?' The detective pointed at Laurel. 'You stay here. I don't want you running off warning your friend. Vicar, after you.' She jabbed her thumb back towards the vestry.

Laurel made a show of slumping where she sat and plastered a sulky expression onto her face, but when Coral turned to walk away, she whispered to Christopher, 'Stall her.'

Christopher winked.

Laurel had no intention of sitting and waiting. When Coral had demanded a cup of tea, it had all fallen into place. She knew what T C stood for, and she knew what Albert had been holding back. She had to get back to Albert's before the police arrived.

Chapter 43

Laurel

Christopher had closed the door behind him as he led the DI away to the vestry to make her calls. The second they were out of sight and out of hearing, Laurel sprang from her seat. She raced back up the aisle, out of the door and around to the back of the church, crouching low so she wouldn't be spotted from the vestry windows.

She would have to be very unlucky for Coral to glance out at the exact time and in the right direction, but she wasn't going to take any chances. It was her fault Coral was headed for Albert's, so it was her job to limit the damage. Sure, Albert hadn't told her everything, but she'd bet on Albert being on the side of the angels over Coral any day of the week.

Bursting through the gap in the graveyard wall, Laurel swung right and ran along the narrow track to Wayback Lane. Darting across the road she passed the primary school and eventually burst out onto West Street. There was no traffic, so she hurried up the middle of the road, past the gates to Elderwick Hall, to the bottom of Birch Lane. She couldn't hear any cars, let alone any sirens, and guessed she was well ahead of a raiding party.

'Please be in, please be in,' she panted as she covered the remaining ground to Albert's front door. She caught sight of him through the window and heaved a sigh of relief. 'Albert, quick.' She banged on the door.

When he admitted her, she was upset by how drained he looked, but she didn't have time to ask after his health. What she was about to do would ease his mind, she hoped. 'Where's the photo?'

'I can't–'

'The police are on their way,' she interrupted.

'What? Again? Why?'

She had to stop and bend over, gasping for breath for a good ten seconds. 'Coral,' she puffed. 'She thinks the key fits the lock on your shed and she's calling...' she paused again, '...I don't know, Hill, I assume, to come and check.' *Maybe Tillow, too,* she thought.

'Well, they'll be disappointed.' He sounded smug.

'I know,' she wheezed.

'Then, why the urgency?'

'The photo. You need to get rid of the photo.'

Albert wavered. Laurel didn't know how to explain quickly enough. Instead, she pushed past him into the living room, but the table was clear, the photo was gone.

'I thought it best it be out of sight,' said Albert.

'It's still here?'

'Yes, but–'

'It can't be here.'

His face fell. 'I'll get it. Can you... I shouldn't ask... but can you take it away?'

'Yes, I'll keep it at my house. They have no cause to search my belongings.' Her instinct was to get rid of it, maybe burn it, but a little voice cautioned that might be considered destroying evidence. Until she heard the full story from

Albert, Dorothy, Jo, whoever, the photo would simply have to remain hidden.

Albert thudded up the stairs and banged around above her head. She crept towards the window and checked up the lane. Nothing was moving, no-one was headed their way. Yet. 'Come on. Come on.' Christopher wouldn't be able to stall Coral for long, and as soon as the DI saw Laurel was missing, she'd know where she'd gone and why.

'Here it is.' Albert handed over the picture with a shaking hand. 'We will explain, I promise. Now go.'

She clasped it and went out through the kitchen. There was a loose panel in the garden fence, and she was sure she'd be able to squeeze through to her own garden.

Aroon, in his favourite spot atop the partition, regarded her with an imperious eye.

It took a fair amount of pushing and shimmying, but she made it to the other side with only a couple of scratches. Letting herself in through her French windows, she was nauseated all over again. What had she done?

She collapsed onto her sofa and waited for the shivering to subside.

The photograph was in her hand. She should look and confirm what she suspected. It was hard to believe she hadn't noticed it straight away, but she was so used to Jo wearing an apron, she hadn't given it a second thought.

Laurel lifted the print up close and scrutinised the image. There it was, plain as day. Jo wearing an apron printed with a simple design: a cup of tea and a name, Tea Cup, T C. It must have been the name of the café before it moved premises and became The Pleasant Pheasant. She could have smacked herself in the head for not figuring it out sooner. It was only the other day she'd been admiring the old photos on the wall of the bakery. Photos in which, if someone looked closely enough, they would see how the bakery was once a teashop, before it had become The Plump Tart. Even if the locks had been changed along with its purpose and name, Tillow would know about it, he'd remember, and he'd hone in on Jo. That was what Albert was afraid of. He was protecting Jo.

Hiding in her living room at the back of the cottage, Laurel heard cars arrive, heard them knocking next door. Tillow's rough voice demanding entry. She pictured them trooping through the garden to try the key in the lock of the shed. It was of great satisfaction to her to know that Tillow and Coral had been thwarted. She wished she could see the disappointment on their faces when the key didn't fit.

For a moment, she enjoyed the schadenfreude, until she remembered that two people were dead and at least one murderer, possibly two, remained at liberty. A black cloud descended. She willed away the minutes until the police would be gone and she could get answers from her neighbour.

The raised voices outside suggested the search was over and the intruders were leaving. Car doors slammed, engines started, then receded into the distance.

Five minutes later, there was a knock at the door.

Albert rubbed a callused hand over his eyes. 'Jurgen's death. It was an accident.'

Laurel sagged against the wall. Never had she been so relieved.

'And Tillow is as much a problem now as he was then.' Albert was shaking. 'Can we sit down?' Once seated in the living room, he continued. 'Dorothy wasn't the only one with an abusive husband.'

Laurel's breath caught. Did he mean Jo? Jo was so small, and the Jurgen in the photo towered over her diminutive form.

'He beat seven shades out of her, and everyone knew it. Dorothy cautioned Jo against going to the police, but – damn it – I talked her into it. I even went with her, and we demanded she be seen by a WPC. But Tillow weighed in anyway and gave her the same short-shrift and threats as we'd known he would.

'It was an accident, Jurgen's death, but we knew if we reported it, Tillow wouldn't believe it. He'd have come down on Jo like a ton of bricks. But after Harold, we couldn't claim Jurgen had also gone missing. Instead, we put it around that Jurgen had abandoned Jo and gone to Germany. Jo knew he had next to no relationship with his brother, and his parents were deceased, so we faked a postcard and sent it to the brother and hoped no-one would come looking for him. And for a long time, no-one did.'

Laurel swallowed the lump in her throat. 'Why didn't you fight against the development of the meadow? You must have known his grave might be uncovered?' Albert had been interested in the plans from the start, but she wasn't aware of him coming out in opposition. Dorothy had, but she was against every change in the village. Her resistance was par for the course.

'We didn't know he was there.'

'What? How?' She'd lost the thread somehow.

'It was Dorothy's brothers again. We owe so much to Dale and Donald, and I never had the chance to thank them properly. Dorothy had known all along what Jurgen was doing. She'd lived that life and saw the signs. It was Dorothy to whom Jo turned when Jurgen died, and Dorothy made the call to her brothers. They cleaned up and said they'd get rid of the body. We didn't ask, and they didn't say how or where.'

'Did you know as soon as the bones were unearthed?'

'When I heard about the ring, I did. The ring and the key are things we should have thought of at the time, but frankly, we were all too rattled to see straight.'

'And you didn't think the body would turn up again at the edge of the village?'

'No, we did not. And then when you mentioned those old photos up in the bakery, I began to appreciate exactly how much bother we were in. How many traces linger in the village. I've been wracking my brains for a way to remove one of them in particular, but couldn't fathom how to do it without arousing suspicion from you or Maggie. Then, old dunce that I am, I left this one lying around where anyone could find it.' He picked up the photo of Jo in her apron. 'I should have burned it the moment I found it. This is all my fault. How Jo has held it together... they're formidable, those women, Jo and Dorothy.'

'Albert, it most assuredly is not your fault, and I am so sorry I doubted you.'

He gave her a sad smile. 'No need for apologies. Besides, I'm afraid you're a part of this now, too.'

Chapter 44

Maggie

The news that Jessica's death was being treated as suspicious had left Maggie itching to speak to Laurel, but Laurel would be busy with Michael for a while and a more immediate issue had presented itself.

'What do you mean, Carter wants to meet? Why would he want to do that?' she asked Constance. Panic fluttered in her stomach.

'That's what he says. Listen:

> Hi Sylvia let's not wait let's meet. Tomorrow 8pm The Queen's Arms in Willerby. What do you say?

'This version of Carter claims to live in Hull, making Willerby reasonably easy for both of us. What do you think?'

'Well, you're not going, obviously.'

'Why not?'

With an effort Maggie didn't say what she really thought, that it was a reckless idea and only a loon would agree to meet with a confirmed scammer. Instead, she focused on an alternative reason for Constance not to go. 'You used Hetty's photo for Sylvia. What's he going to do when someone he's already conned money from shows up and he recognises you? He might hurt you.'

Constance pouted. 'I hadn't thought about that.' She reread the message. 'I still think I should go. I can disguise myself and get there early, then watch for when he arrives.'

Maggie tried a counter argument. 'First, The Queen's is a big place, you might miss him completely. Second, you say he's using the same picture on all his profiles, but it can't really be him, so how would you even know who to look for? And third, I still don't understand why he would want to meet in real life? It's worrisome.'

'Why don't you come with me? We'll just look like two women out having a nice meal together. If there's two of us, we stand a better chance of spotting any man on his own who looks like he's waiting for someone. We might even get a photo of him and then we can report him.' Constance typed and an affirmative reply appeared on the screen.

'You're going to go whatever I say, aren't you?'

'Too right. I want to look this bastard in the eyes. I may be a disabled woman, but it doesn't mean he gets to take advantage of me. I am not inconsequential.'

'Of course you're not. And I thought you were only going to watch him. Now you're talking about confronting him?'

'It'll be in a crowded pub. What's he going to do?'

In her mind, Maggie imagined Constance going to her car and Carter, having lain in wait, appearing from behind and attacking her. She shook her head. It was too awful to contemplate. 'You're not going alone.'

'Great. I'll book a table for two for seven-thirty tomorrow evening. I'm telling him I'll be there.' She hit send. It was done.

Chapter 45

Laurel

Following their talk, Albert had gone to see Jo. He'd asked to go alone and said he'd call round later to let Laurel know what Jo wanted to do. Left alone, her brain went into overdrive. Of all the questions remaining, the one head and shoulders above the others was the manner of Jurgen's death.

The presence of the ring and the key in the makeshift grave, and Albert's knowledge of them, dispelled any remaining doubt that the remains were Sturm's. But how had he died? Albert had said it was an accident, but he hadn't gone into detail. Had Jo, the survivor of Jurgen's fists, and feet, and words, been the only other person present when the fateful event occurred? If so, who was to say it truly was an accident? And if not, who could blame Jo if she had fought back against her abuser?

Tillow, that's who.

As she reached the point where she thought her head would burst, she heard Maggie's knock at the door.

'We need to talk,' Laurel said.

'We have to talk,' said Maggie in unison.

Without even pausing to get tea and cake, they each took a place on the sofa, notebooks open and ready on their knees.

'Should we get Albert?' asked Maggie, her knees jiggling up and down.

Everything she had learned about Jo and Jurgen, and Albert's subterfuge, was buzzing in Laurel's head, but with an effort, she focused on Maggie. 'He'll be round later. But we shouldn't wait. Do you want to go first?'

'No, no, I don't have the news. You do. You met with Michael, and he confirmed Jessica was murdered?'

'How do you... never mind. Yes, it looks like it's official now. Jessica's death wasn't an accident. I don't know half the details, but what I do know doesn't add up.' Laurel walked Maggie along the timeline as she knew it.

'And what parts don't make sense?' Maggie asked, pen poised.

Laurel had been covering the same ground in her head and was increasingly certain that the inconsistencies were the key to identifying Jessica's killer. Whoever it might be.

'According to the police, Jessica was last seen at Drumble's Hive at eleven-thirty on Sunday night and the time of death was around midnight. However, the police told Michael she was killed *before* the downpour that evening, but the rain started at eleven.'

'Why was she going out at that time of night? The pub would be closed, and there's no other nightlife in Elderwick.'

'Best guess, she was going to meet someone, but I've no idea who.' She sketched some boxes in her book and labelled them.

WHO

WHY

HOW

'Let's think about *why*. Why would anyone want to harm Jessica? What do we know about her?'

Maggie peered at Laurel's page and copied the boxes and headings into her own notebook. 'We know she is– was an anthropology masters student at York University, and was invited here by Lin to help identify the bones. She has a colleague, Michael...?'

'Wishart.'

'And based on Jessica's research, and assuming Dorothy told the truth that Harold was still alive when he was run out of Elderwick, we've concluded the remains in the meadow belong to Jurgen Sturm?'

'Yes, we can be certain of it.' After the ritual of swearing her to secrecy, Laurel told Maggie about Jo. 'Albert's speaking to her now.'

'Jo? No, I don't believe it! How ghastly for her. And she's had to keep it secret all this time because of Vincent Tillow.' Maggie's dislike of the man was written across her face.

Laurel was reluctant to voice her next concern. 'Even if Jurgen's death was an accident, would Jo kill to protect her secret?' Anticipating Maggie's shocked objection, she pressed on. 'Think about it: Jurgen's body is dug up. Next Jessica turns up brandishing a file on Jurgen, and then she's killed. It's too much of a coincidence to be unrelated.'

Maggie was staring at her like she had two heads. 'Don't talk nonsense. Jo didn't murder Jurgen, and she certainly didn't attack Jessica.' Spots of colour bloomed on her cheeks. 'And before you even think it, just because Albert and Dorothy know about Jurgen doesn't mean they are suspects in Jessica's death either.'

Laurel put aside her book and pen. 'I don't want to think it's possible, but who else could it have been?'

Maggie's nostrils flared. 'Then don't think it. These people are our friends. I've known them for years. They wouldn't dream of harming another human being. No, we have to go back to the beginning and consider again who could have had reason to harm Jessica that has nothing to do with Jurgen's body being found. What's more, it simply can't be anyone from Elderwick. She was only here a day and a half.'

Stung by Maggie's words, Laurel sat quietly. She wasn't sure she was ready to let go of Jo as a suspect and Jurgen as the link but recognised she wouldn't be able to discuss it further with Maggie.

'The obvious people to look at have to be the others in the archaeology team,' Maggie continued, as though nothing had happened. 'Or this Michael, her fellow anthropology student.'

Laurel had to concede it was a good point. 'We could talk to Dr Delgado, if we can find him before he hears the news...' She trailed off because Maggie was shaking her head.

'He was in the pub when we all heard Michael on the phone telling you the news.'

Of course he was. 'How did he react?'

'He was calm. It was Beth who took it especially badly.'

'She was there too?'

'And Lin and Penelope. Dr Delgado said they should abandon the dig.'

'Did you get a sense the news wasn't a surprise for any of them?' She wished she'd been there to see first-hand how the revelation had been received.

'I'm not sure. They all seemed shocked. As did Sam and Christopher.'

'Was there anyone *not* in the pub?' Laurel groaned. 'Sorry, it's just that now everyone knows the police are looking harder at the incident the guilty party will be on their guard. I bet they thought they'd got away with it when it was blamed on the cows.'

Maggie grasped her by the shoulders and turned her, so they were face to face. 'We can do this. We've done it before, more times than I'd like. We're good at this. Now focus and we'll make a list of possible culprits and go through them one by one.'

A familiar fizz started up in Laurel's stomach. They *could* do this.

'Plus, if we don't work out who it was, the police are going to blame Jo and that would be a hideous miscarriage of justice.'

Was Maggie being naïve to exonerate Jo so quickly? Whether or not she was, it made sense to consider other possibilities. 'You're right; we need to think who else might have a motive.'

'As far as the archaeology team goes, no-one had a reason that I'm aware of, but I don't feel I know Dr Delgado or Beth well enough to be certain.' Maggie flipped to a page near the front of her book. 'However, I wrote down something Penelope told me. It was the Sunday afternoon, before Jessica was... you know... Penelope saw her talking to Dr Delgado and she said they both looked very agitated. No, *shifty*, that was the word she used.'

'Does she know what they were talking about?'

'No, and I doubt Dr Delgado's going to tell us if he was the one who attacked her. Should we confront him anyway? He might give something away?'

Laurel flinched at the suggestion. 'Let's bear him in mind.' She wrote down his name and put a question mark beside it. 'What about Beth?'

'Penelope said that Beth turned up whilst Dr Delgado was talking to Jessica and that he looked tense when she appeared.'

'Maybe Beth had an issue with Jessica, or with Dr Delgado being around Jessica? Let's put it down. We can look into it more if necessary.'

Maggie duly made a note. 'We can rule out Lin and

Penelope, surely? And the rest of the team were sent back to York after the bones were found last Friday. I haven't seen any of them around since then.'

'It was Lin who invited Jessica here, but I don't think she lured her here so she could kill her. Talking with Lin and Penelope, I didn't get the sense there was any bad blood between the three of them?'

'I agree.'

'Who does that leave?' Maggie tapped her pen on the page. 'There are two other people new to the village, your old school friend, Jayne, and isn't there another Dandelions manager?'

'Alex,' said Laurel. 'I haven't met him, but Albert and Dorothy have. As for Jayne, I can't imagine her killing anyone. However, if Alex or Jayne thought Jessica might in some way derail or delay the dig, which would upset the opening of the new centre at Elderwick Hall, would that be motive for murder?' It was a stretch, the dig was on the proposed site of a produce shop, there would be no reason to delay the opening of the centre for the sake of the shop.

'What about Michael?' asked Maggie. 'I know he's Jessica's friend, but what do we actually know about him?'

'Of all the people on the list, Michael is at the top for me. I'm going to call the university on Monday to ask about him. As it stands, I don't even know for sure he is who he says he is.'

'So, we've got Michael Wishart.'

'And Dr Delgado is a maybe, depending on what he was discussing with Jessica.'

'Which we'll probably never know. So, what now?'

'I have no idea.'

Chapter 46

Albert

In a daze, Albert walked back from Jo's house to his cottage on Birch Lane. Whilst they'd been talking, Jo had taken a call from Lin, who was in tears. She was at Dorothy's house where Dorothy was being arrested as a suspect in the probable death of Harold Emmerson. The police had arrived with a key, insisting it was the key to Dorothy's holiday rental, Tulip Cottage. 'It didn't even fit,' Lin had cried, 'but they claimed the locks had been changed deliberately, and took her, anyway. She asked me to call and to tell you both to keep your mouths shut. Sorry, but that's what she said.'

Albert had tried to convince Jo it could still all work out. As soon as they could prove Harold was alive, the police would have to release Dorothy. But Jo was tired of the lies, and the stress caused by the lies. She refused to sit by and leave Dorothy locked up. Besides, it was only a matter of time, she said, before Tillow remembered the Tea Cup café and where it was located. The lock on the antique front door at the bakery had never been changed. The key would still fit.

Jo said she needed to give herself up voluntarily so she

would have a chance to tell her side of the story. Albert had argued, warning she was putting her head in the lion's mouth.

Despite his exhortations, Jo had made the call. He'd stayed with her as DI Coral and DS Hill arrived and formally arrested her on suspicion of the murder of Jurgen Sturm.

There was a light still on over Laurel's front door and he had promised to stop by and let her know what Jo had decided to do. When he was admitted and led through to the living room, he saw Maggie was there, too.

'I regret,' he said, subsiding into the armchair by the French windows, 'I am the bearer of bad news.' Furnished with a large brandy, he told them about Dorothy's arrest and how Jo had reacted by giving herself up. 'Tell me, please, that you have deduced the identity of Jessica's killer. For I fear Tillow, in his zeal, won't shy away from attempting to charge Jo with a second murder perpetrated to conceal the first.'

He saw how Laurel and Maggie looked at one another, and his heart plummeted. He was aware Laurel retained her doubts over the manner of Jurgen's death. If someone who knew Jo could think such things, what chance did Jo have against the police?

But his spirits lifted again when Maggie said, 'We've been making a list of possible suspects for Jessica's murder. If we're going to save Jo, we need to find the killer as soon as possible. Here's what we've got so far.'

They talked him through their thinking, and he had to agree, Rik Delgado and Michael Wishart were the most obvious people to investigate.

'We're just not sure where we go from here,' added Laurel.

Albert couldn't stifle his yawn. It had been a long day, literally and emotionally. 'It's late, I suggest we all get a good night's sleep and tomorrow, how about this: I'll go to church and pick Christopher's brains; Maggie, can you take a wander up to

Drumble's Hive and see if Lin is still there? Better yet if you can get hold of Penelope too. Ask Penelope again about what she saw between Jessica and Rik – Dr Delgado – and see if either of them remembers anything else helpful. Laurel, do you feel up to quizzing Michael further?'

There was uncertainly in her expression.

'If it would be unethical, we'll find another way,' he began.

Laurel waved him off. 'No, he's not my client, not officially, so it's not exactly unethical. I'm trying to think how to walk that line, you know, between him as grieving friend of the victim and him as murder suspect. I'll do it though. This has been a horrible week and if we can get to the bottom of the whole mess and get Jo back home, then I'll do what's needed.'

Their friendship and support warmed him more than the last swallow of brandy from his glass. 'Shall we reconvene mid-afternoon? It's going to be a hot one again tomorrow, so I'll whip us up a spot of homemade ice-cream. Raspberry ripple, I think.'

'I can provide the eggs.' Laurel offered. 'It's taken my chickens ages to start laying, but since they've started, I'm overloaded.'

'Perfect. *Bonne chance, mes amis.*' With stiff limbs, he raised himself out of the armchair and bid them goodnight.

Twenty minutes later, as he climbed into bed, he thought about all he and Dorothy had done to protect Jo over the years. And what he and Jo had done for Dorothy. There had been times when he'd questioned the wisdom of their actions, but on reflection, he was sure in his bones, it had been the right thing to do. And he'd do the same all over again. As, he suspected, would most of the village. Elderwick was a special place, where a neighbour could still turn to a neighbour and be given succour. Something the Tillows of the world would never understand.

Chapter 47

Laurel

She was going to take a stroll and if she just so happened to bump into an off-duty police officer who she just happened to know ran most Sundays on a route that took him past her favourite bench, it would simply be a happy coincidence. It had nothing to do with seeing him in shorts and a tight, sweaty running vest.

'Ben?' She'd practised her surprised tone and thought it came out quite well.

'Laurel, I don't usually see you out at this time on a Sunday.' He jogged on the spot and wasn't even out of breath.

She wanted to get him to sit, but he gave no sign he needed or wanted a break. 'I decided to make the most of the day while it's still cool enough to sit in the sun.' She patted the space beside her on the bench. 'Can I tempt you?' *Ugh, that had not come out as she'd intended.*

He wiped his forearm over his forehead, consulted his smartwatch, and began to slow his jigging about.

'Sure, I've done ten miles. I think I deserve a break.' He plopped down and tilted his face to the sun. 'What can I help you with today?'

'Am I that transparent?'

Now he caught her gaze. 'You do have a habit of only seeking me out when you want information, or when you've found another dead body.'

She swatted him on his shoulder. 'Not funny.'

'Sorry,' he said, not hiding his laughter. 'But seriously, is this about Jessica? I wanted to let you know myself, but it was late when I got home from work last night. Besides, you'll have heard by now, no doubt?'

'Of course.' Living in the village, Ben would know as well as anyone the efficiency of the grapevine. 'She was hit on the back of the head? And it definitely wasn't an accident?'

'Correct, and correct.'

She pictured Jo cooped up in some cold cell that smelled of vomit. It wasn't right. 'And they've arrested Jo.'

That got his attention. 'They've what? Why?'

'You didn't know?'

'I was keeping the peace outside the pubs in Saturday Market last night, and I'm not on the Jessica Marumo case. I was so beat after my shift I didn't hang around to catch up on the gossip. I know they had Jo in to ask about the remains in the meadow, but why would Coral think Jo was involved with *Jessica's* death?'

'I'm not sure she does, yet.' Once again, Laurel repeated what she'd worked out about Jurgen. 'After they arrested Dorothy, Jo gave herself up so she could tell her side about Jurgen.'

Ben raised his eyebrows 'Wait, they've arrested Dorothy too? What for?'

'For the death of her ex-husband, Harold Emmerson.'

'The other name on Jessica's list?'

'Yes, but he's not even dead. He was run out of the village in 1983 by–'

He held up his hands. 'Woah, I'm not the one you should be telling this to. Does Coral know all of this?'

'She will by now, but how much difference that will make...' Laurel shrugged. 'I don't even know if they've let Dorothy go home. We're all worried that Tillow is whispering in Coral's ear, and he'll convince her to charge Jo for Jessica too.'

Ben shifted so he was sitting forward, elbows resting on his knees. 'It doesn't really work that way. For one, Tillow isn't on the force anymore.' He furrowed his brow. 'But you're right, he does like to spread his opinions around. *Is there anything to link Jo to Jessica's death?'*

'Not that we know of.'

'We?'

'Me, Maggie, Albert. Oh, and Dorothy, Christopher, and, kind of, Jayne Clement from Dandelions.'

'The whole village then.'

'By now, probably.'

'I can't believe it. Poor Jo. Living with such an enormous secret all these years. So, she was married to this Jurgen Sturm, and he died in an accident?' He was shaking his head. 'It's good that she went in voluntarily, but it's been a long time she's kept quiet about it. That doesn't look good. We have to hope there's evidence on the body of how he died. Enough to prove it was an accident. Do you know how it happened?'

'No, Albert didn't say.'

His watched beeped and he silenced it. 'How can I help?'

She beamed at him. 'We're already searching for Harold Emmerson, to prove he's alive, but we urgently need to work out who did kill Jessica.'

'I was worried you were going to say that.' He sighed. 'I still can't believe Jo, Albert, and Dorothy covered up a death. They must have had heart attacks when the body showed up. Dorothy's brothers sound a few sandwiches short of a picnic.

They were lucky the Autumn Festival wasn't held in the same place in the years afterwards. I can see it now. They're digging a new fire pit, and there's old Jurgen. Ugh.'

It wasn't an image Laurel wished to linger over. 'Dorothy said Tillow is the type of man who thinks a husband has the right to hit his wife. Is he like that even now?'

Ben pulled a face. 'I expect so.'

'Is there anything else you can tell me about Jessica's death? Anything that would help us find her attacker?' Laurel asked.

'First off, you can't go running around chasing a killer. You could get hurt, and I'd really hate that to happen.'

He was making eye contact as he spoke. Her heart rate tripled. 'Do you... um... do you have any more details?' She was having trouble concentrating.

He lightly and briefly touched her knee, and electricity tingled where his fingers met her skin.

'I'm serious. This person has killed once already. It's dangerous. You could get hurt.'

Not that she wanted to be, but if she did get hurt, he'd probably come to visit her in the hospital. She wondered which pair of pyjamas would be best to wear.

'Laurel, are you listening?'

'Yes, I heard you.'

'But...'

'But we have to do something. What do you know?'

He blew out his cheeks and huffed. 'Honestly, not much, only what we both saw at the scene.'

'Talk me through it again anyway, please?'

'Fine, but if you think you've worked out who it is, you call the station, or me. Promise me that?'

She crossed her fingers. 'I promise.'

The narrowing of his eyes told her he wasn't fooled. Nonetheless, he acquiesced. 'She had no defensive wounds. I didn't see the back of her head, but I understand from DS Hill that the pathology report states there was a single blow. There was no evidence of other injuries from what I could see in the field. The ground immediately around the body was muddy, but there were no footprints other than those matching Jessica's trainers.' He shrugged. 'That's all I've got.'

'Is there any chance your footprints obscured something when you got close to check her pulse?'

'No. There were no other prints. Some hoof prints from the cows, but I'm as certain as I can be they weren't recent and that they weren't covering any prints either. Do *you* remember anything else?'

Closing her eyes, she conjured the image of Jessica's lifeless body lying in the mud and shuddered. 'No. The only thing I would say – and I'm no expert – is if she was hit on the back of her head, she must have turned her back on her attacker. She wouldn't have done that if it was someone she feared, would she?'

'She might if she'd been trying to run away.'

'True.' Laurel scuffed her feet in the dry dust beneath the bench. 'What about this lack of footprints? How can that be?'

'Beats me.' His watch beeped again. He frowned at the screen.

'Do you need to be somewhere?'

'Actually, I do. It's... I'm meant to be meeting up with someone. I should probably get going.'

She hated the disappointment that hit as he spoke. It must be the same person he was on a date with the other evening. 'Sure, don't let me keep you.'

He stood up, and she concentrated on brushing non-existent lint off her skirt.

'Be careful,' he warned.

'Sure.' *You're not even interested in him. Why are you being so pathetic?*

He was soon out of sight, jogging away up the lane. The joy of sitting in the sun had gone with him. She sighed. There was no point in wallowing; she would go and look for Jayne and ask about the search for Harold. That would kill half an hour.

Jayne proved easy to locate. She was painting the gates to Elderwick Hall, just round the corner from Birch Lane.

'Don't you have like a maintenance team to do that for you?' Laurel asked.

Jayne scratched her nose, leaving a smear of paint on her face. 'It's a gorgeous day and I don't do well sitting around idle. Anyway, I was hoping I'd bump into you. I tried your house earlier, but obviously you were out. I have information about Harold.'

Crossing her fingers, Laurel asked, 'You've found him?'

Jayne set down her paintbrush and leaned against the wall. 'Almost. I found a report detailing his sentencing for aggravated assault in 2018. The leopard didn't change his spots, more's the pity. He was sent to prison for five years, which I think is the maximum, so it must have been bad.'

Laurel did a rough calculation in her head. 'He would have been what, seventy, seventy-one, that's pretty old to be sent to prison.' She wrinkled her nose, not willing to contemplate how brutal his crime must have been.

'Trouble is, he's been moved around since he was put away, so I don't know exactly where he is right now.'

'Doesn't matter, we can prove he was still alive long after he left here.'

'I thought you'd be pleased. I don't know how Dorothy will

feel about it, though. We will have to think about how and when to tell her.'

Jayne was right. This could be distressing news for Dorothy. 'We can prove he wasn't killed, though, which is great. Can you email me what you found? I'll forward it to the police. Let me talk to Albert later and ask what he thinks is the best way to break this to Dorothy.'

'Sure thing.' Jayne picked up her brush. 'I'd better get back to this,' she gestured to the gates, 'before the bit I've done gets all sticky and I end up making a mess.'

Taking a deep breath, Laurel said, 'About yesterday. Thank you. I wasn't nice to you at school, and I'm ashamed of that.' She kept her eyes on the wall to Jayne's left. 'Thank you for forgiving me. And if you want, I'd like it very much if we could become friends, since you're going to be around.' Her smile was uncertain, but it was met with a chuckle.

'I'd like that very much, since I'm going to be around,' Jayne teased.

Laurel walked away with a spring in her step. Her earlier disappointment over Ben leaving her to go on another date was already fading. Who needed a man in their life when they had good friends?

Albert's cottage was her next port of call. He'd know how to break the news to Dorothy, and the sooner it was done, the better. The wind needed taking out of Vincent Tillow's sails. Proving him wrong about Harold might throw doubt on his judgment if he was trying to talk Coral into believing Jo had killed Jessica to hide the circumstances of Jurgen's death.

Approaching her friend's front garden, she could hear a voice from the back. She let herself in through the gate and followed the path round to the back of the house. 'Albert? It's me, Laurel.'

'You've got all this space, all the slugs and bugs you could ever want. You know better than to go wandering without me,' a stern voice lectured.

'Hello,' she tried again, emerging onto the patio. She couldn't see anyone, but the voice belonged to Albert, so he was there somewhere.

'Laurel?' His snowy head popped into view from amongst the raspberry canes.

'Do you have company?'

He chuckled. 'I was giving Aroon a talking to. He's been bothering the good folks up at Elderwick Hall. Got into their greenhouse and helped himself to some tomatoes. Naughty rooster.'

'Where is he?' She scoured the undergrowth, expecting him to launch another attack on her sandals.

'He's gone to sulk in the rhubarb.'

The rhubarb patch was further away towards the back hedge. It was probably safe to approach. 'I was chatting to Jayne a few minutes ago. She's found Harold.'

'And?' Albert stopped fussing with the canes, his expression a mix of fear and hope.

'He's been in prison and is very much alive.'

He sagged. 'Thank goodness. I can't say Dorothy will be pleased, but it's a blessed relief all the same to know the old cockalorum still lives... more's the pity,' he added under his breath. 'Tell me what else you know while I change into my good shoes, I'm going to go and give Dorothy the glad tidings.'

'They let her go?'

'With bad grace, I believe, but yes, she's home. After Jo's confession, they could hardly claim the bones belonged to both Harold *and* Jurgen.'

'That's something.'

'But I expect she and I remain at risk. I don't doubt we'll be charged with assisting Jo.' He grimaced and massaged his lower back. 'After I've broken the news, I'll drive her into Beverley, and we can let the bobbies know. That should put a potato into Tillow's exhaust pipe. The bones might not be Harold, but Tillow still believes Dorothy killed him.'

'Will any of this help Jo?'

'In all honesty, I don't know. It may be of use in explaining how Jurgen came to be buried in the meadow without Jo's knowledge. Naturally, we can't ask questions of Donald and Dale since they've passed, but Harold would be able to confirm their involvement with him. It's not so much of a stretch then to believe they would also come to the aid of their sister's friend.'

'*If* Harold's willing to give his side. I'm not sure he'll be eager to help Dorothy.'

'Mayhap he won't, but let's see where we get to, shall we? *If* we can get the police to listen to us. I know we're meant to meet this afternoon, but could we reschedule to, say, lunchtime tomorrow?'

Laurel mentally checked her work diary. 'I have a gap from eleven-thirty until one, will that do?'

'It will do splendidly. Shall we come to you?'

Arrangements made, Laurel followed Albert back to his kitchen, where he gave his hands a wash and switched his gardening shoes for a pair slightly less battered.

He peered at his watch. 'Since I will be otherwise occupied, would you mind being the one to quiz Christopher this morning? If you leave now, you could even make it in time for the service if you think you can stomach a bit of God this early in the day?' He winked. Like her, Albert was a loud and proud atheist.

'I'll skip the sermon. I've got some thinking to do about footprints, or the lack thereof.'

'Godspeed.'

'Yeah, and God be with you, because you're going to need all the help you can get with Coral and Tillow.'

Chapter 48

Maggie

At first glance, Drumble's Hive could be mistaken for a couple of roughly constructed treehouses amidst the woodland that blanketed the side of Elder Hill. Closer inspection, though, revealed well-worn paths between the cosy and determinedly solid huts made from local wood. The roundhouse in the centre of the commune even boasted a thatched roof. Maggie called hesitantly from the edge of the group of buildings. She'd met many of the residents over the years, and had attended most of their spring open days, but it felt impolite to wander in without an invitation.

After hearing from Laurel that their meeting had been postponed to the following day, giving time for Albert and Dorothy to tell the police about Harold, Maggie had opted for a different approach to her own part of the plan. With a thrill of anticipation, she imagined finding a witness, or uncovering a clue, that could crack the case of Jessica's murder.

'Hello there,' replied a young man who appeared by the cider press. He wore cut-off denim shorts and a tattered T-shirt that showed off bronzed, well-muscled arms.

Maggie blushed. 'Hi, my name's–'

'Maggie!' Lin came barrelling out of the roundhouse and rushed to greet her. 'Oh, it's so nice to see you. It's been such a crap week.'

Maggie held out her arms and Lin fell into them. The man by the press faded away, giving them some privacy.

'I'm sorry, it's all been a bit much,' Lin sniffed when she eventually let go and stepped back. 'I still can't get my head around it. That Jess was killed. It's... it's sick.'

'Is there somewhere we can talk?' Maggie asked. 'Jessica is the reason I'm here. We want to find out who it was that hurt her, and we think you might be able to help. If you feel up to it?'

Lin led Maggie to one of the small huts on the edge of a clearing behind the communal structure. 'Come on in. My roommate's out so we can talk. Do you want a drink? They make the most amazing apple juice here?'

Maggie accepted a glass. She was well acquainted with the beverage, Jo sold it at the café, and Sam in the pub. She sipped. It was sweet and earthy with a zing of tartness that lingered on the tongue.

Lin had given Maggie the only chair available while she sat on the bed, her arms wrapped around her shins, chin on her knees. 'I don't think I know anything that will be useful, but I'll try.'

Balancing her glass on a low table made of a tree-stump, Maggie considered the questions she'd prepared. There was no point in beating around the bush. 'Penelope told me she saw a heated conversation between Dr Delgado and Jessica last Sunday afternoon. Did they know each other from the university?'

Lin nodded. 'I would think so. It's not that big and our department is in the same building as anthropology.'

'Did they get on?'

Lin thought for a moment. 'I don't know that they actually

spoke to each other all that much. Jess never mentioned him. You can't think it was Dr Delgado that hurt Jess?'

Maggie chose her words with care. 'We're going through the details, that's all.' Then added, 'But could you keep this conversation to yourself for now?'

'Of course.' Lin bit her lip. 'Should I be worried?'

She looked so young and scared. 'No, I don't believe so.' Maggie hoped it was true. 'Tell me, have the police spoken to you about Jessica?'

'Barely. They were up here the other day, two of them in uniform. They asked how I'd known Jess and if she'd said anything about meeting someone on Sunday night. Which she didn't. I didn't even know she'd gone out.' A tear rolled down her cheek. 'They also spoke to two of the regular people here. I don't think they spoke to Pen at all.'

'Who else was it they spoke to when they were here?'

'Todd and Sparrow. Do you want to talk to them? Todd's who you saw a minute ago. I can get him. Sparrow's away for a few days, though.'

'Before you do,' Maggie said. It was off topic, but there was a different mystery she hoped to clear up whilst talking to the young student. 'A few days ago, Laurel saw you leaving Dorothy Little's house in tears. I know it's none of our business, but if she upset you, or said anything offensive... it's just she's not very...'

Lin groaned and pulled a face. 'Oh god, that. That was so embarrassing, bawling my eyes out. Ugh. What it was, was that DI Coral woman. It felt like she was blaming Jess's death on me, because I was the one who invited her here. I don't know if it was on purpose, but it got to me, you know? Anyway, Dorothy had heard, and she told me I shouldn't give a toss what other people think because they're all morons.'

Dorothy being supportive? That was a first.

'She invited me back to hers for a cold drink and we talked.

She's amazing. Did you know she's been volunteering for women's charities for years? She's even involved in TPSG Hull Dragons who support trans young people, amongst others. I ended up telling her that my parents haven't spoken to me for about two years now because of what they call my *lifestyle choices*. Dorothy just listened, you know? She didn't judge me and... well, I was a pretty emotional. She didn't upset me.'

Maggie was still digesting Lin's account when the young woman bounced up from the bed, stuck her head out of the door and yelled, 'Todd?'

He materialised by the door and stepped inside.

'I'll give you space to talk,' said Lin. 'Back in five.'

Maggie gathered herself and turned her attention to Todd. Keeping her eyes firmly away from his tanned arms and legs, she told him who she was and why she was there.

Todd shared with her how sad everyone in the commune had been to hear of Jessica's death, and how upset they'd been to learn it was probably murder. 'The police have already been to speak with us, but I have to say, they did a rather poor job.'

'Do you know who it was that saw Jessica on Sunday evening?'

'It was me. As I told the officers, I saw her leaving around eleven-thirty.'

'Were you not worried about her, a young woman going out so late on her own?'

He ran a hand through his delightfully tousled hair. 'It used to be safe here, but these last few years...'

'You were concerned, then?'

'Not really. She said she was meeting someone.'

Maggie's breath caught, her heart beat faster. 'Did she say who?'

'No. Sorry.'

Todd had nothing more to add and excused himself when Lin reappeared.

'Any joy?'

Maggie shook her head. 'Do you have a number for Penelope? Do you think she'd mind if you shared it with me? I'd like to speak to her, too.'

Lin rummaged in a backpack by the bed until she found her phone. 'It's useless here so I don't really keep it charged, but I think there's enough battery... yep, here it is.' She found a scrap of paper and a pen and jotted down the digits. 'Pen won't mind you calling. Her parents are keeping her at home since all of this, but she'll want to help too.'

'What about you? Have you thought about going back to York?'

'Beth's cancelled the dig now anyway, so I might.'

'That's a good idea.' She would prefer Lin to be well away from Elderwick until the culprit was caught. 'Until you go, if you need anything, anything at all, you know where to find me.'

Lin's lower lip trembled. 'You know, I don't have many people I can talk to. You, Dorothy, Laurel, and Albert, you've all been so nice. I wish I could stay here.'

Maggie thought of how close she was with her own, now grown, children. She couldn't imagine not being there for them, whatever was happening in their lives. 'I'm sorry you can't talk to your parents.'

Lin's face crumpled.

'Oh, my goodness. I'm sorry,' Maggie gasped. 'I shouldn't have said anything.'

'No, it's not that.' She clutched her stomach. 'It's just, it's all my fault. That police woman was right; Jessica's death is all my fault.'

Thrown by the sudden change of direction, Maggie asked,

'What do you mean?' How she wished Laurel were with her. Was Lin about to confess?

'It's my fault the team came to Elderwick,' Lin croaked. 'It's embarrassing, but I had a pretty awful childhood and years ago, I ended up as a Dandelions kid. It was the best two weeks of my life and ever since, I've tried to do what I could to pay it back, you know. When I heard about the new centre, I mentioned it to Dr Delgado.'

Maggie's panic dissolved.

'And I'm the one who invited Jess here, too, after I found the body. See, it was all me. If it wasn't for me, Jess would never have been here, and she'd still be alive.'

Maggie had shouldered more than her share of misplaced responsibility in the past. 'Lin, none of this was your fault. The only person to blame for Jessica's death is the person who killed her. Do you understand?'

It took a moment, but eventually, Lin nodded.

'And I promise you, we're going to find out who that person is.'

Chapter 49

Laurel

A flutter of apprehension stirred in Laurel as she approached the stile into the field where, almost one week ago, she'd found Jessica's body. So little time had passed, but Elderwick was in turmoil; residents being questioned, released, arrested, suspected of murder. It wasn't the tranquil escape to the country Laurel had dreamed of when she'd moved to this attractive East Yorkshire village.

A familiar unease gnawed. How much of it was her fault? She'd never set out to get involved, but if a murder happened on her doorstep, she could hardly ignore it. But had her interference been the very thing to draw the attention of the police to Dorothy, Jo, and Albert?

However, the blame couldn't be placed solely at her door. For nearly four decades, Jo had hidden the death of her abusive husband, and Albert and Dorothy had colluded. The death, Laurel was desperate to believe, had been an accident, but she had yet to see any proof of this claim.

Then there was Jessica.

Gripping the wooden post with a firm hand, she climbed the two steps up and over, dropping into the cow-free field. The farmer had not returned the animals. For a Sunday afternoon, the footpath was uncommonly empty. The only movement was the fluttering of the blue and white police tape in the feeble breeze.

She'd worn trainers similar to those that had been on the dead woman's feet. In the dry earth and browned grass, they made negligible marks as she walked away from the trod pathway. She lingered by the tape. There'd been no more rain since the night Jessica died. Jessica's prints – clear and well defined – and the hoof marks of the herd were unaltered. Just as Ben had reported, there were no other shoe prints visible. How was it possible?

Laurel retreated once more to the stile where she sat. What was the key to this mystery? Was it Jessica or was it Jurgen?

If it was Jessica, the motive lay with someone who knew the young anthropologist and who had known she was in Elderwick. The suspect pool was small. There were the members of the archaeology team and the few locals with whom she would have crossed paths during her brief stay. Like Lin, she'd been billeted at Drumble's Hive, but the residents of the commune had been there for years, were well known, and she couldn't imagine they had reason to harm Jessica. That left Lin, Dr Delgado, and Beth. Then there was Michael. More investigation was needed before she could rule him in or out.

On the other hand, if Jurgen was at the heart of events, it was those who had known him in life, and were perhaps present at his death, who would have cause to silence the one person in Elderwick who might have spoken out to identify him. She was back to Jo, Albert, and Dorothy.

She sighed and shifted on the bare wooden step, trying to find a modicum of comfort. The answers were there to be found. If only she could put the pieces in the right places.

She closed her eyes and tried to relax. There was something.

Something someone had said that didn't align with the facts she'd recently discovered. Her eyes snapped open. She had it.

Yesterday morning and the gaggle of long-term locals outside The Pleasant Pheasant. According to Maggie, these locals denied any knowledge of Jurgen Sturm ever having lived in Elderwick. But he *had* lived in the village. Were their collective memories so bad, or had they all been lying?

She nearly toppled off her perch when the next realisation hit her. It had to be a coincidence. It couldn't be what it seemed to be. When she'd first understood the initials T C need not refer to a person's name, but could be a building or a business, she'd made the connection with Albert's shed, Tumbledown Cabin, and Dorothy's holiday rental, Tulip Cottage. Later, when she'd worked out there was more in the photograph taken at the Autumn Festival than Albert wanted her to see, she'd known T C stood for Tea Cup, or more accurately, The Tea Cup, the name of Jo's original tearoom. But now she thought about it, Elderwick was strikingly full of T Cs.

Coral's guess had been uninspired, but valid; The Church. The home Maggie had recently moved to was named Thatcher's Cottage, and the allotments were called Turnip Corner, complete with a cute sign depicting an anthropomorphic turnip. There were at least three other buildings whose initials were T C: Turner's Corner; The Copse; and Thistle Crest.

What was going on?

From the far side of the village, the church bells rang. If she wanted to catch Christopher, she'd need to hurry. He invariably vanished soon after a Sunday sermon to have lunch with one of his parishioners.

By the time she reached South Street, her back was unpleasantly damp, and her head prickled with sweat. If her usual luck played out, she would run into Ben and his no-doubt gorgeous, cool new girlfriend. That would put paid to any idea she had of him ever asking her on a date. Not that she had to wait for him to ask her. She could ask him if she wanted, which she didn't.

Relieved, she reached Saint Stephen's without enduring any mortifying encounters and paused in the shade of the stone building to cool down. Congregants were trickling away. The days of there being a crowd were long gone.

'Another visit, my goodness,' quipped the vicar when he saw her. 'God *is* working in mysterious ways.'

'This whole village works in mysterious ways, Christopher. Speaking of, do you have a minute?' She tucked her hair behind her ears in an effort to temper the frizz.

'For you? Always.' He looked behind him, back into the porch. 'I think that's the last of them. Come on in, out of the heat.'

Laurel followed Christopher back up the aisle and down the corridor into the vestry. He was in his day clothes, as she thought of them, so didn't need to change.

As though he'd read her mind, he commented, 'It's too hot for the full get-up. I'm sure I quite scandalised Mrs Bishop, but I think she'll survive. We have to move with the times, and I've never been high church. Lemonade?' he offered, reaching into the small fridge by his desk.

'Thank you,' she held the chilled can against her cheek. 'I won't keep you long, and first, I want to say thanks for distracting DI Coral the other day. It was very helpful.'

He smiled. 'Albert told me as much. It was my pleasure. We're all God's children, but some are nicer than others.'

Christopher had allways been easy to talk to, and had never tried to convert her, which earned him bonus points.

Before saying anything further, she re-opened the vestry door, checked the hallway, then closed it firmly once more.

'Just checking we don't have any nasty little eavesdroppers today.'

'Good idea.'

She grinned.

'So, what are you grilling me about this time?'

'Jessica. Or more accurately, the suspects in her death.'

'Do you have suspects?' He leaned forward, interest written in his features. 'I was shocked to hear that what happened to her was no accident. We said prayers for her today.'

'There are a few people I'm thinking of, but I have no evidence against any of them.' Laurel outlined her central question: was she murdered because of Jurgen, or was her death unrelated to the body in the meadow? 'Have you had much contact with anyone from the archaeology team?'

He steepled his fingers and pursed his lips. 'I know you will appreciate my care in answering your question. What I can say is I haven't come across anyone or anything to make me suspicious or alarmed.'

This was a dance with which Laurel was familiar: professional confidentiality. 'Okay... can you tell me if you spoke with Jessica before she died?'

'I didn't have the pleasure.'

'Outside of the church, in your role as a person who lives in Elderwick, have you had much to do with the team?'

He chuckled, fully aware of what she was trying to do. 'Laurel, if there was anything I thought pertinent, and which I was permitted to share, I would. With you and the police.'

'Fair enough.' She finished her drink and placed the empty can in the wastepaper basket under the window. 'Just one more thing.'

'Yes, Columbo.'

'You mentioned how you like to hide... I mean, spend some uninterrupted time up on the roof? At any point when you were up there, whilst the dig was in progress, did you see anything unusual?'

'I really don't go up there that often,' he protested. 'And no, I can't think of anything. I see they're back at work now, though.'

That was odd. 'I heard they were packing up and leaving after everything that's happened.'

'I could be mistaken, but I'm sure I saw a newly dug patch of ground yesterday.'

'Can we go up and look?'

'I should be heading off. I'm having lunch with Mr and Mrs Canarvon today. Can you come back tomorrow, around about ten?'

Laurel swallowed her impatience. The vicar was a busy man, and she was quite capable of checking it out from ground level.

'Don't worry, I'll go over there and see if I can find it. Do you remember whereabouts it was?'

Without hesitation he replied, 'Top left-hand corner, in the long grass.'

It was time to try her hand at some archaeology, but maybe she would wait until nightfall and the cover of darkness, just in case.

Chapter 50

Maggie

'Are you nervous?' Maggie asked Constance.

'We're not actually going to meet Carter, whoever he really is, remember? We want to get a look at the real him, that's all.'

'You promise me you're not going to give in to the temptation to confront him and give him a piece of your mind?'

'You worry too much. We're going to sit there, see what he looks like, get a photo if we can. Then, once he realises he's been stood up and leaves, we'll have a nice meal. It'll be fun.'

Maggie was sure her blood pressure was rising. 'Taking photos feels like a bad idea.'

'If the opportunity presents itself, it would be daft not to get a snap.'

She huffed. 'What's more, if you're not intending to speak with him, why is it you're wearing your favourite dress?' Maggie had admired Constance's outfit when she'd arrived to prepare for their sting operation. She'd noticed the new strappy sandals too.

'Because I'm going out to eat with my favourite friend.' Her smile was all teeth. 'Come on, we're going to be late.'

Forty minutes later, Maggie pulled her blue Mini into a parking spot towards the rear of the pub car park.

Constance waved a placard at her. 'Park in the disabled bay. I've got my badge.'

'If we do that, he'll know we're here.'

'I'm not the only disabled person in the county, you know.'

'I know that, but shouldn't we try to be as incognito as possible? We can find a table out of the way so he can't see your chair, because if he does, he's bound to recognise you.'

'He thinks he's meeting Sylvia, so he'll be looking for someone who looks like Hetty.'

'Yes, but don't forget, he has also seen your pictures when he was talking to, and scamming, you. So, if he walks in and sees you, he'll twig what's up and run. Or worse.'

'Oh.' Constance's face fell.

'Quite.'

'This is why I need you with me. You're the brains of the outfit.'

Inside, Maggie scoped out the best table, and the bar manager was happy to oblige. Their position, away from the door, gave them a good view of the whole dining area whilst concealing Constance.

'And now we wait,' said Constance as she locked her wheels and studied the menu.

After a plate of fish and chips each, two glasses of Chardonnay for Constance, and a lime and soda that Maggie nursed throughout, they had exhausted their good humour.

'Not only does he scam me, now he stands me up! This man is unbelievable,' muttered Constance, as Maggie helped her back into the car.

Once she'd put Ernie, the lightweight folding chair, away in the boot, Maggie took her place in the driving seat but didn't immediately start the engine. 'Did you get any messages from him while we were waiting? Maybe he got held up?'

'No, nothing. Argh. I don't even know why I'm letting it bother me.' She thumped the dashboard.

'Because you're a nice person and you wouldn't dream of behaving in such a deplorable manner.' Maggie wasn't about to tell her friend how relieved she was that the man calling himself Carter hadn't shown up.

They'd watched the door like hawks and considered every man who had entered the premises since their own arrival, having already satisfied themselves he hadn't been there when they'd arrived. No-one who entered the pub came anywhere close to the person they were expecting. It wasn't as though they believed he would resemble his photograph, but they had assumed he would be an unaccompanied male and so relatively easy to identify. However, there had only been couples, a group of middle-aged businessmen, and a few families with young children.

'You're positive we didn't miss him?' Constance asked for the third time.

'Unless he was dressed as a woman, or is in fact a woman, then no, I think we can safely say he wasn't there.'

'I'm sending him a snotty message.' Constance bent her head to the screen of her phone and spent half of the drive home crafting a note expressing her indignation.

Maggie could tell she was still stewing as they came down the hill towards the village. Indicating to turn right onto South Street, Maggie frowned. 'Constance, I don't want to worry you...' Ahead, the street was blocked by two police cars and a small crowd of onlookers.

The moment they pulled to the curb, Ben was leaning down to speak to them through the window. 'Hetty's fine. She's had a bit of a bump, but she's okay.'

Constance stretched across Maggie. 'What's happened? What's going on?'

'Is your chair in the boot?' he asked.

Maggie nodded and Ben had a colleague remove it and set it up by the passenger-side door.

'There was a break-in and Hetty disturbed him. She got a bit of a knock as he was getting away, but she's been checked over and given the all-clear.'

'Oh my heavens,' said Maggie.

Hetty got out of the police car ahead of them, followed by Laurel and Jayne.

Sporting a lump on her forehead, Hetty reached them and gave her sister a hug. 'I'm fine. I wish everyone would stop fussing.'

'What happened? Ben said there was a break-in? You were meant to be out? Where's Florence?' Constance grilled her.

'Calm down, seriously. I know you love me, but I am injured and can only answer one question at a time.' Hetty feigned a swoon, her hand dramatically held to her head.

'You said you were fine,' Constance grumbled, evidently relieved to hear Hetty joking.

'Are we allowed in the bakery?' Maggie asked. 'I think I need to sit down.'

Ben, who had remained close by, answered. 'No. We're not sure if it was only the flat that was broken into, so until we've checked downstairs, we'll need you to stay out. Hold on.' He moved away to speak to another officer. When he came back, he suggested, 'You can wait in the pub if you like, and we'll come and find you when we're done. Sorry, it might be a while.'

Hetty wrinkled her nose. 'I don't think I can handle The Fox right now.' In spite of her initial reassurances, she was pale and drawn.

'What about if we sit on the bench on the village green?' Maggie suggested. 'It's a pleasant evening.'

Ben nodded. 'Fine by me. Laurel, Jayne, would you go with them?'

Hetty and Constance led the way, but Maggie hung back a few steps to talk to Laurel and Jayne. 'Why do you look like a pair of gardeners with your trowel and spade?'

'It's a long story,' said Laurel. 'Where have you two been?'

'It's a long story.'

With Constance being in her chair, Hetty, Maggie, and Jayne settled on the bench, while Laurel said she'd stand.

'Well?' Constance demanded.

'It's not an exciting story.' Hetty's hands had a slight tremor in them. 'Florence had to cancel dinner. Her mum's not well, so I came home. The back door was ajar, but I thought it was just you, Con. Thank goodness you weren't in. I was terrified you were in the living room and that he'd hurt you.' She had to stop and swallow a couple of times before she could speak again.

'I went upstairs, and I could hear a voice, but it was a man.' She paused. Constance placed her hand on Hetty's knee. 'He was muttering, something like "Where's the paper, and where's the bloody hair". I must have made a noise because he shut up. Then everything happened so fast. I saw him at the top of the stairs. Next thing I know, he's pushing me out of the way, and I banged my head.' She touched the lump. 'Before you ask, I didn't get a good look at him. The light on the landing was on, but not the one on the stairs, so his face was in shadow, and I think he had a scarf over his mouth and nose.'

Laurel frowned. Why would anyone be looking for hair? She wanted to interrogate Hetty further, but Ben came jogging over.

'Have you got somewhere else you can stay tonight?'

Hetty's face fell. 'We can't go home?'

'It's going to take us a bit longer than I thought. Rather than hang around, best you get inside and get some rest, like the paramedic told you.'

'You can stay at mine,' Laurel and Maggie spoke at once.

'Or there's more than enough room at the Hall,' Jayne supplied. 'We're fully accessible and I have clothes you can borrow and toiletries you can use.'

The sisters smiled.

'I've always fancied staying at Elderwick Hall,' said Hetty. 'You okay with that, Con?'

'Try and stop me. Thanks, Jayne. I'll need my other wheelchair, though. Can I get it, Ben?'

'Where is it? I didn't see it in the flat?'

'I left it downstairs, in the bakery kitchen.'

'No problem. Maggie, Laurel, I can drop you both home, and we've got the van, which can take you three to the Hall. Give me five minutes.'

'Rain check,' Laurel said to Jayne.

'Probably best,' she replied.

Laurel turned to Hetty. 'Before you go, tell me again. What was he looking for?'

Hetty shrugged. 'I have no idea. It sounded like paper and hair.'

Maggie clocked the look on Laurel's face. She knew that expression.

Chapter 51

Laurel

'Okay, which of you two are we dropping off first?' asked Ben, once they'd seen Hetty and Constance safely off to Elderwick Hall in the police van with Jayne.

'You know we're fine to get home on our own,' Laurel looked at Maggie, who nodded. 'It's not even dark yet.'

'I'd feel better if–'

'Really, Ben, it's very chivalrous of you, and we appreciate the offer, but Laurel and I have some catching up to do.'

'I'm not going to convince you otherwise, am I?'

Laurel linked arms with Maggie. 'Nope.'

'Well, be careful. We don't know who broke in, and he's probably long gone, but... call me if you need anything.'

'Thank you,' Laurel meant it.

'I've got cake at mine if you want some?' said Maggie. Decision made, they set off for the far side of the village and Thatcher's Cottage.

Their destination made Laurel think again of all the occurrences of the initials T C. 'How did your house get its name?' she asked Maggie as they strolled.

'I haven't got the foggiest. Why do you ask?'

'No reason.' Her frazzled brain returned to puzzling over the break-in. Elderwick was subject to crime the same as anywhere else, but burglary was rare. Given the events of the week, the man in Hetty and Constance's flat smelled like a coincidence too far. 'Now tell me, what were you and Constance up to this evening?'

'I will, as soon as you've explained why you're dressed like Alan Titchmarsh?'

Laurel told Maggie what Christopher had seen from the tower. Adding that she'd press-ganged Jayne into joining her for the foray into the long grass of the meadow. 'We didn't get there, though. We heard the sirens and went to find out what was happening.'

'Should we go there now, to the meadow?'

Laurel admired Maggie's fortitude, but she'd lost her enthusiasm for digging. She might have told Ben she could look after herself, but her anxiety was growing. As soon as she'd seen Maggie to her door – and graciously accepted a piece of cake – she would hotfoot it back to Myrtle Cottage and lock the doors.

'Let's do it tomorrow. We'll see better in daylight, anyway. Now, about you and Constance?'

As Maggie described *Carter's* invitation to Constance and their fruitless stake out at the pub, Laurel's unease increased.

'We were there from half-seven until about nine and he didn't show.'

When she'd finished, Laurel voiced her disquiet. 'Do you think it was a little too convenient that the flat was broken into when both Hetty and Constance were out?'

Maggie's arm tightened against Laurel's. 'You think it was someone who knows Hetty and Constance?'

'Who would have known they were both out this evening?'

'I don't know. We'd have to ask them. Any number of people, at a guess. Although... Constance wouldn't have told anyone about her date, not even Hetty. She's embarrassed about the whole affair, not that she has any reason to be. So actually, no, I can guarantee, I was the only person who knew about our trip into Willerby.'

'Someone could have seen you leaving on your way out, I suppose. They wouldn't have known where you were going or how long you would be, though. Plus, Hetty said the man she disturbed was looking for a specific item, which says to me he wasn't an opportunistic thief. I bet you anything he targeted the flat when he knew it would be empty.'

'It's not possible.'

'Think carefully. When did Constance arrange to go out? Was there anyone nearby who could have overheard?' Laurel's fingers were tingling. She had the sense they were on the edge of a breakthrough.

'It was yesterday. We were in The Fox when she got the invitation from Carter on her laptop. No-one else could have seen the screen and no-one was close enough to have heard us talking about it. I know because Dr Delgado, Beth, Lin, and Penelope had just left, and they were on the only table near to us that was occupied.'

'You're positive?'

'Absolutely, one hundred percent. The only people who knew Constance would be out tonight were Constance, myself, and this Carter character.'

Laurel gasped. 'What if it was Carter?'

'It couldn't be. He thought he was meeting someone called Sylvia.' Maggie outlined the deception and how Constance had used Hetty's photo to scam the scammer. 'He doesn't know Sylvia is really Constance.'

Laurel shivered as she had the sudden sensation they were being watched. She let go of Maggie's arm and turned in a circle. As far as she could tell, there was no-one there, but the feeling persisted. She lowered her voice. 'He might if he's someone Constance knows in real life.'

'Oh no, that's too awful to consider.'

'But it would explain everything. Go with it for a second: Carter knows Constance and one day he finds her on some dating app and decides to con her. Then, suddenly, on one of his other profiles, he sees Hetty's photo pop up, but with a different name.'

'Sylvia. Which he knows is fake because he also knows Hetty?'

'Exactly. And because he knows them, he'll be aware that Hetty isn't interested in men, and she's in a serious relationship, so it's not really her.'

'Right...'

'Next, there's something that one of the sisters has that he wants or needs, and he has the perfect opportunity to get Constance out of the flat. One way or another, he knows when Hetty will be gone, so he proposes the date at The Queen's Arms for the same time. Bingo, everyone is out, he can break into the flat undisturbed.'

Maggie had gone very quiet. 'Let's get inside.' Maggie hurried ahead to the door of her cottage and ushered Laurel inside, bolting it behind them. 'I'm putting two and two together and getting five. I'm sure I'm wrong, but...'

'But?'

'Friday, on the green, Constance dropped a piece of paper. When she got it back, she looked at it and said it was something Jessica had dropped a few days back.'

'What was on it?'

'I only caught a glimpse. I think it was a list of initials. It certainly didn't mean anything to me. But now we know Jessica was murdered. What if it's a clue? What if whoever killed

Jessica saw her drop it, but before they could retrieve it themselves, Constance beat them to it?'

'That's a lot of what ifs...' A lightbulb moment silenced her. 'Which chair was Constance in when she dropped the paper?'

'Her big one. Why?'

'The electric one that was in the bakery this evening and not in the flat?'

'He wasn't saying *hair*, he was saying *chair*!' Maggie paled. 'He was looking for her wheelchair. Whoever he is, he knew Constance wasn't using it tonight, he knew she had her lightweight one, the one you can pick up and put in the boot of a car.' She froze. 'Was he watching us?'

Laurel was already moving towards the door. 'Get your keys. We have to go to the Hall. We need to find that piece of paper.'

Deep within the house, a bell jangled but no-one answered. Laurel yanked on the bellpull for a second time. 'They've probably already gone to bed.'

'Who's there?' Jayne's voice called from inside.

'It's Laurel and Maggie. We need to talk to Constance.'

Jayne opened the door and pulled her robe more tightly across her body. Her eyes asked the obvious question, but Laurel told her they'd explain all as soon as they saw the bakers. The Dandelions manager shrugged and led them to a cosy sitting room on the first floor. When the bleary sisters came in, Laurel asked Constance if she could check her chair for the scrap of paper.

Constance rummaged down the sides of the seat cushion, then her face lit up. 'Is this what you're looking for?'

'You said this chair was downstairs in the bakery this evening?' confirmed Laurel. 'No wonder he couldn't find it.'

'Are you going to tell us what this is all about?' Hetty peered from one to the other.

Laurel winced at the size of the bump on Hetty's head, and how red it was. 'We don't want to say too much yet, in case we're wrong. Can you all take a look at this. Does it mean anything?' She held out the note and everyone craned to get a good view.

Jayne produced a pair of glasses from the pocket of her dressing gown, and Alex – who'd been drawn by the late-night commotion – got up to switch on the overhead light before whipping out a monocle.

Laurel had to pull her focus back to the piece of paper, much as she wanted to stare at his unusual accessory. She had expected to see the initials T C again, but it wasn't the case.

'DDC; HOL; TMF; SNP,' Maggie read out aloud. 'And a gobbledygook word.'

'It's not a word. There are symbols in it.' Alex pointed. 'Here and here. I bet it's a password.'

'Are those letters websites?' Jayne guessed.

Alex had his phone in his hand. 'Let me Google them. Right, DDC, nothing obvious jumps out in the results. What are we looking for?'

'We don't know,' said Maggie, peering at the screen from over his shoulder.

'Next one, HOL. The first result is *Hearts On-line*. It's a dating website.'

'And the next?'

'*There's More Fish*, another dating site.' Alex was typing again. 'Finally, SNP is–'

'*Salt 'n' Pepper*,' finished Constance with a groan.

Yet another unlikely coincidence, Laurel thought

recognising the name of the website which Maggie had told her Constance was using. What had they got themselves mixed up in?

Hetty's muffled voice came from the end of the sofa. 'You're not telling me you're on one of those dating sites?'

'Sort of,' was the meek reply.

'Hold on.' Jayne pushed her glasses up onto the top of her head. 'Constance has a list of dating sites? You dragged us out of bed for this?'

'It's not my list,' said Constance. 'Jessica dropped it last week outside the bakery. This was before she, you know...'

'And we think it must be connected to Jessica's death, or may point to her murderer,' Laurel explained. 'Which is why someone was desperate enough to break into your flat tonight.'

Hetty swore.

Jayne massaged her eyes. 'But it's just a list of dating sites.'

Alex took the paper from Laurel. 'This password here, I'm guessing it's for an account Jessica created on these sites. We could try to log in except we have a password but no username.' He held up his phone screen to show the login page for *There's More Fish*. 'You need both, and even if it's Jessica's list and password, we have no idea what username she chose.'

Constance perked up. 'On *Salt 'n' Pepper*, your username is your email. Does anyone know Jessica's email address?'

Laurel's hope flared. 'No, but I know someone who does. It's probably too late now, but I'll give Lin a call in the morning.' She paused and looked at the tired people gathered around her. 'This could give us the identity of Jessica's killer.'

Chapter 52

Albert

After a frustrating time at the police station the previous day, Albert was in no mood to chase his rabbit, Lago, around the garden when the fuzzy criminal slipped out of his hutch. 'Damn rabbit,' he muttered. 'Aroon, round him up, will you? Or at least make sure he doesn't get into the lettuces again.' The rooster was a smart bird. Albert would swear he understood at least twenty commands, even if he ignored eighteen of them.

Dorothy had been conflicted over the news of Harold's longevity, but pleased he'd been locked up for some of it. However, she was gung-ho for throwing the news in Tillow's face. There was no mistaking her satisfaction at the prospect of proving him wrong in his claim that she had killed her ex-husband.

The officer on the front desk at the station had refused to call DI Coral or DS Hill. Undeterred, Albert and Dorothy had taken up positions on the hard plastic chairs in the reception area and announced they would wait for as long as it took. By mid-afternoon, they were flagging. Albert had nipped to the nearest shop for provisions. Suitably equipped to stave off hunger and thirst, they'd waited a further two hours before a new man on duty had taken pity on them. Apparently, Detective Inspector Coral had been in the building the entire time, and she wasn't happy about seeing them.

Although she had listened, impatiently, to their news, all she would say was that the DNA results for the body from the meadow wouldn't be available for a few days. It being the weekend and resources were stretched and so on and so forth. When Albert had, quite reasonably he thought, asked therefore how they could continue to hold Jo, he and Dorothy had been shown the door.

It wasn't like him to let a setback dampen his mood for long, but until Jo was back where she belonged, he couldn't shake the distress in his gut. It had been so bad he'd foregone his habitual toast and honey earlier.

Feeling all of his seventy-something years, he eased into his favourite chair in the patch of garden that got the best morning sunlight. Eyes closed, he savoured the soundtrack of his home; the soporific drone of the bees in the lavender; the blackbird at the top of the tall conifer singing his heart out; and the distant rumble of a tractor. He had two hours until he was due to meet Laurel and Maggie, two hours in which to fathom a strategy to save his friend.

'Should I harbour the hope of smiling fates and find Laurel and Maggie have solved the case?' he asked Aroon, who had abandoned his guard duties and was scratching for bugs under the chair. 'Perchance, old friend?'

Chapter 53

Laurel

Before her first client of the day arrived, Laurel caught Lin on the phone. She'd given a sketchy explanation as to why she was asking about Jessica's email address, but Lin wasn't to be fooled. Although having already set out on her back to York, she said she had the address, and she would tell Laurel, but she wanted to do it in person. A skilful negotiator for one so young. Laurel had capitulated and invited her to join the meeting at eleven-thirty.

The clock had barely struck the half hour when the gaggle arrived, having gained a member in the person of Penelope.

'I called her,' admitted Lin.

'We waited on the green until we were sure your client had left,' giggled Penelope. 'It was like we were on a stakeout.'

Albert smiled, but Laurel noticed Maggie was apprehensive.

With a bit of manoeuvring and shifting of furniture, they all crowded round the laptop as Laurel brought up the *Salt 'n' Pepper* dating website. Scrolling down to the username box, cursor poised, she turned to Lin.

'It's jess mar anthro, all one word, 393 at gmail.com.'

Laurel typed it in, then the password copied from the slip of paper they'd found in Constance's wheelchair, held her breath and hit enter.

Incorrect username or password flashed up on the screen. Her heart sank.

'Did she have another email address?' Maggie asked Lin.

'There's her uni one. I doubt she'd use that for dating, but we can try it.'

Laurel entered the new address as Lin recited it, held her breath for the second time and crossed her fingers for good measure.

Incorrect username or password

She banged her fist on the keyboard.

Albert moved it away. 'Steady on. This is only a temporary setback. We'll crack this nut yet.'

Lin looked doubtful. 'I don't know any other email addresses for her. I'm really sorry.'

Laurel was frustrated. Whatever was on those accounts had to be important. Why else had someone broken into Hetty and Constance's flat? The paper with the list on it and the fact that it had been in Constance's wheelchair – the chair the thief had been looking for – made it the obvious conclusion.

'Oh.' She hadn't meant to say it out loud, but she had an idea. With everyone staring at her, she asked, 'Maggie, you said Constance dropped the list the other day, and that's when you saw it and what was on it.'

'Yes.'

'Was there anybody else with you who saw it too?'

Maggie's eyes went wide. 'Oh. Could it be?'

Laurel fidgeted, but kept quiet so Maggie could work it through.

'Dr Delgado was there,' she whispered. 'I can't believe I didn't think of it before. He was the one who picked up the piece of paper and gave it back to Constance. He saw what was written on it and he saw her stuff it down the side of her chair.'

'Dr Delgado?' Lin and Penelope repeated, disbelief colouring their voices.

In her mind, Laurel sifted through the data they had collected so far. 'There was that heated discussion between Jessica and Rik.'

'Excuse me,' said Albert.

'Just a second,' Laurel replied. She had to get the events straight in her head. 'Penelope, it was you who saw them, right?'

Penelope bobbed her head. 'Dr Delgado pretended to not remember when I mentioned it to him. I suppose that's suspicious?'

Clearing his throat, Albert tried again. 'Excuse me.' He turned the screen so they could see what he'd been doing. 'You entered the password incorrectly.'

Laurel's cheeks flamed.

'Shall I do the honours?' He hit enter and brought up a new page. He fumbled for his glasses and eventually found them on top of his head. Leaning in, nose almost to the screen, he told them, 'There's a message here that Jessica sent to the website administration team. She sent it last Sunday at one seventeen in the afternoon. She says: *I wish to report the following profile: Carter Braidwood.*'

Maggie leapt from her chair, and in her haste, toppled it over. 'I need to call Constance. Carter Braidwood is the name of the person she's been talking to online. He's the man she was supposed to meet last night.'

'Hold your horses' Albert waved Maggie back down.

She righted her chair and sat, but didn't look happy about it.

Albert kept reading. '*I wish to report Carter Braidwood. That is not his real name, and he has been using this and other profiles on many websites to scam women out of money. His real name is...'*

Laurel's office phone rang, causing yelps of shock and exasperation. The call went to voicemail, so everyone heard the message as she scrambled to silence it.

'Hi, this is Gertrude Bell. Sorry I didn't show up for my appointment the other day. I was coming to see you about an issue between my husband and I, but I think we've sorted–'

She mashed the right button, and the voice disappeared.

'That was so unprofessional.' Her face burned. 'Can you all forget you heard that?'

'Shall I continue?' asked Albert.

'Yes!' was the unanimous reply.

'His real name is Dr Rik Delgado.'

There was a synchronised intake of breath.

The name sank in. Laurel asked Maggie, 'Didn't you say Dr Delgado was in the pub when Carter sent the message to Constance about meeting for a date?'

'No, he'd just left.' The colour drained from her face. 'Before he went, we had been talking about Hetty being out on Sunday night. He would have heard.' She put a hand over her mouth. 'It was Rik that scammed Constance. And he hurt Hetty so no-one would find out he was a low-life con artist? The bastard!'

Laurel got to her feet and paced. 'If Rik is Carter, and Rik engineered this attempted robbery all for the sake of a piece of paper that Jessica dropped and Constance found, then Rik might be far more than a con artist. He could be Jessica's killer.'

Chapter 54

Maggie

Maggie's chair tipped over again as she sprang once more to her feet and announced, 'We need to get to the meadow.'

'We should have gone last night,' said Laurel, struggling to rise while caught between her desk and her laptop power cord.

'Do you have your trowel and spade here?' Maggie was wringing her hands. That Dr Delgado could be behind the break-in, let alone might be a killer, was beyond what her mind could cope with. Least of all, on a Monday morning.

Laurel was shaking her head. 'But I can run home and get them.'

'I don't know why we need to go to the meadow, but if this helps Jess, then let's go,' cried Lin, sporting a fearsome grin.

To the young, Maggie thought, *everything is a grand adventure.*

'What about the meadow?' Albert enquired, unflappable in the midst of the action.

Laurel answered as she untangled herself, 'Christopher said someone has been digging there, even though the archaeology team's work has been on hold. That's right, isn't it, Penelope, Lin?'

'Definitely. We were told to do our own thing until work could start again, but then Dr Delgado and Beth decided to call it and send in a whole new team. But they're not here yet,' said Lin.

'So, no-one should have been digging there, and certainly not in the long grass away from the trenches.'

Remaining in his seat, Albert asked, 'Could it have been the police when they were searching the ground right after the bones were found?'

Laurel shook her head. 'Christopher saw the newly dug earth yesterday. As far as I know, the police haven't been back for a few days now. But I'm willing to bet Rik has, and we need to know why.'

Practically dancing on the spot, Maggie shooed Laurel towards the door. 'Go, get something to dig with. Penelope, you go and help Laurel; Albert, Lin, and I will get over to the meadow and guard the area until you get there.'

There wasn't much to see. A slight depression in the ground covered with freshly turned soil. It had been recently disturbed, but it was a small patch, and Maggie couldn't imagine what could be buried there, if anything. Now they were waiting, poised with garden implements, she was having second thoughts. What if they found more bones, or worse, fleshy remains? She gagged and stepped back.

'Shall I start?' Laurel hefted the shovel in her hands.

Lin raised her hand. 'You might be better off starting with a smaller tool, like this.' She held out the trowel.

Maggie took it and passed it to Laurel. 'Be careful.'

'What's going on?'

Maggie and Penelope jumped, and Laurel dropped the trowel.

'Ben,' said Albert, moving to head him off before he could clock what they were doing.

Maggie shuffled over to put herself between the police officer, Laurel, Lin, and Penelope. Out of the corner of her mouth she mumbled, 'Jayne knows right? We have her permission, so I don't think he can stop us? And at least it's not Coral.'

'Can one of you tell me what you're doing?' Ben was in uniform, on duty.

Maggie raised her eyebrows at Laurel, who shrugged.

'Go ahead, we may as well tell him.'

As she spoke, Ben clenched his jaw, and his body grew still. 'And that's why we're here,' she finished. 'We think Dr Delgado's involved. It could be nothing, but...'

The police officer pressed his lips together and his hand strayed to his radio. He sighed. 'Give it here,' he said, leaving his radio silent and reaching for the trowel. He knelt by the depression. 'At least this way, if there is anything here, and it turns out to be evidence, I can testify that it wasn't tampered with.' Before he disturbed the dirt, he cocked his head and asked, 'Dr Delgado, Rik. Really?'

The blade of the garden tool sank easily where someone else had dug so recently. Ben scraped away a little at a time, and they crowded round to watch.

He was a few inches in when he paused. 'There are two objects in here. Stand back so I can see properly.' He snapped on a pair of gloves and pushed his fingers into the earth.

Maggie craned her neck, but she couldn't tell what it was he'd discovered until they came free of the dirt. 'What are they?'

She didn't know what she'd expected, but it wasn't these muddy lumps of wood.

Ben turned them over and brushed off the biggest clumps of mud. 'I don't know. They've got carved bits and straps...'

'I think I know what they are,' squeaked Penelope. 'Can I see them closer?'

Ben held them up, warning her not to touch them.

'I'm pretty sure they're cow shoes,' she said eventually.

'Well, I never.' Albert rubbed his chin. 'I've never come across a pair in real life.'

'I know horses wear shoes, but cows don't, do they?' Maggie wrinkled her nose.

'We learned about it in school. They were used mostly in the US by moonshiners during prohibition times to disguise their footprints. I doubt these are authentic, but they'd do the job.'

'Why are you looking at each other like that?' Maggie quizzed Laurel and Ben. 'What do you know? Laurel?' She caught her friend by the arm as she staggered. Albert supported her from the other side, and they moved her away to where she could sit. 'You've gone a funny colour.'

'Jessica's killer didn't leave any footprints in the field,' said Laurel. 'Even though the ground around Jessica was muddy that night. There were only hoof prints near her body.'

A shiver ran from the top of Maggie's head down to her toes.

'And you think these belong to Rik?' Ben had placed the cow shoes back on the ground, taken off his gloves, and was unclipping his radio.

'We don't know, but I'd say it's a fair bet if he was the person who attacked Hetty last night.'

'He was? What?' Ben began.

'Oh, they belong to Dr Delgado, I'm like positive they're his.' Penelope was trembling. 'He was the one who came to our school and told us about how smugglers, moonshiners specifically, used to use them.' She swallowed hard and dropped down to sit beside Laurel.

'It could be a coincidence,' suggested Maggie.

'My dear, it is true there have been the most remarkable instances of coincidence in the world. However, in this particular instance, I would hazard that if it looks like a duck, and quacks like a duck, it is most likely a duck,' Albert opined.

'I'm going to need you all to give statements about all of whatever this is.' Ben puffed out his cheeks.

He looked dazed, which was how Maggie was feeling. She didn't understand why a respected archaeologist would be an on-line scam artist, nor why he would kill Jessica. Even if Jessica had stumbled across his secret, was it worth killing for? 'She must have threatened to expose him and his scam. He must have lured her here and...' She couldn't complete her sentence. It was all so ghastly.

Ben finished calling in his report then bagged the cow shoes. 'No more speculation, right? Let's just wait here for the guys from the station to secure the scene, then we'll take those statements.' He looked up, pinched the bridge of his nose, and sighed. 'Where's Albert gone?'

Chapter 55

Albert

'Mind if I join you?' Albert shuffled onto the sun-warmed bench beside Christopher and Dorothy. 'It's always so peaceful in the graveyard, I don't know why more people don't avail themselves.' He thought for a moment. 'But I'm glad they don't.'

'Dorothy was telling me about your sit-in yesterday.' Christopher shaded his eyes to look at him. 'Any news this morning?'

'Not about Jo.' Albert grimaced. 'But there's been some developments in the meadow. It appears the villain who did for poor Jessica may be on course for his comeuppance.'

Dorothy stirred. 'They know who it was?'

'Young Ben is investigating as we speak. And I believe you played a role, Christopher? From your lofty perch, you spied a disturbance in the green, green grass of home?'

'You mean the digging in the meadow?'

'I wish he'd speak plain English,' grumbled Dorothy.

'There was something buried there, then?'

Albert described what had been found and Penelope's

explanation for how they were used. 'A diabolical plot, and clearly premeditated.'

'Lucky I noticed it. If a body can go unnoticed there, a couple of pieces of wood might have rotted away before anyone stumbled across them.'

Albert fancied there was a glimmer of pride in the vicar's smile. 'It was lucky,' he emphasised the word lucky with a grin. 'Lucky you knew it wasn't the archaeology team continuing their work. I presume a new team will arrive soon. Jayne and Alex from Dandelions will want to push ahead with the farm shop, I'm sure.'

'Comes to something when even a dead body doesn't stop city types paving over our green spaces.'

'Dorothy, please,' Christopher admonished. 'I think you're right about a new team, Albert. Beth said goodbye to me on Saturday. She pledged her own group wouldn't set foot in the meadow again. I can appreciate her sentiments.'

'Quite.'

'Enough patting each other on the back. What do we do to get Jo home?' Dorothy glared at them.

'Ben is calling in reinforcements as we speak. Once Laurel and Maggie–'

'I should have known they'd be involved in this mess.' She scowled.

'Once Laurel and Maggie have explained everything,' Albert continued, 'I imagine Rik will be taken in for questioning about the break-in at least. Then, if they can tie him to that crime, I believe they will have cause to question him about the murder.'

'Well, let's pray they arrest him. Jo doesn't deserve to be there because of Jurgen. And she absolutely did not kill Ms Marumo to cover her supposed crime. The police have mud for brains.'

'And when justice is done and Jo is freed, we can thank Laurel and Maggie for bringing Rik's guilt to light,' Christopher needled her.

Albert scratched his ear. There was the issue of proof. They had precious little. Circumstantial evidence, certainly, but it wouldn't be enough. 'We should prepare ourselves for a long campaign if the powers-that-be are unable to show Jurgen died as the result of an accident. Despite innocent until proven guilty, I fear Vincent Tillow will not be satisfied or silenced. He has something to prove, particularly as you, Dorothy, were able to prove him wrong over Harold.'

She flashed a wicked smile. 'I enjoyed that. Pompous ass.'

'Do you know how...'Christopher subsided.

'How Jurgen died?' Albert completed the question. 'Dorothy and I know, yes. Sadly, in the eyes of the law, not only are we already considered unreliable, but we did not witness the event firsthand and can only testify as to what Jo told us.'

Dorothy smacked her hand on the bench. 'Which is the truth and should be enough.'

'He was drunk and fell down the stairs. I'm no expert, but I'd say he broke his neck.'

Christopher blanched. 'You saw the body?'

Dorothy turned away.

'Yes, Jo called Dorothy and Dorothy called me. We went straight over. She was devastated.'

'He deserved to die,' Dorothy said as she gazed across the gravestones. 'He put her through hell when he was alive, and because of how he died, and because Tillow was, and is, a misogynist, Jo has been in hell ever since. If she'd reported it, she would have gone to prison, accident or not. He would have made sure of it.' She sniffed and added softly, 'I saw the blood, the bruises, the pain. If I had been there that night, I would have pushed him down those stairs myself.'

Christopher mouthed a prayer.

Chapter 56

Maggie

The moment Ben was occupied, briefing his colleagues who'd arrived at the meadow, Maggie followed Albert's lead and slipped away. She tried The Plump Tart first, but the bakery was closed. The first time she could remember it ever being so on a Monday morning. There was a note on the door citing *unexpected circumstances*. When there was no reply to her knock on the door to the flat, she reasoned the sisters must still be up at Elderwick Hall. Given the ugly bruise on Hetty's forehead from her run-in with Dr Delgado – Dr Delgado! She was struggling to absorb it – she was glad they'd seen fit to take a break and rest.

Were it not for the thought of a killer on the loose, Maggie would have enjoyed the walk to the Dandelions base. Instead, every trill of a bird and rustle in the undergrowth had her twitching and flinching. When a squirrel broke free of cover and bounded out of hiding ahead of her, she shrieked, startling herself as much as the bushy-tailed rodent.

There was no need to knock when she reached the house. Raised voices were drifting on the breeze from the formal garden. She poked her head round the gate and saw Hetty and Constance flanked by Jayne and Alex.

'What do you think?' Jayne was asking Constance, who was between a series of new raised flower beds.

'It's perfect. I can see and touch everything. You've done an incredible job, Alex.' She trailed her fingers through the greenery, plucked a stem and lifted it to her nose. 'I'm going to need plenty of lavender to calm me after this week.'

'I'll get some cut for you to take home,' said Alex. 'And I'll throw in some camomile. You can make some tea with it.'

'Hi.' Maggie lifted a hand in greeting.

'Hey,' they chorused.

'I have news,' she said, wanting to break the news as soon as possible. Above all, it was important to warn Constance over having any further contact with Carter Braidwood AKA Rik Delgado.

'Judging by your expression, it's bad news?' queried Alex.

'It's about what you found on that dating site, *Salt 'n' Pepper*, isn't it?' Constance's anxious fingers dismantled the flower she was holding. 'I knew it was too much of a coincidence. Do you need me to sit down first?' she joked.

Jayne snorted. 'Sorry. I laugh when I'm nervous, and all this violence and mystery has got me at sixes and sevens.'

'Had Jessica been conned by Carter, too, like me?'

'In a manner of speaking. We now know that Carter was... is Rik Delgado.'

Alex gaped. 'As in the archaeologist bloke?'

Constance reached for Hetty's hand. 'How? I don't... what?'

'We managed to log in to Jessica's account and saw that she'd reported him to the site admin. She named him. If we had her username for the other sites, I think we'd find the same thing. She was tracking him down like we were, only she knew his real name. I don't know how. Rik must have found out that she knew. Maybe she confronted him.'

Hetty released herself from her sister's grip and glared. 'If Jessica was going to expose Rik, then Rik was the one who broke in to try to get that piece of paper back. It must have been. I can't believe it. He always came over as so charming. I gave him the best cinnamon bun the last time he was in the bakery. Do the police know?'

'They do. We told Ben this morning, and he got some other officers down to... oh, actually, there's more you should know.'

'I am rethinking our idea to base Dandelions here,' said Alex, sotto voce to Jayne.

Jayne shushed him. 'Tell me, Maggie, if Rik was willing to break in to steal a piece of paper, injuring Hetty in the process, then are we to assume he is what Laurel suggested last night, a suspect in Jessica's murder?'

Constance groaned. 'I really know how to pick 'em. 'Hetty, I'm so sorry.'

'It's not your fault, you daft bat.' Her sister gave her a one-armed hug. 'Have they arrested him?'

'They hadn't when I left the meadow.'

Jayne interrupted. 'You've been to the meadow? Last night, Laurel and I were going to check out the corner where there's been recent digging. Did you do it today?'

'We did. It was odd that there was freshly disturbed earth, and after finding out about Dr Delgado, we thought we should go and look straight away. And it's a good job we did. We found cow shoes.' After a brief education on the purpose of cow shoes, Maggie put it together for them. 'Dr Delgado even demonstrated them at Penelope's school a few weeks back. It must have been how he got close enough to Jessica to kill her without leaving footprints. He murdered a young woman to prevent her from exposing him as a scammer. It's atrocious.'

Constance leaned over the side of her chair and threw up into the marigolds.

Chapter 57

Laurel

Monday afternoon in the office loomed ahead of her. Interminable, unavoidable, but fortunately, not fully booked. Her usual Monday people included Mary, who she'd seen that morning; Nick and his wife were on their holiday in Spain – which had left her free for the eleven-thirty meeting with Maggie and co. – and Sanjay was her only afternoon booking. She had arranged to meet Michael again at the end of the day, but since he wasn't in therapy, she was under no obligation to provide the complete fifty minutes of total concentration and attention.

She had intended to speak to the university about him before seeing him again, but her dramatic morning meant she had completely forgotten. Thankfully, in light of the revelation about Dr Delgado, it was no-longer necessary.

In the meadow, before she'd returned to the office, Ben had assured her he would provide updates when possible. Maggie, she knew, had nipped away to update Constance and Hetty; and Albert, she presumed, had gone to see Dorothy. Now all she wanted to do was go home and mull over their new discoveries. The idea of Dr Rik Delgado as a conman, thief, and murderer was sinking in, but there were a lot of unanswered questions, and until he was arrested and charged, she wouldn't rest easy.

Her session with Sanjay – who was progressing well – lifted her spirits, and with their next appointment booked in the diary, she walked him out and welcomed Michael.

'I've had another call from the station. They want to ask me about a person of interest in Jess's death.' He sat in one of the low chairs by the window and crossed his legs. 'It means I can't stay long, but I wanted to check-in.'

Laurel noted how carefully he was holding himself. The emotions were there, tightly bound beneath the surface. 'Did they say who?' Ben had made it clear she wasn't to start throwing names around and she had agreed, though the name Rik burned on her tongue.

'No. I just bloody hope it's not me anymore. Have you heard anything?' There was a flicker of hope in his eye.

Laurel did what she did best when confronted with a question she didn't intend to answer. 'Have you heard any more about the body in the meadow? They believe it's Jurgen Sturm.'

'Huh. I didn't know. Since Jess... I sort of forgot about it.' He was wearing grubby trainers which he was scuffing against the carpet. They were well worn, the soles practically smooth.

Laurel tensed, but then chided herself; paranoia wasn't useful and smooth-soled shoes didn't mean anything, especially as Rik was surely bang to rights.

Opening her mouth to ask another question, she was interrupted by a beep from Michael's watch.

He scratched his cheek, then glanced at it. 'Actually, sorry, I've got to run already. I've got to get to the police station.'

He left without making plans for another meeting. He was agitated, probably nervous about the grilling he got the last time he saw DI Coral. Laurel watched from the window as he climbed into a shiny Volkswagen Golf that she hadn't seen before. She couldn't recall what vehicle he'd driven to the village on his previous visits, but she didn't think it was the Golf.

Though her brain ached, and she craved a cool glass of wine with her feet up, Laurel woke her laptop and Googled the admin office of York University. The clock said four-thirty. There was time for some phone calls and a dash of bending the truth. The guilt could wait for later.

'Hi, my name is Doctor Nightingale,' she said when her call was answered. 'I'm a clinical psychologist consulting with the police over the suspected murder of Jessica Marumo.' It was an outright lie and an abuse of her title, but even with Dr Delgado in the spotlight, something about Michael continued to niggle.

'I don't need any confidential information, but I was hoping you could put me through to someone who can tell me about the Lawton Grant?'

Five minutes later, she had all the information she needed. The grant was substantial in financial terms, and prestigious academically. The university, she'd been told, only put one candidate forward each year. This year, that candidate had been Jessica. Now she was dead, the opportunity had been passed on to Michael Wishart.

Not wanting to add to the complicated state of affairs, Laurel decided to sit on her suspicions about Michael until she heard what the fall-out was from the dating website and the find in the meadow. Monday evening, a call from Ben – relayed quickly afterwards to Maggie and Albert – confirmed there was no news, and no arrests had been made.

Monday night was a restless one.

Tuesday was a packed and challenging clinic which

occupied her time and her mind and meant she didn't have the opportunity to reflect on Jurgen or Jessica before getting home that evening. She'd arranged for Maggie and Albert to call round with the idea of pooling ideas and chasing Ben for any developments. As it turned out, Ben was waiting outside her door when she dragged her weary self home.

'Can I come in?'

Laurel thought her neighbour's curtains fluttered as she invited Ben over the threshold, through the living room, and out onto the terrace at the back of her cottage.

'Tea, coffee, something cold?' she offered.

'I'll take a cold drink. Thank you. Non-alcoholic. Take your time. I predict we have around ten minutes or so before Albert and Maggie show up.'

She smiled. He'd caught sight of the curtain twitching too. 'Better make yourself comfortable then.' She went back into the living room, depositing her work bag in the corner, and wandered into the kitchen. 'No hot date tonight?' she called. *What are you doing?*

'I thought that's what this was?'

Butterflies invaded her stomach. He was joking, of course he was, but it was pleasurable to think he might be flirting. Unless he was joking about it because it was too ridiculous to contemplate? 'Argh,' she growled, turning her attention to what refreshments she had to offer.

'Here you go.' Back outside, she handed over a glass of summer fruit squash.

'Thank you.'

As he sipped, quiet fell between them and the butterflies beat faster against her insides. It was no longer pleasant. 'How was your day?' *Kill me now!*

'Good. Busy. Yours?'

'Same.' She opened the sun umbrella to give them some shade and lowered herself into her favourite reading chair.

He drank again.

'Have you read–' The doorbell rang. *Oh, thank god.*

Without waiting to be invited, Maggie and Albert hustled through the house and out to the garden.

'What news?' demanded Albert.

Ben spluttered. 'Give a man a chance to say hello first.'

Laurel offered the newcomers drinks, which they declined. 'You haven't missed anything. He hasn't told me the latest yet, but I assume there have been developments?'

Giving up his place at the bistro table to Maggie, Ben set his glass down and put his hands on his hips. 'Do you promise that anything I tell you goes no further? Or am I being naïve to even ask?'

'Yes,' replied Albert, settling himself next to Maggie.

Ben looked to the sky for a full five seconds.

Maggie had her notebook on her lap, open to a new page. 'Ready when you are.'

He sighed. 'You know what, everyone is going to know soon enough, anyway.' He unfolded the deckchair that had been leaning against the wall and sat. 'You'll be pleased to hear that Rik was arrested on suspicion of burglary, not theft because as far as we can tell, nothing was stolen. DI Coral and DS Hill questioned him, and he confessed.'

Maggie let out a whoop.

'But...'

'There's always a but,' Albert grumbled.

'But only to burglary. When he was asked about Jessica's murder, he denied any involvement.'

Laurel shuffled so she was perched on the edge of her chair. The muscles in her neck clenched and an insistent throb was building in her temples. 'What about the cow shoes? He can't deny they're his and, okay, maybe they don't prove he was there when Jessica was killed, but it looks pretty suspicious, right?' She was clutching at straws. They – she, Maggie, and Albert – had done all they could. Now it was down to the police, in whom she had little faith.

'It's not proof. Even if they can link the shoes to Rik, there's nothing to say he wore them or was anywhere near the footpath the night Jessica died.'

'Ben, can't they compare the hooves of the cows with the cow shoes?'

Laurel loved Maggie for her hopeful question.

'They're not going to... er hoofprint a herd of cows, Maggie.'

'Albert's right,' Ben confirmed. 'And even if they did, I doubt it would stand up in court.'

'How does he explain them being buried in the meadow, then?' asked Laurel, not ready to let go of her prime suspect.

'He doesn't, and he doesn't have to. It's up to the police to provide the evidence. That they were buried proves nothing.'

Maggie's face had fallen. 'When Albert told me you were here, I thought you had good news.'

'I do. About the body in the meadow.'

Already convinced the remains belonged to Jurgen Sturm, Laurel wasn't stirred from her funk. Unless cause of death had been determined and Jo had been released. She perked up at the possibility.

Albert beat her to the question. 'Have they formally identified him? Does it help Jo?'

'DNA taken from a Mr Brendt Sturm at Saint Helen's nursing home confirms a familial match. Jo's statement, the ring, and the key, they all fit so it's been confirmed. The body is Jurgen Sturm.'

'And the cause of death?'

'We're still waiting, but Jo will be released soon. Coral's not saying much, but without cause of death or any evidence linking Jo to Jurgen's death, they can't continue to hold her. You should be prepared, though, that she could be rearrested if additional facts come to light.'

'Do they believe she's responsible for Jessica's death?' Albert asked.

Ben showed his palms. 'I don't know. If they do go on to charge her with Jurgen's death, and if no new suspects have been identified, then I'd say it's a possibility. They would have to consider that she might have killed Jessica to cover an earlier crime.'

Albert slumped back in his seat. 'I thought we'd done it. I dared to hope Rik was the perpetrator and all we have discovered to date would be enough to convince the authorities of his guilt.'

Laurel's eyes pricked with tears as the stress of the week caught up with her. After all they'd done, the clues they'd uncovered which led to Rik. It sounded as though he would not be held accountable, and if he wasn't, poor Jo would be raked across the coals.

'I have to warn you, Tillow has the ear of the current chief inspector and Tillow is a–'

'Snollygoster,' barked Albert.

Ben blinked. 'Me or Tillow?'

'Tillow, of course. Snollygoster, it means a person of *some* intelligence but no principles. Vincent has a low cunning, and he won't want to come away empty-handed. Not when his prize of one day convicting Dorothy for Harold's death has been spirited away. He'll push to pin something, anything on Jo. You mark my words.'

Maggie put a hand on Albert's shoulder.

Laurel looked at Ben. 'Where do we go from here?'

Chapter 58

Laurel

Disheartened, the group disbanded soon after Ben had delivered his news. Laurel showed them out before returning to the garden. The golden hour had arrived. The blackbirds were gearing up for their evening recital, and the robin was out searching for the last few bugs before bed.

She hadn't written anything in her notebook during the discussion, but she opened it now and uncapped her pen. There had to be something she'd missed. Some way of tying Rik Delgado to Jessica's murder. But first, she wanted to review the other people surrounding both cases: the body in the meadow; Jessica's death. Had they missed someone?

Lin was friends with Jessica through university. Penelope had only met the anthropologist when she came to Elderwick. Laurel could think of no reason for either of them to have harmed her. They were far too young to have any involvement with Jurgen's death, so they were off the list.

Michael was a possibility for Jessica's death. Maybe it was weak, but he had a motive. Jessica's death meant he was now the Lawton Grant applicant. And he was driving a pretty flashy looking car. Was he already spending in anticipation of getting a windfall, of not having to worry about paying PhD fees? Or – she blinked as another thought struck her – was there a connection to Jurgen Sturm's wealth? Jessica had known about it, it was in her notes, had she mentioned it to Michael? Had Michael devised a way to get his hands on it? Was that a direct link between the two cases? He would stay a *maybe*.

She made a separate note about the money. Could Jurgen have been killed, not by an accident or in self-defence, but for his money? Was it long gone? She tapped the pen against her teeth. She had no way of knowing, but the police were surely considering that angle.

Back to the suspects. To be thorough, she had to consider Jo. Jo had covered up the death of Jurgen, her husband, and might have had a hand in that death. She had allowed Dorothy's brothers to dispose of the body, and she had allowed Dorothy and Albert to lie for her all these years. Even when the body had been found, she didn't immediately come forward.

Albert insisted none of them knew where Jurgen's remains had been disposed of, but all three of them had to have wondered if the bones in the meadow were Jurgen's. Once the design on the ring was common knowledge – a ring whose description Albert admitted they'd recognised – it would have been confirmed. Yet, it wasn't until the key with the initials T C was in play and Dorothy had been arrested that Jo spoke to the police.

However, Albert was in Jo's corner, and for Laurel, that counted for a lot. Still, Jo would also stay on the *maybe* list.

Dorothy and Albert, they were complicit in the original lie about Jurgen's death. Maybe one of them had even killed him in an effort to protect Jo. She could almost imagine Dorothy being capable – especially given her own experiences at the hands of an abusive husband – but Albert? She couldn't see it. Or didn't want to. Either way, they had a motive to keep Jessica quiet. They had to go on the list, but right at the bottom.

She was back to Rik. She couldn't figure out how he could be connected to Jurgen, but he had an obvious motive for silencing Jessica. He was a scammer, a con man, and Jessica had found out, though, goodness knows how. The list and messages on the dating websites were proof of that. Had she threatened to speak to the police about him? Was that what Jessica and Rik had been talking about so heatedly when seen by Penelope? Had Rik become anxious Jessica would expose him? Leading him to act before she could?

She put her pen down and massaged her temples. The ache was penetrating. She could feel her pulse in her skull. Wine wouldn't help. She needed a tall glass of ice water. Two more minutes, she decided, then she would stop and get that drink.

Rik, as a suspect, felt right, but there were problems.

She printed a heading, *Supporting evidence,* and listed: Jessica being a threat to Rik; his alter-ego, Carter Braidwood; the cow shoes incontrovertibly connected to him via his talk at Penelope's school; and most damning of all, his breaking into the flat above the bakery. Having ensured Constance would be out of the way, and believing Hetty would be out too, he'd gone in search of the note Jessica had made of the dating websites on which she'd found him plying his trade. He'd resorted to violence to escape when Hetty disturbed him. Was it so great a stretch to imagine him raising a weapon and bringing it down on Jessica's head?

Under a second heading, *Problems,* she made another list. Scamming money from women on dating sites was fraud. If exposed, he would have been in bother, but was it enough of a motive to kill a person? He could have lost his job with the university and his wife would have found out, so perhaps he felt he had enough to lose to justify the drastic action to himself. Finally, just how did Jessica know he was Carter Braidwood?

The cow shoes, ingenious as they were for disguising footprints, led immediately back to Rik thanks to Penelope. If he had used them to commit the crime, though, why would he bury them in the meadow? He could have got rid of them anywhere and no-one would have been any the wiser. No-one would have thought of such a thing as cow shoes if they hadn't dug up a pair.

Once the police had taken him in for questioning, why had he confessed to the break-in? Ben hadn't said anything about hard evidence at the scene proving it was him. Had he confessed to the lesser crime in an effort to *prove* his honesty and make it appear less likely that he was lying about being involved in the murder? Or was he panicking, knowing he would be looked at for the murder and afraid to lie about the burglary? After all, if he was caught in one lie, everything he said would be subjected to increased scrutiny.

Lastly, there was a basic and, as yet, unanswered question. Where was he on the night Jessica had been killed? Did he have an alibi in his wife, Beth? Laurel thought she remembered hearing they were staying at a hotel in Beverley for the duration of the dig. That would be costing them a fair amount, but maybe such fancy accommodation was funded by his fraud. If so, did Beth know what he was doing on-line? Four questions, she amended, and a complete lack of answers.

That was enough. She closed her book and put away her pen. Time for a break and a drink.

On her way to the kitchen, she paused by the phone. Two more minutes wouldn't hurt.

Ben answered on the third ring. 'Laurel, miss me already?'

She barely acknowledged his tease and launched into the interrogation.

'Woah, hold on.'

The line went quiet, but there were muffled voices in the background. Had she interrupted another date?

Ben came back on the line. 'Rik claimed he was in bed at the hotel on the night Jessica was killed, but Beth can't give him an alibi because they have separate rooms. Rik says his wife didn't know anything about his on-line side-line, and we don't know how he was paying for the hotel.'

The distant voice sounded again. Was it a woman? She strained to hear but couldn't make it out.

'Uh huh,' Ben replied to whoever was in his house. 'Laurel, you still there? Yeah, someone's looking into his finances. Is that everything?'

'Yes, thanks. Bye.' She hung up without waiting for a reply.

In the kitchen, it was the bottle of wine in the fridge she reached for, after all. Water be damned.

Chapter 59

Maggie

The day dawned ten degrees hotter than any so far that summer. After lunch, her short walk to The Plump Tart left her perspiring, sticky, and longing for autumn. The air in the kitchen was heavy even though she'd opened every window. The fan, doing its gallant best, only succeeded in moving the heat around. The temperatures had taken their toll on her class too. Three of the eight booked in had left messages apologising about the need to cancel. Maggie hoped they were headed for the coast or, at least, a kids' paddling pool in the garden.

Setting up for the baking tutorial and demonstration, her thoughts inevitably returned to Dr Delgado. She wanted it to be him, and she wanted him found guilty so they could put the whole dreadful mess behind them. However, as Ben had so helpfully pointed out, there was no hard evidence.

Laurel's call, when it came, was not a surprise.

'Are you free to meet?'

'I've got a class this afternoon, but I'll be available at four-thirty. We can meet at the Village Hall,' Maggie proposed.

'Why the hall?'

'I've offered to set up the equipment for the mother and

toddler group tomorrow morning. If we meet there this afternoon, you and Albert can give me a hand. I'm assuming Albert will be there too?'

'Of course. Another pair of hands for free labour for you.'

'Absolutely,' she laughed. 'See you later. Oh, and it's lemon curd tarts we're making today in class. Shall I bring some with me?'

'I think you know the answer to that,' Laurel replied.

By the time Maggie got to the hall at four-thirty-five, Laurel was already waiting for her, loitering by the village hall entrance in the shade in an effort to keep cool. Ten minutes later, Maggie was glad she'd suggested the hall because half the village had turned up to hear the latest.

'We heard there was a meeting,' said Constance. 'We thought we should be here since I know the most about Dr Delgado's alter ego.'

'And I want to see justice done.' Hetty bristled, pointing to the vivid bruise on her forehead.

'And I ran into Jayne and Alex,' said Laurel. 'They're on their way, too.'

Albert arrived with his entourage. 'I thought it would be helpful to have Christopher with us; he's anxious to help Jo any way he can. As is Dorothy,' he added, as the latter elbowed her way inside.

Maggie tried counting the milling bodies. 'Anyone else?'

'Lin and Penelope,' Dorothy informed her. 'This isn't the Laurel and Maggie show. You should listen to what others have to contribute.'

Wounded, Maggie didn't respond. *Deep breath.*

Inside, the chairs were soon set out in a rough circle, and

everyone was munching on the lemon curd tarts she'd brought with her.

'I put the box on the table over there,' Maggie told Laurel, nodding to the table by the tea urn.

'It's empty,' Laurel shouted back. 'And when did that bird sneak in?' She pointed at Albert, who was feeding a whole tart to Aroon.

A cheery hello from the doorway announced the arrival of the young archaeology team members. Dorothy saw them and motioned to the two chairs next to her. 'Lin, Penelope, I've saved you seats,' she shouted, then flapped her hand in Laurel's direction. 'We're quite ready to start. Some of us have lives to be getting on with.'

The buzz of conversation died, and everyone stared at Laurel. Maggie mouthed 'Good luck.'

'Thank you for coming along. I wasn't expecting so many of you, but now we're here...' Laurel hesitated. 'We're all here because of the horrible death in our village of a young woman, Jessica Marumo. Like me, I'm sure you all want to know who is responsible and to see that they are stopped from harming anyone else.'

'Punishment is what we want,' said Dorothy. 'And we know who did it. It was Rik Delgado.'

From the rumblings, it sounded as though everyone agreed.

'He is being questioned by the police, but Maggie, Albert, and I met with Ben last night and he said there's no evidence to tie him to the murder.'

There were a couple of exclamations of disbelief.

Laurel raised her voice. 'But, I think, if we pool our knowledge, we have the chance of coming up with information that could help the case against him. Or identify another suspect.'

'Do you have someone else in mind?' Alex enquired.

Christopher stood before Laurel could answer. 'Much as I wish for justice to be done, please remember, we are not the authorities. We must exercise caution in laying blame.'

'This was only meant to be a chat,' mumbled Maggie.

'Speaking of Ben.' Albert nodded to the door where the local officer was scowling at the group.

Maggie jumped up and went to intercept him. 'Hi Ben. It's not what it looks like.'

He stepped inside and closed the door. 'Not a lynch mob, then?'

She thought he was making a joke, but his tone was serious. 'No.'

He bent his head to hers. 'Look, I need a quick word with Albert and Dorothy. Could you ask them to step into the kitchen?'

Dorothy's sharp eyes were watching. 'Whatever you've got to say to us, you can say in front of witnesses,' she said, displaying impressive hearing.

Ben shuffled, clearly uncomfortable.

'Spit it out.'

'I could get in a lot of trouble for this, but I think you have a right to know. It's Vincent Tillow. He's pushing to have you both arrested. He and DI Coral are on their way here now.'

Albert put a protective arm around Dorothy, which she promptly shrugged off, so he scooped up Aroon instead and smoothed his feathers. 'Is this about Jurgen?'

'Yes. They're going to charge Jo, and he wants you both arrested. And...'

'And?'

'And he wants you questioned over Jessica's murder.'

There was a collective gasp then pandemonium as everyone spoke at once.

This was bad. Did it mean they no longer believed Dr

Delgado was guilty? Could they hide Albert and Dorothy? Her knowledge of Tillow told her he would be dogged in his quest. And once they were in the system, would Jo, Albert, or Dorothy ever make it out again?

'Quiet,' shouted Jayne. 'Thank you. Let's get some facts straight. It's Ben, correct?'

'Yes.'

'Come, take a seat and tell us who is on their way, and do they know we're all here in the village hall?'

'It's DI Coral, Tillow, and maybe even the DCI. Tillow and the DCI are... buddies. That's why I'm here. Tillow is not police and it's wrong how much influence he's had over these two cases. They, and some uniforms, will be going to your houses, Albert, Dorothy, but in Elderwick, it won't be long before someone tells them where they can find you.'

'Then we don't have much time,' Jayne confirmed. 'Laurel, you said the police need evidence to charge Dr Delgado. Well, let's see what we've got. The floor is yours. Talk us through it.'

In the spotlight again, Laurel hadn't even opened her mouth when a knock echoed through the hall.

The group went silent. Ben tiptoed to the entrance and snuck a glance out of a small side window. His shoulders dropped and he opened up to let DS Hill inside. 'He's not with them. He's on our side,' Ben reassured as people got to their feet. 'Perry, come on over and let me introduce you properly.'

If she wasn't so worried, she would have found it fascinating. All these people coming together to save three of their own. Maggie's heart swelled. She loved Elderwick more than ever.

'DS Hill and I have been liaising with our professional standards department and meeting up outside of the station since all this started. We've raised concerns over Tillow and his influence in the squad. We'll be in trouble with Coral and maybe the DCI, but we had to act.'

Hill lifted his hand in greeting.

'Laurel was about to tell us what these guys know about Dr Delgado.' Ben brought him up to speed.

'Maggie,' Laurel called, 'can you grab me a flip chart and some pens?'

Maggie set them up and whispered, 'You can do this.' Laurel reached for her hand and gave it a squeeze.

'Okay. I need you all to add information as we go. Let's start with the night Jessica was killed.' She drew a line. 'The police said she died around midnight.' She marked this on the line. 'And she was seen leaving Drumble's Hive at about eleven-thirty. So far, so good.'

Lin put up her hand.

'Yes, Lin?'

'It was Todd up at the commune who saw her go out that night. He told Maggie that too.'

Maggie nodded. 'He said she went out to meet someone, but he doesn't know who.'

She could see this was news to Laurel, and wished she'd thought to mention it sooner.

Laurel continued. 'There's something that bugged me about the police account of that night, though. This comes from Michael, Jessica's colleague from the university. The police told him Jessica must have died *before* it rained. I think they assumed that because of the lack of footprints in the mud near her body – which we'll come back to in a minute. I remember though, and Christopher, you confirmed, it rained at *eleven* last Sunday night. Which gives us this order of events: rain at eleven; Jessica seen leaving the commune at eleven-thirty; killed at around midnight. *After the rain,* so there should have been prints left in the mud by the killer.'

Hill raised his hand.

'Um, no-one has to raise their hand. I'm not a teacher. But DS Hill, what do you want to say?'

'That's one of the problems I had with the scene. The victim's prints were clearly visible in the soft ground, and I couldn't understand why, um, others in the team tried to explain away the lack of the perpetrator's prints.'

Ben gave a harsh laugh. 'They like things simple. No prints, no explanation, so let's ignore it. At least now we've got an explanation in the form of the cow shoes.'

'Right.' Laurel picked up her pen again. 'The cow shoes were found buried in the meadow and they link directly to Dr Delgado, who demonstrated them at Penelope's school. But this is where I have a problem. Why would Dr Delgado use cow shoes when Penelope was a part of his team and had met the victim? She would recognise them instantly.'

'Which is why he buried them,' Hetty declared.

'Why not get rid of them miles from here, though? He and his wife are staying at a hotel in Beverley. He could have hidden them anywhere between here and there and we would never have found them and tied him to the crime scene?' She drew a large red question mark.

'Wait.' Constance put her hand in the air. 'I'm so sorry, I didn't know how important this was sooner. She can't have been killed at midnight, not by Dr Delgado, anyway. I was talking, well typing, to him as Carter Braidwood on-line from about eleven thirty-five until one fifteen in the morning. He wasn't away from the keyboard for more than five minutes during that time.'

More muttering and gasps broke out among the crowd.

Maggie groaned aloud at the disclosure and saw that same sentiment mirrored in Laurel's expression. 'You're positive about the time? And it was him, it wasn't someone pretending to be him.' Maggie crossed her fingers.

'I'm one hundred percent certain of the time. I even took screen shots of our chat, and it was definitely the person I'd been speaking to before. Since we're sure now that Carter is Dr Delgado, then yeah, it was him.'

Constance's testimony had just thrown their theory over the lead archaeologist's guilt into disarray.

The door to the hall banged open.

Maggie jumped, and jumped again when Laurel dropped her pen, which rolled into the centre of the circle of chairs.

'Well, isn't this cosy.'

DI Coral had arrived.

Ben and Hill went over to the detective and commenced a heated conversation. They'd lowered their voices, but everyone could hear what they were saying given the acoustics of the hall.

'The CCTV from the hotel has just come in. We've charged Dr Delgado,' Coral hissed.

'We don't need Albert or Dorothy – Ms Little – then?'

'Yes, we do. Nothing has changed in that respect.'

Ben and Hill looked dumbstruck, and Coral seized the opportunity to push past them and confront the gathered residents. 'I don't know what's going on here, but I'm ordering you to clear out now. Except you and you.' She singled out Albert and Dorothy.

No-one moved. Dorothy folded her arms and Aroon, on Albert's knee, hissed at the police officer.

Hill was at Coral's elbow. In a quiet voice he said, 'Ma'am, you know Tillow is wrong.'

She shot him a fiery glare.

Steeling herself, Maggie chanced a question. 'What did the CCTV show?'

Coral gaped at her. 'This is police business. I am not about to start sharing evidence with you.' Her lip curled.

'Only, we might have a problem with that,' said the DS. 'We have a witness who claims to have been speaking to Dr Delgado at the time of the murder.'

Coral closed her eyes. 'Give me strength.'

Ben gave her the short version of Constance's alibi.

Hill stood next to his boss. 'What did the CCTV show?'

'I haven't seen it. A call came in from the hotel. Here.' She handed a message slip to her DS, who read aloud.

'*Dr E Delgado on video leaving North Bar Hotel at 11.27pm. Footage to be emailed over.* That would have given him ample time to drive to Elderwick and intercept Jessica at midnight.'

'E?' Maggie hissed in confusion into Albert's ear.

'Edrik.'

Of course, she'd forgotten his full name wasn't Rik. How many names did one man need?

'Then we have a problem,' declared Ben. 'Not only could he not have been messaging Constance whilst driving, we're all aware that there is zero mobile signal in Elderwick. Which means he couldn't have been on-line at the same time he was in the middle of the field ending Jessica's life.'

Chapter 60

Laurel

Coral, Hill, and Ben retreated into another huddle and furious whispers leaked into the air around them. This time, no-one could make out what they were saying.

'Laurel.' Maggie nudged her and tilted her head towards the kitchen. There loomed the bulky figure of Vincent Tillow and peering from behind, Beth Delgado.

'DI Coral, a word.' His deep voice cut through the hubbub and the hall fell silent.

Coral's head snapped up and she went scurrying over.

'If I didn't know any better, I'd say busy little bees have been going behind our back,' he growled, indicating DS Hill and Ben.

'Why haven't you let my husband go?' wailed Beth, interrupting the daggers shooting across the room between the officers. 'He's innocent. He did not kill that girl.' Her red-rimmed eyes skated around the room, settling on Laurel. 'It was you. You accused him of breaking into that woman's flat on Sunday night. He couldn't have, he wouldn't.' She stalked closer.

Laurel flinched, and Albert, Maggie, and Ben moved to stand beside her.

'Your husband scammed me out of nearly four hundred pounds.' Constance wheeled over to join them in facing Beth.

'I think he did the same to one of my teachers,' announced Penelope.

'And a lecturer at uni,' said Lin. 'We've been asking around. In fact, I think we've worked out how Jess cottoned onto Dr Delgado.'

'Go on,' encouraged Laurel as Beth hesitated, uncertainty in her eyes.

'Constance, Jess told me she'd seen you on a dating website looking at some guy called Carter Braidwood.'

'That's true. And later I found a second profile in which he was calling himself Evan Arthur,' Constance confirmed.

'That figures.' Lin nodded to herself. 'Jess told me just after she got here about a lecturer who'd been scammed. Do you remember, I mentioned it in the pub that evening when Dr Delgado was there?'

Maggie, Constance, and Hetty nodded.

'I had a hunch and got in touch with the lecturer and checked the name of the person who conned her. It was Peter Wulf, a name which should have been enough to give the game away in itself.'

Beth sagged.

'If you're an archaeologist,' Lin finished.

'I'm not sure I follow?' complained Maggie.

'*It's only hubris if I fail*,' Albert intoned.

'Julius Caeser.' Laurel was excited to recognise one of his quotes, finally. 'Sorry, carry on, Lin.'

But Beth spoke first. 'He wasn't a scammer, he was... he wasn't scamming people.'

'They're all names of famous archaeologists,' Lin explained, ignoring the objection. 'He's changed some of them around, but not much. Carter Braidwood is one of the easiest to unravel, and Jess had heard me talk about Howard *Carter* and Robert *Braidwood* often enough that I think it rang a bell with her. I found out Jess called her lecturer friend on Saturday night and asked her the name of her con man. Peter Wulf is another famous archaeologist. After that, I'm guessing she went onto the dating websites and looked for other profiles of people in this area using names of yet more archaeologists. Pretty easy. I'm embarrassed I didn't catch it sooner, but to be fair, I only had one name to go on, Carter Braidwood.'

Half inclined to clap, and annoyed she hadn't twigged, Laurel asked, 'What put you on to it?'

'It's funny. It was that call you got when we were all in your office. The call from Gertrude Bell. That's the name of *another* archaeologist. Obviously a coincidence this time, but it got me thinking.'

'It doesn't mean anything,' spat Beth, taking a stumbling step forward.

DI Coral reached out and took her by the arm, leading her to a chair. 'He has admitted to scamming women on-line. He's defrauded a lot of people for a lot of money. Are you claiming you didn't know?'

'No, I didn't know.' Beth's voice wavered. 'I was told he'd been charged for burglary and was being questioned about the murder.' She leaned forward, putting her head between her knees. 'I think I'm going to pass out.'

Maggie murmured in Laurel's ear, 'I really don't think she knew what he was up to.'

Laurel twitched. There was a cold sensation creeping outwards from her core. The top of her head went numb, and her fingers tingled. *Gertrude Bell.* Booked in for *relationship difficulties that were now solved.* 'Oh no, we've got it all wrong. We've got it all back to front.' Her throat constricted.

'Will someone tell me what is going on here? Why aren't you arresting them?' Tillow glared at Albert and Dorothy.

'Shhh,' Laurel shushed him. She needed just a moment of quiet to think.

'Don't you dare–'

The hall shushed him louder.

Her head snapped up. She had it. All the pieces fit. 'I know what happened.'

Even Tillow shut up.

With a shiver, she rose and positioned herself so she could see everyone in the hall. She would have one shot at this.

She started with Beth. 'Beth, you knew, didn't you? You did the same thing, used the name Gertrude Bell when you booked an appointment with me to discuss your relationship difficulties. You'd booked some days before Jessica arrived in Elderwick because I think your husband has been keeping secrets from you for a long time. Isn't that right?'

Beth jolted.

'Rik's been using dating sites for quite some time, and what would any of us think if we found out our partner was on those kinds of sites? The fact we now know he wasn't using them to have affairs is irrelevant. What matters is what you believed. I think you suspected him of seeing another woman and the final straw was when Jessica showed up here in Elderwick and you surprised them that afternoon in the meadow.'

Maggie piped up. 'What was it you said, Penelope? Rik and Jessica had their heads together, whispering, but stopped when they saw Beth. And Beth, you saw the guilt on his face–'

'Yeah, he was like super guilty,' interrupted Penelope.

'What else were you to think but that you'd caught him murmuring sweet nothings to his latest lover?' Laurel continued. 'We know there's been tension in the marriage because you've been in separate rooms at an expensive hotel.'

Beth wouldn't meet her eye.

'Beth, did you kill Jessica because you were convinced Rik was having an affair with her?'

Beth sprang to her feet, pushing Coral aside, lurching towards Laurel, hands outstretched, nails like claws seeking to damage and tear.

'No, you don't.' Ben had her contained before she could hurt anyone.

The blood was rushing in Laurel's ears. 'You were being honest when you said you didn't know he was a scam artist. But you're wrong in thinking he and Jessica were having an affair.'

'Are we just going to stand here and listen to this drivel?' Tillow demanded.

'Yes, Vincent, we are. Or you can leave, no-one is asking you to stay,' DS Hill informed him.

Laurel caught Albert sharing a flash of glee with Maggie.

Now came the tricky part. She needed to see if all the details fit if she was to convince Coral and Hill. 'Beth, was it you who arranged to meet Jessica that night? I think it was, and she had no reason to fear you so when she turned her back, you hit her with all your might. We can see you're a strong woman. But that wasn't enough for you. You wanted your husband to pay.'

'That's why you wore the cow shoes!' exclaimed Maggie.

'And it's why you buried them in the meadow, so we would find them and connect them straight back to Rik. That was how you solved your relationship difficulties by framing him for the murder you committed.'

'Oh dear,' groaned Christopher. 'You saw me up on the church tower. You even waved to Laurel and me. You knew I would notice the digging from up there. In fact, in the pub, the day we heard the news that Jessica's death was murder and not an accident, you made a point of telling me that none of your team would set foot on the dig site again. You set me up to find any newly disturbed earth suspicious.'

Beth burst into tears. 'Why are you letting them torment me like this? My husband is arrested for burglary, and now these people are making up this ridiculous story.'

No-one went to her. No-one said anything. Even Tillow kept his mouth shut.

'We know it wasn't Rik in the field that night with Jessica because he was on-line again, messaging Constance. But you wouldn't know that. You couldn't give him an alibi for that night – which you hoped would make him look guilty – but having separate rooms means he can't alibi you either.'

'Do you have an alibi?' asked Coral.

'I didn't leave my hotel room. Ask them on the front desk, they'll tell you, I didn't go out all night.' She lifted her chin.

Albert spoke up. 'I have a friend used to work there. There's a back door to the car park. You wouldn't have to go past the desk at all. Guest keycards open it from the outside, so you could get back in that way too.'

To DS Hill, Coral said, 'Call the hotel and ask if they have a log.'

Laurel thought she saw a flash of relief in Beth's face. 'If you find that only Rick's card was used that night, it's worth remembering it would have been easy for Beth to get a copy of his card.'

'Hold up, what about the CCTV footage?' asked Ben. 'The hotel confirmed Dr Delgado was seen leaving that night. Were they both out?'

'Can I see the note?' Laurel held out her hand and Hill passed it over. 'Dr E Delgado, it says here.'

'Edrik Delgado,' shrugged Hill.

'Or Dr *Elizabeth* Delgado. You might want to check the

video. She might have been wearing a disguise, but I bet it's Beth. Did you know about the CCTV?'

Panic in her eyes, Beth stammered, 'It's not true.'

'Even that must have rankled; everyone calls him *Dr* Delgado, and you're just Beth. You've got a doctorate too though, haven't you?'

'This is all a big mistake,' Beth wailed. 'Okay, I admit, I wanted my husband to go to jail and I planted the cow shoes, but only because he killed Jessica. It wasn't me.'

Tillow nudged Coral who stepped up to Beth. 'Elizabeth Delgado, I'm arresting you on suspicion of the murder of Jessica Marumo.'

Chapter 61

Albert

Out in his garden, Albert savoured a glass of lemonade. Laurel had polished hers off in seconds. He understood; it had been horribly stuffy in the hall and the drama had left everyone wrung out.

Laurel held out her hands. 'Look, I'm still shaking.'

'I'm not surprised. That was quite the performance. When did you realise it was Beth and not Rik?' He'd chastised himself for not seeing through Beth's act sooner, but then the whole case had been monstrously bewildering. And what a couple of ne'er-do-wells. One an on-line lothario, defrauder, and burglar, and the other a killer who had tried to frame her own husband. What was the world coming to?

'It was only after I saw Beth's response to hearing that her husband was a swindler. She was genuinely shocked. Then I understood. She thought he'd been having affairs. Put that together with Beth making an appointment to see me about relationship difficulties using the name Gertrude Bell, and the cow shoes being buried somewhere they were bound to be found. Somewhere Beth knew the fresh digging would be spotted by Christopher, and bingo.'

'Hell hath no fury...'

'Exactly. I mean, there might be one or two loose ends, but who else could it have been?'

'I must say, once more, I am suitably impressed by your dogged determination and powers of deduction.' He was interrupted as the phone rang inside the house. 'Do excuse me.' After a couple of tries, he stood and hobbled inside. The previous week, especially his worrying over Jo, had taken a heavy toll. He was wabbit.

Three minutes later, he was back in his chair opposite Laurel. He'd caught her taunting Aroon by eating a biscuit and not sharing it with him. She'd pay for that; the bird could hold a grudge.

'Is everything okay?'

'That was Ben. They're releasing Jo. Jurgen's cause of death has been determined as a broken neck consistent with a fall. Whether he was pushed, they have no way of knowing without any remaining soft tissue that they could examine for injury or damage.' He was relieved, but frustrated.

'That's great news then, isn't it?'

He sniffed. 'I'm thankful poor Jo will be back home, but it's hardly the vindication she deserves. All these years, and still the shadow of doubt will follow her.' He kneaded his knuckles. The mealy-mouthed conclusion was Tillow's work. He would bank on it.

Laurel put down her glass. 'You, Jo, and Dorothy didn't know what Dale and Donald did with Jurgen's body. If it hadn't been for his ring I guess you wouldn't have known for certain it was him?'

'If this were anywhere but Elderwick, we'd probably have suspected because how many dead bodies are likely to be lying around?' He gave a hollow chuckle. 'We'd all recognise that ring anywhere. The key to The Tea Cup served only to confirm what we already knew.'

'You'd seen him wearing the ring when he was alive?'

'Not only wearing it.' His face darkened. 'That bastard heated it over the fire and...' he had to stop and clear his throat. 'That evil bastard heated it over the fire and branded Jo with it.' Tears spilled down his cheeks, and he fished out a voluminous white handkerchief. 'She's still got the mark to prove it.'

Laurel winced. 'Oh, poor Jo, I had no idea.'

The familiar anger bubbled through his veins. 'How Vincent Tillow could have seen that and not have arrested Sturm all those years ago, I'll never understand not even if I live to one hundred and fifty years old.'

Laurel gasped. Wide-eyed alarm morphed into knitted brows then grim determination.

Unease stirred in Albert's gut; he knew what that look meant. He repeated his own words back in his head, searching for what had affected Laurel so. When it came to him, the wave of devastation was colossal. 'No...'

'I'm sorry, Albert.' He felt Laurel take his hand. 'I'm horribly afraid we're not done yet.'

Chapter 62

Maggie

There was nothing Maggie could do to soothe Hetty and Constance's dismay at the state of their flat. Not that the police had been destructive when gathering evidence, but their presence had left its mark. Rik's too. When he couldn't find the wheelchair, he'd rifled through drawers and cabinets in his search for the scrap of paper.

Wishing to cheer her friends, Maggie said, 'You helped catch a killer today. And I'll help clean up. We'll have this place spit-spot in no time and all the while, we have the satisfaction of knowing that Doctors Delgado, plural, are under lock and key for their crimes. You said you'd track him down, Constance, and you did.'

Constance fiddled with a cushion from the sofa. 'What I don't understand is why Rik targeted people he'd met in real life? Me, Penelope's teacher, and Lin's lecturer friend. What did we do wrong?'

It was a question Maggie had puzzled over. She'd asked Laurel the same thing. Trying to recall what psychological answer she'd been given she settled for an approximation. 'I don't want to throw around unsubstantiated theories, but my guess is he was always on the lookout for single, compassionate women. Knowing his target ahead of time also let him tailor his approach. Constance, he must have found out you were single. He knew where you worked so he invented a lonely chef. He'll have done similar with the others.

'I wonder too, if in some sick way, he enjoyed seeing the effects of his scams first hand. I'm not saying he has a problem with women, but just look at how he was always *Dr Delgado*, but he never referred to Beth as doctor.' She shuddered, then worried she'd gone off track. 'The important thing to know and remember is what he did is on him. You did nothing wrong.'

'Too bloody right! But I can't believe you didn't tell me what was going on,' grumbled Hetty. 'I mean, on-line dating. If you want to meet someone, Florence has a whole station of firefighters she can introduce you to.'

'Ugh, no thanks. I'm not into the hero-type.'

'Evidently,' Hetty came back with, quick as a flash.

Smiling, Maggie went into the kitchen and put the kettle on. 'Let's get some windows open, shall we? It's like a sauna in here. And while we wait for the kettle to boil, tell me all about your stay up at the Hall.'

Chapter 63

Laurel

It was late, a breathless night, and someone was knocking at her door. Laurel had on a cute summer dress and a touch of make-up, but glancing in the hallway mirror, all she saw was a sweaty mess with frizzy hair. *Plus ça change.* Smoothing a few strands down as best she could, she blotted her damp forehead with a tissue and summoned a smile.

'You left a message at the station,' he said his face half obscured in shadow. 'I'm here to put your mind at ease.' His teeth flashed white as he smiled. 'Let's have a chat.'

She shuffled, uncomfortable. 'It's too hot inside. Let's talk in the garden.' She pulled the door closed behind her and walked him round the corner of the house. Their footsteps were soft in the dark, a sliver of silver light the only illumination.

Knowing he was following so close behind, a shiver ran down her spine. When they reached the terrace, she turned to face him. He moved forward into her personal space. She eased back a step.

'I understand that you still have questions. What do you want to know?'

Laurel took a breath and lifted her chin. 'You knew from the beginning that the body in the meadow was Jurgen Sturm.'

He flexed his fingers. 'I don't know what you're talking about.'

'It was the ring, wasn't it? You recognised it straight away. How could you forget? It can't be every day a woman is branded by her abusive husband.' His eyes flashed, but scared as she was, she'd started, and she would see it through to the end. 'What happened to the missing persons report? I know one was made by Jurgen's brother.' It was hard to keep her voice steady.

'And how would you know that?' he growled.

Her mouth was dry. She wished she'd had a drink before he'd arrived. 'I've spoken to Brendt Sturm's social worker. He's in a nursing home with early onset dementia, but the social worker confirmed with him that he reported his brother missing in 1986.'

'A guy with dementia remembers 1986?' he scoffed.

'A guy with dementia and diaries from the 1980s.' She watched a vein pulse in his forehead. 'It's all written down. Brendt even kept the postcard he got in 1985. The one that convinced him Jurgen had gone back to Germany. And he believed it, until he couldn't track him down and started to get suspicious. The postcard he told you about when he reported his wealthy brother as missing.'

'I've never heard of the man.'

'Well, you're in his diary too. He names you. Made a note of your call. *A helpful bloke*, he called you.'

'Anyone could have written those diaries, at any time. It's not proof of anything.'

'You assured him his brother had been located alive and well back in Germany. Told him Jurgen wasn't a missing person, no need to worry. End of story. But I know the postcard wasn't from Jurgen. It was sent by Jo, Albert, and Dorothy. They've admitted they sent it. Which means there's no way you found him alive and well in Germany.'

He snorted.

'Brendt never saw or heard from his brother again, and now he's coming to the end of his life he wanted to make one last effort to locate him or find out what had happened. His social worker contacted the university when she saw an advert for Jessica's research project into people who'd gone missing.'

Nervous of the look in his eyes, she wiped her damp palms on her dress and continued. 'You must have been worried when you ran into Jessica that Sunday afternoon. But poor Jessica was the unlucky one. If she'd spoken to Hill, like we assumed, or even Coral, things might have gone very differently. If we'd known the male police officer Penelope saw with Jessica was you and not Hill, maybe...' she sniffed. 'Unfortunately, it was you Jessica spoke with, and she told you about the two possible matches for the recently uncovered bones: Harold Emmerson and Jurgen Sturm.'

'This is all very entertaining, and completely untrue.'

He wasn't rattled. She needed to unsettle him. 'You had to stop that name getting out, and what better way than to point the finger at Dorothy? Let the bones be those of her ex-husband, Harold. As a bonus, it meant you'd have another crack at locking her up. Anything to stop people learning it was Jurgen Sturm lying in the meadow all these years.'

'Why would I try to stop his identity from coming to light? I was the one running round trying to solve this debacle.' Was it wishful thinking or had there been a hitch in his delivery?

'It was the money, is my guess.'

'A guess? Is that all you have?'

'But I'm right, aren't I?'

He sighed. 'Fine, you got me.' Grinning, he held out his hands as though she were going to cuff him. 'Sure, Sturm was loaded, his brother told me that. Once I'd put him off though, no-one else was looking for Jurgen. Your precious mates, Jo, Albert, and Dorothy, well, they weren't about to spill the beans, were they?'

'Did you know he was dead?'

'It was an educated guess.' He leered at her. 'I figured the daft bat must have snapped and done him in. No way would Jurgen have gone off and let her go. I kept an eye on the bank account, and when the money hadn't been touched for two years, stood to reason he was dead.'

'That was Jo's money, and Brendt Sturm's.'

'Ah well, Jo couldn't touch it without admitting he was dead, now, could she?'

'So, you helped yourself? Maybe just a bit at first, but I'm betting it's all gone now. Maybe in 1986 banks weren't as good at tracing the movement of money, but if they had cause to look now, would there be a trail of breadcrumbs leading straight to your door?'

He chuckled. 'You're so pleased with yourself. But look, we're all alone, I happen to know Albert's out for the evening, and the police have their murderer, thanks to you. It was quite the little plot Beth dreamed up. You can't trust women. Imagine doing that to her own husband; framing him for a murder he didn't commit because she thought he had a bit on the side. No-one's going to look at me. I'm a decorated police officer. What motive could I possibly have?' Metal glinted in the hand that had been empty just moments ago. 'Over by the house. Now.'

Laurel shrank from the blade. She had to keep him talking. 'You must have loved the mess Rik and Beth stirred up? Very convenient for you.' She moved backwards. He matched her, step for step.

'Like I said, I have you to thank for that.'

She blanched. He was right, but she couldn't dwell on it. 'The one thing I can't work out is the lack of footprints?'

He sneered. 'You always did overthink things.'

Tell me, she urged silently.

She felt the rough wall against her back, and he pinned her there, hands either side of her head. She could smell garlic on his breath.

'I told little Miss anthropology – what was her name? Jessica? – I told her I would be off work late, but if she could meet me, I'd dig up the precious missing persons report for Jurgen so she could add it to her file. And, if she came alone, I promised I'd share as much confidential info as I could on Sturm and Emmerson. Stupid cow didn't even blink.' He brought the knife to rest against the skin of her neck.

She tried not to flinch at the feel of the cold blade.

'It was easy. I was there early, before the rain, standing on nice, dry ground. When she arrived, we chatted, I hit her. Not as hard as I should. She didn't go down straight away, she stumbled into the mud, but then she fell and didn't get up. No need for cow shoes or any grand scheme. I kept my shoes clean.' He laughed, his piggy eyes creased in obscene glee.

If she'd had a weapon of her own, Laurel would have attacked him right then.

He sobered but continued to gloat. 'That's your problem, you get most of the way to the answer, then you go off course. Like now. You suspected me, but you're all on your lonesome. No-one will ever find *your* body. I'm going to make sure of it.'

'I left a message at the police station.'

He chuckled. 'You did, but you didn't give any details, did you. DS Hill is planning to come round tomorrow to see you. Unfortunately, I also saw the note, hence this little tête-à-tête, but no-one knows I'm here. You might get lucky, Hill might report you missing when he can't find you tomorrow, or maybe he'll think you forgot and it'll be a couple of days before they start looking for you. Either way, it doesn't matter. You'll be a long way away by tomorrow morning, and you won't be telling any more tales. Ever.'

He moved the knife from her neck, and she knew she had to act or be killed in her own back garden. She went limp and slid down the wall. The stone scraped her skin, but she barely felt it. She tried to push away from him, moving sideways, but fear made her clumsy and she fell. Her hip and shoulder connected with the solid ground, winding her. She flopped onto her back, digging her heels into the ground to propel herself away. Darkness swam in front of her eyes. She could hear his breathing, then his hand clamped onto her ankle. He dragged her back.

Laurel couldn't move, his weight was on her and she was defenceless. She closed her eyes as his breath dampened her cheeks. She braced for the first slice of the knife.

'You nearly died before,' he hissed in her ear. 'But the idiot didn't finish the job. I won't make the same mistake.'

A voice boomed from the darkness and a brilliant light tore through the ink black night.

'Vincent Tillow, you're under arrest.'

Tillow bellowed and lashed out. Without thinking, she lifted her arm to ward off the blow and the blade sliced into her skin. Through the haze of terror, hot liquid poured from the wound, but there was no pain.

Frozen, she watched as men in black wrestled Tillow upright and hauled him out of sight. Then someone was bending over her. Talking. Speaking words she couldn't understand, could barely hear over the thundering in her ears.

'It's okay,' Ben soothed, scooping her into his arms. 'We got what we needed. I've got you. You're safe. You're safe.'

Epilogue

Laurel

The table groaned under the weight of sandwiches, pork pies, quiche, scones with jam and cream, and a rainbow of assorted cakes and sweet treats. There was tea, coffee, lemonade, and seemingly endless bottles of Champagne. Laurel's stomach growled. She coughed, trying to disguise the noise, but Maggie grinned in understanding.

'So, without any further ado, on this glorious autumn day, I declare our farm shop open for business.' Jayne and Alex beamed at their audience and cut the ribbon. The cameras of locals and the local press alike clicked, cementing the moment in Elderwick history.

Laurel, Maggie, and Albert picked their way through the crowd to join Hetty, Constance, and the Reverend Christopher Ibori.

'This place is amazing,' said Constance. 'I'm so impressed.'

'I'm glad they didn't push ahead with building in the meadow,' said Maggie. 'I don't think I could bear to buy fresh produce from a burial site.'

'I'm glad you approve.' Jayne appeared, bearing a fresh batch of macarons in the Dandelion colours of pale green and yellow. 'This way, having it up here, we can properly integrate the village with our centre. It'll be good for the kids to mix with people coming up to the Hall instead of having the shop all the way down by the church. Losing part of the formal gardens is no big deal. The kids who'll be staying with us aren't so fussed about box hedges and neat flower beds.'

'Dorothy,' called Albert, inviting her over. 'What do you think?'

She sniffed. 'It's fine, I suppose.'

Albert poked her in the ribs. 'Come on, you can do better than that.'

Dorothy relented. 'I like it.'

Christopher chuckled.

'High praise indeed,' Laurel whispered to Maggie.

Lin popped up at Dorothy's elbow. 'I got you some of those sausage rolls you like,' she said, handing over a napkin stuffed with four or five pastry parcels.

Even with Lin being a regular visitor to the village now, Laurel had yet to get used to the unexpected friendship between the young archaeology student and Dorothy. Unexpected especially after she'd seen Lin leaving Dorothy's house in tears a couple of months back, though now she understood how shamefully she'd misread the situation. Dorothy was one of the good guys. On balance.

'Lin, I haven't heard from Michael for a while. I know it's been the summer break at the university, but do you know how he's doing?' Laurel asked with a stab of guilt that she'd ever suspected the pleasant young man.

'You'll love this. He's deferred his second year and gone travelling. He admitted he'd been more than a bit in love with Jess and he needed a break from being in the office he shared with her. I think he'll be okay. Also, his family is loaded, so it's not like he's going to have to work while he's away, it'll be one long holiday. He said he'd send you a postcard.'

A squeal alerted them to Penelope's arrival. 'Laurel, you are my absolute hero. How are you? How's your arm?' she gushed.

Disliking the spotlight, Laurel brushed off her concern. 'I'm fine, all recovered.'

Not to be deterred, Penelope peppered her with more questions. 'What happened to Dr Delgado and Beth? How did you work out that it was Vincent Tillow? Have they found the money?'

As if on cue, Ben wandered over, bearing a bottle of fizz. 'Top up, anyone? I pinched this, but I don't think anyone will mind.' He refilled glasses and reported on Dr Delgado and his wife. 'Beth's been charged with wasting police time. It's doubtful she'll get a custodial sentence, but there wasn't much else we could charge her with.'

'Unbelievable,' declared Albert. 'But I have to admire her trickery. It was quite a dastardly scheme to frame her husband.'

'And Rik's been charged with fraud–'

'Too bloody right,' muttered Constance.

'–burglary, and actual bodily harm.'

'Tell us,' asked Albert, 'where did Rik go that night when he was picked up on the hotel CCTV?'

'Nowhere. The original footage shows him go out the front entrance at eleven twenty-seven, but he returned five minutes later at eleven thirty-two. In time to be on-line with Constance at eleven thirty-five. Coral didn't actually bother sending an officer to view the footage first-hand, and the hotel only thought to look to see if Rik had gone *out*.'

'And Jurgen's money?' asked Hetty?

'Gone.' Ben emptied the last of the bottle into Laurel's glass. 'But we can connect it to Tillow.'

'I feel sorry for Brendt Sturm,' said Maggie. 'Imagine finding out your brother's been dead all these years, and that he was guilty of domestic abuse. Then, to rub salt into the wound, all his money has gone and can't be used to fund your end of life care.'

The jovial spirit dipped.

'Why the long faces?' DS Hill, dressed in casual shorts and a polo shirt in a cheery shade of pink, nudged his way into their loose circle.

'DS Hill.' Laurel was surprised to see him. 'How are you?'

'Perry, please,' he implored. 'I'm much better these days. Did Ben tell you? DI Coral has applied for a transfer.'

'That deserves a toast.' Ben accepted a glass from a passing server, pressed it into Perry's hand, then raised his own. 'Cheers!'

'Cheers!' they chorused.

As the chatter continued and people broke away into smaller groups, Laurel and Maggie wandered off, out of the formal gardens and over the parkland to the revamped orchard, now replanted and full of vegetables alongside the new fruit trees.

Laurel remained unsure how she felt about Ben. She hadn't seen much of him since the night Tillow had attempted to end her life. However, she had to admit to having been pathetically happy to learn it had been Perry who Ben had been spending his time with and not a beautiful mystery girlfriend. Whether anything would ever come of their friendship, she was in no rush to find out. Maybe she would talk to Maggie about it sometime, but later. For now, she was simply happy to be outside on a glorious, fresh autumn day, with good company and fantastic food.

Comfortable to wander together without talking, Laurel had thought they were alone. She jumped and her hand flew to her chest when a figure materialised from behind the flourishing greenhouse. 'Jo!' Although they'd spoken briefly after Tillow's arrest, Laurel didn't know how Jo had been coping since. Seeing her there, in the grounds of Elderwick Hall, she was struck by how different she looked. It was probably the first time she'd seen the talented cook not wearing her apron and without some kitchen implement in her hand, but the change was more than the lack of accessories.

'Hey Laurel, Maggie,' replied Jo. 'I see you're also in search of a bit of peace and quiet?'

'Sorry, we can go,' Maggie offered.

Jo removed her glasses and balanced them on her head, nestled in the piles of her salt and pepper hair. 'No, stay, please. I haven't had chance to thank you both properly. Come, sit.' She led the way to a rough wooden bench against the sunny south wall of the orchard.

'You have nothing at all to thank us for,' Laurel insisted. If anything, she thought, Jo had a right to be angry at how their interfering exacerbated an already distressing situation from the moment Jurgen's remains were uncovered. Maggie's face told her she was thinking the same.

'Nonsense.' Jo lifted her face to the sun as a curlew's plaintive cry floated on the breeze. 'Don't get me wrong, it was dreadful to know he'd... come back. And I was terrified I'd be sent to jail. But now... I'm finally free.' She paused.

Laurel didn't speak. She was fighting back her tears, and Maggie had pulled a tissue out of her sleeve and was snuffling into it.

Jo took Laurel's hand in one of hers and Maggie's in the other. 'I have the entire village to thank for giving me back my life. A life in which I no-longer have to look over my shoulder, fear every knock at the door, carry the guilt of knowing my wonderful friends, Dorothy and Albert, lied and continued to lie for me. Now, here and now, I am free.'

'Mind if I join you?' Albert asked, falling into step alongside her. 'It's been a delightful afternoon.'

'It has.'

'Maggie not with you?'

'No, I left her chatting to Jo about mange tout.' Laurel glanced at her neighbour, her friend. The sun hit the planes of his face, causing deep shadows in his laughter lines. His wispy white hair bobbed in the occasional puffs of the breeze making its way between the gnarled oak trees lining the driveway of Elderwick Hall. If she was ever going to ask, now was the time.

'Albert,' she began, 'the letters inscribed on the key found with Jurgen Sturm's body, T C.'

'Yes, the key to The Tea Cup Café, as was. What of it?'

'There are a lot of T Cs in Elderwick.'

'Are there?' He continued to stare resolutely ahead.

'Tulip Cottage; Thatcher's Cottage; Turnip Corner; your shed, Tumbledown Cabin.'

'Mm hmm.'

'Why is that, do you think? Why so many places with those initials?'

He slowed and turned to smile at her. 'Simply a coincidence, my dear. A wonderful Elderwick coincidence.'

Also by Rachael Gray

A Little Bird Told Me

A Turn-up for the Books

From the author

If you need support regarding domestic violence:
(details correct as of February 2025)

Australia: National sexual assault, domestic and family violence counselling service:
https://1800Respect.org.au Phone: 1800 737 732 – online chat also available

Canada: Shelter Safe: https://www.sheltersafe.ca/ - webpage available in French and English
(provides a list of domestic abuse shelters in each province and territory with phone numbers)

New Zealand: It's Not Ok Campaign: http://www.areyouok.org.nz/ Phone: 0800 456 450 – online chat also available

Northern Ireland: Northern Ireland Women's Aid: https://www.womensaidni.org/ Phone: 0808 802 1414 (numbers available for local Women's Aid across NI - online chat also available)

From the author

Scotland: Scottish Women's Aid: https://womensaid. scot/ Phone: 0800 027 1234 – online chat also available

UK: National Domestic Abuse Helpline: https://www. nationaldahelpline.org.uk/ Phone: 0808 2000 247 (British Sign Language support also available, via website)

US: National Domestic Violence Hotline: https://thehotline.org Phone: 1-800-799-7233/1-800-787-3224 (TTY) or text START to 88788

US: The National Deaf Domestic Violence Hotline: https:// thedeafhotline.org/ (American Sign Language support available, or Phone: 855 812 1001) Videophone: 1-855-812-1001

About the Author

With over twenty years of experience working as a Doctor of Clinical Psychology for the NHS and healthcare charities, Rachael Gray is the author of *A Little Bird Told Me*, *A Turn-up For The Books*, and *A Storm in a Teacup*.

Though she'll always be a Yorkshire girl at heart, Rachael now lives and writes from the home she shares with her husband in Normandy, France.

Rarely without her nose in a book, her *Elderwick Mysteries* series is inspired by her love of a good whodunit.

She can be found on:
Bluesky: @rachaelgray.bsky.social
Facebook: RachaelGray_Psy
or visit her website for the latest book news and offers: https://welcometoelderwick.godaddysites.com/

A note from the publisher

Thank you for reading this book. If you enjoyed it please do consider leaving a review on Amazon to help others find it too.

We hate typos. All of our books have been rigorously edited and proofread, but sometimes mistakes do slip through. If you have spotted a typo, please do let us know and we can get it amended within hours.

info@bloodhoundbooks.com